THE BALLAD OF STEVIE PEARL

A NOVEL BY
SW HAMMOND

The Ballad of Stevie Pearl is a work of fiction. The book is based on a multi-cultural encompassment of humanity and pop culture. Names, characters, places, incidents, products, corporations, agencies, institutions, and faith-based organizations either are the product of the author's imagination or are used fictitiously. Any resemblance to actual persons, living or dead, events, or locales is coincidental.

Published in the United States by Surf Star Media.

Title page art by Sean Hammond
Book design by Surf Star Media
Editing by Nicole Acevedo

LIBRARY OF CONGRESS CATALOGING-IN-PUBLICATION DATA

Names: Hammond, SW, author.
Title: The Ballad of Stevie Pearl / SW Hammond.
Description: Farmington : Surf Star Media, [2023]
Identifiers: LCCN 2023904145 | ISBN 9798987937709 (hardback) | ISBN 9798987937716 (paperback) | ISBN 9798987937723 (Apple Books) | ISBN 9798987937730 (Kindle)
Subjects: Fiction. | Drama—Romance.

www.surfstarmedia.com
www.swhammond.com

9 8 7 6 5 4 3 2 1

Editorial Edition

With reverence for the Chemehuevi,
Colorado River Indian Tribes,
and survivors.

WILDEST DREAMS
TAYLOR SWIFT

Stevie stood alone on the patio. An onshore breeze ruffled the hem of her golden dress. She stood like a Greek God; a statue come to life watching over the sea. The salty air brushed her hair and kissed her cheek. She closed her eyes and inhaled.

"We're ready for you, Ms. Pearl." A voice beckoned.

She ignored him and continued to center herself, filling her lungs once more. She focused on the fabric fluttering across her shoulders. She stared into the falling sun until its glow left spots in her mind.

Inside the beach home a camera crew swirled. Techs measured lighting, camera operators studied displays, and sound engineers checked levels. Sarah Jennings sat across from Stevie's empty chair, reviewing her notes and scribbling on index cards with a Sharpie.

The prized journalist was the first to interview Stevie Pearl in over 18 months. The live broadcast was scheduled to shutdown primetime television, every channel carrying the conversation like a Presidential address.

It was Stevie's idea to do the interview live. She demanded no filters. She refused to have her words edited. She was only going to address the matter once.

Sarah sipped from her water and looked at her watch. She stood and rounded the couch, the beach home decorated in white nautical fashion. Her heels clacked against the stone floor, and she paused in the doorway as she consumed the sight of the generation's most prolific artist.

"Stevie…" Sarah was soft. "It's time."

Stevie pressed her lips and turned. She offered Sarah a smile as she returned within her home, taking a seat in the plush cotton chair. The makeup crew fussed with her hair and dabbed at her cheeks. Sarah sat across from her as the final audio and video checks took place.

The producer made an announcement. "Going live…" The rest of the staff cleared the frame and a countdown began. Introduction music played and graphics swirled across the monitor. Stevie closed her eyes once more, conjuring every ounce of courage that remained in her being.

"Ms. Pearl," Sarah began. "Thank you. We're honored to be in your home. It's been a long time since the world has heard from you—I'm thankful for you trusting me and giving us the opportunity to speak with you today."

"Certainly." Stevie nodded. "You've always been fair. I still remember the first time you interviewed me—what was I, 17?"

"You were 15." Sarah smiled. "It was just after your first multi-platinum record."

"That's right…" Stevie's gaze vanished toward memories. "Seems like a lifetime ago."

"I want you to know that I'm here to listen. Guide. Perhaps ask a few questions. There will be no interruptions or commercials—take all the time you need."

"Thank you." The star-shaped diamond earrings glinted as Stevie accepted. "Where shall we begin?"

"Why don't you start by telling me about Alex..."

THE BALLAD OF STEVIE PEARL

Running With The Devil
Van Halen

A rippling tide of scorched earth blurred the horizon. The front tire of Alex's motorcycle balanced the yellow stripe like a gymnast cartwheeling across a high beam. The roar of the engine penetrated and scattered hazy mirages, dissolving mindless daydreams into a lonely stretch of spiderwebbed blacktop. Its molten darkness absorbed the sun and radiated the heat upward; baking chrome, leather, and bone. Alex opened the throttle and charged forward, the hot steel slicing through the heart of the desert.

It was a typical Sunday ride for the hometown hero. He'd leave L.A. shortly after first light, weaving traffic and then racing through Chino and San Bernardino before cutting northeast on Highway 62 out of Palm Springs. He kissed the edge of Joshua Tree and then seared under the late morning sun, pounding east across the Mojave. Each time he approached the *Entering Colorado River Indian Reservation* road sign, his upper lip stiffened and his pace slowed.

An old habit reinforced by his grandmother's superstition, Alex made a wish while crossing the long bridge that separated

California and Arizona. The reservation's lifeblood ran gentle and slow, the river turning like chocolate milk mixed by a lazy spoon. He lingered on familiar sights while crossing into the city limits of Parker, searching for a sign of something new. It had been years since the construction of a building caught him by surprise, or even a fresh coat of paint on a billboard for that matter. He didn't resent his sleepy hometown, but had simply outgrown it.

Alex lowered gears, giving a subtle wave to the people behind the wheel of oncoming traffic. Everyone recognized his motorcycle. It was a source of envy and aspiration, serving as a rolling reminder to the community that he made it out. Some admired him for it, some begrudged him. Most saw the young man as a beacon of hope. They were proud of him and all that he had accomplished. His success had become their success, and while he was still uncomfortable with the attention, he didn't mind sharing it with them.

As with all of his Sunday visits, Alex's one-man parade customarily came to an end by topping off his parched tank at Woody's; a glamorous name for two pumps and a freezer chest. Taking refuge on the side of the gas pump with shade, he used the fill as an opportunity to stretch his legs and pick the sweat-soaked cotton from his crotch.

"'Ey, Nopah!" An old man leaned out the window of a late-60's Ford pickup, limping the clutch toward him. "Hollywood treatin' you good?" He grinned. "I 'eard you're working on movies now."

"Where'd you hear that?" Alex removed his aviators and wiped the grime from his brow.

"Your mother!" The old man sputtered. "She tells everyone!"

Alex smirked, figuring she was the source of the gossip. "Take it easy, Mr. Johnson—tell Mrs. Johnson hello for me."

He stepped back and allowed the truck to coast by. The old man responded by flinging his hand with a half-hearted wave before cutting into traffic. Alex shook his head, watching the Ford ride the breakdown lane.

Refitting the handle to the pump, Alex arched his back once more before entering the gas station. The air conditioning was harsh, freon gripping the back of his throat. The hair on his arms stood on end while his boots scuffed along the worn tile floor. He took his time browsing with the refrigerator door open, the chills settling on his sunburnt skin. Leaning deep inside of the cooler, he grabbed a bottle of water.

Alex immediately cracked the top and began drinking in the middle of the aisle. The cool flow of water ran quicker than he could swallow, sending the rest down his chin and onto his chest.

Sipping the second half of the bottle, Alex looked over the racks of junk food and candy. He selected his brother's favorite, a Mr. Goodbar, and then made his way to the register.

"Alex." The teenager behind the counter finally acknowledged him. "You gonna give me that bike?"

"Why would I do that?" Alex cocked an eye.

"You Hollywood now, man! You can buy another one."

"Your mother would kill me—you still need training wheels for that BMX!"

"Ah, shit…" The kid scoffed. "So, like, you just got all the ladies in L.A., right? Hanging out on the beach, drinkin' bottles?" The boy searched for an ounce of life to live vicariously through.

"Oh yeah, Henry." Alex rolled his eyes. "Three-ways every night."

"Awe dawg—I knew it! This guy here—this guy right 'ere!" Henry cupped his mouth in one hand and threw the other in the air with disbelief.

"You staying out of trouble?" Alex questioned him.

"They don't got nothin' on me. Like I told you—I'm straight, man."

"The deal's still good." Alex eyed him. "Pull those grades up, get the scholarship—you can come stay with me in L.A.. Bitches and beaches."

"You know I'm tryin', man. It's hard… My English teacher is all crazy—she fuckin' hates me, man. She has it out for me."

"Just show up and shut up." Alex slid him a $20. "You can't learn when your mouth's always runnin'."

The young man glared at him and worked the register.

"Keep it." Alex nodded. "Hollywood, remember?" He smiled at Henry. "Don't be a dick—buy dinner for your mother and sister tonight."

Alex gulped the rest of his water while he walked toward the door. "Bitches and beaches!" He shouted back to Henry as he yanked the handle. The heat hit him square in the jaw, almost buckling his knees.

"Bitches and beaches…" The kid muttered as the door swung shut.

Alex slid the candy bar into his vest pocket and fired the motorcycle. Leaving behind the only road that connected the reservation to the rest of the world, he navigated through the small farms and trailers toward his childhood home. Reaching the end of the pavement, Alex wove through potholes and the last stretch of dust until he reached the livestock gate of the ranch. Rusted chains baking in the sun burned his hands as he allowed himself in. He circled the rutted driveway and backed the bike into a patch of shade created by a scraggly ironwood.

"Alecito!" His grandmother shouted from the porch. The worn screen door of the trailer slammed shut, snagging her old white nightgown on the latch.

"Tita!" Alex greeted, swinging his leg in a dismount from the bike.

"I heard you coming—told 'em you'd come today." She tugged at the cloth.

"Here I am!" He leaned down and pawed through his saddle bags.

"You got the goods?"

He ignored her, latching the buckle. His long stride carried him up the porch steps and then he wrapped the frail old woman in his arms. Her hunched back strained to meet his embrace.

"Well?"

"Tita…"

"The glaucoma—my back! You bring it?"

"Jesus. I got your fix, old lady." Alex shook a medicine bottle in front of her face.

"Atta boy." She gave an excited toothless smile. "You gettin' laid?"

"Can we go in?"

"The boy's still not gettin' laid!" Tita shouted back inside of the house.

Alex pushed past her and opened the door, ending their conversation.

"Hey! Get back here…" His grandmother tried to grasp at his leather vest with her boney fingers, wanting her California-grown medicine.

"Mom? Ma?" Alex shouted.

"Kitchen!"

Alex tossed the weed bottle onto the coffee table and let the old woman fend for herself. He then crossed to the back of the small double-wide into the kitchen and found his mother, Kadence, working on Sunday dinner.

"Where's Charlie?" He asked, greeting her with a brief hug.

"Out back. Workin." She nodded through the window toward the barn.

"Thought you moved the cattle?"

"Did. Pump's broken. Horses still need water."

Alex nodded, putting the melted chocolate bar from his breast pocket into the freezer. "How's work?" He sat on a barstool across from the counter where she was preparing dinner.

"It's good… The kids are excited about your movie."

"It's not my movie, Ma."

"Well, they hired you to make sure they're doing it right. It's your movie." She grinned at the thought, her eyes focused on slicing vegetables.

"You can't keep going around telling people about it. They'll fire me—confidentiality agreement. Non-disclosure. You have no idea how strict they are."

"Fire you? It's just superheroes…" She rolled her eyes.

"Almost a billion dollars worth. It's bigger than Batman."

"I'm not saying it's not special—but no one would fire you for talking about superheroes. It's not top secret or something…"

Alex gave her a blank stare, unsure how to even begin his reply. "They're Gods, not superheroes… And, just stop. Okay?"

"I'm not going to stop being proud of my baby boy!" She continued to smile, overly joyed with her son's accomplishment. "Everyone is so happy for you."

"'Fuck sake–" He heard his brother's bark from the front porch. "Alex!" The screen door slammed and heavy steps stomped across the living room.

"You shut the fuckin' gate?" Charlie growled, leaning through the doorway of the kitchen. "'The hell's your problem?" His brother snatched the Bronco keys from the hanging rack.

"Thought you moved the cattle?"

"Did. Still got other animals here, asshole."

"Calm down." Their mother interjected. "It's no big deal."

"I'll help." Alex stood from his stool.

"No—you just sit there. *I got it.*"

Alex was tired of fighting with his older brother about chores. If Charlie wanted to be stubborn and handle it himself, he'd let him.

Alex sat back down without apology. A decade of resentment had divided the two ever since Alex left the reservation to pursue his dreams as an illustrator. Charlie felt he was left carrying the family load.

"Go help him." Kadence eyed Alex as the screen door slammed once more, Charlie running after the horses. Alex sighed, pushing himself up from the counter.

"He's a dick."

"You left the gate open…"

Alex rushed to catch up with Charlie and jumped in the passenger's seat of the old Bronco. The truck thundered to life in Confederate fashion and Charlie spun the tires in the gravel, clearly pissed at this brother.

"This's bullshit." Charlie dug under his breath.

"Sorry, man." Alex looked through the crusted water spots from last month's rain on the side window. "Didn't know it mattered."

"Oh, that's right. Nothing we do out here matters to you anymore."

"I'm out here all the fuckin' time—what are you talking about?"

"You should know better."

"Horses are usually in the corral, dipshit. Not just wandering all over the yard."

"The corral's fence is broken—whole section down—but I thought I'd fix the water first so they don't die. Then I have to fix the wheel on the trailer so that I can pick up material to fix the goddamn fence—instead I'm chasin' fuckin' horses down the road because of you!"

The remaining several hundred yards were silent as the truck caught up with the escapees. Alex jumped out and the two brothers began working the sides of the road, Charlie angling the truck and Alex running back and forth waving his arms to push the horses down the fence line and back into their yard. Once Charlie was through the gate with the Bronco, Alex had the honor of securing it so it wouldn't open back up.

Charlie slammed the door of the truck and stomped back toward the barn without saying a word. Alex contemplated following but decided to give him some time to cool off. The horses, gate, fence, and water pump weren't the problem. Charlie was feeling insignificant with Alex's rising success, and there wasn't much Alex could say that would fix that. He went back inside and found his grandmother hunched over in her chair, staring at the television.

"Thanks for telling me about the gate, Tita."

"Shh!" She pointed at the TV. "Mi Mario…" she whispered fondly as Mario Cordova anchored *TMI*.

Alex stood for a moment, watching the show's daily Stevie Pearl update. All of America, and most of the world, was enamored with the remarkable young pop star. Before she could drive, she was cutting tracks and breaking industry records. A genuine songwriter, Stevie was the youngest artist to win Album of the Year. She continued her exceptional sugary-pop notoriety over the last decade with a dozen more Number 1 singles and countless music awards.

The television program flickered, showing Stevie being bombarded by paparazzi while trying to enter a night club. Alex rolled his eyes and returned to the kitchen.

"What the hell's wrong with Charlie?" Alex asked his mother.

"He's just tired… Sales aren't lookin' good—prices down. Things keep breaking…"

"It's always been that way. We never win, just survive another day."

"I suppose he doesn't like being reminded of that..." She looked over at him with hesitation. "Is that a new vest?"

Alex took immediate offense.

"I'm not going to feel bad about a goddamn vest!" He pulled at the leather around his shoulders. "When will you let me help? I'm finally okay, Ma. The publisher has me on our biggest title, the movie studio finally came around with the consulting money, and I've already pre-sold some of my own work before the gallery opening—"

"We're fine." She cut him short. "We've always made it work."

Alex reached into his breast pocket and pulled out a thick envelope. "You don't have to tell Charlie." He slid the cash across the counter. "Just... get the fence fixed."

His mother looked down at the gesture reluctantly. The family needed some help but she didn't want to turn her son into a bank. The strain between him and Charlie was already at a breaking point and she feared money would only further divide them.

"Take the friggin' money!" They heard Tita shout from the other room.

"Well, her hearing hasn't gone." Alex smiled. "She's right. I want to do this. I want you to have it."

"We'll pay you back..."

"No, you won't. It's yours. Fix some things right. Go up to Havasu for dinner. Breathe a little."

Kadence bit the inside of her cheek as she thought about all the ways some extra money could be put to use. She nodded and forced a smile, tucking the envelope into her back pocket.

"How much he give you?!" Tita yelled.

"Watch your show, Ma!" Kadence hollered back. "Thank you." She looked to Alex. "It will help a lot."

"I know." Alex beamed. "When's dinner? I'm starved!"

REBEL GIRL
BIKINI KILL

The next morning Alex arrived at the film studio for pre-production meetings of *The Final Book*. The movie was being adapted from a series of comics that he had been illustrating since graduating art school. A dozen years earlier, the small publisher he drew for took a chance on an off-beat novel about modernizing the Greek Gods. Zeus was a renowned super-scientist living among the mortals, working to usher in the second coming of Christ—all, of course, in a desperate attempt to save humanity before their self-imposed apocalypse. It was the perfect project for the young artist as no one had high expectations.

However, it took off. The series of comics, much like the novel, had little to do with religious dogma but was rather a metaphor of the human condition, and Alex captured that beautifully. The once small, indie sensation had grown into a world-wide franchise and Alex earned himself a lead consulting role on the feature film, which was expected to be one of the largest undertakings in motion picture history.

Alex had become a well-known, almost mythical creature in the comic sub-culture. While virtually invisible during typical daily life, he was a Sultan at Comic Con. Fanboys and girls would wait in long roped-off lines for him to sign autographs and pose for selfies.

The Final Book pandemonium was feverish and the panels he was a part of always overflowed in capacity—the announcement of the movie eclipsing his wildest dreams. His work on the series propelled his career, and that success granted him freedom as an artist. He was getting to the point where he could pick and choose the projects he wanted to work on, and at this moment he was in the middle of planning his opening night at a hip Santa Monica art gallery.

Alex Nopah had come a long way from his quiet childhood on the Indian reservation. The late nights he spent drawing at his desk, the concerned conversations held at parent-teacher conferences, and the provisional approach he applied to his chores all made sense now. He chose his path from an early age and struggled tirelessly to walk it; the fruits of his intuition finally paying off.

His big brother, Charlie, was the exact opposite. Growing up, Charlie was the star athlete. He was a promising baseball player and always at the center of attention. He'd get busted taking the Bronco filled with girls and beers out into the desert. The rez police were strict about underage drinking, but they usually just tussled Charlie's head and made him clean up the empties. His big brother was likable, where Alex always seemed to be in his own world. Except for his mother, hardly anyone noticed when Alex left home for art school. That was anything but the case now, Alex being the biggest thing to talk about on the reservation since Jacoby Ellsbury.

"What'd you do this weekend?" Celeste asked, reaching over him to grab a sugar for her coffee.

"I worked all day Saturday." Alex replied. "I'm trying to get ready for the opening. I'm so far behind…"

"You go home yesterday? Out to, ah, you know—the desert?"

Celeste was an indie rock glam queen, the type who wore thick rimmed glasses and put chopsticks in her hair. She had tattoos on her forearms and a pierced eyebrow; somehow when it all came together it made her extremely attractive. She was hired as a production assistant for the movie and the two became quick friends. They occasionally shared lunch or a snide comment, he even met her for drinks one evening—only for the two to be joined by her boyfriend.

"I'm not sure which is more offensive," Alex twirled coffee in a paper cup, "you calling my home "the desert" or "the reservation.""

"Hey man, I grew up in hickville too. I've wanted to go to Joshua Tree since—"

"I will lose all respect for you if you finish that sentence with anything related to U2."

"Fuck—The Edge? Now I'm not allowed to like The Edge?!"

"He could be your dad."

"I'd like to call him daddy..."

"I'd like to call that daddy issues." Alex raised a playful eye. "Is that why the tattoos?"

"Umm, yeah, actually. My dad was a piece of shit."

"Mine too..." Alex sighed and took a sip.

"So, what? Like, you have something against sunblock?" She pressed her finger on his forearm.

"Is that a red man joke?"

"It could be. Or you could just be a dumbass that's sunburned."

"Rode the hog." Alex said with mocking arrogance. He leaned back in his chair like a cool guy.

"You're an idiot." She finished stirring her coffee. "Lunch today? You know, if they actually let me have one?"

Alex nodded with acceptance.

"Cool. I'll text you." Celeste put a lid on her coffee and purposefully kicked his foot that had lingered out into the walkway. He couldn't tell if she was flirting or just wasn't putting up with his shit, either of which he liked.

Alex dithered around the craft services table a while longer before grabbing his computer bag and heading into the meeting room. He was still getting comfortable with his roll and the idea of what he was doing. His job really had no duties other than ensuring quality control and striving to capture as much integrity of the original story as he could.

Abstractly, it was an insurmountable task. If the movie fell short of those goals it would lead to a ferocious backlash among faithful fans and humiliate the studio. However, the movie also had to crossover into a mainstream audience and gain world-wide appeal to sell tickets and recoup its insane budget. There was no checklist or order of operations for accomplishing this, not to mention he had never made a movie before.

He took his usual seat at the conference table as the room filled with the rest of the team. The large television mounted to the far wall was turned on and it displayed the desktop of the computer that was sitting in the center of the table. Extra rolling office chairs were being pushed in and the place buzzed more than usual.

"What's going on?" Alex leaned over and asked the person sitting next to him.

"Conference call or somethin'?"

The director, Jim Brigman, entered the meeting room with two executive producers in tow. Alex was a bit surprised to see him. At this point Jim hadn't been involved in the meticulous day-to-days and was more focused on securing locations and other logistics.

"Good morning everyone." Jim brought the group together and began the meeting. "Sorry for the short notice, bit of a change in plans this morning, but we're going to roll with it. This will be the first of several of these types of conference calls—mostly introductory today, but take note on what's expected of you or your department. Devon, you want to connect?" He nodded toward the computer.

The woman worked the trackpad and FaceTime pulsated through the speakers as it rang. The user on the other end stared awkwardly into the camera and then greeted everyone with a large smile.

"Jim?"

"Sean, can you hear me?"

"Loud and clear!"

"Excellent. Let me introduce you to *The Final Book* production team!"

Sean waved to everyone through the monitor. His hair was long and shaggy, his face tan, and he wore an unbuttoned collared shirt. The background of the screen was filled with endless tips of sail masts from what looked to be a marina, the sun's last light glistening across the water.

"Nopah! Is that you?!"

Alex laughed and shook his head at the sight of his old friend.

"Everyone, meet the original author and creator of our story—welcome, Sean!" Jim continued.

Sean nodded with the introduction but persisted with his own conversation. "Alex—you lookin' good, man. Almost as tan as me!" He made fun of the sunburn.

Sean and Alex had become longtime friends from working so closely with each other on the comics. The two had endless conversations about his characters and the overall philosophy of the book. Alex was committed to delivering the most accurate portrayal of Sean's story, and Sean couldn't have been happier with Alex's dedication and visual representation of his imagination. Mutual respect existed between the two, but after a decade they were now almost like family.

"What are you doing?!" Alex flipped his hands at the screen. "Where are you?"

"I'm spendin' my money!" Sean continued to grin, pointing back over his shoulder with a thumb at a blue water catamaran. "Just docked in Corsica, didn't think I'd make the call..."

"You couldn't be bothered to fly back?" Alex was in disbelief that Sean was out of the country while his baby was being turned into a movie. At this point, ultimately neither of them had creative control over the project, but surely the studio would want Sean around as a consultant like himself.

"Nah—you got this! Plus, Jim bugs me all the time—we email. I'll be meeting up with you guys once filming starts in Greece. I'm just getting an early start!"

"Sean will also be joining us on these conference calls for the next few weeks, assuming he keeps an internet connection..." Jim interjected and corralled the conversation. "You guys need to take advantage of him while he's here. Any creative questions you may have, utilize both Alex and Sean. They made this franchise what it is—no one knows this universe better than them."

Jim ran down the agenda and Sean was introduced to the various departments and a schedule was laid out in front of them. A plan was beginning to crystalize for what was to be the most expensive production in cinema history, and Alex's head swam with the notion.

The meeting carried on and began to resemble a marathon. Alex grabbed his phone and quietly checked messages from under the table. "*Is that meeting ever going to end? You guys have been in there forever. Lunch??*" Celeste had messaged.

"*Hell yeah.*" Alex wrote back. "*We're wrapping up.*"

"'*Bout time. I was going to blow you off. HANGRY.*"

"*Let's get out of here, or at least take a sandwich outside.*"

"Aye aye, captain."

Celeste and Alex met once again at craft services and snagged pre-made sandwiches wrapped in paper. They eyed each other's selections and took turns in the mini-fridge, Alex taking an iced tea and Celeste going straight for the hard stuff—an afternoon energy drink. The two abandoned the studio, Alex holding the door for her as they made their way outside.

"Sun..." Celeste moaned. She swapped her Buddy Holly's for a pair of Jacqueline Onassis'.

The two weaved like drunken sailors across the lot, kicking random pebbles and tightroping painted lines. They found a patch of trees and sat on the curb in the shade.

"Only two and a half years left..." Celeste said, unwrapping her sandwich.

"Already counting the days?"

"Nah." She smiled. "I love my job. Pam's a bitch though."

"I'm starting to learn that no one really cares what I say. They want me around, but they're going to do what they want anyway."

"They need someone to blame when it all goes to shit."

"Great."

"Take the money, dude. Maybe you'll end up looking like a genius."

"At least the comics were good..."

"They were really good—" Celeste paused while chewing. "I've finally gone back through and reread them. You're fuckin' talented, man."

"It was a good story." Alex was modest. The two sat quietly and enjoyed their lunch, watching trails of passing jets.

"So what's the deal, man?" Celeste cocked her head. "You, like, the brooding-artist-type cut off from the rest of the world? I never hear you talkin' about chicks."

"Not much to say."

"You should be knuckle deep—working on this movie, everything you've done for *The Final Book*—it's the hottest shit going right now."

"You been talking to my grandma?"

"Is she disappointed in you too?" She smirked.

"I was in a relationship for a while." Alex pressed through her humor. "It just… didn't work. I'm not avoiding it, but I'm not going to force something. Things are good."

"Things can't be good with a babe?"

"You tell me."

Celeste chewed on her sandwich. "I've dated some shit guys." She said. "You're not a shit guy."

"So glad I've met your standards!"

"Oh no, you haven't met my standards." She looked over at him. "I'm just saying, you're not awful. I dunno, Nopah, maybe you just need to get laid?"

"Again, grandma…"

"I want to meet this lady."

Alex took a long swig from his bottled tea and looked across the pavement. "Why does everyone care so much about relationships? It's like I'm an outcast because I'm not miserable."

"We just want to make you one of us. It's not fair."

"Things with you and what's-his-name good?"

"Troy? That guy I've been dating for, like, ever?"

"Yeah. Him."

"Sure, man. We have couple shit, but I tend to like him."

"How'd he win you over? Maybe I could use some pointers?"

"Well, first off, I'm not one for *winning*. Second, he plays guitar. Third, he's honest. We just 'get' each other. He's really thoughtful. Not only about me, but life."

"He's a cool dude." Alex admitted. "I didn't want to like him, but I do."

"That's pretty shitty, man! Why didn't you want to like him?"

"I don't know!" Alex tried to defend. "You're like the cool chick in the movies, the one that the guy like me always pines over."

"Jesus, man—you've known me for, like, 10 minutes. Watch something other than a chick flick!"

"Don't tell me you don't play it up—the cool girl who's just one of the guys. Miss *I know every comic and like gutter punk, by-the-way did you pre-order the new* Star Wars *video game?* girl."

"Fuck you, man! I'm allowed to like that stuff and not be a nerd stereotype of desire! Hundreds of millions of people like *Star Wars* now—get over it."

Alex rolled his eyes. "When you bought that band shirt, you didn't think to yourself *this will let the world know I'm cooler than the rest of them and at the same time be a mega high-five to the one person who gets it?*"

"It's a t-shirt, Alex—not Marcus Aurelius! I like what I like." She looked down at the faded white screen printing. "Gardening, Not Architecture—it's Sarah Saturday—she's solid. The Bouncing Souls wrote a song about her for Christ's sake."

Alex simply stared at her as if she had proven his point.

"What about you, *Mr. I Always Wear Black?* You doing some stupid Johnny Cash metaphor?"

"Yeah, all the injustice of my people."

"...Nice downer."

Alex paused and tongued his cheek. "I'd be lying if I said you weren't pretty. And apparently everyone knows you're rad... but I am happy for you. And Troy. I guess I'm jealous. Not of him—but what both of you have."

"Fuck. Some honesty. It's about time." She smiled. "You're cute too, tiger." She leaned over and nudged him with her shoulder. "There's a party Thursday in The Hills. You should come. I have a friend you should meet."

"What, now you're setting me up?"

"What's wrong with that?"

"I usually save pity dates for Tuesdays."

"Well, shit—I'd hate to fuck up your melancholic week… She's an old friend, we went to high school together—we're both in L.A. now."

"Does she have awful, awkward teenage stories about you?"

"I was never awkward."

"Why do I believe that?"

"You want to come or not? I think you'd like her."

"I don't know…" Alex rubbed the back of his head. "I've got my opening next week. Plus, that shit's weird."

"She hates blind dates too. It'll be perfect."

"Now it's a date?"

"It's a party, man—just stop by and meet her. Third-wheel it with me and Troy for a bit." She jabbed.

Alex rolled his eyes.

"Yes or no? It's one of those posh ones—I have to put you on the list."

"Oh god…"

"Don't get there before 9:00. You'll be the only jackass at the bar."

"Is she going to bust my balls too?"

"In her own way… She's a lot more sweet than me. At least she'd like you to think."

"So, she's fake?"

"We're all fake, Nopah. You tryin' to pretend you weren't chasin' pigs yesterday."

"Horses… How'd you know?"

"Lucky guess?" She raised an eye. "Anyway, she's nice, Alex. She's… got a lot going on but could use a guy like you. And you could get laid."

"I'm not looking to be used…"

"That's why I want you to meet her."

ROCK SUPERSTAR
CYPRESS HILL

Stevie Pearl's Beverly Hills estate was patrolled by private security. They took shifts walking the perimeter, handguns concealed under sport coats. Security cameras covered all 2.5 acres of the prime real estate, her fortress sealed by a massive cement privacy fence. Double embossed wrought iron gates equipped with a checkpoint controlled the flow of traffic. The young pop star had become a prisoner of her own life, and she was smoldering with contempt.

"Not today, Dallas..." She scowled at her PR manager from across the patio.

"What's the matter, darling?" He placated. "It's a beautiful day, what could possibly be wrong?"

"It's Taco Tuesday and I can't go to Yuca's."

"We've been over this—you can't be seen just anywhere. You can't associate your brand with that."

"It's a taco!"

"How about we have some delivered? You want me to send one of the boys? Or perhaps the chef can make tacos here..."

"No. I don't want them delivered… You're missing the point—I'm an inmate! When was the last time I went out? That wasn't a scheduled appearance? Even my *dress-down pop-in shopping* is arranged by you!"

"Stevie, dear—everything you do is news. We have to be careful of who you associate yourself with. You know this."

"It's only news because you call the paparazzi ahead of time! You make it news!"

"It's the game—and that's why you hired me."

"I didn't hire you." She folded her arms. "My label did."

"That's right. I'm the *big bad man* that makes every teenage girl *want to be you*. Enjoy it, Stevie. It won't last forever."

She shot daggers at him. "It's been a decade, maybe that's long enough. I love my fans… I am proud that they look up to me—but you need to remember it's about the music, not which lipstick I'm wearing."

"Should I look at the schedule? Maybe in a few weeks we can arrange tacos."

Stevie began to grit her teeth. "*Maybe in a few weeks I'll want to go for a walk on the beach, or go out for a run!*"

"You're *so* tortured." He rolled his eyes. "Did you see the latest *Star*? They've got you on the cover—your lunch with Jason Saint worked beautifully."

"You're disgusting. He's a nice guy."

"Is he? Maybe you should read the article…"

Stevie snatched the magazine from Dallas's hands and began skimming the piece. Her eyes narrowed and a lumped formed in her throat.

"Asshole…" She shook her head as she read the lies. "This is such bullshit."

Stevie had become thickened to the media scrutiny and journalists slinging sensationalism trying to make a name for themselves. However, she kind of liked Jason and a tiny piece of her heart broke by the betrayal.

"Everyone's a climber, dear. That one date alone made him hundreds of thousands of dollars."

"Yeah, but how did it help *me*—PR Man? How is this 'protecting my brand?'" She flung the magazine on the table.

"It's perfect." Dallas sneered. "Another heartbreak for America's sweetheart. Your relationship status gets more coverage than the Dow."

"That's so messed up..."

"They're all on your side, sweetie. Jason's the villain here. Now they'll have more to agonize over, figuring out who's who in your lyrics. They just want to see you fall in love and be happy."

"Yeah, but you don't. You wouldn't have much of a business plan if I did."

"I suppose there's always the music..."

Stevie was beginning to loathe Dallas and his PR firm. Sadly, she knew that anyone else she found to replace him would be no different. At least they weren't in the past.

She flopped down on the cushioned chaise lounge and curled up beside her dog. Gibby was a medium sized speckled border collie that she rescued a couple of years back. He knew it too. The dog had wandered the streets for weeks before spending about a month at the shelter—his time running short. One afternoon the most unimaginable woman walked into his life and she took him far away from the piss-covered concrete floors and chain-link cages. He loved her without question ever since.

Stevie dug her fingernails into Gibby's long shiny coat and scratched his neck, his eyes shifting back and forth as the two spoke.

"We've got to talk about your party." Dallas continued to push her. "Finalize the guest list."

"Well, take Jason off of it..." She flicked her finger toward the magazine. "Dick."

"Perfect. I assumed as much and already sent an email to his people."

Stevie twisted her head. "Taking liberties?" She was direct, upset that he didn't bother to consult with her first. This type of behavior was becoming a trend since he had been assigned to represent her, and one that didn't sit well.

"We obviously couldn't have allowed him here after those things he said about you..."

Silence fell upon the patio while Stevie contemplated the various ways that this man was handling her affairs.

"Try to keep your hands off of Thursday night." She directed. "I just want to have fun. Everyone on *the list* meets your *approved branding*—just let people be."

Dallas gave an unimpressed sigh. "Speaking of which, a Celeste Ashby requested an additional guest. Supposedly her, her boyfriend, and some guy from the movie she's working on. He checks out. An artist or something."

"Yeah, that's fine. Whatever she wants. I saw I have a voicemail from her—I'll call her back in a while and let her know myself."

"The winning fans from the online contest, the Pearl Party Crashers, we're restricting their access to just the pool area. Some of the other celebrities don't want to be associated..."

"Pfft—screw that! It's my party. My guests—all of my guests—can go wherever they want."

"Monique Stewart specifically said that she will not attend if she's being bothered by groupies."

"Monique can sit home then—I'm not getting into this with her."

"A feud with Monique could be good... The timing isn't perfect, but—"

"It's not a feud, Dallas! *I just don't give a shit*—they're my fans, this is my party—she can come if she wants to have fun. I'm not going to make some little girl feel bad because Monique doesn't want to take a selfie."

Dallas turned his attention and pressed some buttons on his phone. "Have you decided who you're wearing?"

"I dunno. I guess…"

"We partnered with several designers for this, you should have plenty to pick from."

"Is Levi's one of them?"

"No. Of course not."

"You got anything else today, Dallas? *It's been such a pleasure talking with you…*" She desperately wanted him and his arrogance gone from her patio.

"Yes, dear—one more thing. The Grand Ole Western is honoring you with a Lifetime Achievement Award. Is that something you want to be a part of?"

"I'm only 26…"

"Yes, but commercially you've already surpassed all of the other recipients. Apparently they felt it was appropriate, your name is the only one that continued to come up when narrowing down the field."

"I can think of a lot of other great artists much more deserving… I'll call Walter directly and we'll talk about it."

"Well, that's what I'm here for—"

"I'll call."

Dallas pressed send on his phone and an email whooshed away. He finally looked up and nodded. "Okay then. I'll, ah… leave you to it." He clasped his hands. "Anything else before I go?"

"Remember—Thursday's a party. Not a promotional event for you. Just take it down a notch."

Dallas raised an eyebrow and turned his back, leaving Stevie with her dog and thoughts. She sat in silence for a few moments before reaching over into a flowerbed, gently rubbing a petal between her fingertips.

"What do you think, Gibby?" The dog twisted his head as she spoke. "I'm not sure about Dallas…"

"Psst—Ms. Pearl." She heard a low vibrato summoning her.

Franklin was Stevie's longtime personal bodyguard; he had been with her since she was 17. Now in his mid 40s, Franklin was the closest thing she had to a true friend.

It was an odd coupling, a lanky young white girl and a three-hundred-and-twenty-five-pound middle-aged black man who devoted his life to saving hers. He was tender and candid with Stevie; always being straight with her when others weren't, and always having her best interests at heart.

Deep down, Franklin felt bad for Stevie. He saw how isolated and alone her fame had made her, and how very few people in the world truly looked after her. Franklin was nothing short of a grizzly bear who made it his mission to protect her both physically and emotionally. In doing so, he afforded Stevie something she rarely had—the ability to be genuine.

In turn, Stevie shared her most vulnerable moments with him. She cried on his chest over boys and forced him to celebrate with her when she won awards. Franklin traveled the world with Stevie Pearl, and she always made him feel appreciated for it.

"Miss Pearl—yo, Stevie." Franklin's deep voice beckoned once more.

Stevie looked around the patio and across the courtyard for anyone milling about. She casually got up from the chaise lounge and walked toward the pump-house of the pool. Franklin poked his head through the door and met her with a grin.

"You want tacos???"

"You know it." She smiled back.

Franklin stepped aside, trying to make a gap big enough between his belly and the doorframe for Stevie to squeeze through. Once she was in, he shut the door and pushed some boxes that revealed an unassuming bulkhead—a simple metal hatch in the floor that looked like a service panel to the pool equipment.

He opened it up and held Stevie's hand as she dropped down the metal ladder. The enormous man followed behind, pushing himself though the tight opening and pulling a rope to close the panel door above them. Stevie used the light on her phone to find a switch on the wall. She flicked it and lit a long underground corridor that lead out of the estate. Franklin carried the keys and kept the door to the outside world locked; the portal hidden by thick bushes and invisible from typical street traffic. If anyone did discover the door, it appeared to be nothing more than an old service entrance for landscapers.

Stevie's secret tunnel was on the far side of the estate and well out of the eyes of prying paparazzi with telephoto lenses prowling the main gated entrance. Still, Franklin made sure the coast was clear before taking any chances.

He looked up and down the street, paying close attention to parked vehicles. Satisfied, he hit the unlock button on the key ring and a silver Honda Civic chirped on the side of the road. He nodded to Stevie and she darted from the bushes, jumping into the passenger seat. The unassuming car had blacked-out windows like a limo and sank three inches when Franklin got in.

"Oh girl, we gonna have some Taco Tuesday!" He announced with full steam. "With the lime! A little fresh squirt of lime!" He kissed his fingers like a gourmet chef.

"Yuca or Henry's?"

"Shit, you kiddin' me? Yuca all the way." Franklin pushed the button on the dash and the car came to life. He then reached into the back seat. "Here, put on your hat and sunglasses."

"Hell yeah, Yuca's!" Stevie grinned, knocking dust off of her Astros hat. "You read my mind!"

"Turn your phone on—get some music up in here!"

"What can I torture you with today..." Stevie flipped through a playlist. "Ah, got it!" She hit play and slowly cranked the volume knob to build anticipation.

"Ah—fuckin' Justin again? C'mon, Stevie—c'mon!"

"Okay, not that." She quickly changed songs.

"This better not be none of that trance bullshit neither. Some stoopid ass robot music..."

Stevie giggled, always overly amused by their little game. She loved playing DJ, choosing a song and torturing Franklin into guessing it. "You know this one, Franklin—I know you do!"

Franklin started to groove and shake his shoulders with the tambourine. He pumped his fist in unison with the gong as Stevie raised the volume. "Ah, you done did it! Walk Like An Egyptian?"

The verse hit and both Stevie and Franklin began a duet.

"*All the old paintings on the tombs, they do the sand dance—dontcha know? If they move too quick—*" Stevie pointed to Franklin who, with an angelic voice and wide eyes, hit the "*oh-way-oh*". She then followed with, "*they're fallin' down like a domino.*"

Franklin muttered some words he thought were lyrics, hitting each "*oh-way-oh*" right on cue until they both paused and gave each other their sexiest, "*walk like an Egyptian... walk like an Egyptian...*" Both flashing their eyes back and forth like Susanna Hoffs from the music video until Stevie could no longer contain herself. She cracked up and they both laughed hysterically.

"Taco Tuesday!" Stevie shouted.

"Taco Tuesday!"

The modest car pulled off the road and rounded the little walkup taco stand, parking by a large white building. Franklin got out and sashayed over to the window, whistling the solo from the song that continued to play in his head.

"Ay ay, Thelma—what's cookin'?" He knocked on the window.

"Whatch you doin', big man? Where you been?"

"It's Taco Tuesday—gotta make my girl happy."

"Yeah, I'm sure she twisted your arm..." The woman smiled, giving a coy look down at his gut.

"We goin' there, Thelma?!" Franklin played offense and cocked his eye back at her. "The usual. Don't forget the lime."

Franklin sat under the frayed canopy of the covered patio while Stevie remained in the car and played on her phone. She twisted around in her seat and snapped a pic of the Yuca's sign out of the back window. She hesitated a few moments with the photo app open, deciding if she should share it. It had nothing to do with associating *her branding* by publicly liking the little mom-and-pop taco shop, but she knew the moment the pic hit the internet, the place would be crawling with paparazzi. Stevie sighed and closed her phone.

Franklin forced himself into the car like a circus bear, handing her the white plastic bag of food.

"Home or picnic?"

"Picnic."

Franklin backed out of the spot and pushed the car through L.A. traffic, Stevie getting lost in thought while looking out the window. They paralleled the concrete ditch of the Los Angeles River and then he turned down a service road, bringing the car to rest at the top of the cement bank.

He looked over at her and killed the engine. She smiled but didn't say much, just took the bag of food and met him out in the sun. They used the hood of the car as a tabletop and watched the heat bake the graffiti on the cement walls.

"Paradise?" Franklin looked over at her, wiping the taco juice from his hands.

She shrugged. She thought about her thirty-million-dollar estate while looking at a pile of broken bottles and beer cans. "It's just good to get out."

"You turned that normal chip in, soon as you wrote the first single…"

"I'm grateful—you know I am." She looked over at him. "I wouldn't change it."

"What's the matter then?"

"I'm just bummed about Jason."

"Jason? Man, fuck that guy. He's a loser."

"I don't really care about him… it's just the same old story. There's no one I can trust. No one that isn't trying to use me. I can't even have lunch…" She looked down at the soggy taco. Her precious addiction tattered by the steamy styrofoam container.

"You let Dallas creep into yo' head. He's used to managing people that got no talent. They need all that other glitter n' shit goin' on." Franklin waved his hand while he talked. "Do whatch you do, Stevie. Write your songs, live your life—it ain't no game. You know what's best. Always have."

Stevie lingered on his words. "It'd just be nice to go on a real date…" She hesitated. "Not a normal one—I understand nothing will ever be normal—but a real one."

"Find a real guy."

MAYBE TONIGHT
NICOLE ATKINS

The sun was losing its evening glow. Landing lights dotted the horizon along the LAX flight path while headlights flowed like a river down distant hills. Alex flicked back to his low-beams and coasted up to the guard shack.

"Good evening, sir!" The security guard tried to shout over the popping exhaust of Alex's motorcycle.

"Howdy." Alex nodded.

"Name?" The man gave up on yelling and mimed with his mouth, pointing toward his clipboard.

Alex killed the engine so they could talk. "Alex Nopah—with Celeste Ashby."

The security guard looked the would-be biker up and down. "ID?"

Alex rolled his eyes and leaned forward, pulling his wallet from his back pocket. He handed the man his license and waited for him to give it back.

"We have a valet tonight. Talk to the attendant about what he wants you to do with... this." The man eyed the metallic monster.

Alex gave a waggish thumbs up and then fired the bike. He revved passed the gates and up the driveway, his loud exhaust turning the heads of arriving Hollywoodites.

The entrance was wide and bold with massive flat stone pavers that circled a misting fountain in its center. Exotic cars lined the pathway to the party, the valet milking the egos of their owners for tips and forcing all who entered to walk by and admire them.

The estate was pristine and enchanting. Gentle landscape lighting brought to life exotic plants and flowers that otherwise would have gone unnoticed in the fading twilight; their sweet bouquet masking the Los Angeles air quality. The valet trotted over and met Alex before his crackling tailpipe made another lap around the fountain. The teenager waved him in over by the exotics.

"What the hell am I supposed to do with this, McQueen?" The kid gave him shit and pointed to a spot next to a Bentley. "Back it in over here, plenty of room—don't scratch it."

Alex pulled the clutch and did as he was directed, suddenly feeling the peculiar pressure of keeping the bike upright. His reflection in the midnight blue paint job of the three hundred-thousand-dollar car made the earth under his boots feel like marbles. His quads strained while easing the chopper back. Finally settled, he killed the engine and flicked the kickstand with his heel simultaneously.

"The great thing about a bike," Alex removed his aviators, "I don't have to tip you." He playfully jested to the kid.

"You do if you want any of that chrome to be here when you get back…" The valet was quick.

"When's your break? Maybe I'll sneak you a beer instead."

"I'm not lookin' for a date, mister." The valet smirked.

"Love it—which comedy school did you fail out of?"

"The same one that sold you that coat."

"Nice." Alex grinned. "I like you." He wagged his finger.

"Look. I told you—you're just not my type… Now, move it along, Mary—there's actually some important people here."

Alex twisted his head, amused but befuddled by the reception. The valet ran off, chasing a massive blacked-out SUV coming up the driveway before he had the chance to sling another comeback. Alex laughed as he watched the kid work, the valet now suddenly oozing charisma with a guest who he assumed had money.

Alex stepped back and admired his bike, wiping a few fingerprints from the chrome mirror with his shirtsleeve. Before he was done, he found his gaze resting upon the cars that surrounded him. He fell for the contrived trick of their parking placement, and his imagination, like many others, ran for a moment. A fantasy played out in his mind of racing up the PCH to Malibu, blonde hair flowing in the passenger's seat. The dewy ocean air mixed with perfume and obnoxious music. He contemplated the thunder he could create from his right foot, the g-forces pressing against the small of his back. He lingered on the thought for a moment before finally noticing the entrance of the home. He then headed up the stone steps of the estate and never looked back.

"Good evening, Mr. Nopah." He was greeted by the doorman.

Alex nodded, finding it suspicious that the man knew his name. He hadn't attended many parties with professional greeters, but after noticing the man's earpiece he assumed the security guard at the gate radioed up about his arrival.

"You can check your jacket over here—"

"I'm good."

"Very well." The man nodded. "The bar is in the back by the pool, however there's waitstaff walking around taking requests. Cuisine is being prepared by Chef Roman Frost. Help yourself or let one of us know about any special dietary needs and we'll be happy to accommodate. Ms. Stevie Pearl welcomes you to her home and wishes that you enjoy your evening."

"Stevie Pearl?"

"Umm—yes, sir. This is her party…"

Alex nodded as if he knew that. "Thank you."

"My pleasure…"

Alex took it slow walking through the entry, his hard-soled cowboy boots clacking on the marble floor with each step. He had been introduced to wealth since coming to L.A., but even still, this was impressive. Tall walls were capped off by a fresco dome that was laced with thick white trim and elegant crown molding. In the center of the room hung an unmistakable Dale Chihuly blown glass chandelier. A wide, long staircase curved up toward the second floor and beautiful flowers bloomed from what he assumed were expensive vases.

Trying not to look like a gawking Midwesterner in Manhattan, he followed the hum of the party and headed straight to the backyard and searched for the bar. Having a drink in his hand made him feel more sociable, or at least like he was trying.

Finishing up with the bartender, he felt a hand on his shoulder. "Alex?"

"Oh, hey, ah—" he drew a blank. He knew he recognized the face but couldn't place the name.

"Troy—Celeste's boyfriend—"

"Troy! How you doin'?"

"I'm good, man. You made it!"

"Yeah, sorry—my head's out of it. Stevie Pearl's house?? I don't even know where I am right now." Alex looked down at himself and what he was wearing. "I also didn't know this thing was a gala… Celeste just said it was party."

"You're fine, dude. No one gives a shit—plus, you look good!" Troy gave him a reassuring smile. "So, how you been? Are you just going insane with this movie, or what?!"

"It's unbelievable—I never imagined I'd be doing something like this. And after our meetings this week, I'm scared as hell... but it's awesome."

"Well, the comics were fantastic—we had them on the road with us and I read every single one. Honest. You're really good, man. Serious."

"Thanks." Alex avoided his eyes. "How's work with you? Celeste said you got to record some tracks at Sound City?"

"I shit my pants, dude! No lie! I'm shitting in them right now as I talk about it. I mean, it was just studio work, not my own material, but fuck—just to be in that room!"

"Oh, I can imagine... It's still all analog, right?"

"As pure as baby Jesus himself!"

Alex smirked, he was beginning to feed off of Troy's easygoing optimism. He briefly wondered if that's how this guy caught the eye of Celeste.

"What's the deal with the band?" Alex asked.

"Ah, we're doing our thing. Going on the road with the boys late this summer—play some festivals, shitty casinos—it's fun. I'm just so happy to have this studio gig. Never thought I'd hear myself say it, but consistency is good. I'm being paid to play guitar —might not be my songs, but at least people are hearing them!"

"You ever played for Stevie?" Alex nodded toward the massive house.

"Ha—noooo! I'm not even going there, bro. Both Celeste and Stevie know I play guitar—if she asks me one day, cool, but I'm not bringing it up."

"Celeste knows Stevie?"

"Fuck man, why do you think you're here?"

"I have no idea! I didn't even know where I was—Celeste doesn't tell me shit! I just knew it was some big house in The Hills... They all look the same."

"Yeah, dude, Celeste and Stevie go way back. You knew Celeste is from Austin, right? That's where we met—my band was in town recording, we've kinda been together ever since."

"Well, I get it now…"

"Nah, dude—I don't think you do." Troy smirked.

"Hey, boys." Celeste put her arm around Troy. "Alex, nice boots."

"What the fuck, Celeste?! You can't give me a heads up—I didn't know what to wear!"

"It's fine!" She laughed. "The motorcycle was top notch. All the priss bitches were snickering."

"Dude, you rode your bike here?" Troy laughed.

"It was nice out." Alex shrugged. "If I'da known anything about tonight… Fuck you both." He snarked at their mocking laughter.

"You look good." Celeste assured him. "It's a music industry party—what's wrong with a little rock n' roll?"

"I tried to tell him." Troy agreed. "He looks like a walking Levi's ad. You know the black and white motorcycle one, the guy riding through the desert? The dude stops at some shit gas station and always finds the hottest chick—she's wearing Levi's too… It works man, don't worry about it."

"Right—the kid out front just said I wasn't his type. He called me Mary!"

"Who, Joey?" Celeste asked.

"The surf punk playin' valet."

"That's Joey." She laughed. "And that's awesome."

"That's Stevie's little brother, man. He's, like, 17." Troy laughed along with her.

"I didn't even know I was at friggin' Stevie Pearl's house." Alex flipped his hand at Celeste. "Again, wasn't informed."

"Yeah, dude. He likes driving the fancy cars. His parents keep him on an allowance—believe it or not—and he gets off on the tips."

"Ha!" Alex swigged his drink. "I told him I wasn't going to tip him either!"

"Better hope that bike's still waiting for you!" Troy playfully shrugged.

"That's what he said!"

Alex looked around at the courtyard and pool area that was decorated for the event. White paper lights ran the length of the house, draped between marble columns that held up the high arches of the upstairs balconies. Hundreds of tea-light candles sprinkled the edge of flowerbeds and walkways, gently flickering in the night air. A few bushes were wrapped in white lights and the infinity pool glowed a magnificent purple. It was elegant, modern, and profoundly tranquil; the subtle glow transforming curves and angles into a conjuring of depth and beauty.

There were celebrities mingling that he recognized but couldn't remember their names. They were all dressed in thousands of dollars' worth of dresses, suits, and jewelry—wearing their Ray-Ban's at night and spilling drinks. He still couldn't believe he was standing in the backyard of one of the world's biggest pop stars, and felt just as insecure about it.

"What the shit?" Alex said under his breath as he soaked in the moment. "Why didn't you tell me this was Stevie Pearl's party?" He looked to Celeste.

"Would you have come?"

In her spiked heels, Celeste was about as tall as Alex. Her dark eyeliner and smoky eyes dug into him. She wore sheer black tights with stars woven through them, her legs capped by a black mini skirt. She layered a pink lace tank top with an old cut up band t-shirt that you could see through. Over that, an unzipped tight faux-leather jacket reflected the purple light of the pool. Her sleeves were pulled up and one hand was pushed into a pocket while the other held a beer. She radiated late-80's Sunset Boulevard, but the gentle features of her face made it clear that she had never partied with Guns N' Roses.

"Well, you know, I'm such a big fan…"

"That's the spirit." She mocked him. "I need another drink."

Alex looked down at his glass that was still half full.

"Pound it." She demanded. "Have another one with me and Troy, and then I'll introduce you to my friend. Troy, you want another?"

Troy weighed his beer bottle and gave her a *might as well* shrug.

Celeste lead Alex through the crowd toward the bar. He awkwardly smiled as he scooted past what he assumed were record label executives. He noticed people glancing at him and couldn't tell if they were trying to figure out if he was someone they should recognize, or if they were caught off guard by unexpected denim and leather. Either way, it made him self-conscious.

Finding a place to stand at the bar, they had a minute to themselves while they waited for drinks.

"You could have at least told me to wear something nice. I feel like a jackass."

"You even own anything nice?" She smirked.

"Well, nothing that would be considered nice here…"

"Exactly, man. Me either. Stop worrying about it. You look good." She nodded. "Classic. Timeless."

Alex rolled his eyes. "So, who is this chick?" He fished for information. "What makes you think I'll like her?"

"I'm going out on a limb here. Promise you'll give her a chance, okay?" She actually gave him a look of sincerity. "Don't be judgmental with first impressions."

"What? She have a club foot or something?"

"So what if she did? I'm telling you you'll like her—trust me."

"You're kinda freakin' me out... What's with all the mystery?"

"She's beautiful, Alex. She's the warmest, sweetest girl I know —be nice to her." Celeste was stern. "I'm serious."

Alex gave a dismissive nod to appease the conversation.

"She's got a complicated life. She has walls—we all do... She's just been hurt a lot. I told her you're not into the bullshit."

Alex used his tongue to play in his cheek. He knew what it felt like to be guarded. His heart left his sleeve a long time ago, and he had no intentions of getting into another bad relationship. "I'll be nice..."

"I know you will." She raised an eyebrow. "Now act like you're having fun!" She grabbed him by the coat and tried to push some life into him. "This's a good thing."

The bartender delivered the drinks and the two wove back through the party to Troy. They found him consumed in conversation with another musician. Celeste handed him his beer, but hung next to Alex as she had little interest in the endless debate over Gibson verses Fender or their favorite pedal mods.

"See those girls by the pool?" Celeste pointed at a group of teenagers that seemed as out of place as he felt. "Pearl Party Crashers. They won some contest to be here. Kinda cool."

Alex watched the three girls for a moment, they looked like they had been picked last in gym class. They did their best to look beautiful in their dresses, but something off a rack never fits as good as the designer gowns that were tailored for the celebrities that surrounded them.

The girls had bright smiles, but were obviously shy and only whispered to one another. He could sense that their overblown expectations of the Hollywood party fantasy were melting into the realities that they were unknown little teenagers and that no one could care less about them. While the young girls were allowed through the gate, little would suggest that they were being accepted.

"Let's go talk to them—pretend we're famous."

Surprised by the suggestion, Celeste returned his devilish smile. "Lead the way!"

The girls were huddled around each other like they were avoiding boys at a middle school dance. They met Alex and Celeste with wide eyes as the two approached.

"Hey—I heard you guys were the big winners?" Alex was direct but friendly in his delivery.

"Yeah…" One of them replied awkwardly.

"Right on. You havin' fun?"

"It's SUPER cool!" The other interjected with an enormous grin.

"Oh, this is my friend, Celeste. I'm Alex." He made the introduction.

"What's your names, girls?" Celeste smiled and reached to shake their hands.

"I'm Rochelle. That's Stacy, and this is Tamrin."

"Well, it's nice to meet you!" Celeste was warm. "I love your hair! All three of you—it must have taken all afternoon!"

"Yeah—Tamrin's mom helped. She's a stylist." Rochelle said.

"She's a good one—you're all so beautiful."

"I like your tattoos." Rochelle returned the compliment, doing most of the speaking for the girls.

"How come you're not out there dancin'?" Alex nodded to the courtyard where the DJ was set up.

The girls giggled. "I'm not goin' out there!" Tamrin said.

"Aww, why not? You need to show 'em how it's done!" Alex moved like a robot. The girls laughed again but shyly avoided eye contact. "So, have you met Stevie yet?"

"Well, we talked to her online when we won, but we haven't seen her tonight." Rochelle said.

"She's here, you'll meet her soon enough." Celeste reassured. "After all, this is her house!"

"Do you guys know Stevie?" Stacy finally eased herself into the conversation.

Alex shook his head. "Nope. No clue!" He grinned.

"Alex will get to meet her tonight too—just like you guys!" Celeste playfully elbowed him.

"Yeah right..." He rolled his eyes. "But, apparently Celeste knows her!"

"Is she cool?" "What's she like?" "How'd you meet?" The girls bombarded her with questions.

"She's the best—you'll love her, I promise!" Celeste tried to settle them. "Alex is the one who you should be really excited to meet though. He's a world-famous artist!"

"Really?!" The girls lit up.

"No, no..." Alex downplayed.

"It's true—his big gallery opening is next week!"

"That's so cool." Stacy giggled awkwardly.

"Celeste works on movies." Alex passed the attention. "Big ones!"

"Really? That's awesome!" Rochelle said.

"What do you wanna do when you get older?" Alex asked.

"I want to sing." Tamrin said.

"Comin' after Stevie." Celeste smiled.

"I want to work with animals." Rochelle added. "Horses maybe. Dogs are cool."

"Have you met Gibby?" Celeste asked. "He's usually running around here somewhere..."

"I've seen pictures of him online—he's so cute!" Rochelle gasped.

"I like his spots." Stacy said.

"Well hey, would it be okay if we all took a picture?" Alex asked the group. "I need proof to show everyone I met the coolest girls at Stevie's party!"

The girls blushed but were giddy with the proposal. "Who has the longest arms?" Alex teased as they all crowded in. "Get in here, Celeste!"

Everyone gave big smiles and the phone flashed as it took the picture. "One more—I was closing my eyes!" Alex laughed with all of the girls hanging on him. They held their pose once more and took another.

"What's this? You stealing my fans?!"

Everyone's eyes tried to readjust from the blinding light, unable to put a figure into the silhouette that was standing before them. All of a sudden, the girls started squealing, leaving Alex and Celeste in a cold squat.

"Oh my god—oh my god—oh my god!" The teenagers pranced their feet.

Stevie gave the girls a big hug.

"Oh, you're so beautiful! Your dresses! Look at you—I love your hair, those shoes!" She did her best to make them feel welcome and special. "Thank you for comin' to my party! I'm sorry I took so long."

Alex steadied Celeste in her high heels, helping her regain balance. He then rubbed the back of his head as he caught a glimpse of the pop star. She was even more beautiful than she was on TV.

"I see you girls met my best friend!" Stevie leaned in and gave Celeste a hug, whispering in her ear. *"Glad you're here too."*

"You guys are best friends?" Rochelle's jaw dropped. "We were hanging out with Stevie's best friend?!" She looked to the other girls with excitement.

"You know it! We've been friends since we were your age." Stevie smiled toward Celeste. "Younger even. We grew up in Austin."

"I've been to Austin." Tamrin said.

"Did you like it?" Stevie humored.

"It was okay. We didn't do anything."

"Not much to do." Celeste interjected. "Girls—Alex and I are gonna go find my boyfriend—let you hang out with Stevie for a bit. Promise to save me a dance later?"

"Wait a minute." Stevie slowed. "Who's your friend?" She reached out to shake Alex's hand.

"This is *Alex*." Celeste emphasized with her eyes. "I was going to introduce you a little later..." She nodded.

Alex met her grip, their touch sending chills down his spine. Her hands were thin and soft, her eyes welcoming and kind. Stevie's blonde hair fell just beyond her shoulders and she smiled at him brightly.

"He's a world-famous artist." Stacy informed.

"Is he?" Stevie held her grip, forgetting to let go.

Alex shrugged, not wanting to disappoint the girls.

"He's got some fancy gallery thing next week." Tamrin added. The girls had obviously taken an instant liking to him and were proud to feel in-the-know.

"Which he will tell you all about a little later." Celeste eyed Stevie once more and regained control of the conversation. "Have fun with the Party Crashers—they've been dying to meet you. We'll meet up in a little while. Do your thing, dear." She briefly hugged Stevie once more.

"Don't leave." Stevie whispered to Celeste. "I want to spend time with you and Troy. With Alex." She looked toward him. "A few loose ends and I'll find you?" She begged with her eyes.

Celeste nodded with acceptance but tapped a pretend watch on her wrist. Getting alone time with Stevie, especially at a party, was next to impossible. She had sat backstage by herself many late nights waiting for Stevie to finish working before the two could enjoy a simple conversation.

"Party Crashers—save me that dance!" Celeste pointed at the girls and lead Alex away. They found Troy standing in the same spot, but now with three guys around him all talking shop.

"More drinks?" Alex suggested.

"More drinks."

They went back to the bar where Celeste began flamingoing. "Fuckin' heels."

"Well, so, I guess you really do know Stevie Pearl…"

"You think?"

Alex ignored her tone and sucked on an ice cube. "Figured that would have come up at some point—oh hey, my best friend from childhood happens to be Taylor Swift."

"It's Stevie fuckin' Pearl."

"Right. Like there's a difference. So, when am I going to get to meet this chick? It's getting kinda late…"

"Wow. You really are that dumb guy from the movies."

Alex scrunched his face, confused as to what she was talking about.

"You just met her!"

"They were a little young, don't you think? I mean, I'm pretty sure Stacy liked me, but shit…"

"Oh my god…" Celeste rolled her eyes. "You deserve to be single."

"What?!"

Celeste glared at him until it finally started to connect.

"My friend from high school—known her forever—doesn't have the best track record with dudes…" She talked down at him as if he should have pieced it all together from the start.

Alex choked on his drink trying to find words. "Wait, what?! You being serious?"

"From Austin—we're both living in L.A. now…"

Alex suddenly felt like he got punched across the room. "You —fuckin'—want me, to date Stevie Pearl?!"

"Shh—keep your voice down!" She glanced around to see if anyone was eavesdropping.

"You're insane!"

"Probably."

Alex stepped back and studied her, trying to figure out if she was busting his balls like usual or being real. "What the hell, Celeste?! When were you going to tell me?"

"I wasn't! I was going to let you two meet and hit it off. I should be home by now."

"Is this a joke?" He stammered. "That's not the most absurd shit in the world?"

"What are you talkin' about, man? You're a cool guy. A nice guy—us dumb chicks are finally at the age where we want that."

Alex was starting to feel the full weight of what she was proposing. "I'm dirt fuckin' poor, Celeste—a nobody—I don't think you get it. I can't date her..."

"I told you not to be judgmental. You promised." She glared at him.

Alex held his breath. "It's just...it's different worlds... I don't think I qualify."

"Alex, if she had to date someone with as much money as her, there'd be like three dudes in the world she could go out with. They're all pieces of shit. Don't ruin something because you're insecure—I've done that, you'll regret it."

"I don't even know what to say..."

"I don't get why you're so worked up about this—you don't even like her... her music anyway. You never get star struck. What do you have to be nervous about?"

"Because..." He gave her a blank stare. "It just seems like something I should be nervous about." He couldn't think of a better response.

"Dude, if you pretend that all of the bullshit, all of her fame and money doesn't exist—the things you don't care about anyway

—I promise—I promise you'll find a normal girl in there. Better than normal... Someone just like you. Gotta give her a chance though."

Alex took a breath, allowing her words to settle. "Did you just call me a normal girl?" He deflected, twisting words to help gain his own composure.

"You're fuckin' actin' like it... A lil' bitch."

"You're unbelievable." Alex tried to swallow the proposition. "Does she know?"

"Know what?"

"Why I'm here? That you're setting us up?"

"Of course. I talked to her last night..."

"Ah, fuck me... That's not awkward."

"Jesus, Alex. This isn't jr. high lunch. You're my friend from work—I like you. I think you have a lot to offer. She's my friend from high school, I've known her forever. You're both single. Work it out. Or don't." She shrugged. "Your loss."

Alex pulled from his whiskey. "I can't believe you're legitimately doing this..."

Celeste stared at him.

"All right." He nodded. "I'll meet your fuckin' friend. I'm just feelin' a little blindsided."

"You would have talked yourself out of it if I told you."

"Damn right." He put his fingers through his hair.

"Let's go find Troy."

NEW ROMANTICS
TAYLOR SWIFT

"Hey, man—" Troy grabbed Alex's shoulder as they walked up. "Where you guys been? You meet Stevie yet?" He grinned.

"He knows too?" Alex's condescension was directed toward Celeste. "Am I the only one who doesn't know?" He facetiously looked around the courtyard.

"Know what?" He heard a soft voice from behind.

Alex closed his eyes and let out a deep breath. "She's right behind me, isn't she?"

Celeste nodded with a shit-eating grin.

Alex forced his legs to step aside, opening up room for Stevie to join their little group.

He looked to her and nodded slowly, unsure of what to say. She looked back at him with a subtle smile, her eyes half hid behind her hair.

Alex gestured out into the crowd. "It's, ah, a very nice party, Ms. Pearl—"

"Ms. Pearl?!" Celeste sputtered, trying not to shoot beer out of her nose. "I told you he was going to act like a goober. Just let him get it out of his system."

"Thank you." Stevie replied, but her eyes plead with Celeste to stop embarrassing him. "Did you find it okay? Things can get twisted up here."

"Found it fine… Parking was interesting."

"Joey wasn't out there?"

"No, he was…" Alex smiled.

"Ooh… What'd he do this time? I told him—"

"He's fine!" Alex laughed. "Funny kid."

"Little wise ass is what he is." She smiled.

"Alex decided to ride his motorcycle." Celeste interjected.

"That was you?" Stevie laughed. "We—we heard you comin'."

"Sorry, I didn't know." Alex shook his head and pointed at Celeste. "She didn't tell me anything, I just thought it was some party… I would have dressed better."

"Don't you think he looks like that dude from the Levi's ad?" Troy jumped in and tried to bail him out. "You've seen that new commercial, right? The black and white one?"

"I don't know…" Stevie raised an eyebrow. "I think he might be a little cuter."

"Gross." Celeste rolled her eyes. "Sorry, can't help it. All this awkwardness."

Stevie blushed. "You have to put up with her every day at work?"

"Unfortunately." Alex nodded. "Sounds like you've been dealing with her since you were kids?"

"'Bout right. My best friend since junior high." She looked toward Celeste. "We were together every day before I started touring."

"Finally, some dirt." Alex raised an eyebrow. "I wanna hear all about lil' Celeste!"

"Well, don't let all this fool you—she wasn't that cool." Stevie smirked.

"Hey!" Celeste pretended offense.

"Neither of us were. We were so awkward!" Stevie laughed.

"Who introduced you to Automatic Loveletter?" Celeste bobbled her head. "Cat Power? All you listened to were boy bands!"

"Oh, don't even start!" Stevie scoffed. "You want dirt, Alex? Don't believe her when she talks about The Smiths or Pixies—this girl's favorite band was the Jonas Brothers! I swear that's the only reason she moved to L.A.!"

Alex grinned, he loved seeing Celeste's cheeks turn pink.

"Hey—Kevin's my one true love! Sorry, babe…" She looked at Troy.

"Remember when we skipped class for the first time?" Stevie continued. "I convinced you to sneak out so we could watch the boys play soccer—you basically had a panic attack the entire time thinking we'd get caught!"

"Awe—you're so cute!" Troy joined in the ribbing. "Celeste The Badass afraid of the hall monitor!"

"We were freshman, and I cried." Celeste admitted. "I used to care about things until I met this bad influence." She grabbed Stevie by the hand. "But then you left me…"

"It was hard, always being gone—it happened so quick…" Stevie squeezed back and reminisced. "But we stayed friends. I love having you here in L.A." She gently lifted her eyes toward Celeste.

"Still never get to see you though." Celeste nudged Stevie with her shoulder. "You're so busy all the time."

Silence fell over the group as their memories faded and the present grabbed a hold of them. Stevie looked out across her party and weighed all the sacrifices she had made and how many of them were unfair to those she cared about.

"Troy, you're playin' still, right?" She deflected the consuming thoughts.

"He just finished up some tracks at Sound City." Alex jumped in with a nod, returning the favor of being compared to the Levi's ad.

"I heard somethin' about that. I'm proud of you, Troy—that's an amazing studio. Heck, I'd love to record there someday."

Troy tilted his beer at the compliment. "I'm sure you could make that happen..." He jested.

"Did you say hi to Jimmy? I saw him here earlier. You never know when he's lookin' for someone."

"Kinda..." Troy blushed. "We were both getting food and I nodded to him."

Stevie laughed. "You gotta do more than nod! I'll talk to him for you. There's always something happenin' in this city."

Jimmy was one of the most successful record producers and executives in the industry. He made the careers of countless musicians and ran the label that publishes Stevie's records.

"You don't have to—" Troy was quick. "I don't want you to think..." He looked over at Celeste. "Let's just have fun tonight."

"It's no big deal!" Stevie beamed. "If he does, he does." She shrugged. "But I'm pretty sure he will."

"Well, thank you." Troy was sincere. "I appreciate it."

"Stop hitting on my boyfriend." Celeste smirked, her words were sharp as usual but her eyes thanked Stevie as well.

"That was really nice what you guys did for the girls—the Party Crashers." Stevie turned toward Alex. "I'm always afraid it's going to be so boring for them."

"I don't think they're bored..." Alex remarked.

"Well, regardless. Some people aren't as nice... Plus, I think one of 'em liked you." She gave a coy smile.

"Only one?" Alex regained a bit of his wit. "Thought I did better than that."

He had a difficult time reading Stevie. She had become naturally good at conversation with strangers, making those around her feel noticed and included. He wasn't sure if this was part of her charm or if she was showing interest in him.

"I don't think I'm willing to share…"

Alex bit his lip and latched upon the comment. It gave him the nudge he needed to continue testing the waters. "So, then you're willing?"

"Well this is cute…" Celeste couldn't help herself. "You two, umm, so yeah… By the power vested in me, Troy and I are gonna go visit the bar—anyone need anything?"

They each had full drinks and shook their head.

"Okay, Alex—" Celeste cleared her throat. "Remember what I told you—just try not to be yourself."

Without another word, the four became two and Alex found himself standing at the edge of the party alone with Stevie Pearl. She was radiant. Never in his life had he been around a woman dressed to the nines.

"Well, this isn't uncomfortable…" Alex immediately approached the elephant in the room. "What'd she tell you?"

Stevie smiled. "Enough. What'd she say to you?"

"Opposite of that." He laughed. "Apparently the less I know, the better. You do look beautiful though…" He muttered while taking a sip from his drink.

"What's that?" Stevie heard him just fine, but much like Celeste, she enjoyed putting people on the spot. Perhaps it's where Celeste picked it up, but Stevie had her own flare. Rather than coming across as ball-busting, she was coquettish. She was always able to walk a fine line of semantics, her words mistaken as sweet and often naïve, but their meaning filled with depth and possibility. It was the *possibility* that drove men nuts. The way she was able to dance with an idea without ever clarifying its intent.

"I said you're very pretty." Alex over enunciated loudly and clearly, doubling down on the compliment. "Serious though, you do look very nice in your dress." He tipped his glass.

Stevie blushed and pushed her hair to the side so she could get a better look into his eyes. "Thank you. Wish I was wearing Levi's like you though."

"I'll share." He looked down at the faded denim. "You're more than welcome. But I don't think I'll fit into that dress."

Stevie bit the inside of her cheek and blazed past the idea of him undoing her dress. "I dig the boots. Reminds me of home."

"Really? I hoped you'd notice. I woke up this morning and asked myself—you know, how could I catch the eye of Stevie Pearl today? *Boots.*"

"Oh yeah?" She giggled. "Well, you have my attention—now what are you going to do with it?"

"Listen." Alex looked over his shoulder. "I've gotta tell you something." He leaned in. "It's been eating at me since I walked through the door." He hesitated, then nodded toward her beautiful glowing home.

Stevie paused and looked at him with curiosity.

"I want to make sure we're always honest with each other. No bullshit." He held her eyes. "...I've never listened to one of your songs. Ever. I mean, like, I'm alive—so through osmosis, I'm sure I heard some of them, but..." He grinned.

"Ha!" Stevie scoffed. She was caught off guard by his brash approach. "Well, since we're being honest... I've never read a comic book in my entire life. I mean, I saw Jughead once standing in line at the supermarket when I was a kid... But, yeah. Not one."

The two grinned as their claws dug into each other.

"I'm okay with it if you are." Alex lifted his glass.

"Cheers to us having nothing in common!" Stevie met him.

The two sipped their drinks.

"You do like to dance, right?" Alex asked. "Why don't we start from there." He was bold and grabbed her hand, stepping toward the DJ.

"Uh oh—I don't think you know what you're in for..."

The entire party erupted when Stevie Pearl stepped onto the dance floor. The DJ sliced and immediately dropped bone-rattling bass, cranking the volume that ended any remaining conversations that may have been happening in the neighborhood. The tranquil courtyard exploded into a fireworks display of Las Vegas lights and glitter, brief moments of darkness becoming consumed by blinding strobes and neon colors that shimmered all of their focus upon Stevie.

She was right, Alex was completely out of his element. Quickly drowning in a club scene that he was never a part of, he did his best impersonation of Jimmy Fallon awkwardly snapping his fingers to the beat. Thankfully he didn't have to keep up for long as glittery dresses with wild legs swarmed the dance floor, working in and out of their slits in rhythm. With Stevie's approval, it now seemed everyone, sport coats included, wanted to be out on the dance floor next to her.

"These all your friends?" Alex shouted, stumbling in and out of time.

"Everyone's my friend if they want to be!" She backed into him and then spun around, a piece of hair sticking to the corner of her lip.

The two tried to outmaneuver each other, Stevie looking like a music video and Alex killing the cabbage patch. The DJ stuttered and warped, sending Alex into a horrendous rendition of the robot. Stevie loving every second of his playful effort.

"I see you do this all the time!" She grinned.

"I only draw to support my dancing!" He grabbed her hand and twirled her back into his chest. "You haven't even seen my Rain Bird yet." He whispered into her ear.

She twirled back around and pushed him, smiling ear to ear. At this point she was surrounded by five or six of her back up dancers from the last world tour. Alex couldn't tell if this was choreographed for the party or just a force of habit. Using up his bag of tricks, he attempted something that resembled the Charleston and desperately looked for an exit.

"Rochelle!" He shouted and waved. "Party Crashers!"

Alex shrugged his shoulders toward Stevie and acted like he was bored with her, doing an epic moonwalk fail toward the teenagers. "Oh, thank god…" He said under his breath.

The girls beamed and formed a circle around him, keeping time in their sparkly heels.

"No more, no more!" He shook his head with his hand on his hip.

"Go Alex, Go Alex!" The girls began to chant. He was now starting to feel more like Hashtag The Panda than Jimmy Fallon.

"Who the hell's goofy ass Tonto?" Franklin muttered to Celeste. He stood next to her and Troy at the bar while keeping an eye on the party that had moved to the dance floor.

"That would be my friend… Though I accept no responsibility."

"I don't like the way she lookin' at him…"

Stevie danced over and joined the Party Crashers in their chant. Alex responded by shaking everything he had.

"Here—you've got a gun." Celeste nudged Franklin and held out her hand. "Can I shoot him? Somebody needs to shoot him. Look at that."

"Yeah, I'll fuckin' shoot 'em…" Franklin grumbled, witnessing another heartbreak unfold before his eyes. "Why you do this to me, Celeste? 'The fuck I ever do to you?"

"He's a good one, big man. Stamp of approval."

"After the last one? Your stamp don't mean shit…"

"That was years ago! And that guy was hot…"

"Yeah, you and 'hot guys'—Troy over there looks like a fuckin' muppet."

"Yeah, but which muppet? That's either a compliment or highly offensive."

"Go save your boy." He nodded toward the dance floor. "He's makin' a damn fool of himself."

"Fine… Gimme the gun first though."

Franklin gave her what he thought was a gentle push but sent her striding to catch up with her feet.

"Your girl's crazy…" Franklin cocked an eye down at Troy.

"Yep."

Celeste found Alex wiggling in the middle of the dance floor, Stevie and the teenagers squealing with delight. "My girls!" She included Alex in her greeting.

"Dance with us!" Tamrin shouted, making room for her.

"You do this? This your fault?" She circled her finger around the dance floor and began to bump hips with Alex. "Hollywood, not Bollywood. Wrong kind of Indian."

Alex laughed, finding humor in the burn.

It didn't take long before Celeste fully relented, letting go just as Alex had but looking much better while doing it. The whole group moved together in motion, Alex stumbling while Stevie and Celeste shared playful glances as they had in junior high.

Absorbing the sight of her friend grinning and flipping her hair, Stevie too lost herself. Her life had become about moments; special instances where the world melted away and all was forgotten. Slices of life that contained no past or future, where time's only function was rhythm and the motion she created from of it. In this moment, Stevie appreciated her friend more than she'd ever know, and relished the thought of the handsome man that she was just introduced to.

It was closing in on 2 AM when Alex was finally able to pull Stevie aside once more. Their little dance group had been overrun with people wanting their own moment on the floor with Stevie Pearl.

"Hey—"

"Hey." She smiled at him.

"This was a… great party." He was sincere. "Thank you for having me."

"Of course. Glad you had fun." She looked down at her shoes.

Stevie found herself transformed. The ease and confidence she carried herself with when meeting new people had melted into an attraction. Being captured within Alex's attention suddenly made her feel shy, and she loved that he possessed the ability.

"I… don't dance." Alex bit his lip, thinking of how he had made a fool of himself. "Ever."

"I dunno. I'd say you danced tonight…"

"Ah, you see… My plan worked perfectly then. Now we've got somethin' in common."

Stevie blushed and twisted the bracelets on her wrist.

"I think your Party Crashers had a good time."

"We all did. The night of our lives."

The two stood quiet. Words, thoughts, and emotions were being mixed with subtle cues buried beneath context and trepidation, paralyzing each from any form of action.

"Hey—umm, I've got this thing next week… my showing. It's going to keep me pretty busy until then, but I thought if you'd like to come? I mean, I'd like you to come. Celeste will be there…"

Stevie lost her breath with the invitation, as ragged as it was. She exploded at the proposition and her face beamed.

"I'd love to!" But then she caught herself and paused. Looking over her shoulder at the ancient ruins of her party, the reality of her world flooded her. "But I don't know if I can…"

Alex's face remained expressionless as the limb broke from underneath him.

"No!" She read his eyes. "I want to—I'd like to... It's just... difficult. It requires an Act of Congress for me to make an appearance."

"Appearance? I don't want an appearance..."

"I know. That's not what I meant... I just... You wouldn't want me there, trust me."

Alex tried to swallow the lump in his throat. He only heard rejection, not her words. "Oh... I get it." He nodded. "No worries."

"It's not like that."

A consuming blend of embarrassment and shame penetrated Alex's brain and melted into his chest. *How dare he allow himself to believe that he would ever have a chance with Stevie Pearl.* His ears burned. The audacity rippled. The moronic disbelief echoed, the notion that he had actually convinced himself that she would have any interest in him.

"It's complicated, Alex. PR, attorney clearance to make sure I'm not competing with my other contracts, security..."

"You don't have to... make excuses." He looked down at his scuffed boots. "I just thought...it doesn't matter. Thanks again for tonight."

"Alex, I'd like to—I would... It's just business. There's a lot of people who want me to go to things. I have to protect myself."

Alex was further taken aback.

"You—you think I'm trying to get publicity out of this? Use you?" He twisted his head. "I asked you 'cause I liked you. I thought we had a good time tonight." He gestured back toward the party.

"No, you don't understand, we did—"

"I don't know why Celeste brought me here—"

"I can't do things—I can't just show up at places."

The two stood silent. They studied each other in the dim L.A. skyline.

"Stevie, it's simple. I just wanted to see you again." He limped. "I wanted to show you my work…"

She maintained her silence, unsure of what to do. Unsure of how to explain herself.

"Yeah… Okay." He nodded at her lack of response. "I realize how foolish that sounds now that I've said it out loud."

Stevie's shimmering golden dress hugged her. The slim strap that wrapped over her shoulder seemed tailored specifically to hold her back. She looked like a confused piece of art; beautiful in its curves and tones but its meaning and intent lost upon the audience.

Dejected, and with a bruised ego, Alex turned his back.

"I'll see ya around…" He began to walk away.

"Hey?" Stevie plead to his fading silhouette.

Alex facetiously waved his hand in the air and disappeared into the darkness.

He fought with himself as he walked around the side of the mansion, back toward his motorcycle. His mind played the night over and over again. The way she looked at him, flirted with him. It seemed real? Was it a cruel game? A prank only seen in teenage movies? He felt so embarrassed. He loathed his boots, his worn jeans—would a suit have made any difference? You can take the boy out of the trailer, but not the trailer out of the boy. He was right all along. He didn't belong there. He was angry with Celeste for thinking any different; for filling his head with ridiculous Cinderella fairytales.

He slowed as he approached his bike, taking a hard, long look. Tampons had been tied and were dangling from the side mirrors and handlebars.

He clenched his jaw with tooth-splitting force. Alex snatched the final insults and ripped them to the ground. He fired the engine and tore down the driveway.

EFFECT & CAUSE
THE WHITE STRIPES

The next morning Alex woke up to a pounding head. His lack of sleep mixed with a couple of drinks only reminded him of his own foolishness.

"Stupid..." He hunched over the sink and looked into the mirror.

"*What am I doing?*" He thought.

He finally had an amazing opportunity at work, and he was now risking it by showing up faded from a night of partying. He had to be sharp—he wanted to be sharp for this job. He whipped himself with guilt while splashing water onto his face.

He walked across the apartment and slumped back onto the bed. He reached to the nightstand and then looked at his phone. He rubbed his eyes and looked at it once more.

Every social media app had exploded.

"What the hell?" *7,496 New Followers.* He tapped to see himself tagged in dozens of photos from the night before. He began to read the comments but suddenly dropped the phone. He sprang to his feet, rushed back to the bathroom, and emptied his stomach into the toilet bowl.

Studying the shapes and stains left behind on the porcelain, he wasn't sure if it was the top-shelf bourbon that brought him to his knees, or that he was now the overnight trending story on *TMI*.

Pulling his laptop from its case, Alex sat at the kitchen table and began wading through the digital trash. He clicked on a link that took him to a video posted by a web-based news agency. The screen glistened and popped as it showed various celebrities posing for photos prior to entering Stevie Pearl's party.

"Hollywood shut down last night as everyone who's anyone was at Stevie Pearl's private residence for an exclusive backyard barbecue. No messy faces and sticky fingers here, only A-Lister's dressed to the hilt. Many brought their dancing shoes as this Pearl party was one to be remembered. That's right, Chuck— especially the dance moves of this lead-footed guest." The video cut to a handheld cellphone clip of Alex dancing. He was horribly off beat and flailing like an idiot compared to everyone else.

"Oh no! Somebody cut the music, please! But don't count this mystery man out just yet. Numerous photos have been posted across social media showing him and Stevie Pearl exchanging scandalous glances." The video blended into a montage of him and Stevie dancing close to one another.

"Could this be America's sweetheart's newest man? Some say a definite yes after witnessing the two last night. So, who is this guy? We did some digging and twinkle toes turns out to be Alex Nopah, comic artist most notable for his work on *The Final Book* series."

The video cut to him sitting on panels at Comic Con and posing in nerdy pictures with cosplayers. "Big production dollars have been spent turning this franchise into Hollywood's next big blockbuster, and Alex is working as a lead consultant for the studio. How he caught the attention of Stevie Pearl is not yet known, but stick with us as the story unfolds."

"Fuck me…" Alex put his fingers through his hair. The internet had already exploded with gossip and he was still sitting in his underwear.

He tried to pull himself together to make it to work on time. He jumped up into his Jeep, tossing his laptop bag on the passenger seat. Alex had an older SUV that he had converted into an expedition vehicle during college. It had thick metal bumpers, big tires, and a modest lift kit. It was designed to take him deep into the desert, and did many times—it wasn't a road queen like the other lifted trucks he saw getting groceries throughout L.A..

He backed out of his spot and made a few turns on his normal route to the studio. He hesitated, looking in his rearview mirror. A sinking suspicion fell upon him as he studied the vehicles. Was he being followed?

Still not thinking straight from his late night and rough morning, he convinced himself that he was being paranoid. He arrived at the production lot as usual and checked in with security at the gate. He parked in his normal spot and got out of the Jeep, slinging the computer bag over his shoulder. Immediately, someone began calling his name.

"Alex—Hey Alex!" A man beyond the fence leaned from his car and waved.

Unsure of who he was, Alex stopped and instinctively waved back at the guy.

"Thanks, fuck nut!" The man opened the shutter on a camera and captured his every move.

"Jesus Christ…" Alex ducked as if he was avoiding incoming fire. He looked over his shoulder and back toward the guy, taking a deep breath. He pushed himself from the Jeep and maintained a brisk stride all the way through the office doors.

Finally at the reception area, three of his co-workers stopped in their tracks and stared at him. Alex looked back at the glass doors, his breath short but he did his best to conceal the panic on his face.

"There he is—fuckin' Fred Astaire!" One of them mocked and they all laughed.

"Cute, Tommy." Alex began to walk. "What'd you do last night? *Call of Duty* in your mom's basement?"

Alex tried to act as natural as possible, consciously reminding himself of his typical morning routine. *Coffee.* The lightbulb went off and he directed his feet toward craft services.

He stood at the table, his back purposefully pointed toward the soundstage. He felt a slight tremble reverberating through his hand as he reached for a cup. *Fuck, I did not have that much to drink...* He tried to recount his trips to the bar the night before. The coffee glugged into the cup, his memory assuring him that he had done nothing terribly excessive.

Suddenly, mid fill, music ripped out of the loudspeakers. The sound startled him and the reflex caused him to jerk and miss the cup, the hot liquid scalding his thumb. He didn't even recognize the song until he heard her voice, the subtle cadence of Stevie's vowels cutting into him deeper than the joke. Alex threw the stir stick on the table and whipped around, giving everyone the middle finger.

"Jim!" Alex stood face to face with the director. He quickly changed his gesture and began rubbing the back of his head.

"You're a meme, Nopah. Congratulations." Jim held up his phone and presented a dancing gif of Alex doing the cabbage patch on repeat. "Stevie Pearl, huh? Good work..." He slapped him on the back with mocking approval.

Alex closed his eyes, summoning all of his composure. His mind raced seeking a moment of reprieve, a place where he could avoid all human contact. Within seconds he found himself hiding in a bathroom stall. He took out his phone and began to text Celeste.

"This is bullshit. Fuck you. Oh, and come find me. I'm hiding in the bathroom."

"I got a text from Stevie." She replied. The pulsing dots of her continued typing felt like an eternity. *"How'd you screw that up? Seemed so good when I left."*

"Fuck Stevie—my life is ruined!" He typed back.

"Whatever. I like your dance a lot more than The Carlton…"

"This isn't cool, Celeste."

"It will pass. Tomorrow everyone will be talking about a dumb panda video."

"Where are you? Are you at work yet?"

"Kinda overslept… Cover for me?"

Alex slid down onto the toilet seat and wiped the clammy hangover from his forehead. All of the apps on his phone continued to rack up notifications like the national debt ticker in New York. He placed his head on the side of the stall, the cool vinyl laminate feeling like morphine. He closed his eyes and thought of Stevie. She had made her way under his skin. He tortured himself with thoughts of her blue eyes digging into him. The way she'd smile, revealing a depth never captured by the camera.

Alex spent the rest of the day avoiding people and trying not to go online. An impossible task when his sole purpose was to answer questions, primarily through email. Each time he looked at his phone he had more followers, now up to 213,858.

Celeste eventually showed up, but she worked through lunch in an effort to make up for her late morning. Physically, she was hurting worse than he was. The more he thought about it, he was pretty sure that he remembered her puking in the bushes. She stopped by his workspace while on the way to the supply closet, offering little clarity of the night before.

"I don't know, dude. I haven't really talked to her. Doesn't sound like you gave her a chance though…"

"That's bullshit. She totally blew me off. Excuses."

"I told you, it's complicated. I just can't see her acting that way. There has to be a reason."

"Yeah—I'm not fucking good enough."

"I can't do this today, Alex… Just lay low, go home and take a nap. That's my plan."

Alex did go home immediately after work, quickly closing blinds all around his apartment. There was no way he was going to fall asleep though, his mind was reeling with the garbage being spun about him.

His feelings had mostly dissolved into a helpless desperation, hinging on his inability to do anything about the situation. He wanted to defend himself. He wanted vindication. He wanted the truth to be known—still naively holding on to the misguided notion that truth meant anything to these people. At this point he had become a narrative, and only a more interesting narrative could derail the train and grant him asylum. He wasn't prepared for this type of attention. He wasn't trained or equipped to manage it.

His idle hands shook, eventually finding use by wrapping the last of his canvas prints around wooden frames. Fortunately, his procrastination left a fair amount of work to be done for the gallery showing and he found the busyness to be a relief. The work acted as an escape and he fully devoted himself to it.

He savored the tension that built in his forearm, holding tight until the loud clack of the staple gun released. He commanded the spring to pop, sending a metal shard through the canvas and penetrating deep into the wood. This was something he could control. As foolish as it was, in that moment, this was a task that empowered him.

The phone broke his concentration, its plastic case vibrating on the side table.

"Ma?" He answered.

"Alex—what's going on?" Her voice was concerned.

"Just framing some prints—getting ready for the showing." He answered casually.

"No. Tita… She's watching *TMI*—you're all over the news!"

"Fuck me…" He hadn't even considered his family catching wind of the night before. "Oh… I, ah, went to a party last night."

"Stevie Pearl? These pictures, Alex… What's going on?" He could hear his grandmother in the background yelling something about him finally having sex.

"They're nothing. Just some dumb Hollywood thing."

"The TV says you're dating. They're talking all about your gallery opening next week."

"What?"

"Stevie's PR agent released a statement denying your relationship and said that she has no intention of attending the opening, but unnamed sources state that her security has been spotted around the Santa Monica art gallery—scouting it out." His mother repeated what she was hearing from Mario on the television.

"What the fuck?" He gasped.

"You need to turn on the TV…"

Alex hunted for the remote control but then stopped mid-motion. "No. Screw it." He caught himself. "Yeah. I had a great time with Stevie last night—I didn't know what I was getting myself into. She blew me off, Mom. There's no story. We're not dating. She's not coming."

"How'd you meet her?"

"A friend through work…"

"She always seems so nice on TV. I like her songs."

"It's all an act." Alex was bitter. "She only cares about herself. Just a typical spoiled brat… I wasn't good enough for her."

"Honey…" Kadence searched for words.

"It's ridiculous! Me—dating Stevie Pearl? How fuckin' dumb is that?"

"You're a nice guy—why not?"

"If one more person tells me I'm nice… Jesus, Mom—where am I going to take her, McDonalds? How am I supposed to date Stevie Pearl? I can't even afford the gas for her limo."

"That's bullshit!" He heard Tita yell in the background. "That skinny bitch wants him—eyes don't lie!"

"It doesn't matter…" He sighed. "She rejected me anyway."

"What do you mean? You're handsome. You've accomplished so much." She said, like any mother would.

"We're a bit different, don't you think? I don't know anything about that world…"

Kadence paused, allowing her son to speak.

"You should have seen it, Ma—I didn't belong there. My clothes were all wrong, my drinks were all wrong, my words were all wrong… Have you been online? Have you seen the things people have said about me?"

A long silence filled the line.

"I've never experienced so much hatred in my life. I feel as big as an ant. And the worst thing about it is I allowed myself, for a brief second, to think that it might actually be different."

"You're not an ant, Alex…"

"I don't even know what to say… I mean, I've gotten glances—we've all gotten the looks—but this stuff online is pure unfiltered evil. Just because I danced with a girl…"

He could hear heartbreak forming in his mother's voice. "Someday you'll find a girl who likes you for you. I know it."

"It's not that… It's not her fault… Yeah, I feel like a dumbass over Stevie, but this whole thing has been a brutal wakeup. No matter what I do, the world will always see me as some low-life savage. That I'm stupid—uncultured. The only reason I'm allowed at a party like that—allowed to have the job that I have, is because of affirmative action—because I surely didn't earn it." Alex clenched the fist in his free hand and dropped his head. "Fuck, Ma..."

"That's not true, Alex—you know it. You're so smart and talented—your work is proof of that. It speaks for itself. When you paint and draw, no one knows who you are—they just see the beauty you create."

"And that's exactly how I want it... I gotta go. Finish this stuff up. I'm sorry I didn't call, but it's been a bad day."

"Things will get better. We love you."

"I know."

"We'll see you in a couple days at the gallery."

"I'm sure I'll talk to you before then..."

"Cheer up. Don't listen to those people, Alex—we're so proud of you. I'm proud of you."

"Yep..."

"Stevie, I released the statement because that was the right thing to do—that is what *I was hired* to do. To protect and promote the brand." Dallas argued with her.

"This is my life, Dallas! Not a brand—not some PR bullshit!"

"Exactly! I'm not going to allow this guy to turn you into that. You don't know him—the first night you meet and he wants you to go to his opening? It's clear, Stevie—he's using you! Why not the movies, ice cream, or dinner for god's sake?! He's not trying to get to know you—he's just looking for the Pearl boost."

Stevie was seething, unsure what to believe. Dallas was right. It had happened so many times before and it always cut her deeply. It made her feel cheap, embarrassed—her fame and notoriety being exploited for quick sales at the expense of her kindness and friendship. However, there was no way that Celeste would put her through that. She wouldn't set her up with a guy just so he could sell a few more prints.

"*This guy's a nobody*." Dallas continued. "His art isn't going to sell—you're his 30 seconds of fame. Why do you think he was acting like such an idiot last night? Drawing all that attention? This one day of media gained him more exposure for his little art show than he would have gotten in his entire life otherwise."

"Not everything is an angle! What if he just doesn't know how to dance? What if he really did like me? Asking me to his showing would have been a big deal for him—a special night. *This is his art.*"

"Ah, sweetie… *He's no good*." Dallas now spoke soft, his condescension palatable. "I didn't want to tell you this, but we did some digging. He's nothing but reservation trailer trash. Some scrap heap from the desert. We shouldn't have allowed him on the list in the first place… In fact, I need to have a word with Celeste."

"Get out." Stevie pointed at the door. "Now!"

"Allow me to remind you that we have a contract."

"Fuck your contract. I own your contract—I own that whole fucking label! *They going to pick me, or you?*" Stevie's chest heaved, adrenaline surging through her veins.

"There's not a professional in the world that would have handled this any different."

Franklin stepped into view, making sure the weight of his presence was felt. "She said get the fuck out. Now get the fuck out."

Dallas eyed the most lucrative client he ever had, and in a split second witnessed the opportunity go up in flames.

"Go back to *Austin*—get a fucking trailer with him!" He tossed his hands and walked toward the door.

Stevie maintained her strength until the door slammed. She then collapsed into tears behind her desk. She was exhausted. Like her friends, she was nursing a cloudy mind and lack of sleep. While an uptick in publicity after such an event was expected, the forest fire that ensued following the electricity between her and Alex was almost uncontrollable. Even for her team.

"Hey…" Franklin moved toward her, taking a seat across the glass table. "That guy's an asshole. Right or wrong, he never cared about you. Just saw dollah signs."

Stevie huffed, anger consuming her. "He's probably right!" She lashed. "Alex is probably just using me like all the others!"

"'Ey, this ain't nothin' to do with Dancin' Feet. Dallas' the one using you—how many things gone bad behind your back? He never consulted with you on nothin.'"

She looked at him and wiped the tears from her cheek with her sleeve.

"We don't know Alex—but we do know Dallas' a piece of shit. You ask me, it was the right move either way." Franklin leaned back and nodded his head. "Alex, no Alex—Dallas never helped you. Dallas only help Dallas. Don't need that in yo' life."

His calm words did make her feel a little better.

"I don't know what to do…" She said. "Everything's tied up at the lawyer's. At first look they said I shouldn't go—possible conflict of interest and *fucking code of conduct* issues with sponsors… Code-of-conduct, Franklin." Her rosy eyes and quivering lip conveyed the hidden racism that her lawyers were unable to speak.

"Stevie, now, I ain't talkin' this guy up, okay? I got my sights into him too." He spoke with his hands. "As security, I ain't comfortable with him neither. Ain't no one's gonna like this dude. But that don't make him a bad guy…"

Stevie sniffled, the tears in her eyes being replaced by focus.

"His family's poor—I'm talkin' you white folks stripped everything his culture had, decimated his people—his tribe almost went extinct—oh-here's-some-dried-up-desert-land-out-in-the-middle-of-fuckin'-nowhere type of poor. Yeah, I Wikipedia'ed that shit… Us black folk, we were at least valuable as property—get some work out of us—keep us around... Not him. Not his people..." Franklin shook his head with a humble stare. "Different childhood."

"I don't care about that. I mean, it's awful—but—"

"Now, hold on. There's a fat little black kid that grew up all messed up too. On the streets, gettin' into *bad trouble*. Military fixed 'em up, added a few more scars. Somehow he made it into this palace..." Franklin looked around the room. "'Cause you allowed him into this palace...

"There's two ways to look at it, Stevie—no one can fault you either way. This world was fucked up long before you and you've got to hold onto your little piece. Alex could be that fat kid—grew up with what he know, worked hard to get good at somethin', then found a way out. He could also be seein' an opportunity—because this here, this is a big fuckin' opportunity. You've got a billion-dollar empire to run, and he ain't makin' that no easier. Who you date affects your bottom line—I ain't got those worries. I don't bring those worries on you. Just bein' seen with that dude caused the stock to dip."

Stevie sat in silence, contemplating his words. "I don't care about the money."

"I know you don't. 'Cept everyone else around you does..."

The two remained quiet. The weight of Franklin's words drumming in Stevie's ears.

"What's Celeste say 'bout this dude? Why she bring him here?"

Stevie bit the inside of her cheek. "She wouldn't expose me, Franklin... She wouldn't even ask me to help Troy out by getting him some guitar work—her own boyfriend. Some art scam for Alex doesn't make sense."

"I know... But maybe you two should talk. Shit's real now—it ain't high school no mo'."

"I will. She didn't do anything wrong."

Stevie's gaze became distant. She watched the palm fronds tap lightly against the window. She then followed the speckles of dust swirling in the sunlight as it pierced through the room.

"It's like I knew nothing and everything about him all at once... I saw him misinterpreting my intent about his art show, but I couldn't find the words that would allow him to hear me. It was pretty crappy how he walked off—though I don't know if I can blame him."

Franklin moved in his seat, lifting a foot across his leg. "You did nothin' wrong... The only thing you're guilty of is liking a fool—he naive. He don't know how this shit works... The world's biggest pop star just drop in at some art show at a beach shack? 'The fuck's he thinkin'?"

"That he wanted to see me again... And I said no."

THE ECSTASY OF GOLD
ENNIO MORRICONE

It was late in the afternoon. Alex worried himself while pacing around the gallery, making final preparations for his opening night.

He agonized over the track lighting—how the color smeared oddly across the canvases, his work reacting strangely beneath a foreign glow. He was accustomed to the cheap fluorescents of his workspace, their harshness providing the tenuto that illuminated his angst. He then tinkered with the sound system that pumped music overhead. He turned it on. He turned it off. He changed the playlist. An off-kilter smudge on the large window that faced the street sent him searching for paper towels and glass cleaner.

Celeste's arrival was a welcome reprieve. He helped her lug in cheap beer and boxed wine from her car. The two arranged the social lubrication, working in silence until she mentioned the one thing on both of their minds.

"So, you never heard from her?" Celeste maintained her attention on filling a tin trough with bottled waters, getting the drinks ready to be put on ice.

Alex tore through the cardboard boxes that held the beer. "Nothing."

"That's pretty shitty…"

"She's your friend."

"I told you she asked for your number—figured she would have text or something?"

"Fuck, I dunno?" Alex stepped back and rubbed his face. "This last week has been a nightmare. I wouldn't have anything nice to say to her anyway."

Celeste read his posture—the dark rings under his eyes, and his pushed back hair was messier than usual.

"I loved the article about you in *Valley Jagg*." She tried to lift him with sarcasm and a grin.

"So fucking stupid…" He rolled his eyes. "Like anything Ronnie Doll ever said matters. Fuckin' hack… We danced—I can't imagine actually dating her. *I can't handle this shit!*" He emphasized the words by tossing a sack of red plastic cups at her.

Celeste's fingernails ripped into the cellophane. With one motion she tore the bag and created a neat stack of party cups that piled high next to the beer. "You did sell everything though, didn't you? Even your prints for tonight?"

"Yeah… Got a couple more commissions too." He thought for a moment. "I don't know how to feel about it. The money's great —you have no idea how much that will help… Mom, Tita. But I always thought if my art ever sold, it would be because it resonated—it spoke to someone. Not because people are gambling on Stevie Pearl's love life… She turned my career, these pieces I've been working on for years, into a carnival show."

Celeste sighed and avoided his eyes. She understood the sentiment and was feeling guilty for how everything had worked out.

"I'm sorry, Alex. I didn't know… She's not a bad person—"

"There's paparazzi outside right now hoping she shows up—even though her people made it *very clear* that she won't be." He glared out of the freshly cleaned glass window toward the creeps with cameras that were lurking in their cars as if it was an FBI stakeout. "This has been the most miserable week of my life."

"Shit, man..." Celeste chewed her tongue, absorbing the bitterness in his tone. "I don't know what's going on with her—things are always difficult because she's Stevie Pearl, but I never saw it going this way."

"It's not your fault..." Alex turned, relenting a *Walking Dead* themed daydream where he was bashing in the brains of paparazzi zombies. "There's not much more to say." He shrugged. "Yeah, maybe I read the whole thing wrong when I walked away—but she didn't stop me. If she couldn't come to the gallery tonight—if she wanted to see me again—she could have suggested something else. Said something, anything, else."

"Well, you were just kind of... gone—weren't you? I mean, you both said you just walked off—"

"She had her chance. I told her I just wanted to see her again. She left me standing there—twisting in the breeze... Nothing. Not a word. It doesn't even really matter about her anymore..." The focus in Alex's eyes fell upon Celeste and his snicker was poignant. "I mean, yeah, I felt like a total jackass for *you* letting me think that I *actually had a shot with the biggest pop star on the planet.* But now I just want my life back... I can't even go the grocery store."

"It's fuckin' stupid, dude—I don't get it!" Celeste protested, her neck snapping toward the sky as she pleaded with Eros. "You both tell me the same story—you're both clearly dumbasses—I thought you'd be perfect for each other."

Alex ignored her usual sass and instead sought insight. "You're, like, her best friend—how'd you deal with it? All the media and drama?"

Not receiving her desired reaction, Celeste's tone weakened. "I just don't let it bother me, man. It's not her doing it."

"Well it's certainly not me!"

"Alex, she didn't plan this. The drama is this beast with a life of its own—she's gotten better at controlling it, but she's not a mastermind. She didn't mean for any of this to happen to you. She doesn't want those guys camped out in front of your house—getting in the way of your big night—prodding and harassing everyone who walks by."

Alex struggled to find compassion, but he knew she was right. This wasn't Stevie's fault, but that wasn't going to stop him from blaming her.

"It was hard at first—no one can prepare you for it. When we were kids and she was blowing up, it was exciting—seeing myself beside her, or in the background on TV—my name in magazines when she'd talk about her best friend in interviews… but then it all got really scary. Creepy dudes showin' up at my house. Literally. My step-dad freaked." She smirked. "You think one house party is bad—try a weekend in Vegas when you're 19."

Alex attempted to mask the thought by returning an uncomfortable smile. He couldn't imagine the gossip escalating, or being 20 years old and trying to deal with the relentless attention.

"I eventually became old news." Celeste continued. "I've been friends with her for, like, 10…15 years? There's not much of a story with me anymore. They try to get me to comment on boyfriends or a breakup once in a while, but Stevie is pretty good about protecting us. She learned the hard way—we all did. She laid down a firm rule with the media to stay away from friends and family, anyone going against that is hardcore blacklisted. And of course, any reputable journalist does not want to be on Stevie's blacklist."

"So why me? I'm not protected?"

"The world's just reacting right now—no one on her team was prepared for you, or your little dance number. You just dropped in that night and everyone was blindsided… including her." She smiled. "She likes you, Alex. I don't know what the fuck's going on, but I know my friend."

A loud thump startled their words. Rustling toward the back of the gallery sent their attention to make sense of the noise. The latch of the heavy metal door snapped open and the hinges squeaked.

"Alex?! You here?" A voice shouted. "Hello?"

"It's just my mom." He reassured. "Yup! Out front!"

Kadence cautiously poked her head in through the backdoor and then followed her son's voice, Tita shuffling behind.

"You guys made it!" Alex greeted. "Good, and you're early—I can put you to work!"

"Your brother's trying to park the truck." His mother leaned in for a hug. "We circled the block a couple of times—who are all of those people?"

"Tita!" Alex ignored the question and welcomed his grandmother. "This is Celeste. Celeste, this is my Mom, Kadence, and that's Tita."

"Tats, huh?" Tita lifted an eye at Celeste. "Got one on my inner thigh. Looks like melted putty now."

Celeste burst into a cackle.

"Jesus, Ma…" Kadence glared down at her. "It's nice to meet you, Celeste." She extended her hand.

Celeste pushed the hand aside and wrapped Kadence in a warm hug. "It's great to meet you too—you did a good job with this one. He gets me coffee at work." She gestured toward Alex with her thumb. She then leaned down and held Tita extra long. "And I've heard quite a bit about you!"

"Shit…" Tita squinted through her cataracts.

"The place is lookin' good, Alex." Kadence complimented. "I haven't seen some of these." She moved around the room, examining his work.

"Gettin' there. Still have to wipe down a few counters—get these beers on ice." He patted the top of a box.

"You can give me one of them." Tita flicked her finger.

"No—" Alex snapped. "I'm not giving you any beer—your meds. Don't let her have any." Alex eyed Celeste.

Later. Celeste mimed with her lips. *Once he's gone.*

"I like this one." Tita struggled forward, reaching toward the tower of cups. "Why don't you date her instead of Miss Priss?"

"I'm not dating Stevie—for the *millionth time!*"

"That's not what Mario says..."

"Tita, I don't care what Mario says! I'm standing right here and I'm telling you that we're not dating."

"Pussy."

Celeste beamed toward the old woman. "I call him that too! We're gonna hangout tonight." She grabbed Tita by the hand. "Maybe we can get you laid."

"Psh—I don't need your help." Tita jerked her hand back and gave a gummy smile. She used her tongue to slide along the gaps in her missing teeth.

"Yup..." Alex imagined the train wreck that was about to unfold. "I've got shit to do."

Alex's opening night was beyond a success. All of his close friends and family came to support him, some of the production crew from the movie showed up, and countless strangers that he could only attribute to the Stevie Pearl phenomenon. Eccentrics, a few minor celebrities, and a lot of climbers created only elbow room within the tiny Santa Monica art gallery.

He felt spread thin, rushing to shake hands and meet introductions. Naturally, everyone he talked to asked him to dance —a joke that quickly grew tired. However, he did secure several more commissions and obtained countless phone numbers and email addresses for future print runs.

The night was more than he could have hoped for, though it did lack one guest in particular—Stevie Pearl's PR department remaining good on their word. There was no sign of the pop star, and he almost felt relieved. Perhaps, finally, the world would realize what he had known all along—that Stevie Pearl had no interest in him.

"Thanks for coming, Charlie—driving Mom and Tita." Alex found a quiet moment off to the side with his brother.

"This place is a shit show." Charlie looked around the room with a beer in his hand. "These the people you hang out with here in L.A.?"

"I don't know most of them…"

Charlie nodded slowly, studying an art crowd he had only seen in movies. "Some babes here though."

"That's one thing L.A. doesn't lack."

"Where's your girlfriend?" His brother's gaze met him square. "You show her your tiny ding-a-ling and she split already?"

"Yeah. That's exactly what happened."

"You don't actually like her, right? Stevie Pearl? Fuck, man— that'd be stupid."

"It is stupid. It's been about the worst week of my life, Charlie… Though today turned out pretty good." Alex looked out across the room with him. Never had his own work brought so many people together, or made him as much money. "Just different worlds. Seems you've kicked me out of yours, and she won't let me into hers."

"Don't even start that shit." Charlie was gruff. "Look at you, Alex… You don't think any one of us would trade places with you in a second? No one crowds around and claps when I unveil a new pump for the well."

Alex remained silent.

"I know you gave Mom money."

He turned and met Charlie's eye but didn't offer a response. The two stood still in silence.

"There's my boys!" Kadence approached, putting her hands on both their shoulders. "Isn't this great, Charlie? Can you believe your little brother pulled it off?!"

"Seems he always does."

Alex shifted his weight and sought peace. "Charlie was just telling me how he got the well back up and running—fixed the fence. I'm sure it looks really nice."

"It does." Kadence agreed. "He keeps that place going. He's been busy since... well, we came into *some money* when Tita got an increase in Social Security. I guess they messed up a long time ago..." She eyed Alex.

"I keep saying that we should seek back-payment," Charlie interjected, "but Mom doesn't seem to think we should. All these years with the government stiffing her—I want to go down there and raise some hell. What do you think, Alex?"

"I think you should just let some things go, Charlie." Alex said. "Speaking of which, I'm gonna go find Celeste and Troy—make sure they haven't gotten Tita too drunk."

Alex nodded toward Charlie and then crossed the room, shaking off his brother's disposition by shaking a few hands as he walked. The warm praise and compliments of his work quickly melted any animosity that was carried with him. He looked back toward his family and saw Kadence smiling. Charlie had his tongue in his cheek. He knew he eventually needed to talk to his brother, but tonight wasn't going to be the night.

"You guys don't have to stick around." Alex said to Troy. "The cleaners will get most of it, I just don't want to leave a disaster." He walked around the room filling a trash bag with empties.

"You did good!" Celeste hung on her boyfriend for balance. "Good night. T'was a good night..."

"It sure was for someone!" Troy laughed, straining to hold on to her.

"She gonna be okay?"

"Looks like your grandma drank her under the table."

"I love Tita!!!" Celeste slurred, dragging Troy as she staggered a few steps.

"Jesus." Alex laughed. "Have fun with that."

"Tita!!"

"Fuck!" Troy lunged as Celeste's limp body flopped like a cadaver. He maneuvered and managed to avoid colliding into a floor display with Alex's artwork.

"Alright—yeah, dude—I need to put her to bed..." Troy finally got her arm around his shoulder. "Congrats on the opening, it was great. You're super talented, man—you deserve this."

"Thanks, Troy. I'm glad you came." He nodded. "You guys get home safe."

Troy mustered his strength and propped Celeste for the walk back to the car. The two squished through the front door and then Troy raised Celeste's arm like a puppet to wave goodbye. "Alex's Grandma!!" She shouted. Alex laughed and watched the two sway down the sidewalk, Celeste pulling Troy out into the streetlights before they disappeared around the corner.

Alone in the gallery, Alex was a bit more deliberate while taking in the sights. On each wall, every angle that caught his vision stood a piece of his own creation. He almost didn't recognize some of the work anymore. It no longer belonged to him, or he no longer identified with the younger man who had created it. There were a few pieces, or at least parts of pieces, that awed him. Several moments within a particular work that he was truly proud of. These glimmers fueled a bi-polar confidence, picking apart each notion of his talent while also giving him the courage to host a night like tonight.

He welled with satisfaction and relief, though not through a sense of accomplishment. Anyone can hang images on a wall and host a party. The relief came from acceptance. Whether people were there on the hopes of meeting Stevie Pearl or not, by the time they left they were consumed with his art. They saw what he had created and at least for a moment forgot about their motives, their problems, and their life. They became absorbed in his visual experience, and Alex witnessed their transformation. These people allowed him to contribute to their existence—his work had inspired contemplation, emotion, and conversation. These were the things that made him feel like he belonged. These are the things that gave Alex his place in the world.

He grabbed a couple of trash bags and carried them to the backdoor, propping it open with a cinderblock. The night air felt cool and damp, its scent mixing with the salty spray from the ocean that was only a couple of blocks away. He crossed the alley and approached a container that was tucked into the shadows. With a heave, he tossed the bags into the dumpster. The clashing of aluminum cans disturbed an eerie peacefulness, Santa Monica having gone to bed for the evening.

He went back inside, double checked that the front door was locked and then killed the lights. He slung his computer bag over his shoulder and twirled the Jeep keys around his index finger. Kicking the brick from the backdoor, he noticed that a car had stopped at the end of the alley. The headlights were out, but its parking lights remained dim. He looked down the other side of the alley, it was barren except for a puddle reflecting the moonlight.

He saw a flicker from the parked car and then heard a door shut. Alex looked back at the gallery, the heavy metal door now locked from the inside. He felt the steps getting closer, unable to make out the contours coming toward him. Alex locked his jaw and balled his keys inside his fist. With two long strides he stepped out into the middle of the alley and faced the footsteps like a gunslinger at high noon.

Alex stood like a weathered rock, waiting for the shadow to approach. With his eyes adjusting to the darkness, he began to see the outline of a hoodie that was pulled up over a head. A long, thin frame with small steps carried the figure toward him, the gait soft and unsure. Alex looked back over his shoulder to see if a crew was trying to bait him, using the decoy's trepidation as their distraction. No one was there.

"How you doin' tonight?" Alex spoke into the darkness, testing for friend or foe.

The shadow continued toward him, unaffected by his words. "Could be better—looks like I missed the party."

He eased as the soft voice hit his ear, strands of blonde hair catching the moon. Alex pushed the keys into his pocket.

The woman stopped about ten paces out, centering herself with Alex.

"Miss Pearl."

"Mister Nopah."

The two continued to stare at each other, unsure of exactly what it was that they wanted to say.

"I don't like how you left things the other night… Storming off in the dark." Stevie shot first. "Is that the type of behavior I can come to expect from you?"

Alex was immediately struck and a gasp of air spilled between his clenched teeth.

"Probably wasn't my best moment…" He admitted. "But I didn't need your excuses."

"You feel I owe you somethin'?"

"That night I didn't. I just wanted to see you again... Now I do. An apology, perhaps."

"You first."

Alex's weight eased to his hip and he bit his lip at the thought of saying sorry.

"Okay." He nodded and composed himself. "I've thought about that night over and over. Seems I can't get away from it. And you're right... our conversation... I wasn't listening to you. All I heard was *no* and it crushed me. I'm sorry."

Stevie moved in a few steps closer, her red lips and smoky eyes coming into focus in the ambient light. She was stunning. Once again Alex lost his footing and began to drown in her beauty.

"I'm sorry too." She said softly. "I'm sorry for all of the unwelcome attention. But I'm the most sorry about missing your night."

"I think you made it pretty clear that you weren't going to be here."

"Still didn't stop the cameras though, did it?"

"I'm not sure how you live like that."

Stevie paused, twirling the long white string that worked her hood. "It makes moments like this feel like they mean something."

"Yeah, but you still got people watching..." Alex nodded down to the car that was running at the end of the alley.

"That's how it'll be if you hang out with me. They're not going anywhere."

Alex studied her and the string wrapped around her finger. It made him smile. He knew from the moment the car door shut that it was her walking down the alley toward him. He also knew that the string she was playing with had a better chance of walking out of this relationship alive.

He was about to trade everything to be with her. And she, just by standing across from him, was proof that she was doing the same.

"It's not over, you know… My night, that is."

"I didn't miss it?"

"Not all of it."

HOLLYWOOD NIGHTS
BOB SEGER

Alex trembled. His fingers tangled as he grabbed at leftover party supplies from the front seat, trying to make room for Stevie to hop up into the Jeep.

She loved his truck, it reminded her of Austin and skipping class with the cool guys from school. Celeste would sit in the back seat and immediately rip open her backpack, digging around until she found a corded cassette tape that plugged into her iPod. She'd push her way up over the center console and take charge of the stereo. Even though Stevie had the big dreams of being a musician, Celeste was always the DJ.

Circling through an old click-wheel, Celeste would eventually find the right song and the two would sing along at the top of their lungs. Stevie loved playing along, this becoming the inspiration for the games she subjected Franklin to.

The memory was effortless. She could almost feel an entire car full of friends bouncing down an old dirt road. When the chatter faded, Stevie would silently craft her own melody while gazing out the side window. Weaving rolling hills with split-rail fences became her trademark, but even then she was looking well beyond the horizon of big Texas skies.

Stevie never let go of the moment, hanging on to the notion of being young and reckless without consequence. She lingered on the thought, this time looking across the colored lights of Santa Monica. The view wasn't what she had imagined. Like any tale from Delphi, nothing could have prepared her for the reality of what her life would become. The amount of money, influence, and fame that she carried wasn't natural. Never in human history had a woman of her age, one without royal blood or being the offspring of a deity, been so obsessed over. The realization terrified her to the core and her thoughts began to spiral.

In the same moment, like a lighthouse giving hope to a lost sailor, the driver's side mirror caught the moonlight as the door swung open. The beacon shook her from the creeping horror, Alex's presence providing salvation from her thoughts. He pulled himself up into the Jeep, turning the key in a single motion.

He had upgraded the entire rig, doing the work himself a little at a time. It was far from the original gift his grandfather had given to him before going away to art school. Besides being a vehicle that gave him the freedom to go just about anywhere, the old Jeep now served as a rolling memorial. It was one of the last great memories he had of the man who used to take him out into the backcountry, teaching him about the importance of nature and the resilience of his people.

Tita's husband was short with a thick, powerful frame. His fingers were like iron hooks from a lifetime of raising cattle and mending fences. The faded scar above his right eye came from clearing tunnels in Vietnam. The old man didn't speak much, but he taught Alex a lifetime of virtues. The two would be gone for a week at a time, surviving deep within the inhabitable desert.

Alex learned a lot about himself through the continual tests the wilderness would put them through—his most important lesson being that of self-reliance. When things broke, they fixed them. Neither were the best bush mechanics, but only once did they ever have to walk home. Those basic skills served as the foundation of his grandfather's certain, unshakable demeanor. He knew he could take care of himself and those he loved, and he instilled that quality within Alex.

The greatest gift that Alex's grandfather had given him, well beyond any Jeep, were lessons in developing his awareness. Cultivating the presence of mind to understand a situation, and the confidence to handle things that went beyond his control. A valuable skill when finding himself a hundred miles from the nearest cellphone signal, or when sitting next to the world's biggest pop sensation.

The last week had tested his resolve. There were no physical or mechanical challenges to overcome, nothing that prepared him for the overwhelming attention. He thought of his grandfather arriving in Saigon. Not that the situations were comparable, or their magnitude equivalent, but they did share the same hapless feeling of being beyond control. A situation was moving forward with or without them, and he could look to his grandfather as an example. His role model had adapted to the challenge that surrounded him, and he survived.

The dash lit up, the interior resembling the cockpit of a fighter jet. Lights blinked; systems went through diagnostic checks as the engine turned and all of Alex's off-road accessories came to life. Immediately, the wireless signal that linked his phone to the over-amplified stereo connected automatically. Music blared, the track picking up from where it had left off earlier.

Alex moved quick to work the volume knob, though not without a subtle smirk from Stevie.

"Thought you never listened to my music?" She was coy.

Embarrassed, Alex pretended to be fixated on the rearview mirror as he shifted into reverse. "Research."

"And what is it, exactly, that you're researching?"

THE BALLAD OF STEVIE PEARL   99

"The downfall of modern music." He crafted a smile. "Something I'm working on for my next exhibit."

"Uh-huh—hipster…" She rolled her eyes. "You artist-types are so pretentious. Self-righteous in your *purity* of music…"

"*Hopscotch, kickin' rocks—ooh ah, ooh ah—baby, you're a fox…?*" His tone was dead as he looked over at her.

"I was 15!"

"Uh-huh…" Alex rolled his eyes back at her.

"Let's see your sketchbook from back then!"

He shifted gears, taking a right onto PCH. "*December Sun* is good. I know I'm totally ruinin' my street cred, but I actually like most of them…"

"It's weird." Stevie's eyes now panned out the window, the two still listening to her old song. "It's like having a diary that the whole world has read. Could you imagine people reading the stuff you scribbled in a notebook back in high school? Most of it doesn't even feel like me anymore. Like a stranger wrote all of it."

"I—I actually know what you mean… And who are you now?"

"I ask myself that question more often than you know… Grateful. At least I know I'm that."

A long pause filled the cab. "Torn between two worlds?" Alex asked, though the question was mostly self-projection.

"Not really. Not anymore. It used to feel that way." She looked over at him. "This is my world now—my reality. Someday it may change, and that's okay. But right now, this is how it is."

"Doesn't seem easy, Stevie… I got a little taste this week. I'm not sure I could deal with it—the relentless attention and scrutiny."

"You get used to it—learn how to control it. Manipulate it. Ignore it… It's just like anything else, there's good and bad. I mean, come on—my life's *not that bad*… it's just… weird. What about you? Story is, you're also a world away?"

"That I am." Alex swallowed. "I'm not sure what Celeste has told you."

"Enough."

"L.A.'s definitely different."

"Tell me about it..."

"I left home after high school, went to art school out here on a scholarship. Been lucky to find work since."

"Ah!" Stevie jumped and pointed through the windshield. "Animal fries!!"

"What? In-N-Out?"

"Hell yeah! You want some?"

Alex laughed and quickly flicked the blinker, jerking the Jeep into the turn lane.

"Drive-thru, though..." She looked down at her hoodie. "Just, can we keep driving? This is nice."

Alex circled around the burger joint and waited in the line of late night cars. The place was always busy, it didn't matter the time of day.

"Hey, so, I'm going to be straight with you about something." Stevie said. "I know a lot about you—facts and figures, logistics... the boring stuff. Things sorta went crazy there after my party. I have people that—well, they're basically required to keep tabs."

"Keep tabs, huh? People? I was going to ask how long that car would be following us? The silver Civic?"

"That's Franklin." Stevie looked over at the Honda that was parked in such a way that would keep them in view. "He's my bodyguard. To be honest—he's, like, my best friend. I love him."

"That's comforting..."

"Sounds crazy, I know... a bodyguard. But he's a good guy. I just wouldn't mess with him." She raised an eye.

"Welcome to In-N-Out! What can we make for you tonight?" The loudspeaker rang.

"Hey—umm, large animal fry, vanilla shake—what else do you want?" He looked over at her.

"Strawberry shake!"

"—and a strawberry shake. Mediums." Alex finished the transaction and pulled around the side of the building.

"So, what does *look into* mean? What sort of stuff do you know about me?"

"Warrants, blood type, ex-girlfriends—I mean, the people at the NSA usually give me what I want..."

"What the shit?!"

"I'm joking! Well, kinda... I really don't know how Franklin does what he does. He might have a Bat Cave at this point."

"That's pretty... not normal." Alex was visibly unnerved.

"It isn't. There's very little that's normal anymore... I've been trying to think of a better way to explain the other night— remember, when you stormed off like a child?" She fired her blue eyes at him.

"Jesus, I said I was sorry... I mean, you kinda forced me to."

"Do I need to call Franklin?"

Alex smiled. "This won't be the last time I hear about it, will it?"

"Quite astute... So, there's two big things that everyone around me is concerned with—growing the business, and protecting the business."

"So... I guess I passed the test with *your people*—I mean, if you're sitting here."

"Ha, not really." She laughed. "Let's just say you're bad for business."

"What does that mean?"

"At this point in my life, absolutely nothing."

The drive-thru window sprang open. "Couple of shakes? Vanilla, strawberry?"

Alex grabbed the cups, taking a big swig of Stevie's through the straw before handing it to her.

"Hey!"

"It's good!" He mumbled through the thickness, squinting his eyes. "Ah, brain freeze!!"

She laughed at his scrunched-up face. "That's what you get!"

The fries were delivered and they pulled back out onto the Pacific Coast Highway, the silver Civic leisurely falling in behind. Stevie beamed, giving Alex the brightest smile as she pulled French fries from a white paper bag.

"Better get in on this." She pointed down to the pile of mess that she was picking through.

"What, and lose a finger??"

"It's so good!" She talked with her mouth full. "Here—" she pushed the sagging carton decorated with red palm trees toward him.

"Okay, okay!" Alex went for it, getting special sauce all over his fingers. "They are good."

"Right? Food's my life!" Stevie was still overly excited about the fries. "Franklin and I sneak out all the time—we go to all sorts of these little spots, get tacos and stuff."

"Sneak out?"

"Yeah, dude—it's ridiculous." She continued to chew and then swallowed. "I told you—I can't, just like, do stuff. It's a big deal to go get tacos."

"Glad to know you're easy to please…"

"Shut up." She simpered.

"What's your favorite taco?"

"Like, where? Or, what kind?"

"I don't know!" He found amusement in Stevie's specificity. "Both?"

"Well, you can't do that. I mean, comparing a fish taco to a chicken taco is just absurd, Alex. Get with the program."

"Well, excuse-me-all-to-hell!"

"We're all about Yuca's right now. I think Franklin just likes the old lady that works there."

"Not Taco Bell?"

"Shut your mouth when you're talkin' to me!"

"What? Those little soft tacos? I could eat like eight of 'em…"

"Yeah, I actually like Taco Bell. Celeste worked there."

"What?! You serious?"

"I ate so many bean burritos…"

"You are a bean burrito."

"So true!" She settled into the seat, holding her shake. "It's a good night, Alex. It's a good night."

"It's definitely been like no other night of my life…" He thought back to the gallery, then his mind weighed Stevie Pearl sitting in the front seat of his Jeep eating French fries. "That's for sure."

"How was your opening?"

"Good—good." He stuttered. "Beyond anything I could have hoped. My plan worked out after all…" He glanced over. "Got that big Stevie Pearl boost I was angling for."

"Did you sell something?"

"Sold everything."

"Really?!" Her excitement was genuine. "Good for you. I'm happy."

"You know, I wasn't trying to—"

"I know." She cut him short. "I know you weren't trying to get anything out of it. Again, I'm sorry about that whole thing… As I said, I just—it's complicated."

"I'm starting to realize. Didn't know you couldn't even get tacos—animal fries."

"It's not that I *can't* get them—or I couldn't have gone to your thing—it's just a whole mess that I need to figure out. If I change my lipstick it sends the financial advisors into the hospital. There's a lot more people involved than you'd think. It's not your fault—and I appreciate you asking me—my heart leapt when, well, you know, you asked.."

"Mine broke… when, well, you know, you rejected me…"

Stevie pushed past the comment by shaking her head. "Do you follow the rumor mill? Like, have you paid attention to all the stuff that has been said this last week?"

"I don't know." Alex stared beyond the windshield. "I never used to… I read more this week than I ever have, but it got to the point where I just couldn't do it. It's all such garbage. Literally, the only time you and I have ever talked was at your party, right? It was a good party—no doubt—but how do people go from that to stalking me outside of my work? Writing articles about us? Spending hours making these stupid web videos and memes?"

Stevie snickered. "The memes were pretty good. Franklin couldn't get enough." She teased. "I think he even started a Reddit."

"Someday I'm sure I'll find that funny…"

"I remember it so much different—we were having so much fun."

"Yeah, I wasn't planning on that moment following me around for the rest of my life."

"That why I block it all out. I just couldn't anymore either… It has to be something major before I hear about it. See this thing—" She pulled a smartphone from her pocket. "It has, like, 5 apps on it. Serious. I deleted everything—I have my camera, calendar, and contacts. I just couldn't do it anymore."

"What bugged me the most about the whole thing was my mom… My grandma watches those entertainment shows. Every night they have their *Stevie Pearl Update.* Suddenly I was on TV and, well, there were those few pictures of us… It was just this big thing with them. I don't bring girls home often."

"Why not?"

"Different worlds…"

Alex let the conversation fade and took a right turn along the marina.

"Chemehuevi." Stevie said. "Am I saying it right?"

"Close enough." Alex glanced over at her. "I'm Native American, yes. Most people think I'm Mexican." He laughed.

"I'm not going to lie, I've never heard of it before…"

"It's okay—no one has. I grew up on the reservation out east, on the Arizona border. The Colorado River. My family has a little land, we tried to farm but things always break down—now we raise a bit of livestock—mostly just surviving. It's hard… my brother hates me for getting out."

"Celeste said you go home a lot."

"Every couple weeks, probably—unless something big is happening and I'll go out to help."

"That's nice. I'm sure they like seeing you. I haven't been to Austin in forever."

"It's different out there, Stevie…" He was earnest. "I felt like Katniss walking through your house."

"It's not the Capitol of Panem, you dork!" She giggled. "But I'm still not used to it either… What's your brother's name?"

"Charlie." Alex looped the Jeep back, now following Pacific Avenue toward Venice and the pier. "Speaking of brothers, tell that little shit who was parking cars the other night that it's on— tampons on my bike. Nope!"

"What??"

"Leaving your party. I came out to find my motorcycle decorated like a vagina Christmas tree."

"Huh?!"

"Strings. Lots and lots of dangling strings."

"Oh my god…" She laughed.

"Yeah. Little bastard."

"He's a funny kid." Stevie rolled down her window, taking a breath of the waves falling onto the shore. "Always in his own world—and a total smart ass. You should pull over up here—let's go out on the beach!"

"Franklin cool with that?" Alex looked in his mirror at the car following them.

"Probably not. We could make him chase us through the sand —that'd be fun!"

"Great. I'm the one he's going to shoot—not you."

Alex slowed the Jeep, and then pulled down an alley for a place to park. The silver Honda did the same.

"C'mon, I'll introduce you." Stevie said as she unbuckled.

"Huh?"

"Come meet Franklin." She jumped down, using her weight to shut the heavy door.

The two walked over to the car. The driver's side window lowered.

"Well, if it ain't Dancin' Feet." Franklin's sarcasm upstaged his greeting. "You okay, Stevie?"

"No…" She fake-conjured tears. "This man, Franklin—he tried to get me to touch him… in the bathing suit area!"

"Shit, no one's ever touched that dude's bathing suit area…"

"Cute." Alex said. "So, you're the creep that likes following people around at night?"

"Did this muthafucka just call me a creep?"

"I… I don't know why he would say such a thing. Alex… I'm a little embarrassed." She basked in a long pause.

"What? You were giving me shit, so I gave you some shit—" Alex looked back and forth between them.

"You fuckin' with Stevie?" Franklin glared at him.

Stevie couldn't hold her laughter from the tense exchange. "Why didn't you get animal fries?!" She pushed Franklin's arm that was hanging out of the window.

"Boo, you know I only do that with you…" Franklin turned his attention to her. "You got twinkle toes takin' my spot."

"This is fun…" Alex muttered and swung his arms. "You two have your own little thing."

"What—you got a problem?" Franklin went after him again. "Celeste said this dude was cool. He don't seem that cool."

"We're going out on the beach." Stevie said.

"Bullllllshit." Franklin looked at her. "You know I don't do sand."

"Exactly." She smiled.

"Stevie, not with this dude. C'mon…"

"Let's go, Franklin—you can hold my hand." Alex jabbed.

Franklin scowled. "I got somethin' you can hold."

"The lady wants a moonlit walk on the beach…"

"You got any shake left?" Franklin ignored Alex. "Strawberry, right?"

"Half a cup!"

"Yeah, okay then." He nodded. "Prancer, you go get me that shake. I gotta talk to my girl for a minute."

Stevie looked at Alex and reassured him with a nod. "Please?"

"Will it put him in a better mood?" Alex said while slipping away back to the Jeep.

"Better fuckin' walk away." Franklin growled. "What up, Stevie. This kat as stoopid as he looks?"

"He's sweet. He bought me animal fries."

"That's all it takes, huh?"

"What would you do if a babe bought you animal fries?"

"I would eat every last one." He pretended to lick his fingers. "But this ain't 'bout me."

"He apologized—straight up—for how we left things the other night."

"Mmmhmm."

"I think we should go out on the beach—when was the last time we were on the beach?!"

"You got that crazy look—I don't like the crazy look—I forbid the crazy look."

"He's just another guy, Franklin. A really, really pretty—smart —talented guy."

"You done talking about me, or can I come back yet?" Alex shouted from his car.

"You're the one who said I should find a real guy—you know he's way better than Jason Saint or any of the Douche Crew."

"He fucks with you, I'll kill 'em."

Stevie smiled, knowing she had her answer. "That's what I pay you for."

Franklin put up the window and pulled himself out of the car.

"Get over here with that shake—the fuck's takin' you so long?" He barked back toward Alex. Franklin then looked down at Stevie. "Gonna have to get this car detailed now—you know how I feel about sand."

The three walked down the side street until they reached the concrete bike path and then the beach. Stevie kicked off her flats and skipped across the cool sand.

"It's the best!" She giggled. "Between your toes!"

Alex hopped around, losing his balance as he took off his boots. He then stuffed his socks inside and rolled up his jeans— the sand feeling soft as powder.

"Uh-uuh." Franklin shook his head and walked straight out onto the beach with his shoes.

Stevie frolicked ahead of them, weaving back and forth as she ran toward the water. The two men followed, walking together but remaining quiet as they watched her dance.

"How's your shake?" Alex finally broke the silence.

"Fuck." Franklin stopped walking. "Here, hold this." He pushed the cup into Alex's chest. "This ain't gonna work." He kicked off his Jordan's while holding onto Alex's shoulder.

"Yeah, Franklin!" Stevie yelled back. "Ow ow!"

"It's got to feel better, dude." Alex handed him back the shake.

"Not too bad." He lowered his nose at Alex. "Now I can do this!"

Franklin cradled the cup like a football and then stiff-armed Alex with his free hand, the blow almost knocking him over.

Franklin sprinted like a running back toward Stevie and she squealed as he got close, running in circles trying to avoid him. The big man moved well, surprising Alex who trotted to catch up with them. The three made it down to the water's edge, the sand becoming hard and damp from the tide that had gone out earlier. Stevie chased the waves, the Pacific running over her toes and up to her ankles.

"You used to play?" Alex asked.

"Football?" Franklin asked. "Nah, man—my school didn't have no grass."

"Where'd you grow up?" Alex seemed confused.

"The ghetto, man—ghetto ain't got no grass."

"Oh…" Alex nodded.

"Brooklyn—the projects. Jay-Z ain't got shit on me."

"I got to go to New York a couple of times for work… It's nuts, man. Nothin' like where I grew up."

"Yeah, I know 'boutch you." Franklin eyed him. "We both poor." His laugh was deep. "Different kind of poor though."

Alex smiled with him. "Ain't that the truth."

"What—you miss rollin' 'round with tumble weeds?"

"Nah, man… the beach is good." Alex stretched his toes into the velvety wet sand.

Franklin took a long breath, sucking in the salty sweet air. "Ain't that the truth. The beach is good…"

The two stood in silence, watching Stevie play in the water.

"She can be a big kid sometimes. She's missed out on a lot…" Franklin finally commented, fiddling with getting the last bit of ice cream from the bottom of the cup. "Then again, she done things neither of us could dream. She ain't your typical chick." Franklin eyed him. "I'm gonna find a trash can." He then turned and lumbered back across the beach from the way they came.

Stevie kicked at the water and then skipped over to Alex. "Where's he goin'?"

"Find a trashcan or somethin'."

"Isn't this amazing? Can't really see the stars, but look at that moon."

"Beautiful." He didn't take his eyes off of her.

"You come to the beach a lot?" She asked.

"You know—I don't. Not sure why."

"You might have to start. Even try it with sun sometime."

"Nah." Alex shook his head. "That's just way too much shiny-happy all at once."

"*Shiny happy people holding hands.*" She sang. "Gross, right?"

"Rem's a good band."

"Ha—Rem..."

Alex's pocket buzzed. He took out his phone and saw a text message from Sean.

"It's my buddy who wrote *The Final Book.* He's asking how tonight went—the gallery. He just woke up, it's morning for him —he's on a boat over in the Mediterranean or something."

"Tell him Stevie says that she's totally in love with Josh and Cloe and they made her cry... I mean, the illustrations really captured it—his writing kinda sucks." She smirked.

"You read it?"

"Research." She leaned in with a whisper. "Let's go find Franklin. It's past his bedtime."

WHAT WOULD I'VE BECOME
RYAN BINGHAM

"There she is!" Alex's tone was overly chipper as he tossed Celeste a paper coffee cup. It bounced off of her. She didn't even flinch. "And how are we feeling this morning?!"

"Like a fuckin' rock star…" Celeste didn't bother taking off her obnoxious Pit Viper sunglasses and tried to correct a sway within her remaining steps toward craft services.

She clutched the edge of the table, studying its layout for coffee before pushing off. She labored pulling a cup from the stack and struggled sourcing the right sugar and creamer. Once all were lined up, she allowed muscle memory to prepare the rest.

"That's twice in one week, Nopah. You're a bad influence on me."

Alex looked on with amazement. "I can't help it if an 80-year-old woman can out drink you."

"She's not human." Celeste took short breaths and steadied herself. "I think Troy's gonna divorce me."

"You're not married, are you?"

"Breakup—whatever, Alex—Christ… I puked in his car. Well, my car, actually—but he drives it around. I did tell him to stop, but he just kinda slowed down and opened the window. Once I started, it was like *The Exorcist*… You know those mini sandwiches? I'm pretty sure there's still a whole one if you want it—why the fuck are you so happy?"

"Lovely… I'm not happy." Alex shrugged.

"I see, like, teeth. You're smiling. Why are you smiling?" She stirred the coffee. "You didn't put something in this, did you?"

"What? No."

"Alex…?"

"It's… you know—it's Friday! TGIF!" He continued to grin.

"Say that again and I'll punch you."

He couldn't see her eyes but the angle of her jaw made it clear that she was glaring at him.

"Now listen—I'm gonna drink this coffee and there better not be shit in it. Okay?"

"There's nothing in your coffee."

"Alex, this is no time for tom foolery—if you've done something to my precious morning beverage, I will make it *my life's mission* to relentlessly spoil each and every movie before you see it. I swear to God."

"Celeste—I don't give a crap about your coffee."

"Yeah…" She stared him down through the florescent sunglasses. "That's right you don't." She then tossed the straw on the table. "So, why do you look, like, normal? You know, cheerful or something?"

"You're still drunk."

"I'd be in a much better mood if I was."

"Okay—" Alex was quick to relent, unable to contain his news. "So, after you and Troy left, you'd never believe who stopped by."

Celeste gave him a blank stare. "You're right. And I'm not about to play Twenty Questions."

Alex looked over his shoulder and then back at her. "Stevie."

She let out violent gasp. "Ohhhh, I should've known… God. You guys didn't already have sex, did you?"

"Shhh…" He tried to temper. "And no."

"Then why are you so… glowie?"

"What? I don't know… it was awesome. We played on the beach and had animal fries."

"You played?"

"You know, ran around in the sand—whatever."

"No, I don't believe I do. Play-by-play, sports fan. I don't associate you with frolicking."

"Jesus. She, like, creeped up on me in the alley behind the gallery, all hidden in the shadows and shit. We had this really blunt conversation where I apologized for storming off like a jackass at her party—"

"Good move."

"Then she said she was sorry for making my life a living hell. So, then we drove around, talked, went to the beach. Franklin's kinda a dick, but you know, I think he's supposed to be."

"Wait, what? Franklin was there?"

"Well, yeah—that's like, her bodyguard, right?"

"So, you basically just played third wheel while him and her had animal fries?"

"No—I had the animals fries! Me!"

"Yeah, sure you did, bud…"

"He got a fuckin' leftover milkshake! Me and Stevie, Celeste—it was me and Stevie eating animal fries!"

Celeste lifted the coffee to her lips. "You're really starting to creep me out, dude."

"Yeah—that's what I said to Franklin because he was followin' us around all night in that little car!"

"You're a dork."

"I know—"

"I thought you basically hated her? She ruined your opening night—shat on your pea-size heart, and writes dumb pop music for teenage girls?"

"I'm a teenage girl, Celeste—deep in my heart. You know this."

"That's unfortunately true."

"I never said I hated her…"

"You said just about every bad thing you could about her."

"That's only because she rejected me. Take-backsies."

"Take-backsies?"

"Yeah. What don't you get?"

"Oh my god… This might be the worst thing I've ever done. I feel like I need to puke all over again."

"Here, have a muffin!" Alex stuck a blueberry muffin out in front of her and she immediately slapped it from his hand.

"You stop it! Stop it right now—no one likes it when you're thoughtful! …I'll, ah… I'll clean that up."

Celeste grabbed a napkin and picked the crumbled pieces from the floor. "How'd it end?"

"What do you mean?"

"The night. How'd the night end?"

"She went home with Franklin."

"What?!"

"Yeah, I mean, it made sense—I had no reason to go to Beverly."

"So that's it? That's your big night? Franklin took her home??"

"I… I laid the groundwork." Alex hesitated, now questioning what he thought was a perfectly acceptable end to their evening.

"You laid nothing but your hand—like always!"

"What was I supposed to do? We don't even know each other —and Franklin was hangin' around the entire time. It's not like we had any privacy."

"You let him watch, like every other weirdo."

"Stevie lets him watch…?"

"No! God, you're an idiot. She'll find a way to lose him, but you've got to take some friggin' initiative!"

"Hold on, hold on—" Alex stepped back. "She came. She came to the gallery. I won." He flipped his hands in the air. "Don't ruin this for me, Celeste. She likes me—on some level, Stevie Pearl likes me."

"Yeah, and what do two people do who like each other?" She pushed her tongue in and out of the side of her cheek.

"I'm not going to rush into something."

Celeste let out a long, dissatisfied groan. "I've gotta get to work." She shook her head and began to walk off. After a few steps she stopped, then turned back around to face him. "I mean, you disappoint the fuck out of me as a storyteller, but I'm glad I was right about you. Thanks for being nice to my friend."

Alex stood perplexed.

"Don't do the waiting game—text her a meme or something." She held up her phone and turned to walk away once more. "You've got plenty of them floating around…"

Alex's eyes followed her until she passed through the double doors that led to the offices and then out of sight. He took a moment, sipped his coffee, and then picked up his computer bag.

Following the same route that Celeste took through the double doors, he turned right and then went down the hall. He claimed a spot in the shared workspace next to the conference room, but today the gait that carried him there was a little lighter and more effortless.

It seemed everyone he passed along the way gave him a smile and welcomed him good morning. His disposition was infectious. Alex paused in a doorway and briefly conversed with Tommy, thanking him for attending his opening the night before. He stopped and made jokes with Rita, Jim's personal assistant. He even gave a high-five to someone he didn't know.

Sliding into the office space where he worked, Alex twirled in the rolling chair as the wheels glided across the plastic liner on the floor. The motion was fluid, a seamless act of grace as he set his coffee on the desk while pulling the laptop from his bag. Tugging on a knot of earbuds, he picked at the rubbery string until he had enough length to get them in his ears. Alex leaned back in the chair and began playing Stevie's latest album, melting as soon as he heard her angelic voice.

He ignored his work. He didn't even bother to check emails before typing www.steviepearl.com into the browser. He was instantly greeted by a high quality black and white photo of her glancing out of the corner of her eye with a subtle smile. The banner was an advertisement for an upcoming video experience that was going to stream live in theaters for one night only. The image then rotated. Next was a big welcoming banner for her fan group, the Pearl Party Crashers. You could click the link to sign up, automatically being entered for a chance to meet Stevie. He couldn't help but think of Rochelle, Stacy, and Tamrin.

The memory struck him and he held his phone to his nose, scrolling through to the photos app. His thumb hovered over the picture of him and Celeste huddled with the girls next to the pool at Stevie's party. He grinned at their bright smiles, and then shared the pic. *"You guys got it all wrong, these are my girls! #BestPicOfTheNight #PearlPartyCrashers."*

It was the first post about the party he had made since the internet firestorm. It had taken an incredible amount of discipline not to engage with the trolls, but mostly he couldn't bear to look at all the hatred that consumed his profile. But now he felt vindicated. Even if things with Stevie never developed, last night assured him that he didn't read her wrong at the party. Her coming to him in the alley confirmed his sanity, something he felt he had lost ever since being dubbed as her new fling.

His attention melted back into the computer and he clicked on the *Events* tab at the top of the website. An aerial image of a sold-out stadium glistened with tiny cellphones lights, the sea of people easily eclipsing the size of Alex's hometown by twenty fold. A giant *"Thank You, World Tour! XoXo"* was written in cursive over the top. There were no upcoming concert dates, but a message told her fans to check back soon.

Next he navigated to the *About* section. Another polished, fashion-magazine-like photo of her splashed across the page. There was no denying that she was incredibly attractive. However, as he studied her, he seemed to like the way she looked in real life more. She was more facetious without a camera lens, and definitely a lot nerdier than these photos gave her credit for.

A couple of paragraphs topped the page, Stevie writing a direct message to her fans:

You hear me on the radio. See me in magazines. I've even been on TV a few times. Besides that, we're not that much different. Well, that's presumptuous of me… I like to think I'm just like any girl, but that's not true. I'm really fortunate. I have a mom and dad who love me—support me, sacrificed for me. I have a little brother that I love. Before my fame, my family was never rich—but I've also never been hungry. I was able to go to school. I was told that I was special and I was encouraged to pursue the things I love. Now that I think about it, what I had before you heard me on the radio is incredibly rare.

I say that because I know not everyone grew up that way. For me to say that I'm just like you diminishes your own special story—the hardships you've faced, the happiness you've shared with those you love, and the sad moments all by yourself. I'll never pretend to know how you feel, but having these emotions is what has connected us.

Whether you have posters all over your bedroom wall or don't have a bedroom at all—together, we feel. That's all I'm doing in my songs, I'm telling you how I feel… and so many of you have told me that sometimes you feel the same way too. Because of that, we share something. I'm here because you're here—and I'll thank you each and every day for it.

Stevie ~ XoXo

Alex could no longer ignore his buzzing phone, all of the notifications popping up since he posted his photo. He opened it up and began reading the comments:

Fuck you tribe nigger

Pedophile! those girls are 16

Ur so hot! DM me

Go back to Mexico wetback

Stevie used to be so hot. Can't even look at her now.

wanna dance?

Who's the hot chick in the leather coat?

hihowareya hihowareya

Die. Indian. Fuck.

"Jesus." Alex dropped the phone. "*What the fuck?*"

The likes and comments continued to pour in, the counter jumping exponentially with each second. He took a deep breath and concentrated on Stevie singing to him through his earbuds. He suddenly had a greater understanding of why she seemed so isolated. Why all of the little things seemed so insurmountable. If this was the reaction to a harmless photo, why would he ever post anything again? As far as the world knew, he was old news and there was nothing to suggest that he'd ever be anything more.

His phone began buzzing once more, this time with a call. He picked it up and saw that the number was blocked. He contemplated if he should answer, eventually relenting just before it went to voicemail.

"This is Alex."

"Hi, Alex Nopah?"

"Yeah."

"This is Emily Dickerson, I represent Hodges & Rhode Entertainment Law. I'm calling on the behalf of one of our clients. It seems you've posted a photo to your social media account, is that correct?"

"I'm not sure…" Alex refused to bite.

"This is a courtesy call, we'd just like to notify you about usage."

"Usage of what?"

"Well, there is a photo on your social media account that was taken at a closed—private event. Exclusive photography rights were given that evening. Also, the young women in the photograph are underage—do you have release forms signed by their consenting guardians?"

"Excuse me?"

"The reason I ask is because I don't seem to have you on file— have you signed a non-disclosure agreement with Austin Lyric & String Holdings? Have you received any sort of likeness authorization that would grant you permission to disseminate such photos or media? Have you read over the code of conduct policies and agreed to them?"

"I think you've got the wrong number—"

"Mr. Nopah. There is an order of operations here. We need to protect our client—we hope you want to protect her too." A long paused filled the line.

"And all of those photos and videos of me that flooded the news and internet were authorized? That's protecting your client?"

"By agreeing to be on the premises, you relinquished your rights. There was a sign posted with security at the gate."

"So if all of these photos from the party had to be authorized, how'd they leak? How did I wake up to see them published all across social media?"

"Each photo is subject to the rules I'm sharing with you now. We are following up with other potential violators as well."

"There were cellphones everywhere—you're telling me that each person that took a picture violated some exclusivity rights? That they're going to be held liable?"

"Many of the guests have a long-standing relationship with our client—they have received authorization to associate likeness, agreeing to the terms and conditions. According to my records, you have not been given such permission. Guests that violate the exclusive photo rights may be subject to litigation."

"So, you guys—her team—wanted this story in the media? You could have shut it down, but you didn't. You allowed the photos to circulate."

"Sir, there's two options. You take down the photo and never associate yourself with Stevie Pearl again, or you do it correctly."

"What's your name?"

"Emily Dickerson. From Hodges & Rhode."

"Do you have a number I can call you back at?"

"Certainly..." The woman rattled off the string of digits. "However, this issue is time sensitive."

"I have 30 days after receiving a formal cease and desist letter... I haven't signed for any certified mail. I think we've got some time." Being an artist himself, Alex was competent in copyright law. However, he wasn't sure why they were coming after him about it. Even if Stevie or this woman did own the rights to the photo, enforcing it would be next to impossible. The woman on the line was clearly trying to intimidate him, though he couldn't understand why.

"It's not only a copyright issue, Mr. Nopah—it's become much more complex than that. You see, it's now a code of conduct issue. Austin Lyric & String Holdings is a subsidiary of Cosmopolitan— the same parent organization that owns the rights to *The Final Book,* the film currently under production—where you have signed a non-disclosure agreement."

"Excuse me?"

"You're in violation of your non-disclosure with Cosmopolitan—the agreement you signed when you took your consulting job with the film studio."

"This movie has nothing to do with Stevie—it's not competing or associated."

"That's irrelevant, Mr. Nopah—"

"What are you saying—I'm fired?!"

"I'm not involved with your studio's staffing contracts or HR. Like I said, my concern is that of my client's. However, if pressed, Cosmopolitan's non-disclosure policy is extremely clear—in addition to the damages caused to our client."

Alex fumed. He was at a complete loss for words.

"As of now, this is just a courtesy call to make you aware that you're in violation. We do strongly urge that you refrain from associating your likeness with our client in the future. If you do not comply, swift action will be taken to ensure that your contract is terminated."

Alex remained silent.

"I will be sending a record of the non-disclosure violations to Cosmopolitan's corporate office to be kept on file. Consider this a warning of your copyright violation–further use of unauthorized photos will result in a cease and desist letter and possible litigation. Do you have representation where I should forward these records to as well?"

"Me. Send them to me…"

"We prefer electronic correspondence—what is your primary email address?"

"Just use my personal—alex@alexnopah.com."

"Thank you, Mr. Nopah. You'll be receiving an email from me with several attachments. Thank you for your time."

The line went dead before Alex could respond.

You've got to be kidding me.

Alex ran his fingers through his hair. *My job? Non-disclosure?* He slammed his computer closed.

"Gibby, whatch you doin'?" Franklin leaned down and scratched the dog's head. Gibby looked up at him with fond eyes and used his nose to urge him to continue scratching. "'Ey, 'ey! I think he missed me!"

"Of course he did—you're, like, his daddy." Stevie was overly amused by her joke. "Did you miss Daddy Franklin?" She teased the dog.

"Don't be sayin' shit like that... It's creepy."

"He loves you—you're the only one who takes him on a real walk."

"That's just 'cause I keep hopin' to run back into J-Law out joggin'." He grinned.

"Whatever." She rolled her eyes. "You love him. Don't lie."

Franklin passed through the massive double doors that were open to the balcony, the infinity pool trickling beneath.

"I need a nap, Stevie! You kept me up too late last night..." He slumped down into a lounge chair, wiggling himself into the cushion to fit just right.

"It wasn't that late..." She frowned.

"Outta my sun—can't you see I'm tryin' to get a tan?"

Stevie stuck her tongue out at him and then moved to quit hovering.

"You're smilin' a lot this mornin', Stevie... I don't like it when you smilin'."

"That's an awful thing to say!"

"Mmmhmm. Both know why you're smilin' too."

"It's no big deal..." She was coy.

"And who you gonna come to when this one break yo' heart? Big Daddy Franklin."

"You act like I'm still 17!"

"Look at that goofy-ass grin—you look like you're still 17!"

"Shut up!" She giggled. "I like him—he's just so, cute. He's real."

"He's real all right… Real pain in my ass…"

"Unaffected, you know? Never pretending. Do you like him?"

"I dunno, Stevie… He's a guy. A dude. He's all right, but…"

"But what?"

"Nothin' special. I mean, I see why girls would like him… I guess. Need mo' meat on his bones, like me." Franklin put his chin on his wrist and acted like he was posing for a camera.

"I don't know… I think his art is pretty special. Have you looked at any of it?"

"Squiggles and comic books? That's your thing now?"

"He's just able to capture a mood. When you see it, you know what the character is feeling… Or what he's feeling."

"I'll wait for the movie."

Stevie scowled and tossed a pillow at him.

Franklin's tone became a bit more committed to the conversation. "You seemed like ya had fun last night."

"Oh, I did!" She twirled. "When was the last time we ran on the beach? The salty air?"

"I didn't get no animal fries…"

"That's your fault." She said without sympathy. "They were so good!"

Stevie looked down at her phone, it buzzed with a text message from Alex Nopah.

"Oh my god—it's him!" She squealed. "No waiting game!"

"Such a gentleman…" Franklin rolled over.

Stevie unlocked her phone and tapped through to her text messages.

"*Suing me??? Not sure what I did. Thought we had a great time last night.*"

"What?" Stevie said out loud.

"What he say?" Franklin asked.

She read the message out loud to him. "I don't know what he's talking about."

"*What do you mean? We did.*" She wrote back.

"*This is fucked up. I just got a phone call from Hodges and Rhodes threatening to get me fired for posting a picture.*"

"Here—get on your phone." Stevie motioned to Franklin. "Pull up Alex's profile. Did he post something?"

Franklin sat up and worked his phone. "Yeah—pic from your party. Those little girls and Celeste." He showed her the picture.

"What's wrong with that?" She asked Franklin. "They're all having a great time."

"I dunno—I don't see nothin' wrong with it."

"He just said that Hodges and Rhode called and are threatening to get him fired—that I'm suing him."

Franklin remained quiet, looking more intently at the photo. He saw the angle. Alex was bad for the brand. Her business partners were trying to get rid of him. Scare him into running away by threatening the best job he's ever had.

"*I don't know anything about this, Alex. I'm not suing you. Promise.*"

"*Your girl made it pretty clear that I'm not allowed to associate with you—I wasn't sure I should even text you.*"

"Screw this—" Stevie swiped through her phone and then held it to her head. The ringing pierced her ear as she waited.

"Hey…"

"Alex, are you okay? Tell me what's going on."

SHUT UP AND GET ON THE PLANE

DRIVE-BY TRUCKERS

Questions continue to mount this afternoon as Stevie Pearl was seen entering the law offices of Hodges and Rhode. Rumors from those close to the law firm report that the meeting was unscheduled and that Pearl demanded to speak with senior partners immediately. This coming less than one week after the firing of notorious PR agent, Dallas Sachs.

To add fuel to the fire, what was thought to be a simple re-signing with Kismet Records continues to remain in question—Pearl's contract with the label expiring in the coming months. Stevie Pearl's home for more than a decade, Kismet Records is responsible for releasing all 6 of her award-winning albums, containing 11 Number 1 Hits and 29 Top 10 Hits. If Kismet is unable to lock down a deal, and soon, it will make Stevie Pearl the most sought-after free agent on the planet.

Markets reacted drastically as instability within Pearl's organization has led to panic among investors. Cosmopolitan's stock alone—the umbrella media conglomerate that owns Kismet Records— dropped by almost four points today. Frustration mounts among business partners as Pearl's camp has remained tight-lipped. No statements have been made by the artist or her representatives explaining the release of Sach's PR firm, nor has any indication been given about her plans for the future.

Other than being seen exiting from this SUV at Hodges and Rhode, Pearl, herself, has remained out of the public eye since the star-studded party at her Beverly estate. Seen dancing with graphic novel illustrator, Alex Nopah, there are no reports placing the two together since; Pearl notably not in attendance last night at Nopah's Santa Monica art gallery opening.

This has been Mario Cordova for TMI's *Stevie Pearl Minute. Follow us online for breaking Stevie Pearl news and sightings.*

"Hey—" Celeste put her hand on Alex's shoulder. "I thought you stopped watching that shit?"

Her touch sent a jolt through him and he immediately removed his earbuds, a reflex he had picked up in high school while being scolded by teachers for escaping into his doodling rather than paying attention to their lectures.

"Oh." He looked up at her. "I couldn't really help it… it's been a *crazy* day."

Alex closed the laptop and then pivoted in the chair to face her. "She texted me a bit ago. Said that everything was taken care of—I have nothing to worry about—my job or the non-disclosure."

"Yeah—I just talked to her—she gave me a call. Why would her team be going after you like that? I mean, I get the paparazzi, but not her own lawyers…"

"I have no idea… That picture was so harmless. If anything, you'd think they'd love it—showing the Pearl Party Crashers having a good time."

"That's scary, man. I know how much this job means to you. I'm sorry."

"Yeah, I'm totally confused. That *fuckin' lady on the phone*—she was definitely trying to intimidate me. "Immediately stop associating *my likeness*.""

"Hmm… Speaking of which—I don't think Stevie feels the same way."

Alex didn't offer a response.

"She asked what we were up to this weekend…"

"What do you mean?"

"Stevie wanted to know when we got off work… and then when we had to be back…"

Alex continued to stare at Celeste. "It's Friday. I wasn't planning on going back."

"Good. You like pizza, right? New York has the best…" A subtle smile formed in the corner of her mouth. "It's one of the perks of having a gajillionaire as your best friend. A weekend in The City? You, me, Troy, and Stevie?"

"What?!"

"Yeah, man—you've got nothin' else goin' on."

"Just like that? Off to New York?"

"The jet's waiting. Apparently she's got some business to do, but wanted to know if we'd like to come along." Celeste cocked an eye and poked him in the chest. "I think she's just using me to get to you."

Alex hesitated, rubbing where she jabbed him. He then leaned back in the chair and shook his head. "After everything that happened today? I don't know… Maybe I shouldn't go."

"What are you talking about?"

He looked around at an office that was set in a different century compared to the barn his brother was working in. Thoughts swelled within his head, contemplating gambling his career for a slice of pizza.

Celeste pressed him. "She said it was taken care of, right? Nothing to worry about."

"What if it's not taken care of next time—or what if she can't?"

"You don't think that Stevie Pearl can handle a few lawyers—or get her way when she wants?"

"Yeah but, what if… she doesn't want to?" He looked down at his faded jeans. "When she gets sick of me? It's not just a normal breakup—avoiding the same bars or laundry mat. This is my job —my life."

Celeste twisted her head and thought about his words. "Don't fuck her over then. It's one thing to realize you're no good with someone, it's another to bring fire and brimstone down upon them. I know breakups can be petty, but she'd never ruin your life —not unless you gave her good reason."

Alex shifted his weight in the chair. "Well, that's a pretty messed up position to be in, don't you think?"

"Yeah. It is. Welcome to being a woman. Doesn't feel good when one side has all of the power, does it? Our jobs. Our money. We make pennies on the dollar compared to you assholes—you don't think any of that enters into our mind when we start relationships, or want to end them? *This guy is a real fuckin' douche, but I need a place to live for the next few weeks...* Might make you think a little differently on how you're gonna end it."

Alex remained silent. He loathed feminist lectures, mostly because he wasn't allowed to participate in them. However, there was honesty in her words. A perspective of love and life that he had never considered—that had never even crossed his mind.

When deciding if he wanted to date a woman, he never thought about what sort of impact she would have on his career. It never applied to him, as it doesn't apply to most men. He never had to contemplate the chances of being fired if they broke up. He never worried that her friends in powerful positions might take her side and consider him tainted—blacklisted and unable to find new work. He never once had to ask himself if he would be able to survive, support himself, if a relationship ended.

Alex's mind spun. Conversely, he never thought of a girlfriend as being able to help his career either. He never considered dating someone to help him get a job. He never considered using a girlfriend's money to pay his bills. He never thought that a girlfriend could help the sales of his artwork… He never thought that a girlfriend could *hurt the sales of his artwork.*

"Fuck." Alex said.

"I know, right? Fuck men!"

"No…" He wrinkled his brow. His jaw ground to a close as he thought about the lawyer threatening his job.

Of course, that was the reason for the call. He was bad for business and everyone close to her knew it. The first chance they had, the first excuse he had given them—they leapt. The epiphany nestled itself deep within his mind, curling up next to a long list of insecurities and triggers of low self-esteem.

"N-never mind…"

"Well, I think you're getting a bit ahead of yourself anyway. You're not even dating and you're already talking about breaking up."

"Statistically speaking…"

"Fuck, Alex—I told you not to sabotage it before it begins! And the only way it can begin is if we eat pizza in New York this weekend. You're good to go, right? I'll tell her that we'll meet her in, like, two hours?"

"I think I should talk to her first."

"That's what this weekend is for. Talking. Also eating. As soon as fuckin' Pam leaves for her Friday afternoon spin class, we're out. Go home, pack a bag—this place can burn to the ground for all I care. You know, as long as it's rebuilt by Monday…"

"Jeez, Celeste—hold on a minute. I don't know…"

"Nopah! Wake the fuck up! The biggest heartthrob since Norma Jean wants to take you to New York, along with what I can assume are your only two friends—me and Troy." She batted her eyes. "Go pack your handbag and makeup—we're goin' to New York, mothafuckah!"

She kicked his chair and sent him rolling across the slick plastic mat. Alex scrambled to grab the corner of the desk before crashing into a trashcan.

"God damnit, Celeste..."

"New York! New York!" She chanted like a frat boy as she marched back down the hall toward her side of the building. "Ow —hey, Mr. Brigman..." He heard her cross paths with the director. "Sing it with me—*In New York, concrete jungle where dreams are made of, there's nothing you can't do...*"

Alex rolled his eyes and then continued looking at the ceiling. "She's out of control. *This is out of control.*"

He picked up his phone and sent a text to Stevie. "*I just talked to Celeste. She's already wearing a Yankee hat.*"

"*Can you make it? Are you going to come?!*"

"*Well, I wanted to talk to you first. I'm not used to being sued, and then hopping on a private jet with the person who sued me all in the same day.*"

"*That's why I was hoping you'd come—I wanted to talk to you too.*"

"*I'm...*" He knew the ghostly dialog dots were pulsing on Stevie's end as he hesitated, "*not feeling very comfortable.*"

Damnit. He wished he could undo what was already sent.

"*Oh. I understand.*"

"*No! I mean, not with you—just, this whole thing!*"

"*Well, to be honest, neither am I. That's why I'm going to New York. I need to straighten some things out with my manager.*"

"*I... don't understand?*"

"*That's ok—I don't expect you to. But I have to see him immediately. Normally, I'd make you take me out so we could get to know each other better, but I won't be around for a few days... and I couldn't stand the thought of not seeing you...*"

"*I'm not used to all of this, Stevie. I really need this job. Are you sure we're all good?*"

"Absolutely. Promise. I want to explain everything in person—I've got some documents you can sign so this never happens again."

"That may be the most unattractive pickup line I've ever heard."

"Yeah, but did it work?"

"Barely."

"Excellent *evil Mr. Burns voice* So you're coming? I'll send a car. It makes everything much easier. What's your address?"

Alex unintentionally impersonated Hunter S. Thompson by inhaling long and deep, holding onto the air until his body reminded him to let it out. He replied with his address and then locked the phone.

His knees bounced with a nervous imbalance. A steady stream of adrenaline had been percolating within his veins throughout the day and was now bubbling over at the thought of a cross country flight on a private jet. His mind was useless and he knew the rest of his workday would accomplish nothing.

He slipped his laptop into its bag and straightened the workspace, taking extra care to not leave anything behind. He was still skeptical that security would let him back into the building on Monday morning. If Stevie's lawyers couldn't run him off, perhaps the director, Jim Brigman, would just outright fire him for code of conduct issues.

"Nopah, have you seen the internet? Your life's a circus. I can't have these distractions." He imagined how the conversation would go. Jim would look at him with sympathy but then hold up a tablet with Mario Cordova ranting about the two being seen at Famous Ray's and describe how a bomb threat got called into the movie studio because some psycho couldn't handle the color of his skin. An artist's imagination is vivid, and he saw the scenario play out all too clearly.

Dusk was being overrun by the stars as Stevie's impenetrable blacked-out SUV traversed along Mulholland Drive toward the 405. Stevie's eyes were locked on nothing in particular as she faced the window. Her thoughts were lost in a sea of thieves, her own crew quietly conducting a mutiny under her command.

Her visit to Hodges and Rhode earlier in the day began to uncover just how deep the treachery sank. She assumed that Dallas's brazen manipulation of all that surrounded her, along with his questionable neglect of keeping her informed was an isolated incident. However, Kismet didn't rush to replace him. Their peculiar silence over her outburst was unsettling, combined with Lisa Rhode's reluctance to dismiss the pursuit of an absurd technicality within Alex's non-disclosure agreement flirted with outright insubordination.

The copyright clause brought up against Alex was to help mitigate her rampant exploitation. It mostly served so that she could have some sort of recourse against the most blatant abusers —it never prevented anything. There were tens-of-thousands— hundreds-of-thousands—of unauthorized photos taken of her throughout the years that went unexamined. Beyond that, she didn't even appear in Alex's photo—it was Celeste and the young girls—the photo merely occurred on her property. The girls in the photo weren't upset that he had posted it. Not that it mattered, their parents had signed away those rights long before they were allowed through the gate.

While the logic and intent behind Hodges and Rhode's decision to flag the violation was confusing, it wasn't the most disconcerting. Going after Alex for the non-disclosure with Cosmopolitan was a strategic move. It wasn't a lapse in judgement made by an overly thorough staff member that happened across a copyright violation; it was a calculated attack by someone exploiting an angle. A well-thought-out loophole to serve a purpose, executed by someone highly competent with Cosmopolitan contracts.

Emily Dickerson, the woman who threatened Alex over the phone, was nothing more than a young attorney clamoring for partnership. She has no stake in protecting the name and honor of Stevie Pearl. It was clear she was following orders, and Stevie didn't begrudge her for doing so. At this particular moment, Stevie actually admired her for it. Lisa, however, ran the show.

Lisa Rhode had represented Stevie since the beginning. She oversaw the first contract Stevie had ever signed with Kismet, which was grossly disproportionate. Most are for young, unknown artists. Though Lisa administered the deal, there was no negotiation or earnest thought given to protecting her client. Her firm served as nothing more than a liaison with a stiff percentage.

As Stevie's popularity grew, Lisa became more interested in the novelty of pop stars. For a time, and a more lucrative percentage, she represented an entire horde of young women eager to take Stevie's place. As they failed and Stevie's wealth and staying power became undeniable, Lisa became resolute in her representation. The bottom line is that Lisa was capable of executing contracts that made everyone wealthy. Hodges and Rhode did their job and Stevie's relationship with them was transactional. When she needed their services, she got them. Now, it seemed, she was also getting their services when she didn't need them.

A sudden slowing in 405 traffic woke Gibby and the dog stood up to get a better look. He shook a few times to straighten his coat, craning his neck that freed the collar to jingle as he twisted. Realizing they hadn't arrived wherever they were going, the dog laid back down. Stevie looked over at Franklin who had been staring at her. She forced a smile and then adjusted herself in the seat.

"Promise me you'll go see your mom while we're out."

"What? Don't want me 'round?"

Stevie smirked. She read his innuendo and blushed. "Pfft—I'm a lady! He hasn't even taken me on a date yet…"

"Animal Fries don't count with you no mo'?"

"Seems like a week ago and it was only last night. I want you to see your mom—she made me promise every time we come to town."

"I'll see her." Franklin nodded. "Don't need both of you mad at me."

"Good." Stevie returned to the window, noticing the exit sign for Van Nuys Airport.

"How 'boutch you? You good?"

She considered his words as the SUV took the off ramp. "I'll be heartbroken if Shane is anything less than honest with me tomorrow."

"Honesty is hard in this business…"

"Shouldn't be. At some point, beyond the tour buses and stock tickers, it has to come down to two people agreeing on something. I need to know that he still agrees."

"Don't let this be 'bout defendin' some boy you just met."

Stevie turned and glared at him. "It's unfortunate that Alex was the catalyst, but *my business* will never be about some boy."

Franklin sat quietly. He knew he was reaching beyond his role. "Stevie, we both know what's goin' on here—"

"We do. And it disgusts me."

"I know it does, boo. But they just doin' what the focus group says—they followin' the money. Plain and simple. It ain't personal."

"Of course it is, Franklin! It's very personal! He's smart, he's talented, and he's worked really hard to get to where he is. But all they see is, is what—he's poor? He's an Indian?"

"Stevie…" Franklin chewed the inside of his cheek. "You represent an idea—you a dream. All American girl, singin' all American songs, sellin' all American cola. Any change from that path and everyone with money on the line is gonna be pushin' back. Alex seem like a nice dude, but make no mistake—he ain't part of that vision."

"I don't want racists controlling me! They can't handle the thought of me dating him—him touching me—it's as simple as that!"

Franklin shook his head. "It ain't just them, Stevie. They a reflection of society—givin' the people what they want. Dallas Sachs' a snake—that's fo' sho'—but he ain't got no principles. Racists, now *racists* got tons of fucked up principles. They all about *their principles*… Hodges and Rhode, they don't care he's Indian— they do care about the money you bringin' in. I told you, ain't no one gonna like this fool. He don't fit the image."

"I can't believe you're defending them—"

"I ain't defending 'em! No way… I just want you to see clearly."

"So, I should go along with systemic racism because it's profitable?!"

"Stevie." Franklin softened his tone. "It ain't right—them makin' these decisions behind yo' back. Okay? *You need to take care of that.*" He nodded with his full weight pressed upon the words. "But, if you turnin' this into a peace march—you better make sure he's worth it."

The SUV pulled into the hanger, tires chirping as it circled on the smooth concrete. The driver pulled next to the ladder that extended from the Dassault Falcon. The front doors of the car opened and the driver and another man stepped out.

Celeste stood next to her bags, leaning against the handrail that lead up into the plane. She cast an impatient stare while Troy waved like an idiot.

Stevie let out a breath of air and closed her eyes. It was the same moment she gave herself before going on stage.

"I'm not mad at you, Franklin... I just worry—how many others have they done this to? How many times have I allowed this to happen?"

Franklin didn't offer a response, knowing he had said his piece.

"Thanks for being there with me today..."

He nodded, then focused his attention at the people milling around the plane.

"Look like Dancin' Feet's late... Yo—have fun with your friends this weekend, okay? I know you got a lot on yo' mind, but those kats right there care 'boutch you. It's okay to enjoy it. Ain't everyday these kids fly to New York for dinner." He then scowled at Troy through the tinted glass. "Look at that fuckin' muppet..."

Stevie snorted, unable to contain her smile at the sight of Troy's goofy grin.

"You'll figure it out, Stevie. Always do."

She didn't offer a reply, stepping from the vehicle with Gibby pushing past her feet. The dog posted a few steps out, scanning the area and taking in the scent of jet fuel.

"Stevie!" Troy shrieked.

Celeste remained indifferent, kicked back against the rail.

She gave him a quick wave but then leaned back into the car, searching for her purse.

Celeste couldn't contain herself and sprung from her cool-guy pose, rushing over to greet Stevie with a hug. Gibby pranced with excitement, Troy following behind. The dog yelped and swung his paws, playfully raising his haunches and arching his back while Troy wrapped the girls in his arms.

"Hello, hello! I see you made it." Stevie's voice was muffled through the arms and hair.

"This is crazy!" Troy stepped back. His eyes were wide and he started robot dancing. *"Like a G6, like a G6!"*

Celeste slapped him in the stomach. "I told you not to embarrass me!"

"Feelin' so fly, like a G6!" He ignored her and continued pivoting his arms.

Stevie laughed. "You ready, or what?! I see Troy's ready!"

"Nopah's almost here. There was traffic on the 101." Celeste informed.

The driver of Stevie's car and his partner in the front seat, both longtime players of Franklin's security team, began rounding up baggage. They organized the suitcases in an orderly row, placing them on a piece of purple carpet that was rolled out toward the aft of the plane. Once everyone's luggage had been gathered, one of the men disappeared inside the plane while the other lifted bags up to him.

Headlights blinded the group as Alex's Town Car pulled into the hanger and parked toward the front of the plane.

"He's such a goober—look at him, he's sitting up front!" Celeste pointed.

The group could see Alex fist bump the driver, and then he stepped out. Slinging an old gym back over his shoulder, Alex's steps were long and lean as he approached them.

"Fuckin' cowboy boots and motorcycle jacket... This dude's my hero." Troy stared.

Celeste frowned and gave her boyfriend another disappointed look.

"I agree..." Stevie awed.

Alex's dark hair was pushed back and he was wearing silver rimmed aviator's. The slap of his boots created an echo that reverberated off the high tin ceiling.

"Oh, Raúl..." Alex snapped his fingers. "Take my bag, would you?" He mocked with decadence. "C'mon, c'mon—what are you waiting for, darling? I've arrived!"

SHE'S A SENSATION
RAMONES

The group arrived at Stevie's Greenwich Village townhouse around 2 A.M. They all felt three hours younger with the time change, leaving enough fuel in the tank to pacify Celeste's incessant babbling about pizza.

"Game time, 'za czar. What's it gonna be?" Troy put his girlfriend on the spot. "Joe's or Bleecker Street?"

"This is all on me, huh?"

"You're the one who's been talking about it for the last 10 hours!"

"Okay…" Celeste bobbled her head. "Fuck it. Bleecker."

"You're kidding me!" Troy shook his head. "Everyone knows that Joe's is the best."

"Oh, c'mon—the Nonna Maria!" Stevie interjected with her hands.

"Your taste is so juvenile, Troy." Celeste belittled. "Yeah—of course we'd all be happy with Joe's—it's the safe call. It's a quality pizza, no doubt, but no one's in the mood for *goddamn training wheels*."

"You talk so much shit! Act like you even know—Stevie, you got any pizza rolls in your freezer for this *Chicago-lovin' deep-dish poser?*"

"Oh, it's on now..." Franklin stepped back. "I ain't gettin' between this. Plus, everybody know Tony's in Brooklyn is the joint..."

Celeste squared off. "We really gonna break up over fuckin' pizza?"

"Settle it, Alex. You pick." Troy looked to him.

Alex's eyes were buried in his phone. "Both."

"What?"

He held up the map app. "They're, like, a block apart—we grab a slice at one, then walk over to the other."

"*Fuck this guy*—both?!" Celeste scoffed. "Can't do that."

"Why not?"

"I don't know... it's, like—it's an unwritten pizza rule. You have to pick one and defend it to the death."

"I like it." Stevie nodded.

"Don't have to tell me twice." Franklin began moving as if the decision had been made. "I'll eat the shit out both of 'em."

"This is sacrilege, Alex. You've offended the pizza Gods." Celeste shook her head. "Though your decision will make my belly very, very happy."

Stevie put on a beanie and then zipped up her hoodie. "Let's do this!" She hooked Gibby to a leash.

The entourage shuffled toward the door and then down the stone steps of the front entrance and out onto the street. Stevie and Celeste skipped ahead with Gibby while Alex and Troy tried to keep pace behind them. Franklin and his two former Rangers brought up the rear, keeping an eye on the group but maintaining their distance.

"You ever been to The City before?" Troy asked Alex.

"Twice. Once was for comic con—I never left the show. Didn't get to go out or see anything. The other time was for work too—but it was meetings. We had some fancy dinners at good places, and I walked around Times Square, but I've never really *seen* New York."

"Gotcha. You could live here your whole life and never see it all."

"You play shows here?"

"Yeah—a lot. Been coming since I was 17. Even got to play one of the last shows at CBGB."

"Shit?! Are you kiddin'?"

"Place was a total shit hole, but, you know, that's why everyone loved it."

"That's incredible, man! The history—absolutely legendary."

"To be honest, I didn't even know who the Ramones were when I played the show. Fuck—now it's the coolest thing ever—but I didn't appreciate it back then. I was so stupid, dude!"

"How'd you not know e*l Ramonés*?!" Alex gasped with a Spanish flare.

"*Ramonés?*" Troy repeated the accent.

"Yeah—we didn't know any better either. All my friends growing up thought that's how you said it." He laughed. "I even wore their t-shirt and had no clue. I was in college at some bar and a guy gave me a high-five—'Yeah, Ramones!'—and I was, like, what?"

"That's hilarious! We're so dumb!"

Gibby's nose stretched outward as the girls passed streetlights and oncoming strangers. The dog recognized where they were. He had spent a lot of time at the second home.

Stevie fell in love with the beatnik lifeblood of Greenwich, the home of Bob Dylan and Pete Seeger. She'd walk along and be captivated by jazz billowing from every corner.

The neighborhood became renown as the command central of avant-garde artists, Marcel Duchamp declaring Greenwich's secession from the rest of Union while taking the Washington Square Arch hostage. This tiny nation within a city invigorated American literature, music, and social enlightenment for more than a century. Critics declared its death upon Stevie's arrival, citing her commercial-gumdrop-tween-musings an insult to the true musicians that struggled within its streets.

That hurt. Stevie was proud of her music and the emotional connection it created. Trivializing her was to mock and shame the genuine thoughts, hopes, and coming-of-age struggles that encapsulated an entire generation of young women. The lack of consideration these critics had for millions of young girls only fueled Stevie's desire to celebrate them and remind them that they mattered. That girls have a place in the world and a future to look forward to. Stevie's musicianship wasn't a revolution against the government or status quo, but rather, it was a uniting force of camaraderie and empathy that crossed gender boundaries, racial divisions, and age gaps.

Stevie's lyrics gentrified an industry that had done nothing but exploit young woman before her. In doing so, her true New York neighbors—not the people writing from some magazine in San Francisco—were proud that the majority of the songs from her last two albums were written from Greenwich. While she wasn't a native, and never claimed to be, she continued to serve the rich legacy of pioneering artists that came from the neighborhood. Those who passed her on the street knew she was kind. She contributed to the community. She reinvigorated the district while its heritage and bustling student body continued to inspire her.

Greenwich Village also hosted the driven and freethinking spirit of NYU—a drastically different path of a young person's life that Stevie observed from afar. Regret wasn't the proper word, but she imagined attending class like a normal college student. Living in a dorm, worrying about exams, fussing over what her major would have been if she had never discovered music. She imagined participating in pompous intellectual discussions outside of a bookstore, summoning the words of Jean-Paul Sartre and casually purporting his nihilist attitudes in hopes of impressing the cute guy with glasses and messy hair from her psychology class. Stevie read the title of book covers that the students carried around with them throughout town, later filling up her tablet with the ones that appeared to be interesting. She actually managed to get through a few of them on the long flights back and forth to L.A..

While Los Angeles remained ground zero for Stevie Pearl logistics, she did her most recent writing from the New York residence. Her manager, Shane Atkins, lived only a few doors down. He was the one who had introduced her to Greenwich, leaving Nashville once the royalty checks allowed him to do so.

Shane lived with his family in a brownstone, juggling a dichotomy between suburban chores and preschool worries with an upper-crust persona reserved for only the city's most elite. Stevie had become an additional member of the Atkins' family. Babysitting, changing diapers, and always having an open invitation to enjoy a home-cooked meal any time that she was in town.

New York filled a hole for Stevie. It served as a sanctuary. A place so chaotic and consumed by progress that it almost made her own achievements seem normal. A place where just by looking up, she felt small. A place where she could blend in.

Stevie hopped down the wide sidewalk, playing a game to avoid the bubblegum stains on the concrete as they walked. Gibby trotted next to her, keeping a watchful eye so that their legs wouldn't tangle and trip each other up.

"How's your mom?" She asked Celeste.

Celeste bit her lip and then looked over at her. "Scared. She calls after each treatment. I think seeing the other patients freaks her out."

Stevie's game of hopscotch came to an abrupt end. "I still can't believe it…"

"The doctors are hopeful. Everyone is *hopeful*… They got to it early, so the odds are good."

Stevie let the words sink in, unsure of how to offer a response. "How are you doing?"

Celeste cursed under her breath and looked off into the distance, summoning composure. "It… sucks. It's just the most helpless feeling in the world. There's nothing I can do."

Silence fell upon them for several strides. The weight in Stevie's chest barely allowed words to escape. "When was the last time you saw her?"

"Couple weeks ago, right before she started chemo. I'm going back next weekend."

"Good." Stevie nodded. Her eyes were wide and welled with tears. She spent countless hours at Celeste's house as a kid— sleepovers, dinners, and movie nights. Celeste's mom always being the cool parent, allowing them to stay up late and watch shows that weren't allowed at her house. "If you want to go more— sooner—just say. Anytime. I'll go with you. I'd love to see her too."

"Thanks. I know I need to get back to Austin more, but it's just been a lot… Fuckin' step-dad is a wreck in the most unhelpful way. It's like, *this is your time to shine, buddy*—suck it up. Be someone this family actually needs."

"Celeste, if there's anything I can do—if you need more help. If the doctors need more resources—please tell me."

"Nothin' you can do either, Stevie." Celeste looked over with desperation and shook her head. "Welcome to my future, right? I mean, that's how my grandma died."

Stevie reached for Celeste's hand and squeezed. "She's gonna be fine. You're both gonna be fine."

A tear ran down Celeste's cheek and she quickly wiped it away. "Ugh! Don't ruin the Nonna Maria for me..." She sucked at the air and squeezed back. "I need this goddamn pizza."

The group bunched together at 7th Avenue waiting for the light to change.

"'Ey—check it out." Franklin nodded. "Drunks ain't here yet—line ain't bad at all."

"Hell yeah!" Celeste hopped up and down, trying to shake off the conversation.

"What are we doing? Getting slices or a pie to split?" Troy asked.

"Lemme handle it." Franklin pushed toward the front. "They know me."

The signal changed and the walk light beaconed like the *Welcome to Las Vegas* sign, a simple gesture announcing their long-awaited arrival to over-indulgences and parmigiano-reggiano debauchery. Their feet were light, toeing across the white crosswalk stripes painted on the street. The green canopy of Bleecker Street Pizza popped against rust-colored paint, the tiny building cut on an angle like the slices it was serving from the counter.

"We. Are. Here." Celeste approached the joint like she had arrived at the Wailing Wall.

"That's it?" Alex cocked his eye. "Looks like Woody's back home."

"Don't matter what it look like, young man." Franklin eyed. "It's what's on the inside... Nonna Maria's?"

"Stop talking, Franklin—" Celeste pushed him. "Get in there!"

Alex trotted a few steps to catch up with the big man. "Hey," he reached for his wallet. "Let me get it." Alex handed him a couple of $20's.

"'Preciate the thought. Though that ain't gonna cut it." Franklin smirked. His eyes told Alex that he was being sincere and not belittling the gesture. "Keep it. We take care of this sorta thing."

"I got more…" He thumbed through his wallet. "I want to."

"Nah, man—we good. Not many even offer."

Alex stood with the money in his hand, staring at Franklin.

"Put it away. Go have fun wit yo' friends."

"…Thank you."

"You welcome."

Franklin's large shoulders brushed against Alex as he reached for the door. He pulled it open and the two were struck by a wave of bubbly cheese and freshly baked dough.

"Ey yo, Marco!" Franklin shouted.

"Franky! Where ya been?"

"Couple of pies for my girl—you got time 'fore the rush?"

"Always got time for you—"

Alex overheard the exchange before the door swung shut. He took a few steps back and watched the workers sling slices through the glass window. *Christ, how much does pizza cost here?* He thought, putting the money back into his wallet.

The girls and Gibby had found a couple of open tables outside on the sidewalk. Troy was busy taking photos of the place on his phone.

Alex approached the two men that been walking with Franklin. Everyone had been introduced on the plane but Franklin and his crew sat up front for the flight and they hadn't talked much.

"Mateo, right? And Knox?"

"Yes, sir."

"I know we met earlier, but I never really got a chance to say hello."

"Hello."

Alex smiled at the uncomfortable exchange. "This place any good?"

Mateo smirked. "It's pizza."

Knox shifted his weight and looked down at Alex. His glare was like a bronze statue and his build was even more impressive.

Alex nodded. His friendly advances being swatted away. "How long you guys known Franklin?"

"A long time."

Silence fell upon them and Alex swung his hands.

"Yeah… we go way back, too. I met him last night."

"Knox!" Celeste shouted. "Be nice, you G.I. Joe mothafuckah!"

Knox ignored her and continued to stare at Alex.

"Well…" He chuckled. "Good talk. Thanks for, ah, looking after us?" Alex shrugged and stepped back. "I'm just gonna… go sit over here."

Mateo laughed as Alex weaved through the patio chairs.

Gibby wagged at his arrival and nosed him. He scratched the dog on the head and then wiped a goober that had formed in the corner of his eye.

"Have a seat, Mr. Nopah." Stevie motioned.

"That went well." He looked back toward Knox while sitting down. "I think we really hit it off."

Stevie laughed but didn't offer him any reassurance.

"It's the steroids." Celeste was loud so that everyone could overhear. "Bulk, Smash!"

Knox pointed a finger at her in a stern manor.

"You know I love ya, big guy."

Knox smiled. The first human expression he had given since Alex said hello.

"Hey, Celeste?" Mateo raised an eyebrow. "What about me?"

"Shhhhh—Troy is standing right there!"

"Funny, hun." Troy said from a squat, capturing just the right angle of the Bleecker Street Pizza sign. "Me and Mateo are homies."

"That's right." Mateo raised his inflection. "When shit goes down, he's the first one I'll use as a human shield."

"Oh, real nice!" Stevie snorted.

"Dude—your words hurt, Mateo. They cut me deep." Troy stood up and slid his phone into his pocket.

"'Ey, Muppet—" Franklin leaned out the door. "Got a couple pitchers here—gimme a hand."

Troy held the door with his foot, accepting the beer in each hand. He was conscious not to slosh as he walked, setting them on the table. Franklin tossed a stack of clear plastic cups to Mateo.

"Whichever one of you pours me that first can sleep with me tonight." Celeste eyed the lager.

Mateo grinned. "Easy." He playfully cradled the cups to keep them out of Troy's reach.

Troy gave him a puzzled stare. He then turned back around, picked up the entire pitcher and placed the beer in front of Celeste.

"Ding ding ding, winner!" She shouted.

"Guess I know my girl better than you think."

Mateo laughed and then handed him the cups. "Match made in heaven."

"Why, thank you, good sir!" Troy accepted and began filling the cups. "Stevie—thank you so much for the impromptu trip." He placed a full beer in front of her.

"Certainly."

"Celeste, the love of my life." He handed her the next one.

"Alex—here's to the *Ramonés*!" He added the Spanish flare from earlier while handing him the beer.

"Knox The Ox." Troy delivered another.

"And Mateo—" Troy poured a little dribble into the cup. "You can go fuck yourself." He grinned.

Alex laughed.

"The fuck you laughin' at?" Mateo eyed him.

"You. You got burned. Twice."

Mateo smiled.

"Looks like you're their bitch." Knox finally spoke, making fun of his partner.

"Awe, poor Mateo!" Stevie leaned over and patted his knee with sarcasm.

"Alright. I see how it is." He snatched the pitcher from the table and finished the pour. "It's fuck with Mateo night. It's cool."

"Guys—" Celeste gathered attention. "I think we need to say a big thank you to Stephanie. It's absurd how well she treats us—my other best friend was only going to take me out on their yacht tonight. We love you, dear—thank you." She held up her plastic cup.

"Yes, Stevie—thank you!" They all agreed out loud.

Alex met her eye and nodded sincerely before taking a sip.

Alex and Stevie walked side by side, Gibby pulling at Alex's arm as the dog led the way back home. The group had abandoned their plan of hitting both pizza shops. The drunks were beginning to wander from the bars and the Nonna Maria from Bleecker Street was more than enough to satisfy their pizza craving.

"You're pretty good with animals." Stevie looked up at him.

"This guy's easy." Alex flicked the leash like reigns. "How'd you come up with Gibby?"

"My guitar. Gibson."

"Ah, shoulda known... Could have called him Flyin' V."

"Les Paul, nerd."

"I miss havin' a dog. Always grew up with 'em—animals were all over the place."

"I love him. He's so unconditional."

"I'm sure he leads quite the life..."

The two took a few awkward steps as they formulated something to say. It was their first moment alone since their walk on the beach. The conversation wasn't labored, but they were still trying to read each another.

"Ugh, gotta get back into tour shape." Stevie patted her belly. "Animal Fries last night, pizza tonight—what are you doin' to me?"

"I believe the fries were your idea!"

"I'd weigh 300 pounds if it weren't for this job."

"I'd weigh 300 pounds because of it... All I've done is stress eat since your party." Alex laughed. "I've eaten more doughnuts in the last week than I have in my entire life."

"What kind?!" Stevie's interest perked.

"Of doughnut?"

"Yeah. What's your go-to?"

"To be honest, I love just a plain glazed doughnut—if it's done right."

"Oh, I agree!" She beamed. "All of the sprinkles and toppings, jellies and frosting—gross!"

"Have you seen those places where they load 'em up with bacon and all this stuff?"

"Yeah. Not into it. Just give me a plain doughnut. Well, more like seven of 'em."

Alex smiled. He loved how overly intense Stevie became about food. It was such a contrast from the persona he knew of her from TV, the way that the news portrayed her.

"Tell me about your family. What are your parents like?" Alex asked.

"Hmm... Let's see. They met in college. They both worked— my dad still does. He's in tech—Austin was huge in the 80s for all the big companies—still is. My mom got me into music. She has this huge vinyl collection—she's been buying records her whole life. She taught me the piano. I began reading music right along, like, learning how to *read regular...*"

"English?"

"Yeah, that's the word." Stevie laughed. "They were good. We had a nice house. They had a couple of kids—me and Joey. I'm lucky. I really love them."

Alex nodded. "Sounds pretty nice."

"It was—still is." Stevie thought about Celeste and her mom. "How about you? What's your family like?"

"A little different." Alex chuckled. "It wasn't bad though. I never really knew my dad. He stuck around for a while after Charlie was born—my older brother. They couldn't make it work. They tried to get back together a couple of times, I assume that's why I'm here. Eventually he just split. My mom always worked—she had a variety of odd jobs but now she's at the community center. She really likes that. We lived with my grandparents—"

"I've heard about Tita." Stevie smirked.

"Jesus… Yep. Her and my grandfather took care of us. He was the one who ranched. That's how we made a living—he taught me and Charlie everything. He was basically my dad. It was hard, we were poor, but I didn't know any different. I remember being happy as a kid."

"Tough for someone in my position to say that money doesn't matter." Stevie looked at him. "It can solve problems. Can cause a few too… but I've learned it's all about the people. People make you happy."

"Yeah, things really went downhill after my grandfather passed. We were all older, I was off at school, but he was the glue."

"I'm sorry…"

"Nah—it's just life. Charlie took it upon himself to continue the ranch. He would have anyway, he never really had any other options. His grades sucked. He was a good athlete but he partied way too much. For some reason I'm the asshole because I didn't drop out and run it with him."

"You're not an asshole…" She smiled.

"Give it time." He smiled back.

Stevie turned and faced him, side stepping as she began to sing.

"*But I see your true colors, shinin' through. So don't be afraid, to let them show—your true colors, true colors are beautiful… like a rainbow!*"

Alex blushed, unaccustomed to be serenaded on sidewalks. Especially by someone who can actually sing.

"You left out the best lyric…"

Stevie really got into it. "*And that's why I love you! So don't be afraid, to let them show. Your true colors… True colors.*"

"You're a dork."

"Yup." She skipped ahead and tussled Gibby, the dog nibbling at her fingers. "I've got a meeting in the morning, but you're welcome to make yourself at home. Celeste knows the routine. I'll hit you guys up and see where you're at when I'm done."

The two approached the steps of her townhouse and Gibby lurched forward. He knew he was home and began scratching his toenails on the cement as he climbed the stairs.

"Pretty crazy night, Ms. Pearl. Thank you."

"Certainly, Mr. Nopah. Thank you for coming."

He leaned down and stroked Gibby's ears as she unlocked the door. The rest of the group caught up and waited to be let in.

"Were you just singing Cyndi Lauper?" Celeste mocked. "Without me?!"

"*And I see your true colors, shining through.*" Stevie began again.

"*I see your true colors, and that's why I love you!*" The two sang together. "*So don't be afraid to let them show—your true colors—true colors, are beautiful like a rainbow!*"

BLUE MOON
BECK

Franklin worked the buzzer of Shane's door.

Stevie stood expressionless, her eyes looking through the cracked spiderwebbing of the brick and mortar brownstone. She fidgeted with a ring on her finger, reviewing talking points within her mind. She was frustrated that she even needed to have this conversation with Shane—that somehow their relationship had come to this point.

Stevie's father jumpstarted her career. Like most involved parents, he supported her wholeheartedly. However, to his credit he wasn't naive. He understood the larger architecture of life and his role as father and husband. From conception, Benjamin doted over her mother, Kristen. There was no reservation within his affection, and equally no compromise within his authority. Stevie's father was the law, but he reigned with supreme justice. He commanded respect because he gave it.

Early on, Ben recognized Stevie's passion, but that had little effect on his devotion to her. Regardless of the task, his job was to challenge his daughter. He taught her the importance of competition and tested her ego to instill selflessness. He also gave her the freedom to play and imagine. Without a thought, he would wrap pink scarfs around his neck and create gravely voices for her stuffed animals. Through him, she learned quickly that were consequences to her actions. Life lessons ingrained because her father led by example. Stevie's existence motivated him to work harder. The thought of being unable to provide the tools and education to foster his daughter's undeniable talent was unacceptable. Ben knew a lifetime with Stevie would be too short, and that he had a very small window within her young life to demonstrate that.

The man had a keen ability to balance observation with action. When the time was right, he took her into the studio to record her first song, long before she ever had a record contract. To build her confidence, he arranged live performances well before any agent expressed interest. He was responsible for getting her played on the radio, and most importantly he created the viral videos and internet marketing campaign that launched her name into the zeitgeist.

Benjamin handled her affairs and money for several years, and did a remarkably good job for having no experience in the music industry. However, when talks of world tours emerged and corporate sponsors approached her for commercials, he knew he was beyond his ability. He was so proud of his daughter, but he had the wherewithal to know that he was now the one holding her back. That's when he introduced her to Shane Atkins.

Shane was in his early 30's when they met. He had graduated from Berklee College of Music, and shortly thereafter earned his MBA from NYU. He interned at a couple of record labels in Manhattan, eventually landing a job at an entertainment management firm in Nashville. He was still building a name for himself when they met, but he was tenacious and had achieved success with several other young artists. Stevie's father saw something in the young man, and as difficult as it was to do, he let

go. He made the introduction but allowed Stevie to make the decision. Shane looked good on paper, but his daughter also had to trust him.

The heavy door sprung from its latch and a tiny human pushed its way through. The little boy squealed and wrapped his pudgy arms around Franklin's leg, hugging him deeply.

"Frank-lin!" The little boy giggled as large meaty fingers tickled his back.

"Hey guys!" Shane's wife opened the door the rest of the way. "Aiden, aren't you going to say hi to Stevie too?"

Aiden continued to giggle. "Hi, Auntie Steve." He squirmed under Franklin's large hands.

"Aiden!" Stevie bent down. "No hug for me?"

"Ahhhhhhhh!" Franklin continued to tickle the boy.

"Come here!" She grabbed him and pulled him close, holding him extra-long. She was actually jealous that the boy was more excited to see Franklin than her.

"Did you miss me?"

"Yeah." His hug in return was quick and forced as he was more interested in playing with Franklin.

"Can't have all the fans, Stevie." Franklin teased.

The three entered the home, Aiden clinging to Franklin's leg like a barnacle as he walked.

"Don't worry." Niko shut the door and then welcomed Stevie with a warm hug. "He insists that we watch one of your videos each night before bed so he can say goodnight to Auntie Steve."

"There they are!" Shane rounded the corner. He shook Franklin's hand while placing the other on his shoulder. "You can just kick him, you know?" He looked down at Aiden. "He'll slide right across the hardwood. He loves it."

"What?" Franklin twisted his head.

"Show 'em your new trick, Aiden. Do your slide!"

Aiden stepped back and took five or six running steps before flopping onto his bottom, sliding across the smooth hardwood. The child giggled and Franklin bellowed with laughter.

"That's new! He wasn't doin' that last time!"

"You miss a day in this house and it's like missing a month. Stevie, how ya been?" Shane hugged her.

"It's been a long few days." She hugged back. "Glad we're here."

"You guys want coffee? I'm gonna have another." He offered.

"Sure." Stevie accepted and Franklin gave a thumbs up.

"I'll get it." Niko said. "You guys do your thing—I know you've got work. I'll make sure Franklin is still in one piece by the time you're done."

"She only offers when you're around!" Shane joked. "She never gets me coffee…"

"Good." Stevie teased. "You should be getting it for her."

"Ain't that the truth. Malee's down for a nap—she's been up since 3. Between the newborn and that one." He nodded at Aiden. "She needs it… C'mon. Let's hit the office. Franklin, you good for a bit?"

"This lil' mad man'll keep me busy."

"Give Niko the nod if he gets to be too much."

"He fine. I missed 'em."

Shane owned two sprawling levels in Greenwich, the rear of the home opening up so that the upstairs looked down upon the living room. Massive windows out the back connected both levels, and giant sliding doors opened up to a patio that served as a mini backyard. The decor and angles were clean and modern, contrasted by several of Aiden's toys that were strewn about.

The two remained quiet as they walked. Shane knew Stevie was upset. He could tell by her tone on the phone the day before. They talked regularly, daily, but it wasn't like her to fly out just to see him. He kicked a stuffed animal from their path and opened the French doors into his office.

Stevie circled the couch, taking in the familiar sight of her multi-platinum records hanging from the walls. She sat in an armchair and Shane stepped around a coffee table and took the couch next to her. He studied her for a moment and then crossed his legs, putting a foot up on his knee.

"Didn't go well at Hodges and Rhode?" He spoke first.

"No." Stevie shook her head.

"It's this deal, Stevie—everyone's on edge. Cosmopolitan thought it was a slam dunk, re-signing with Kismet."

"Why would Lisa Rhode care who I signed with?"

Shane shrugged his shoulders. "I don't know. She shouldn't... but I think everyone cares at this point."

"Why hasn't Kismet replaced Dallas Sachs yet?"

"What happened between you two? I mean, I know he was an ass but he's no different than the rest of them."

Stevie stared at him. She needed to know who's side he was on.

"Shane, do you remember when I was 16—when you and I first met?"

"Of course."

"I don't think either of us thought we'd be here." She looked around the room.

"I did." Shane was unaffected. "I had no doubt."

"That's flattering, but no one can plan what we've achieved. You can work hard, and we did—but there's no equation for this."

"Stevie, you're no accident. Your talent as a songwriter appears to be an otherworldly gift to anyone outside of this room—maybe it is—but I also know how hard you work at it. How many songs that have never seen the light of day. I know the amount of time and care you place into every performance. From the stage, wardrobe, lighting, props, and dancers—down to the facial expressions you make while singing a particular word... the moment you allow yourself to breathe between them. There's not a single thing you haven't thought of."

"My father sat across the table from us. He was absolutely terrified, but he did his best to compose himself—to reassure me that I was making the right decision."

"Stevie, what are you saying?"

"I need to know if the man who promised my father—the man who looked me in the eye and pledged to always be open and honest with me—is still sitting in this room."

Shane swallowed hard and twisted in his seat, dropping the foot that was balanced on his knee.

"Knock, knock." Niko said, opening one side of the French doors. "Coffees—just how you like 'em." The tension fell upon her like a wave and she abruptly stopped in her tracks. Stevie didn't break her stare on Shane.

"It's okay." Shane motioned for his wife to come in. He sat forward and pushed a few magazines on the table to make room for the cups.

"I didn't mean to interrupt..."

"You're fine." Stevie looked toward her. "Thank you, Niko." She nodded sincerely.

Niko placed the cups on the coffee table and then straightened her shirt. The expression on her face was uncomfortable as she searched for a pleasant word.

"Let me know if you need anything else. I'll be helping Franklin keep the monster at bay..." She nodded, then left the room as quickly as she had entered.

Shane leaned forward and blew on his coffee.

"She's always been my savior. Impeccable timing." He smiled. "I'm serious. She has literally saved my life. You remember how I was—young with money, somehow managing your explosion... We met at NYU, but I was always too driven—or stupid—to think about a relationship. It wasn't until I was back in town, negotiating one of your tours, actually, that we bumped into each other. I was pacing Washington Square Park, over by the Holley Monument. I had never been so in over my head… Niko was reading a book. She made fun of my new sunglasses and slicked back hair. Best thing that ever happened to me…"

Stevie remained expressionless, unaffected by the story.

"I've only made a handful of oaths in my life, Stevie. One was to Niko—my children. The other was to your father. I told him no matter what you did, where you were in the world, that I would stand beside him and fight to protect you. I promised him, as long as you would allow me, that I would look after you—just as he has. There's a lot of shitty things that go on behind the scenes—the world has offered me nothing but temptation since you entered my life—but I have never broken my oath to Niko, Aiden or Malee, to your father—and I have never broken my oath to you."

Stevie's chest pounded. Fear, anger, frustration, relief, trust, and thoughts of her father combined to create a nonsensical cocktail of emotion that she buried within her throat.

"Tell me what this is about." Shane looked to her.

"What do you know about Alex Nopah?"

Shane leaned back with a look of ambivalence. "The guy from your party? Just the report Franklin sent out…"

"What—do you know—about Alex Nopah. I will not ask a third time."

Shane pressed his lips together and bit the inside of his cheek. Her words were cold and calculated, a side of Stevie he had seen several times but rarely was such focus directed toward him.

"I didn't know anything about him until you fired Dallas Sachs." Shane shook his head. "Apparently, Dallas went straight to Cosmopolitan from your house. His brother-in-law is an executive at the Music Group—real high up—probably how Dallas got the job in the first place. He told him a bunch of garbage but the crux came down to you taking an interest in some poor Indian kid—enough interest that this new guy was the reason Dallas was fired.

"It's not just with the media or your fans, but *everyone* seems to take a great deal of interest in who catches the attention of Stevie Pearl… Cosmo execs quickly put a lot of resources into figuring out who this Alex guy was and what he would mean for the brand—apparently they didn't like the numbers. I learned a lot more yesterday afternoon—after you stormed in on Lisa Rhode. She called me and we had a very, well, *frank conversation*."

Stevie remained motionless. Her posture was straight and her eyes latched onto Shane like an eagle. She wanted to hear what he had to say.

"Lisa, who now, curiously, all of sudden decided to take it upon herself to enforce our copyright contracts—you remember how long it took me to get any action out of her when we were going after the fake porn sites—anyway, she must have agreed with Cosmopolitan's assessment of Alex. That he was bad for business. She went along with what I can only assume was a plan hatched by Cosmo and Kismet to get rid of Alex. Scare him away. They kept tabs on his behavior and as soon as he did something they could pin him on—posting a stupid photo from your party—they went after him… Get him out of the picture before he had the chance to charm you with any more dance moves.

"What they didn't anticipate was that the two of you continued to talk—all indications being that neither of you had spoken to each other after the party. Lisa, to say the least, was surprised to see you in her office defending him—she assumed he simply would have disappeared without a word. You forced her hand into dropping the copyright charges and not filing a non-disclosure violation with Cosmo. After all, legally, she works for you."

Stevie let out a breath of air, disgusted that she had been spied on. How did they know who she was talking to? Did Franklin know about this? Someone had to be helping them. Her flickering eyes moved past Shane and onto more of her memorabilia that sat on a bookshelf.

"That's not all." Shane leaned forward. "With the contract up, I've been testing the water with other labels. I just wanted to make sure that you knew your options when the time came to make a decision. Yeah, I'll admit, I've dropped the ball on getting the numbers to you—it's been a little busy around here with the new born—my fault. Right now there's two offers out there besides re-signing with Kismet that I'd take seriously—ballparks at the moment—but they are *very good*."

"Good." Stevie's nod was slow and deliberate.

"Well… things are getting tricky." Shane shifted once more and began talking with his hands. "I've never wanted to kill anyone in my life, but if I could have reached through the phone and strangled Lisa yesterday—I would have. Kismet won't re-sign you if you continue to associate with Alex."

"Then we won't resign with them. Done."

Shane paused, trying to find the appropriate words. "Lisa… gave the impression, she did a lot eluding—but if you don't re-sign with Kismet, they will do everything they can to devalue you to the other labels." His tone became low, as if that would help soften the blow.

"The ballpark numbers I got—Lisa said they won't mean anything once they rip you apart in the media… If you leave, they'll paint you as completely unhinged—firing Dallas, your lawyers, your label, and everyone else as you're going through your Britney-head-shave moment. They'll make sure that the new labels and investors conveniently find their projections and focus-testing of Alex. Even if you and Alex don't, you know—date—they'll keep him in the press and the rumors going anyway—perception being reality…

"Your erratic behavior, the *image of the brand*—it will create uncertainty among investors, making it impossible for the new labels to pay you what you're worth. Cosmo's stock will also take a hit—but they fully plan on blaming you. They'll broadcast every sob story, showing people's lives being ruined by your careless actions and abandonment—they can only hope that Wall Street starts jumping out of buildings.

"Lisa said they'll make it their mission to end your reign as the biggest pop star on the planet—and, without a doubt, they'll absolutely destroy Alex in the process… So, I guess I need to know from you, who is Alex Nopah?"

Stevie closed her eyes. A rage filled within her like she had never felt in her entire life. Her ears burned and scalp tingled. Adrenaline coursed through her, giving her the strength to flip the solid oak coffee table and couch right along with Shane sitting in it.

However, her voice remained calm. It was the mastery of her vocal cords that afforded her all she had ever known in life, and her next words came out slow and sweet like honey.

"When you say protect me—your oath to protect me—what, exactly, does that mean to you?"

Shane was caught off guard by the question. Not the response he was expecting after the news he had just delivered.

"I… I don't know what you mean?"

"Do you believe that you are protecting me by securing my most lucrative and stable business future? Or do you believe you are protecting me by moving my business partnerships away from extortionists? There's two very logical ways to look at this—two ways of how you *might believe* that you are protecting me…"

Shane took a deep breath and looked her in the eye. Without a single accusation, she had cornered him. Her words left no room for deflection. Her question was ideological and he knew the answer had to align with her core values. It had to confirm that they were both on the same page.

Given the stakes, in the midst of a massive contract negotiation and her lawyers and label turning against her, he could understand where the paranoia was coming from. However, he hadn't expected it to be directed toward him. He wasn't a part of Kismet's coup.

It didn't matter though, there was no explaining away the situation. Shane knew in that very moment that he only had two options. If he chose wrong, their relationship would be over. She would walk out the door and all of the success he had seen in his life would go with it. The young girl that he thought of as a little sister would be gone. Sure, he was a competent and capable manager—but she was the only Stevie Pearl.

He continued to study her, searching for any sign or a poker tell that would help push him toward the right decision—a nod in the direction of what she wanted from him. There wasn't one. There was nothing. Her stare was stone and she wasn't going to say another word until he answered her question. His survival depended solely on how well he knew her. His own moral compass—the decision came down to what he believed was right and wrong.

"Extortionists, Stevie. I'm protecting you from extortionists. I can't do business with people who would treat you in such a way."

Stevie honestly didn't know the right answer. She knew what she wanted, but she didn't know if she was willing to risk everything to have it.

As a manager, Shane should have chosen the other option. He was supposed to allow her to have emotional outbursts and moral crusades, but his job was to protect the empire. He was supposed to be sensible. He was supposed to rise above childish idealism and broker deals that worked in the real world. He was supposed to convince her that bowing to Kismet was the right move for her career.

Had Shane become a *yes man*? Had she molded him into someone who agrees with her no matter the cost? Was he her own personal Conrad Murray, pumping her full of approval because that was the mellow she wanted? A manager is supposed to have discipline. A manager should have better judgement. A manager —a manager—a manager—a father shouldn't be afraid to tell their children no!

Stevie sucked air and dug her fingers into the armrest.

"Good." She began. "I think they're underestimating my willingness to burn them to the ground. As of now, make sure that Lisa is fully aware that I will expose her, Kismet, and all of Cosmopolitan for racism, collusion, and egregious extortion if she mentions another word of Alex or the prospect of me re-signing with them. I'm sure she can get the message to the rest of *the team*. I will command every single camera lens, I will go on every single talk show, and I will tell the entire story. I will do a primetime two-hour-long-sit-down with Sarah Jennings. I will make sure the world knows what my lawyers have done to Alex, what Cosmo intended to do to him, and what type of disgusting cattle-call polling they conducted about a human being. I will lead a march to Cosmo's doorstep by women tired of being manipulated—I will tell the world how they sat in a boardroom and decided who I can and can't date like my love is a prize for their shareholders. How they threatened my career—my entire professional and personal life—unless I went along with their twisted demands. Oh, the recourse will be tremendous! Maybe my brand will take a hit… maybe I won't sign with anyone—*no one said I had to*. They think they got me by the balls? I will shame every single sponsor for sticking with a company as unethical as them and I will plead with every single artist to leave their roster. They want to take this public? We can take it public!"

Shane had sunken into his seat, his eyes and ears heralding the apocalypse. A wretched sickness penetrated his marrow as his mind tried to accept that he was now Kennedy in the midst of a full-on nuclear missile crisis. Stevie was lit, ready to burn the world to the ground over a mistaken sneeze.

"Okay. Okay." He said aloud though it was mainly to calm himself. "Let's not go there yet—though it's good to know how you feel. All options are on the table."

"Shane. I will not tolerate one single bad word about Alex, or my reputation, leaked to the press by them. Got it? They do, and it's all over."

He nodded erratically. "Got it."

Stevie sat back in her chair and huffed. Her stare seared him. She studied all of his movements, absorbing the panic across his face.

"I need to know you're in this."

"Stevie, I don't know what you've heard… but I've always been in this."

She allowed the words to settle. Her mind calculating his tone, the way his words fell from his tongue.

"I don't know what Lisa told you yesterday, but her and I haven't been talking. That's probably the problem… Kismet gave me their price months ago—obviously I was talking to other labels—and we're supposed to circle back to see if they can match it. The longer we've waited—which, I know, is my fault—the more intense the bidding war got. The offer from Apollo Records is *staggering*…"

Stevie saw that he was being genuine. She felt it.

"Late yesterday—you were on the plane, on your way here—that's the first time Kismet pulled this shit. Actually threatened you."

Stevie's eyes left him and they moved across the room. The electricity she had conjured for battle, the tremendous strength it took to confront Shane's intentions was melting into the notion of actually losing him.

"Obviously they got word of Apollo's offer and went into crisis mode. They can't come close to matching it."

Stevie's head swam—betrayal, anger, and the absolute depravity that Kismet was capable of mixed with a dreadful sense of vulnerability. The root of Stevie's fear had been rubbed raw, and the salt caused her to face it. The reason she had flown to New York—the reason she was sitting across from Shane was all about trust.

"I'm sorry." Her words were soft.

Shane cocked his eye and hesitated.

"I'm sorry, Shane."

The man dropped his head as the words rang in his ear. He allowed it to hang for a few moments before he wiped his chin. He looked up at her and then waved his hand, dismissing the possibility of career-ending trauma like it was no big deal.

"I know you've been busy with Malee—you should be. I'm not mad at you... but I don't know who's on my team anymore. Who I can trust..."

"Stevie..." He looked at her square. "You're a part of this family. You're at my house all the time—you change my son's diapers for Christ's sake. I don't know how I can let you know any more than I have that you're part of this team—and I'm part of your team. Ride or die."

"Fo' sho'..." Her voice finally cracked, a sound heard by few.

"I love you, kid."

A couple of loose tears bubbled over and dripped down Stevie's cheek.

"I'm sorry." She breathed deep, trying to slow her heart rate. "I love you too... Niko, Aiden, Malee—I love all of you. You're family. I was so scared I was gonna lose you... *all of you.*"

The levy broke as she admitted what was truly bothering her. The prospect of being left all alone. The tears were uncontrollable.

Shane stood up and opened his arms. "Come 'ere."

Stevie pushed herself from the chair and fell into his chest, tears soaking into his t-shirt. The thought of losing the man and family that offered her a shred of meaningful human connection sent her trembling.

"You're never gonna lose us—no matter what happens."

"I'm sor—ry." She huffed between sniffles.

"It's okay." He hugged her tight.

Stevie balled the back of his shirt into her fist and squeezed, holding on to him with all her might. "It's lonely, Shane. It's so lonely. I can't lose you too."

He continued to hold her until she released the clutch of cloth from her grasp and stepped back.

"Quite the mess we're into this time." He smiled while holding her by the wrist.

Stevie just shook her head. Her eyes blackened from smeared mascara.

He let go and she flopped back into the chair. Shane then crossed the room and grabbed a box of tissues from his desk. He handed it to her before returning to the couch. The two were quiet while she calmed herself.

"Are you going to tell me about Alex?"

Stevie dabbed the tears from her eyes but couldn't keep a small smile from returning to her face as she thought of him.

"I don't know… It's all so new. He's gorgeous." She looked up.

"There's never been a shortage of *gorgeous* guys…"

"Whether we date or not, what Kismet has done is unforgivable… All because of who he is."

Shane watched her twist a tissue around her finger, cutting off the circulation. She was the most troubled he had ever seen her.

There had been plenty of tears over the years, but none that had carried the weight of her mind and conscience with such anguish.

"Niko and I had that…" He offered a moment of vulnerability. "I mean, there wasn't tens of millions—hundreds of millions of dollars on the line, but our families were… *skeptical*. She's Vietnamese. Her parents barely speak English, they came over when she was a child. The missionaries got to them, they're super religious… I am not.

"I don't know what they wanted for her, but I'm pretty sure I'm not it. My parents, god love them, were so confused by the whole thing. Trying to explain to them that she was a good person —that her family being poor, or having such a different childhood… Jesus, the food. None of it mattered to me. Waking up and going to work and doing all the things you're supposed to do—she gave it meaning. All of a sudden it all meant something. My life mattered because of her."

"I didn't know your parents didn't want you to be together?"

"It's not that they didn't like her… They were just… scared. They wanted the easiest path for me and their future grandchildren. Less complications. Less struggles because marriage is hard enough as it is. But what they didn't seem to realize is that's why I wanted to marry her. She makes my life easier. She makes me such a better person."

Stevie let out a breath of air as she thought about Alex.

"I don't know if he's your Niko, but as magical and unpredictable love is—it's also a choice. Niko and I can approach things very differently. After dinner she'll just throw a lid on the leftovers and call it good. I'm like, 'hun, we have a refrigerator…' but her parents didn't. That's how she grew up. So, I just don't eat as many leftovers…" He smiled.

"I know she gets totally pissed at me for being wasteful— throwing things away. She'll box up the dumbest stuff and send it back to Vietnam. I don't mind sending care packages, but let's at least send them something good!"

Stevie laughed.

"Guaranteed there's times when she thinks I'm a total spoiled snot. I know this. But I also try to make her feel loved. Let her know that we can get mad at each other, but I'm not going anywhere. We made that choice, and that's why we can laugh about most things."

Stevie absorbed his words. She had never considered the most obvious challenges of Shane and Niko's relationship. Of course, they had issues. Each would occasionally confide in her during a moment alone, but she also witnessed their love. She saw them date, get engaged. She was a bridesmaid at their wedding. She was there when they bought a house, and brought children into the world. To her, they were an example. A model. They had the type of relationship to strive toward. Thoughts of race and money seemed so insignificant in comparison.

"Alex is real." She reflected. "Authentic. He's not caught up in all of the drama and nonsense… I worry he won't date me because of it."

"He'll see you're not caught up in it either. Once he really gets to know you."

"He's here…"

"In New York?"

Stevie nodded. "Him. Celeste and Troy… Speaking of which— I need a favor. I want you to send someone to Austin for a few months."

"Okay?"

"Janet, Celeste's mom, she has cancer."

"Oh—oh my god."

"Yeah… I want someone to help out the family. Buy groceries, medicine—help get her to doctor's appointments—pick up around the house. Whatever. I also want you to follow up with the doctor. Make sure they know that resources are not a problem—get them anything they need."

"Yeah… Yeah. No problem. Is she…?"

"Well, it's never good… but they're hopeful. Celeste doesn't talk about it and she won't ask for anything, so we just need to handle it."

"Done." Shane looked at Stevie. He could see the weight of the world resting upon her shoulders. "What are you guys doin' tonight? Want to come over for dinner, spend some time with the kids? I'd love to meet Alex."

Stevie lifted her head at the proposition.

"I'll bring in a cook. Niko won't have to worry about a thing. We'll get Franklin—I'm sure his goons are here too. We can all just hangout—Aiden will go crazy."

"Knox and Mateo."

"Jesus, Knox is here?"

Stevie chuckled. "I'd like that. I'll run it by the others."

WOLVES
RYAN BINGHAM

The sun crept through the curtains, its rays warming the corner of the bed. Alex rolled over and buried his face into the oversized comforter. The duvet was smooth and plush. He stretched his legs and the sheets felt like butter.

He rolled once more, the tiny slits in his eyes trying to focus on the ceiling above him. A pressed tin design made him go cross-eyed before its pattern came into focus, an elegance he hadn't noticed the night before. He yawned and then forced himself out of bed, nature inspiring him to leave the cocoon.

A bathroom was connected to the bedroom and Alex made use of it. He turned the water on to the shower and a massive fixture created a warm and soothing rainstorm. The soap was fluffy like whipped cream and smelled like exotic flowers mixed with citrus. The lather from the shampoo was thick and full, tingling his scalp.

Once finished, he crossed the tile for a towel. Its weight and density feeling like a blanket. He ran the terrycloth across his skin and then wrapped himself up while staring into the mirror.

Where the hell are you?

Alex leaned in for a closer look, paying attention to his pours and the stray hairs around his eyebrows. He used his fingernails to pluck and press, suddenly becoming self-conscious about his appearance. Discovering there was little he could do about a lifetime of indifference in a single morning, he gave up and dug through his toiletry bag. He brushed his teeth and then splashed on some cheap cologne, his grandfather's recipe found in any supermarket. He then bent down and used the towel to wipe up his wet footprints and stray drops, making sure to leave the bathroom just as he had found it.

Alex pulled on his jeans and wrestled with his boots. He took a fresh shirt from the gym bag and then grabbed his jacket before leaving the bedroom. He cracked the door and peered down the hall, listening for signs of life. There was no one stirring so he stepped lightly down the wide wooden staircase, its curve leading him to the main living area.

Stevie's Greenwich townhouse was a hip Victorian palace. Rich, dark wood molding encased every surface. Accent lighting blended with the morning sun that fell through massive paned windows. Plush leather furniture filled the room and invited a passerby to run fingers along their seams. A centered fireplace separated the living room from the kitchen, two large arches guiding the flow of traffic on each end of the room.

Alex had never been alone around such wealth. He had seen money, attending the welcoming party at director Jim Brigman's house and wandering through the lobby of Stevie's L.A. mansion, but they were both full of people. He was afraid he would embarrass himself by gawking. No one seemed to be marveling at what surrounded them, so he too acted as if it was normal. He played it cool. Now alone, he allowed himself to admire details that he had never even considered.

The handcrafted woodwork was superb. He respected the skill because he understood how difficult it was to achieve. He and

Charlie decided to build an addition off of the barn one summer, extra space to keep tools and equipment from baking in the sun. Charlie was a perfectionist, insisting that the siding and trim match his grandfather's work on the existing structure. It was one of the last times Alex picked up a nail gun.

Alex moved deliberately. He took in the rich embossed damask fabric that was stuck to the walls instead of paint, a touch only suitable for royalty. He then leaned down and examined a couple of photographs that were placed on a side table. He wondered if their frames were made of actual silver. He assumed the people gathered in the picture were Stevie's family, the little boy vaguely resembled Joey—the valet punk who desecrated his motorcycle. He then turned and smirked at a large canvas hanging on the wall. He leaned in to read the signature, knowing his own work was much better—though this one was sure to have cost exponentially more.

Toenails scraped against the hardwood, the unexpected tapping of paws startling Alex. Gibby had caught him lurking and offered a wag as good morning.

"What's up, Gibby?"

The dog stood in the sunlight that beamed through the oversized windows, twisting his head at the words.

Alex smiled as he approached, squatting down so that he was at the same level as the dog. Gibby buried his head into Alex's chest and his wag became more devoted. Alex reached forward and ran his hands in long strokes over the dog's back. Gibby arched and then looked up, licking Alex's ear.

"Gross, ya sicko!" He tussled the dog. "Anyone else up yet?"

Alex heard the clearing of a throat and the sound of paper rustling. He gave the dog another quick scratch on the head and then stood up, crossing through the sunlight and around the corner into the kitchen. Knox was sitting on a barstool reading a legit newspaper. He had a cup of coffee steaming in front of him.

"Mornin." Alex greeted.

Knox bent the page so he could see and nodded. He flicked the paper to re-straighten it and began reading again.

Alex circled the large island countertop that penetrated from the center of the kitchen. He paused and looked around.

"There's juice 'n shit. Coffee. Whatever." Knox said.

Alex considered the vast amount of cabinetry that surrounded him. The refrigerator even blended in with the woodwork and he had no idea where to begin or end.

"Stevie and Franklin are over at Shane's. They left just a bit ago, so I imagine they'll be a while. I don't expect Celeste before…" he paused and twisted his wrist, looking at his watch. "I dunno, noon?"

"Oh…" Alex hesitated, unsure what to do with himself.

"Want to get breakfast? Decent place 'bout a block from here. The flight last night was spur of the moment so the house didn't get stocked like usual."

"Where's Mateo?"

Knox moved the paper again and raised an eyebrow.

"Need to know basis… and I don't need to know?"

He folded the paper and placed it on the counter. ""Lil' bitch is still sleepin'. He's got errands to run anyway. It's just you and me."

"Yay…"

Knox took a slug from the coffee and then got up and tossed the rest into the sink. "Let's go."

Alex followed him through the house and then down the steps onto the street. Knox immediately put on a pair of sunglasses. The two walked side by side, the buildings and sidewalk looking older and more worn in the daylight. Alex was decently tall, about 6 feet, but Knox stood an entire head above him. His strides were long and with purpose, his torso twisting with each step. Alex had to adjust his normal gait just to keep up.

"That place." Knox pointed to a bodega as they approached the corner of the street. "It's like a gas station without the gas—coffee, candy, chips. Typical bullshit. Get yourself a slushee." He then checked the traffic before crossing the street. "Down that road, you can catch the subway. If you keep goin', there's food."

Alex smiled. Knox was playing tour guide and he appreciated the gesture. It was the first nice thing he had said to him since they met.

"You don't eat weird shit, right? We can just have a normal breakfast?" Knox looked down at him.

"I'll eat whatever."

"Good."

The two walked in silence until they arrived at the breakfast spot, a tiny diner with the smell of coffee and bacon wafting out onto the street. Knox about tore the door off of the hinges letting himself in. He then scooted into a booth, his frame taking up both seats.

Alex sat across from him and looked around. For being a New York dive, it was still nice compared to the tiny greasy spoons that dotted the California desert along the highway out to Parker. Knox glanced at the menu and then set it down, Alex suddenly feeling urgency to make a decision.

The waitress arrived. "Drinks, fellas?"

"Bacon. Eggs—over easy. Coffee." Knox said.

"Straight to it—want toast?"

"Yup."

She didn't bother asking him what kind. "What can I get for you, hun?" She turned her attention to Alex.

"The Denver omelet, hash browns, wheat toast. I'll have a coffee too, please."

"You got it."

Alex looked at Knox sitting across from him. He was still wearing his sunglasses and he noticed a faded scar that ran down his neck and passed the collar of his shirt toward his chest. His forearms were tattooed and covered with thick hair.

"Where you from?" Alex attempted small talk.

"Give ya a guess."

"Knoxville…" Alex put it together as soon as he had asked the question.

"Ain't the fort. Only Stevie got that kind of money."

"That house—her place—it's insane."

"You ain't seen half of it…"

Alex fiddled with a wire caddy holding extra napkins and ketchup, running his fingers through the Sweet'N Low and jelly.

"So, why are you special?"

Alex raised an eyebrow, not understanding the question.

"What's a girl like her see in you?"

"I have no clue." Alex could only laugh.

"Lot of guys been through here—way better than you."

"A lot?"

"You don't own a TV?"

Alex didn't offer an immediate reply, unsure if Knox was just an uncontrollable asshole or intentionally belittling him. "I never really kept up on it."

"Couple of coffees." The waitress placed the thick ceramic mugs in front of them. "Breakfast'll be up in a minute."

"Thank you." Alex acknowledged.

"I ain't gonna let you get nothin' out of her."

Alex sat back in the seat.

Knox stared at him.

"I—I don't want anything from her."

"Good."

"I'm tried of this shit…" Alex's tone turned. "Everyone accusing me of being a dirtbag—fuckin', just trying to use her for something. She's the one who's just about ruined my life. Twice. And I've only known her a week."

Knox folded his arms. "So, don't hang out with her then."

"Fuck you, Knox. What you got against me?"

"Better watch that mouth."

"What are you gonna do? Beat the shit out of me in front of all these people?"

"It ain't my job to like you."

Alex remained quiet. He looked down into his coffee.

"I'm rootin' for you." Knox took off his sunglasses and stuck them between the buttons of his shirt. "There's been some real pieces of shit that have come through here—only after one thing. You ain't earned trust yet, Alex. But I sure hope you do."

"What the fuck does that mean?" Alex flipped his hands. "Is this some Army interrogation bullshit?"

"It means I'll fuckin' gut you." Knox growled.

"Yeah—how many of her boyfriends have you gutted? I'm sick of everyone around her trying to intimidate me."

Knox smiled at the venom. He sat back and stared at Alex, not offering a word.

Alex stared back.

The two sat in silence until the food was delivered. Knox didn't hesitate and dug in. Alex just looked at his omelet.

Knox slurped at runny eggs, dipping his toast in the yoke. "Bacon's good." He nodded. "Not too crispy."

Alex pushed his hash browns around, only taking a few bites.

"I'm gonna give you some advice." Knox continued to focus on his food. "She's lonely. She's lookin' for someone she can tell secrets to—who won't tell them to the rest of the world. She's lil' boy crazy, but what she really wants is a friend. A person she can rely on... Always know your place—don't ever offer her business advice. Her favorite flower is the Indian Blanket."

Alex looked across the table at him, his brow wrinkled with confusion.

"Go on. Eat your breakfast."

Alex couldn't understand Knox or his disposition. He continued to push food around, trying to find words for his thoughts. "You don't think I know that I'm way out of my league here? I don't know what the fuck I'm doin'?"

Knox looked up. He wrapped his hand around his coffee cup and brought it to his mouth.

"It took me five minutes to figure out how to turn the shower on. I've never been on a private jet. All the while I'm tryin' to make sure I don't say somethin' stupid… which is impossible because she's so fuckin' beautiful… powerful. I'm under the microscope with you guys—is he gonna steal something? Is he going to post something online? Yeah, Knox—I don't belong here. No one is more aware of that than me."

"You done bitchin'?"

Alex shrugged, his eyes faded around the diner. "Probably not."

Knox threw a wad of cash down next to his plate.

"No one's ready for Stevie. Don't be somethin' ya ain't." He got up from the table. "I got shit to do. Think you can figure out how to get back?"

Alex's expression was filled with desperation, his head wobbling in what was an attempted nod.

Knox towered above him, raising an eyebrow as he put on his sunglasses. He then started toward the door.

"Thanks for…" Knox was several steps down the sidewalk before he could finish, "…breakfast."

Alex looked at the empty space across from him. He took a few more bites and then pushed his plate to the center of the table. He pulled his phone from his pocket and scrolled around. No new messages.

He let out a sigh, unsure of what to do with himself. He thought about seeing some of the city, taking a walk along its fabled streets. He pulled up the map app and dropped a pin on his location, insurance so that he could figure his way back to the same block that Stevie lived on. He then began scrolling the neighborhood, reading the different names of businesses and parks that surrounded him. Something felt familiar and he opened up his text messages.

"*Hey dude, what's the name of that bookstore you love in New York?*" He looked at the time and did some quick math before sending the message. There's no telling what Sean would be doing over in the Mediterranean, but at least he knew it wouldn't be too late.

After a few minutes his phone buzzed. "*Nopah! Three Lives and Company. Are you in the Oversized Macintosh?*"

Alex smirked. "*Yeah. I'm actually right by that place—I'll check it out.*"

"*Hit up Joe's Pizza for lunch. You'll thank me.*"

"*Psh—Joe's is shit. Had Bleecker Street last night! It was definitely good.*"

"*Well shit, look at you! Sounds like someone knows the neighborhood—is your tour guide who I think it is?*"

"*Maybe…*"

"*Dude—you're crazy! You guys have fun. You going to be back to work on Monday? We got another one of those video calls, right?*"

"*Yep. I'll be there.*"

Alex got up from the table and thanked the waitress while walking out. He stood on the sidewalk in front of the large window, squinting through the sun in each direction before deciding on one and heading out.

He was unhurried. His steps were without purpose as he allowed the leather-soled boots to slide along the concrete. He wasn't used to the flow of a walking city and absorbed the different way of life. Trees stuck up through the middle of sidewalks, the roads were narrow with cars parked bumper to bumper, and bike traffic navigated like kamikaze pilots missing their mark. L.A. was huge, but no one actually walked anywhere.

Downtown L.A. was nothing but business centers and retail, actual living was pushed off into towering condos and apartment complexes. This was different. As he scuffed along, one door might lead to someone's house. A few more doors down might be a variety store or business. The next was a restaurant or bar. Then another big building where people lived.

Nearing an intersection, he made a turn and then ducked into a corner coffee shop. Alex waited in line to place his order, the guy working the register complimenting his jacket once it was his turn. He nodded and then looked around at the other customers. What seemed to be hipster-chic in Greenwich was Alex's everyday attire. He hadn't seen so many boots in one place since he left the reservation. He laughed at the thought, but then realized his own boots hadn't been protecting him from snakes or tumbleweeds for at least a decade.

Alex took the coffee and continued his walk. The sun and air felt polarizing. The rays on his back wrapped him like heavy electric blanket while the bits of shade were as crisp as leaning into Woody's cooler. He avoided the path of people walking the other way, their hardened stares making it clear that they weren't out for a stroll. He then weaved effortlessly with the flow of dog walkers, steered around mid-morning joggers, and smiled at those suddenly stepping out of storefronts onto the street. Alex had found the rhythm. It was a brief taste, but he saw why Stevie liked it here. The city was an endless crescendo of motion with countless conductors, all orchestrating a story of their own.

He rounded another corner and saw the red doors of Three Lives & Company, the tiny bookstore and Greenwich hometown staple for the last 50 years. Approaching the large glass storefront, he took in the book covers and read the new titles that acted as an invitation. The window was decorated proudly in hopes of enticing a New Yorker out on the street who never seemed to stop or look around.

The double doors of the store were pinned open, welcoming customers and letting in the fresh morning air. Alex went inside and could immediately see the appeal. The place was quirky. He imagined beatniks wearing black turtlenecks with stupid hats carrying on a conversation about Joyce Johnson. Anything related to Kerouac made Alex's eyes roll and of course Three Lives had all the premier titles you'd expect. However, the store also specialized in books not typically found. It wasn't afraid to dedicate some of its shelf space to an unknown author, if its litigious workers made the case for it being there.

A middle-aged man behind the counter greeted him while a younger woman carried a stack of books out onto the floor. She was refilling stock and fiddling with arrangements, Alex said hello to both of them and then tried to stay out of the woman's way as she worked. He picked up a couple of hardcovers that looked interesting, briefly reading the dust jacket before placing them back on the shelf. He wasn't after anything in particular.

Alex's boots twisted on the hardwood as he turned up and down isles, the leather coming to an abrupt halt as he was struck by an entire end cap filled with *The Final Book*. The store carried each of Sean's novels along with a vast collection of the comics they both had worked on. The display was impressive, and he couldn't control his smile. It was still surreal to see his work in a real shop and he couldn't get over the sight.

A handwritten sign flew like a flag above the display; "Read The Book Before Hollywood Ruins The Movie!"

Alex belly-laughed out loud, causing both workers to look over at him. He excused himself by nodding and then picked up his favorite issue, thumbing through his artwork. Hera was engulfed with rage, seething with fury over William's encounter with Anu. Memories consumed him as he relived the hours that were spent getting her to look just right, getting her to move in a way that carried the weight of the world. Getting her to look like a God.

Releasing the memories, he noticed that the workers were whispering to each other behind his back. Uncomfortable with their stares, he placed the comic back onto the rack and moved toward the back of the store. Now browsing the non-fiction section, he came across a block of scandalized books about Stevie Pearl. The covers were all brightly colored and most featured a closeup headshot of Stevie with a curious look on her face. Alex reached for the copy sitting front and center and flipped it over to read the back.

All the dirty secrets! The true side of Stevie she doesn't want you to know! The further he read, it became clear that the book was a tell-all confessional written by an ex-boyfriend. He recognized the name, some talentless DJ that pushed play on a computer for crowds of douchebags. *"The sex was mediocre at best. Yeah, she's hot, but deep down she's a damaged prude desperate to be loved. I just couldn't handle her brand of crazy."* Alex clenched his jaw and scowled.

"Excuse me, sir?" The clerk behind the counter had now creeped up beside him.

Alex was quick to put the book back onto the shelf, a little ashamed to have been caught reading such dumpster garbage.

"Are you… Alex Nopah?"

Alex took a step back with confusion. "Umm, yeah?"

"You're right, it is him!" The man attempted to whisper back to the young woman who was stocking shelves. "Sir, it's a pleasure. We're huge fans of your work!"

It took Alex a moment to process the words. He didn't expect to be recognized, especially not for his work. "Oh. That's awesome! Thank you."

The girl set aside her books and moved toward the conversation. She stood behind the bearded man and leaned her head out around him so she could see Alex.

"Your illustrations… I mean, the novels were good, but you turned it into the phenomenon."

Alex grinned but then looked away. "There were a lot of us who worked on it."

"You signed my first issue." The young woman's voice was meek. "I went to comic con three years ago and you signed it."

Alex searched his memory, trying the place the girl. He had met and signed for thousands of fans over the years and all of the shows had blended together. "You had glasses then, right?" He asked.

The girl blushed and covered her mouth.

"Yeah. Black rims. Weezer style. We talked—I know we talked… What did we talk about?"

"You—you encouraged me. You gave me hope." The girl's eyes began to well as she was filled with the memory. "You told me the story of the Coyote and Broken People."

Alex smiled and nodded.

"The Coyote ruined everything." The girl relived their conversation with great clarity. "He had a simple job but he made a promise and broke it. He was supposed to deliver a basket, but he was curious. He wanted to see what was inside, so he opened it up. When he did, he unleashed all the people of the world… Humanity. At the bottom of the basket were all of the trampled, broken, and cripple humans that got caught in the fleeing stampede. They were dying and suffering and the Coyote felt bad for what he had done. He took them to his brother—"

"The wise Wolf…" Alex filled her words. "My grandfather told me this story many times."

"Yes! The Wolf—the Wolf cared for these people. He healed them. He taught them all the skills they'd need to survive in a harsh world… Once they were better—smarter—stronger—the Coyote returned these people to the desert where they'd be able to live and thrive in such a hard place. Their damage ended up saving them. Everyone who had rushed out of the basket, that trampled all over everyone else, they died. They didn't have the wisdom of what it takes to survive in such a cruel world."

"I remember." Alex nodded. "Once broken, they were now stronger than ever."

Tears fell down the young woman's cheek and her eyes bore into him.

"I was… It was a bad time for me. I didn't kill myself because of you… You cared about me, in that moment, when no one else did. You took the time. You were my wolf.." She quickly used her sleeve to wipe her cheek and turned away. "Jesus—I'm so sorry. That's so heavy."

Alex stood in shock.

"I'm sorry… I shouldn't have said anything—I'm so embarrassed."

"No—" Alex reached for her. "It's okay."

The girl's face was flushed pink and she had dark streaks running down her cheeks.

"Come here." Alex put his arms around her, hugging her tight. "Don't be embarrassed. Shit's fucked up and hard."

"Thank you… It was just so hopeless… until you gave me hope." She held him back.

Silence fell upon the bookstore. The middle-aged man's jaw was slack as he stood by and watched.

"Glad you didn't do it." Alex rubbed her back "That you're still here."

"Me too."

Alex let go and looked her in the eyes. They were a rip tide, filled with a pure sincerity. He then motioned to the clerk. "You got any tissues?"

"Oh—yes. Yes!" The man hurried behind the counter and grabbed a box.

Alex let out a sharp breath of air as he continued to look at the girl. "Phew—my heart's pounding!"

The man delivered the box and the girl tore at them to cover her face.

"I think I'm gonna need one too." Alex smiled. "Come here, sit down." He juggled a round scooter step stool toward her with his foot.

She sat and wiped her nose. "I'm sorry about all of this..."

"You're good." Alex reassured. "Thanks for telling me... I—I never knew my words had an impact..."

The woman nodded. "You saved my life."

"I think you did all the hard work."

"You took the time. I know you were busy, but you treated me like a person. In that moment, I mattered to someone."

A long paused filled the air. Alex tried to think of something to say, anything to ease her before the silence became awkward. "Of course you matter... Are you doin' good now? You look good."

She nodded again. "Yeah. I am. I got this job. I'm in school. Going to graduate next semester."

"That's awesome!" Relief poured from his voice. "Good for you."

"I mean, I'm not sure if it's something I'll ever get over... I work at it every day. But I want to help other kids. Be someone who knows what it's like... We'll see. That's a long way away."

"Do it. Just gotta keep workin'—keep goin'. You'll make it happen."

The woman let out a long breath of air and shook her head. "I wasn't expecting to see you today." She smiled, trying to regain composure. "You caught me off guard. Brought up a lot of feelings."

"I didn't mean to upset you."

"No—no. That's not what I mean. You—those comics and books—I know it's foolish, but that was my escape. The one thing in the world that wasn't… just a lot of bad things happened. Then I got to meet you. You were so kind. Thank you. You don't know how much it meant."

Alex couldn't offer any words.

"I'm glad you're here. I'm glad you came in."

"I just kinda stumbled across this place. Sean, the author," Alex used his thumb to point back over his shoulder towards the display, "he told me to stop in and check it out… I'm glad I did." He raised an eyebrow at the girl, letting her know that he meant it.

She then stood from the stool, crumpling the tissues into her fist.

"Yes." The middle-aged man finally spoke. "It's been a while, but he's been here a few times. Nice guy."

Alex smiled. "He's okay."

The young woman straightened her shirt and walked behind the counter, throwing away her tissues. She then cleared her throat, attempting to speaking in a professional manner. "Well, Mr. Alex Nopah—what can I help you find today?"

Alex rubbed the back of his head. "I don't even know any more…" He smiled. "This is a little… because, well… what's your name?"

"Isabelle. Izzy."

"Izzy." Alex nodded. "How about you?" He looked toward the man.

"Jeffery."

"Well, what are you guys reading right now? What do you recommend, Isabelle?"

She came from around the counter and began scanning the shelves. "I assume you enjoy mythology, seeing as you're now the king of it?"

He shrugged. "Sean writes the stuff, I just draw it… But yeah. I've come to like it."

"Have you read *Circe* by Madeline Miller?"

"No…"

"Done." She reached up and plucked the book from the shelf and then handed it to him.

"It's good?" He looked at the cover.

"Very."

"Okay."

Alex brought the book to the register.

Jeffery shook his head. "It's on the house."

"It's fine, really."

"No. Thank you—for being kind. I had no idea." He looked over at Izzy. "She's one of our best employees. We'd do anything for her."

Alex nodded.

Jeffery wrapped the book in a paper bag and handed it him. "Oh." He hesitated. "I hope it's not too much to ask, but before you go, would you mind signing some of your work? Maybe taking a couple of pictures with us in front of the display?"

"Yeah—no. Of course not."

Jeffery smiled and then searched the register for a Sharpie. Alex signed a dozen issues across the cover, he even flipped through to certain pages and left special notes. He then took photos with Izzy and Jeffery, both exchanging their phones so they could pose with him in front of his work.

Before he left, Alex wrote his email address on a scrap piece of paper and handed it to Izzy.

"I'm sometimes slow to reply, but *I'll always reply*. You're never alone."

SIMPLE KIND OF LIFE
NO DOUBT

"He's quite handsome." Niko spoke under her breath. Her wine glass was held close to her lips to conceal the gossip. Stevie blushed, gently rocking Malee in her arms. "You like him, don't you?"

"Aiden seems to." Stevie remarked, observing the boys playing with a plastic golf set in the middle of the living room.

"He's a real-life Calvin Klein ad…" Niko's eyebrow raised.

"Eww." Celeste faked a gag from across the dinner table. She wasn't entirely involved in the conversation but knew exactly what the two were talking about.

"Levi's." Stevie corrected. "A real-life Levi's ad."

"Ah yes, you're right."

A plastic ball whizzed passed Celeste's head and bounced off the hanging chandelier.

"Jeez!" Alex cringed and looked around the room with a guilty shrug. "Dude, you're not supposed to hit so hard!"

"Are you kidding?!" Shane grinned, leaning back on his rug-burned knees. "Aiden, that was your best hit ever! Good job!" He gave the boy a high-five. "Do it again. Try to hit Celeste!"

The boy wound up to drive the ball once more, this time hitting the carpet a foot behind the mark. The force of the swing jarred him and he fell over, giggling.

"They're gonna break something." Celeste pleaded, pointing toward the glittery light that was lurching above her.

"It's worth it." Niko sipped. "At least he'll be tired when we put him to bed."

Stevie swayed while Malee's eyes flickered within a dream. "This one's out."

"For now... So, have you two, you know?" Niko prodded with innuendo.

"Ha—no. This is pretty much our first date." She laughed.

"And you're torturing him here? Are you trying to scare him away?"

"Don't lie." Celeste scowled. "Unless it's the longest first date ever—you guys have hung out the last three days in a row."

"Ohhh..." Niko swallowed. "So she does like him."

"Obviously." Celeste rolled her eyes. "The problem is they're both goobers. *Oh, what does it mean—are these feelings? I don't know what to do.*" She mocked.

"I'd know what to do..." Niko continued to eye him. "Jesus, how much of this have I had?" She put down her glass and pushed it toward the center of the table. "Go for it, Stevie. Don't you want golf balls smashed around your living room?"

"Shane's so good with him." Stevie deflected with a compliment. "He reminds me of my dad with Joey."

"Alex looks like a natural as well..."

Stevie smiled and looked down at Malee. She watched her little chest rise with each breath.

"That's it—give the baby here." Celeste motioned. "I see what's happening and you're not getting one before me."

Stevie was gentle in the transfer, Celeste welcoming the infant into her arms.

"When's it gonna happen, Celeste?" Niko tilted her head. "You and Troy have been together forever, you must have thought about it?"

Celeste looked over at her boyfriend who was playing a blue putter like an electric guitar. His long hair covered his face and he head banged to whatever country song Knox had put on.

"Babe. Hey, babe." Celeste beckoned. "I want one. Put one of these in me tonight."

Troy gave an awkward smirk. "No way—you crazy."

"Celeste…" Mateo popped his collar. "I'll be yo' baby daddy."

She looked down at Malee. "Done."

Another ball went whizzing across the dining room.

"Yeah-ha!" Shane cheered.

Alex rolled on the carpet laughing, the ball rattling between furniture. Aiden stepped back and aimed, pouncing on Alex's stomach. Alex lifted the boy into the air and he squealed, flapping his arms and legs in flight.

Knox's phone buzzed and he stood up from the couch to dig into his pocket. He answered the call and the conversation was brief. He then signaled to Shane.

"That was Franklin—he wants you to turn on the *Stevie Pearl Minute*."

"Is it bad?"

"Don't know—ask Dancin' Feet." He nodded at Alex.

Aiden came to an abrupt mid-air halt and Alex lowered the boy to ground. Shane rocked over onto his side and navigated his phone. Suddenly the massive flat screen TV that was embedded within the wall came to life with Mario Cordova. The surround sound pumped with a breaking news style intro and then the segment began:

Mario Cordova here with breaking news about your favorite pop star, Stevie Pearl. Photos surfaced this afternoon on social media placing the possible lead-footed heartthrob, Alex Nopah, near Pearl's New York residence. Seen here posing with fans in front of his work at Three Lives & Company bookstore in Greenwich Village, Nopah is the illustrator who helped launch The Final Book *into the mainstream and the creative talent many are crediting for its international success. Curiously, the bookstore is only several blocks from Pearl's Greenwich townhouse. It is unlikely, given Nopah's consulting role and the aggressive production schedule of the feature film, that he would be in New York for meetings—so was this trip for pleasure? We did some digging and obtained these photos of Pearl's private jet at Teterboro Airport just outside of the city. We cannot confirm if Pearl or Nopah were on the flight—Pearl last seen Friday afternoon leaving the law offices of Hodges and Rhode in Los Angeles. Both the sightings of Nopah and the jet do beg the question if the two have been in contact since the party at her Beverly estate. No official reports have placed them together, but this reporter is sensing that there's a little more to the story… Always the first to bring you the latest celebrity news, this has been Mario Cordova for the* Stevie Pearl Minute.

Alex's eyes darted around the room at all of the faces staring at him. "I—I didn't know. I didn't mean to."

Shane's attention was now fully focused on Stevie who had moved over into the living room to get a better look at the TV. "You're fine." He dismissed toward Alex out of the corner of his mouth.

"You didn't do anything wrong, Alex." Stevie's words reassured, though her eyes were locked on the screen that had reverted back to a submenu. "The photos were great—those people looked really excited to see you." Her mind was clearly reeling.

"Jesus—I was in a bookstore. I never have to worry about this stuff." Alex tried to explain. "I mean—this girl—she… I just, I didn't know it mattered. I take photos with fans all the time… well, not all the time." He corrected himself as he realized the company he was surrounded with. "For someone to recognize me, especially outside of a comic con—of course I'll take a picture with them if they ask."

Stevie tried to shake the thought of Lisa Rhode from infiltrating her brain stem. "It's okay." Her eyes were sincere and she leaned down to gently push the hair from Alex's forehead. She could feel the heat radiate as her fingernails curled around his ear. "No one's mad at you. You did the right thing. You have a career too—these are your fans."

Alex looked toward Shane. "It doesn't feel that way. I don't mean to keep causing problems."

Shane smiled to ease his tension. "This isn't a problem, man—you're not a problem. It's a heads-up, and now we'll plan accordingly. You should take it as a compliment—Cordova actually gave you some pretty good props."

The words did little. Worry was stricken across Alex's face.

"Didn't the douche say something about you being the reason for *The Final Book*'s international success?" Celeste chimed in. "Fake news—totally irresponsible reporting."

Troy laughed. "That's the type of shit that will go to your head." He teased. "What's your buddy Sean going to say about that?"

Alex took a breath and then tried to smile. "I don't know, but I'm definitely going to make sure he sees this…"

Stevie laughed, but her jaw tightened. Inside she began to burn.

"We'll increase security." Knox said. "The pap's going to be everywhere—close the blinds, use back entrances—no one in or out without one of us. Everyone be conscious of what *you post online*." He eyed Alex. "You know the drill—Franklin said the street's crawling to be first to catch these two together."

Stevie folded her arms. "I see no reason why we can't walk outside right now. I have no problem being seen with Alex."

Shane squinted and pressed his lips together. His tongue ran on the inside of his cheek as he conjured the appropriate words. "I don't have a problem with it either… I just want to make sure that we do it on our terms—that it benefits the both of you. No sense in being reactive here. We still hold all the cards."

"This is all pretty messed up, guys." Alex looked back and forth between Stevie and Shane who were clearly expressing different opinions.

"Exactly." Shane said. "It is messed up. We're just hanging out… still getting to know each other. No need to add any pressure."

Stevie knew that Shane was deflecting a much larger issue by taking Alex's side and she glared at him. "I'm happy to be seen with my friends, Shane."

"Give me some time, Stevie. *Please*." He spoke earnestly.

She took a deep breath and continued to stare at him. "Only for the right reasons, Shane. *Only for the right reasons*."

The entire dinner party sensed the two were talking about something much larger than a paparazzi photo but no one dared to question what it was. Silence fell upon the room and Stevie tried to conceal her flushed pink face.

"Did you like the bookstore, Alex?" Niko stepped in. "Three Lives? It's one of my favorites."

"Umm, yeah…" Alex nodded, turning his attention toward her. "It was cool. Super local vibe. I actually kinda met one of the clerks a few years ago. I didn't really remember it, but I can't stop thinking about her now…"

"That place always seems to attract the strangest encounters— Shane, remember when we bumped into your childhood friend there? What was his name?" Niko pressed, trying to refocus the energy of the dinner party.

Aiden smacked the ball again and it whipped around the room.

"Alright, buddy." Shane gave an uncomfortable laugh. "Why don't you show Auntie Steve your new game? He's got this new game with ladybugs. It's awful but will knock him out."

Stevie cocked an eye at Shane with displeasure, but then put on a smile as she leaned down to face Aiden. "Ladybugs, huh? Let's do it."

Aiden dropped the plastic golf club and ran over to the toy chest, Stevie following behind in an effort to cool off. The boy dug through the pile of toys like a raccoon digging through a trashcan.

"Got it!" He held up a neon colored game box with pride.

"Make sure to get the other pieces too, buddy." Shane directed.

Alex moved over to the dinner table and sat next to Celeste while Knox and Mateo worked their phones like operators.

"Good one, dingus." Her words were cold but the inflection was that of baby-talk as she continued to cradle Malee.

"Fuck…" Alex muttered under his breath.

"Wha?!" Celeste faked a gasp. "Poor virgin ears." She bounced the sleeping baby. "Uncle Alex is a filthy sailor."

"Yep—now insert a joke about seamen…"

"And he thinks he knows us so well!" She ogled her. "Oh, come here, you've got something on your face." She motioned toward Alex with the spit-up rag. "My joke about semen."

Alex rolled his eyes. "I didn't mean to mess things up—I didn't even think about it. Usually photos of me don't mean too much."

"Yeah—they shouldn't. What's this world coming to? And what's with this *international success*? I mean, I didn't realize I was friends with such a heavy hitter. Think you can get me a job on the movie?"

"You bet—be at the studio by 9 on Monday."

Celeste mocked a surprised expression. "Think you can fire Pam too?"

"I'll call up Mario Cordova. See what I can do." He was bitter.

"Dude, chill. It's no biggy. You're allowed to be a person. No one's in hiding here."

"I knew coming here was such a bad idea—Brigman's going to fire me, I know it."

"For what? Giving him more publicity? That was a fucking glowing endorsement for you and the movie."

"He should give you a friggin' raise." Niko injected herself into their conversation, pushing her weight against the table while picking up her wine glass.

Alex was unsure how to reply.

"I'm sorry. Don't listen to me, I'm drunk."

"Yeah you are." Celeste laughed. "Speaking of which—here, hold this baby thing." She pushed Malee towards Alex. "I'm gonna get some refills."

Alex panicked, trying to avoid the reception.

"She's not a football—here, cradle the head." Celeste moved quick, not giving Alex a chance to back away.

"Damnit, Celeste..." His grip was awkward and Malee's face began to curl as if she was going to wake up and cry. "There, there..." He soothed, rocking the newborn with a scowl on his face.

Celeste twirled around the dinner table, plucking wine glasses as she went.

"No more for me." Niko covered her glass with her hand. "I am out of practice."

"Oh, come on! Shane's fine—he can put everyone to bed, including you."

"Nooope. Hangovers with children are a divine punishment. You go ahead though."

Alex nodded as she approached his glass. "I think I need it."

Celeste slid the stem between her fingers. "Oh no—someone said my name on TV!" She mocked as she skated across the hardwood in her socks toward the kitchen. "Life is such torture to be associated with Stevie Pearl…" She trailed off rounding the corner and out of sight.

"You don't have to hold her." Niko offered to relieve him.

"It's okay. I was just afraid she was going to wake up."

"Aiden would have. He was so fussy. Not her… You're pretty good with kids."

"They freak me out. I've never really been around them—I was the youngest."

"It's not complicated. They just require a tremendous amount of time—which, when they're yours, you're usually pretty happy to give."

Alex gave a ruffling of his brow as he contemplated Niko's words. Looking into the baby's face, it seemed everything in the world carried more weight.

"She's worth it." Niko assured with a nod.

"Hmm?" Alex looked up.

"Stevie's worth it." Niko allowed her words to settle as she studied Alex. "It's all noise. When I first came to the city, it was so loud. The traffic, horns, crackheads yelling, sirens, subways, stereos blasting… I thought I was going to go crazy. The sound was all I could focus on. It was sweltering. All the noise made me feel like I was trapped inside a sauna. Then, slowly, I just stopped noticing it. Then one day it was gone. It's like a refrigerator running, your mind can filter it out. Just like mine has done with Mario Cordova."

Alex listened to her words and was slow with his response. "I hope you're right. I feel like the sauna is locked inside of a vault."

"You're cooked?" Niko chuckled.

"Something like that."

Stevie arranged round wooden pegs that were painted like ladybugs. Shane approached and hovered above her, searching for words. "It's a memory game. I hate it." He said.

Stevie didn't offer a reply and continued to set the game up. Aiden rambled with instructions of how to play.

"I've thought a lot about our conversation this morning—it's all I've thought about… And I'm going to ask something of you."

Stevie's hands settled and she looked up at him.

"I want a meeting with Cosmo. Not with Kismet or the Music Group, but I'm talking about top Cosmopolitan Global brass— head of the entire conglomerate—movies, video games, electronics. I know a woman on the board, and I want to have a conversation with her."

Stevie shook her head with disgust. "I can't believe you'd still consider working with them."

"I'm not sure that I am. But I am asking for your permission. This conversation—I don't know what will come of it, or if she'll even meet with me… but I couldn't live with myself if I didn't try."

"Why, Shane?"

"Stevie, it's time we start working on something bigger than a record deal. If you sign with Apollo, it will be the same thing all over again but with different people. The money is—*my god the money is good*—but you need a future."

"I—I don't understand."

"As it sits now, you'll be in your 40s when the Apollo deal expires. Do you want to be dealing with this until then?" He looked across the room over at Alex. "He's a good guy—a great guy as far as I can tell… but the two of you are strangers. Our fight isn't about him, but this is certainly about someone like him. I want you to be happy, Stevie—as long as some focus group is controlling your destiny, I don't think you ever will be."

"So, what? We start our own label? I don't want to deal with that."

"Me either. But I do want you to have control."

"Steve—put the bug in the hole." Aiden said impatiently. "It goes here."

Stevie looked down at Aiden. "You're supposed to show me how." She handed him a ladybug. "Shane, I'm gonna let you do what you think's best. But know I meant every word this morning. I will not tolerate an attack on me or Alex."

Shane nodded in agreement. "I've already spoken with Lisa— she is crystal clear about where we stand. But ceasefires are only good until someone pulls the trigger. That's why I don't want any unnecessary attention. I need a few days, Stevie. Please, help me."

She looked over at Alex. He had a beaten look on his face, but the vision was endearing. Malee was swaddled, still fast asleep and he balanced her between his forearm and chest. In that moment all she wanted for was his happiness, and she questioned if bringing him into her life would ever allow him to have that.

"Protecting him from the press right now is my biggest concern. No unnecessary attention." She agreed.

"What is this—you have your own movie theater?"

Gibby pushed past Alex's legs as the group clogged the entrance. He stepped into the room and ran his fingers along the back of a plush leather chair. The awe in his gaze followed the tiered stadium seating and then became consumed by the massive screen at the head of the room.

"I love it." Stevie beamed, fiddling with futuristic accent lighting. "Joey mostly plays video games in here, but I've been known to binge some shows."

"I'd never leave…"

"I'm cooped up inside more than you'd think. It's worth it."

"You should see the one in L.A." Celeste made her way front and center, flopping onto a loveseat. "Gimme." She pointed to a blanket that sat on top of a chest and then beckoned to Troy by opening and closing her hand.

"You'll be asleep in 10 minutes…" Troy grabbed the fleece.

"Let's hope."

Troy teased by pulling the blanket away each time she reached for it. This went on for several seconds before Celeste whipped her legs around and kicked him in the thigh.

"Ouuu!" Troy laughed and limped, Gibby scurrying to get out from under his hobble. He then opened the blanket like a net and used it to smother her. Celeste squealed while trying to fight him off, limbs tangling in the fabric.

"'Ey! 'Da fuck you doin'?" Franklin leaned into the doorway. Gibby let out a couple of excited and confused yelps. "Sound like a whole fuckin' football team comin' in 'ere."

"They're just playing…" Stevie leaned down and tried to calm the dog. "How's your mom?" She asked Franklin.

"She good."

"You guys have dinner?"

Franklin nodded.

"Didn't miss much. Aiden played golf in the living room."

"Fuckin' kid about hit me six times." Celeste finally won the battle and curled up into a cocoon.

"Too bad he didn't put a hole-in-one in yo' mouth."

"I swear to Sweet Baby Jesus, Franklin—speaking of baby, did you see Malee this morning? It's the first time I saw her… I love her."

"Yes, we all got to fawn over Malee." Stevie said. "Even Alex held her."

"Mmmhmm." Franklin muttered. "I'm goin' to bed. 'Ey yo, Stevie—shimmy shimmy coco pop, shimmy shimmy rock."

"Ice cream soda pop, vanilla on the top."

He paused and then lowered his brow. "You sure?"

She reassured him with a nod.

"Yeah, okay… See you kats in the mornin." Franklin bobbed his head around the casing and then disappeared out of sight.

"What the hell was that?" Alex asked.

"It's their fucking stupid little code." Celeste slurred. "You don't have a broken arm right now, so apparently she said *open sesame*."

"A code?" Alex looked at Stevie.

"Remember the movie *Big* with Tom Hanks?"

"Sure?" He shrugged.

"Well, that's how they let each other know that everything was okay… It's how I let Franklin know I'm okay."

"Different lyrics mean different things," Celeste talked into a pillow, "I can't keep it all straight."

"And what does *ice cream soda pop vanilla on the top* mean?" Alex added some sass to his sarcasm.

"*Don't worry about it*." Stevie was coy. "What are we watching? Here, Troy—find somethin' good." She tossed him the remote.

Troy's hand sprung like a cat as he snatched the remote in mid-air. He then twirled and fell on Celeste with all of his weight.

"Ugghgh!!! You suck…"

"Move over!" Troy elbowed as he wiggled in. "Stop hogging the blanket."

"Make yourself comfortable. I'm going to freshen up." Stevie looked to Alex. "Back in a few!" Her inflection raised as she tilted her head toward his blank stare.

Alex looked around the room. He always hated this stage of dating. Something as simple as choosing a seat carried with it so much symbolism.

On the floor, down in front of the screen was an oversized plush bean bag. The thing was the size of a Prius. On the first row was Celeste and Troy tangled in the loveseat with two big reclining chairs on each side. In the back row was a long, oversized couch with a chaise lounge attached to it.

He went for the chaise and sat on the edge, further absorbing the hardwood details and accents of the theater. Subtle purple and cyan lighting were woven throughout the room, everything seeming to lead toward the screen where the colors glowed their brightest. He leaned back and pulled off his boots, realizing the entire ceiling resembled a starry night sky. Tiny pinholes of light created constellations in black fabric, the imagery sending him longing for late nights lost in the desert.

Gibby came over and hopped up onto the couch. The dog scooting between him and the backrest, taking the space where Alex was going to sit back.

Alex grabbled a fist full of fur and playfully roughed the dog's neck. "You're in my way!"

Gibby licked the back of his hand and then looked up at him with what appeared to be a pearly white smile.

"Dude, what are we watching?" Troy scrolled through movies.

"No. No. No." Celeste directed as he scrolled. "Eh, maybe."

Alex ran his fingers behind Gibby's ears, the dog's smile transforming into a limp grin of indulgence. Gibby then flopped his head onto the cushion and settled his weight to his side with raised a paw, enjoying the attention and further solidifying his spot on the couch. Alex continued to run his hands through the soft fur of his belly, studying the gray speckles and almost finding as much comfort in the moment as the dog.

"What about that new comedy special?" Alex suggested.

"Thalia!" Celeste slapped Troy on the thigh. "Yes, yes—make it happen."

"Matt said it wasn't that good." Troy surfed the icons.

"That's because he didn't get it." Celeste was sharp. "What do you call a drummer with half a brain?—Gifted."

"You liked *Rough Nothin'*. He told you about that."

"Really going out on a limb by recommending something with Keanu. I'd watch him do laundry."

Troy found Thalia's new standup special and started it, pausing at the beginning for Stevie to return.

"Shane seemed nice." Alex filled the silence.

"I've only met him a few times." Troy replied. "Always busy."

"Malee…" Celeste sighed. "Don't you want one?"

"A baby?" Troy's voice raised.

"Yeah…"

"I dunno… I mean, you're the only person I ever thought about it with. You'd be a good mom."

Celeste rolled out of the little spoon and turned, her sleepy eyes studying the scruff on Troy's face. She kissed him. "I don't think we're ready, but that's all I needed."

"I brought a surpreat!" Stevie bounced into the room with a white box in her arms. She was wearing pajama pants and a worn Ramones t-shirt. "Eww—were you guys making out?"

"*A surpreat*?!" Troy arched his back and reached upward with his free hand. "I want one! What is it?!"

"I can't tell!" Stevie teased.

"What the hell's a surpreat?" Alex continued to scratch Gibby.

"It's a surprise and treat all mixed in one!" Stevie's smile was bright as she pirouetted around the chairs. "Franklin brought us home the best cookies in the world!"

"Levain? Oh my god!" Celeste groaned and sat straight up like a zombie resurfacing from the earth. "Chocolate chip. No. Dark chocolate peanut butter. No. Chocolate chip—it's classic. Just gimme a goddamn cookie!"

"They're so big!" Stevie held one up, covering her face.

"Thing's fuckin' huge!" Troy's excitement grew.

"Let's split them up so we can have a bite of each." Stevie suggested.

Celeste nodded intently, satisfied with the plan.

Stevie sat in the center of the couch next to Alex and Gibby army crawled next to her so his nose could get a better sniff. She broke a chocolate chip cookie in half and handed it Alex.

"Try it." She smiled.

The entire group watched, Gibby raising his ears, as Alex took the first bite.

"Wow…" He chewed. "I don't even like cookies," he swallowed, "but this… holy shit."

"Okay, gimme!" Celeste became impatient.

"I'll do one of those dark chocolates." Troy eyed.

Stevie fulfilled the requests, handing off the fabled surpreat like a priest giving communion.

"What—no one wants a walnut? I'll have the walnut." Stevie took a bite.

"That's 'cause you're… nuts!" Celeste punned.

The silly amusement got the better of Stevie and she shot crumbs out of her mouth as she laughed. Her cheeks turned red and she tried to cover her face with her hand.

Celeste rolled her eyes as she chewed and Alex laughed at the sight, rubbing Stevie's back. "Don't choke!"

Stevie coughed and then grinned with purpose, walnuts and chocolate chips all through her teeth. "What? Do I have lil' somethin' in my… teeth?"

"Hawt." Alex smirked. "Come on. Dark chocolate—do it up!" He motioned toward the box of cookies. She handed him his next flavor and he took a bite, pushing the black gob of dough into his bottom lip.

"I hear you're from Texas, lil' lady." He cocked an eye and the cookie overflowed from his lip like a giant wad of chewing tobacco.

Stevie spat again, trying to catch the crumbling cookie in her hand as she laughed.

"So gross!" Celeste laughed. "You look like fuckin' Knox!"

That sent Stevie laughing even harder. She had caught the giggles and fell over into a ball on the couch. Gibby pawed at her backside as she convulsed, forcing air in and out as she tried to breathe. Troy lost himself a moment later when Alex tried to use his tongue to push the wad of cookie back into his mouth. It was a failed attempt, a large chuck of the half chewed black mess falling from his lip with Gibby quick to clean it up.

"Big Daddy Franklin comin' through…" Celeste remarked, lost in late-night sugary ecstasy.

"He hates it when I call him that." Stevie was still on her side but now able to breathe. She pushed herself upright and nudged Alex with her shoulder. "Pretty good, huh?"

He nodded. "I didn't know a cookie could be a religious experience…"

"It's the water, right? Like, pizza—bagels—cookies—pasta—anything with dough is always better in New York."

"Witchcraft."

"Or that. Fire it up, Troy. What are we watching?"

Troy reached back for another piece of cookie. "Pay the toll first." As soon as his fingers grazed the treat, he started the comedy special.

FIRST SIGHT
THESE UNITED STATES

"Oh my gosh—" Stevie gasped. Her head was dangling upside down off the seat of the couch, her feet flung over the backrest. Her eyes were wide as she grabbed Alex's arm. "Knox is up! What time is it?"

Alex picked up his phone. "Don't know—my battery died hours ago."

"It's gotta be, like, 6 in the morning!"

"No way…"

"Hear that? That's the coffee machine!" She whispered. They both listened intently through the open door of the movie theater.

"You're a bad influence on me, Ms. Pearl…"

"It's all your fault, Mr. Nopah." Stevie swung around and scooted toward him.

Alex was still lying in the chaise lounge and she used his thigh as a pillow, her legs running down the normal length of the couch. They each had fuzzy blankets and looked up into the faux night sky of the ceiling.

"It makes me miss home." Alex commented. "It's been such a long time since I had a night out in the desert. Used to go out every weekend—shoot, sometimes just for an evening drive to get out of the house."

"It must be beautiful."

"There's moments when it's surreal—nowhere else like it."

"I love focusing on a black spot. Allowing your eyes to slowly become flooded with millions of stars. I haven't seen that since Texas."

"Don't get many stars in L.A."

"Or New York."

"Maybe I can show you some time? We'll take the Jeep."

"I'd like that." Her attention moved from the ceiling, her eyes looking up passed her brow to find his gaze. His head was propped by a pillow and his eyes were heavy, lost between a dream and fighting to remain present in the moment. He looked down at her and a subtle smile formed in the corner of his lips.

"What?" Stevie's voice was soft and knowing.

Alex sunk deeper into the cushions and closed his eyes. He placed the weight of his lifeless arm across Stevie's stomach and found her hand, weaving his fingers between hers. "You're gonna be the death of me." He whispered.

Stevie rolled to her side and brought his arm into her chest, wrapping him up like a stuffed animal. "I'm quite fond of you too." She settled and yawned, their fingers tangled.

The two laid motionless, sleep muddled by pangs of adrenaline and anticipation. The touch of Stevie's soft and slender fingers made Alex's spine percolate. His entire consciousness was warmed by the rhythm of her shallow breaths.

He hadn't felt the primal rush of affection in years, the weight in his chest sorting through momentary spikes of anxiety and supreme content. Since arriving, his mind had been playing an ever growing game of *should I or shouldn't I?*, tallying a lopsided balance sheet between his id and egos. The rational, the grounded intellect that had warned him of getting on the plane—the sensible trepidation that reminded him of all that was at stake had become muffled by the weight of a fleece blanket and Stevie's head in his lap. Regardless of any notions of past and future, right there—right then within that moment—there was nowhere else he wanted to be.

Stevie sensed the electricity pumping through Alex's veins and organically positioned her lips for reassurance. Her nose brushed against the soft underside of his arm and she controlled the intensity of air that passed from her lungs. Her hold on him was deliberate, the warmth of her breastplate and gentle pulsing of her heart conveyed unclouded intent. Stevie's tenderness for Alex was guiltless, her attraction fostered by admiration and a fundamental sense of guardianship. Without the need of a mental dissertation, a preparatory act of justification that had become routine around the recent guys she had dated, Stevie instinctually enveloped Alex. Deep within she felt secure, and that reassurance allowed her to thaw his tensed quads. It melted the goosebumps from his forearm. Stevie felt the power within his posture release as she lulled them both to the brink of sleep.

"You're quite special…" The words were faint that fell from Alex's fading thoughts.

She nuzzled with her cheek and pulled him in closer.

A blacked-out SUV pulled into the hanger and parked next to Stevie's jet. The group took turns getting out, everyone moving a little slower and with less enthusiasm than their flight in a couple of days earlier.

It was mid-afternoon and Celeste was still licking her wounds from a hangover. Alex was quick to help Knox and Mateo with the bags and used his initiative as a mask, still very much unfamiliar with the routine of private jetports. Stevie was visibly tired, but her smile radiated. She moved slow across the concrete while the plane was preparing for flight, positioning herself between the massive sliding doors of the hanger to absorb the sunlight.

"'Ey, 'ey." Franklin came up beside her.

Stevie nudged him gently with her shoulder.

"You doin' good?"

She closed her eyes and inhaled for what felt like two breaths, then nodded. "I am."

"Yeah, ya are..." Franklin squinted into the sky.

"We just talked. All night."

"Ain't no one got that much to say..." He bit the inside of his cheek and then looked down at her. "Glad to see you happy, Stevie."

"But...?" She used her hand as a visor to shade the sunlight, looking for a glimpse of his expression.

"But I'll still break his fuckin' jaw."

She smiled. "I don't think you'll have to."

"Mmhmmm... Let's getch you back to L.A." He motioned toward the plane.

Stevie turned to see Knox securing the cargo door. Alex was leaned up against the SUV, his boots heal to toe and arms folded. Even through his sunglasses it was apparent that his gaze was upon her. Gibby stood by his side with a wag, both waiting for her to join them. The sun's embrace warmed her and just like a light breeze, Stevie rose to her toes and skipped toward them. Gibby twirled and pranced as she got closer, Alex pushing himself from the car.

"Last one on has to sit by Knox!" Stevie was loud so the Ranger could hear.

Gibby darted up the stairs of the plane, Stevie's knees nearly clipping the dog's rear as she raced behind. Alex grinned, grasping the rail and lumbering up the steps as he was clearly defeated.

The trio moved to the back of the plane next to Troy who was already fiddling with the TV. Celeste was in an oversized chair and had her shade pulled down, pretending to be asleep until the constant slap from Gibby's wagging tail forced her to smile.

"Ugh, sleepy." She pushed the dog away. "Mimosa. No alcohol."

"It'd probably make you feel better." Troy scrolled through shows.

"I'm not going down that road. Once I start doing that, I'll have to admit I have a problem."

"I'm not sure what we've got." Stevie said. "They usually keep the galley pretty well stocked. Let me look." She moved further aft, rummaging through a built-in bar with mini kitchen. "Want a ginger ale? Looks like Mateo put in some kind of energy drink… Oh wait, there's juice." The plane lurched forward as it began to taxi. Stevie grabbed ahold of the counter and quickly regained her footing, giving a surprised and awkward snort that turned into a laugh.

Alex grinned. "Ma'am, please return to your seat. The fasten seatbelt sign has been illuminated."

Celeste sat up, her eyes clouded and puffy. "Yeah, juice. Thank you." Her hair was frizzed and her absent stare was diluted. "Guys. I'm not handling this well at all… My mom."

Troy stopped his search. He looked over at her while shaking his head. The obvious "no, you're not" within his bobble put her on the immediate defensive.

"Fuck you, man."

"Babe, it's heavy shit. No doubt. But you've been drunk—like, really drunk—more days this week than you've been sober."

A confused look came over her face. "Yeah, well, my world's crumbling—it's the only time I'm not thinking about it."

"I know. I get it. I haven't given you any shit about it."

"Well, seems like you've got a problem."

"…I did spend all Friday morning cleaning your puke out of the car."

"I told you to pull over!"

"It's fuckin' California traffic—where am I supposed to go? There's no pulling over!"

"So, what? I'm just your dumb drunk girlfriend that you have to clean up after?"

"Really, babe? C'mon. This isn't you."

"What? Throwing myself a fuckin' pity party? Is that what you think?"

"Whoah. Okay? Whoah." Troy took a breath and adjusted his tone. "I don't know how I would cope with what you're going through either. I'm sure I'd feel pretty damn helpless… and if there was anything out there to not make me feel that way—I'd go for it too."

Celeste huffed. Her eyes dug into him as her fogged mind tried to process his words.

"I love you, babe. You're not alone. I'll clean the puke out of the car everyday if that what it takes."

Alex looked back and forth between the two, feeling the weight of the conversation but unsure of its context. He then turned toward Stevie for relief.

"We both know getting blackout drunk isn't the answer." Troy continued. "Right now, it's a release. Yeah, it's helping you cope, but it's not helping your mom—and I know you want to do everything you can to help her."

"Fuck…" Celeste's eyes welled. She forced her head upward to focus on the ceiling. "I am *so mad* at you right now."

"No, you're not." Troy slid to the edge of the couch so he could be close to her.

Celeste swallowed hard and fought back tears. "I've never been more angry in my entire life."

"I know you're mad. But you're not mad at me."

Celeste's lip curled and she clenched the armrest, imaging slamming her fist through Troy's face. "Fuck..."

"I'm mad too." Stevie eased. "It's... it's not fair. She doesn't deserve this."

"You don't know..." Celeste shook her head. "I want to tear this plane apart. I want to burn the whole world to the ground. I want to stick a fork in God's eye. I want to eat cancer and shit it out like Taco Bell. I just...." A single tear ran down Celeste's cheek and she quickly wiped it with her sleeve. "There's just nothing I can do... Fuck, my head hurts."

Stevie handed her the orange juice. Celeste took two big gulps as she tried to calm herself.

Alex cocked an eyebrow, finally understanding her desperation. While he has sensed something had been going on with her, she had never told him about her mother's diagnosis. He studied her flushed face and tried to conjure words that would resonate.

"You're right... There's not much you can do—except be there for her. My grandfather—that's how he, well... He was basically my dad. He raised me and my brother. I wish you would have told me. I've been there, too."

"I didn't want this." Celeste looked aimlessly around the cabin and then settled on his face. "I don't want you guys feeling sorry for me—I'm not the one who's dying."

"She's not dying." Troy reassured.

"You don't know that."

"Celeste, you don't have to hide from us." Stevie said. "Especially this. We're here for you."

"That's nice—but you're so busy. I don't blame you. It is what it is, but..."

"I am—but I've always been there for you. Being busy's never stopped us."

"I don't want to add more—you're dealing with the biggest record contract in history. Everyone's always after you for something. I didn't want our friendship to turn into that. Another one of those people."

"You're my best friend, Celeste. You're not just anyone. I'd do anything."

The group was silent until the pilot interrupted and announced that they were next for takeoff. Stevie took a seat next to Celeste and grabbed her hand.

"I'm sorry." Celeste looked down at their tangled fingers, her eyes landing upon the contrast between the chipped paint on her nails and Stevie's unblemished gloss.

"You have nothing to be sorry for. I like you when you're drunk." Stevie said out of the corner of her mouth.

"You must really like me."

"I sent help." Stevie squeezed. "Someone'll be there tomorrow. Shane's arranged an aide to do errands. Drive her around—cook and clean—help with the meals."

"What?" The plane straightened itself on the runway and its engines began to wind.

"It's not much, but I thought it would take some of the burden. I want her to have the best treatment—anything she needs, Celeste. I mean it." Stevie nodded.

The weight of their bodies pressed into the cushions and the plane rumbled as it tore down the runway. Celeste turned to meet Stevie's eyes, tears falling freely down her cheeks.

THE SIMPLE TRUTH
TSUNAMI BOMB

The lights were low in Alex's apartment. His computer screen glowed from the coffee table but his eyes were absent upon the retro popcorn that speckled his ceiling.

He pushed himself deeper into the couch and imagined the weight of Stevie's head on his chest. He longed for her flowery perfume, holding on to each moment of the memory from earlier that morning. He closed his eyes and put himself below the artificial star covered canopy, consumed by purple and cyan that circled her theater room. One night. One sequence of beautifully constructed snorts, tiny laughs, and sarcastic proddings melted into total surrender. When hours became minutes and, suddenly, he despised the sunrise.

Alex reached over and picked up his phone, the motion illuminating the screen as he checked the time. 10:30 PM. He quickly calculated how long it had been since the plane landed— how much time had passed since his car had left the hanger. It had only been a couple of hours, but the thought sent anxiety pouring through his chest.

An hourglass filling with millisecond withdrawals turned to bone chilling panic as his mind conflated imagination. What if he never saw her again? What if the zombie apocalypse happened right now? What if the biggest earthquake in Southern California history split the earth wide open between them? The devastation creating a bottomless chasm between him and Beverly impossible to be crossed? He'd never be able to reach her... What if she just decided she didn't want him?

He held the phone in his hand, wrestling the urge to call her.

Play it cool, bro—no one likes a stage five clinger. A louder voice within caused him to squeeze the phone even tighter. *Fuck the games, if you want to call her you should call her—be honest for once. What would you even say?* He argued with himself. *I need to come up with some reason, an excuse—dude, you have no reason, you literally saw her a couple of hours ago.*

"Jesus. I'm like a goddamn teenager." Alex verbalized the words aloud and set the phone back onto the coffee table. He then sat up and rubbed his head. His eyes were heavy but he fought the notion of sleep. He wanted to live in the moment from earlier that morning, somehow capture it, and he was afraid putting something like sleep between him and New York would cause him to lose it forever.

Alex got up and paced with purpose to his bedroom. His steps carried conviction as if his feet had brought him to the nightstand for a reason. He paused and looked around, surely there was a reason why he was standing there. Impatient to remember, Alex then went into the bathroom and looked into the mirror. He leaned in and examined his skin, just as he had done in Stevie's New York bathroom. He pushed at several imperfections and scowled, imagining her floral curtains and thick towels. Flipping off the light, his aimless motion returned him back to the living room. Scanning the room, his eye caught the shine of distant kitchen lights reflecting off the glass of his cellphone.

"Fuck it."

He snatched the phone from the coffee table. His fingers brawled with the icons, the losing side of his conscience struggling to stop himself from what he was inevitably going to do. The ringer pulsed in his ear.

"Hey—" The voice was soft on the other end.

"Hey." Alex was paralyzed. He didn't actually expect her to answer. Now what was he supposed to do? *Say something.*

"Miss me already?"

Alex let out an awkward chuckle that was mostly a gasp of air. "Yeah, right..." Silence fell over the line as he struggled to correct himself. "Maybe a little."

"Mmmhmm." Stevie was coy.

"Are you sleepin'?"

"Not yet... I am quite sleepy though. Someone kept me up all night."

Alex smiled. Stevie's kittenish tone filled him with validation. "Well, I just... I never got to properly thank you—for this weekend. Everyone was standing around after we landed, I didn't want to make a big deal of it. I just... I appreciate everything you did. Thank you for inviting me."

"Well, you're certainly welcome. I'm glad you could come."

"My first time on a private jet."

"Your first time eating Bleecker Street Pizza."

"That was good..."

"The best." On the other end of the line Stevie's heart was pounding like a jackhammer. Alex's name appearing on her phone flushed her cheeks and she used all of her years as a performer to regulate her composure. She too was lying in bed, pretending Gibby's warm body was his pressed up against her. "I had fun too, you know?" She added.

"You did?" Alex settled back down into the couch.

"Well, it's been a long time since I hung out with friends—spent time with Celeste. It's also been a really long time since I enjoyed getting to know someone so much…"

"Who? Me?"

"Stop…"

"Yeah… I enjoyed that as well. Doesn't happen often."

"Not at all."

Silence filled the line as Alex poised himself to step further out onto the limb. "How is it that we could talk all night long, spend the day together, and here I am still wanting to talk to you some more?"

"I'm not sure… but I'm glad you called. I was thinking about you."

"Were you? What were you thinking about?"

"You're really gonna make me say it?"

"Uh huh."

"Well, I just can't stop thinking about your terrible movie choices. What was that awful '80s garbage after Thalia?"

"I'm crushed. How could you not like *Over The Top* with Stallone?"

"A movie about arm wrestling?! You truly know the way to a girl's heart."

"Oh, I think I've wiggled my way in there…"

"You think?"

"I do. See, I'll be nice—I was laying here thinking about you too. But instead of making fun of you, I was trying not to forget this morning."

"I'll never forget this morning." Stevie's voice was velvet. "Makes me wish…"

"Wish what?"

"If I tell you, it won't come true."

And again, with what seemed liked minutes, hours had passed and Alex was trying to say goodbye.

"You've got to go to sleep!" Stevie giggled. "If you go to bed right now, that's like four and half hours before you have to wake up."

"I know—stop reminding me!"

"For real this time. I don't want you blaming me for making a bad movie."

"As if they even listen to me... You're right though—god, we've been on the phone for, like, ever!"

"Go to bed!"

"What's Gibby doing? Tell him goodnight for me."

"He got sick of us a long time ago. He left back when you were telling me about the Royalty Pageant."

"I can't believe I told you about that—so embarrassing."

"It's cute. You totally made that little girl's day."

"Tayla... My brother still makes fun of me."

"...So, I'll talk to you soon, right?"

"Is when I wake up too soon?"

"Probably."

"Psh, you can't resist me!"

"We'll see about that..." Stevie toyed. "Text me."

Alex yawned and he rolled to his side. With hushed words he conveyed his deepest sincerity. "Goodnight, Ms. Pearl."

An audible warmth was returned, filling his ear and chest. "Sleep well, Mr. Nopah."

"I didn't see you getting coffee this morning." Celeste gnawed on a sandwich. The two had taken their lunch out at their usual spot on the lot underneath the trees. "Ew, gross." She pealed a slice of tomato from the soggy bread and flung its remains over the bushes.

Alex chuckled and shook his head.

"What? It's totally nasty."

"You're gonna have a sandwich graveyard behind there. Celeste's pile of unwanted cold cuts."

"Don't. Now you're making the bush sound like the Isle of Misfit Toys. All my little mutated babies coming to life."

"No doubt something's growing back there."

"Growing's fine. It's the animated voyage to find their mother I'm worried about... Dude, so give me the deets. You've been curiously quiet about my friend."

Alex couldn't hold his smile at the thought. "That's why no coffee, I barely made it in on time."

"You guys hung out more last night?!"

"No. Just on the phone."

"What? You called her? So lame."

"Why's that lame?"

"Because you're not a friggin' teenager. Plus, that's, like, *so soon*. You know the rules, you've got to wait a couple days."

"I know, that's what I thought too—but then I was like, screw it. No games. I wanted to call her, so I called her."

"Look at you, growin' a pair of balls. It's still creepy. Sweet, but creepy."

"It wasn't creepy..."

"Let me guess, you started off the conversation something like, 'gee willikers, Ms. Pearl. I sure 'preciate you takin' me around on your flyin' machine to the big city...'"

"You already talked to her, didn't you?"

"Yes."

Alex rolled his eyes.

"What? I talked to my mom this morning to check about the aide Stevie sent. She was all worried and reluctant, but knew it'd be a huge relief—so I called Stevie to thank her. Of course she had to mention you…"

Alex blushed and quickly took a bite of his lunch.

"You two are gross."

"What'd she say?" Alex forced his words through the gob of sandwich that was lodged in the roof of his mouth.

"Mmhumgmm?" Celeste mocked his chewing. "That you guys talked 'til 3 in the morning. That's two nights in a row, Nopah. I've known you for a while now and I'm pretty sure I've never heard you string together more than a few sentences."

He swallowed hard and then cocked an eye. "It's weird, you know? Like, I'm not sick of her."

"Ohhh, your pea-sized heart—it's growing."

"Shut up…" His dimples turned away, the curl in his lip falling as the conversation caught up with him. "Hey… I get it—not talking about your mom. But, if you ever want to, you know you can—right?"

Celeste slowed her chewing. Her eyes were hidden behind sunglasses, but Alex knew they were focused on him.

"I just mean, you've become a really good friend. That type of thing is okay."

Celeste contemplated for a moment. "I should have said something sooner. It was just nice to have one person where that wasn't lingering in the back of their mind."

Alex nodded and looked across the lot. A light breeze rustled the leaves above them.

"After I found out about your grandfather, it made me want to tell you even less. I didn't want you to relive it—I also didn't want to hear your stories and think about my mom going through it."

"You've got to face it." Alex said. "You'll regret wasting time if it comes to that. I wish someone had said that to me."

Celeste squinted or winced, he couldn't quite tell behind the glasses. She then sipped from her afternoon energy drink. "These things are just as bad as the booze."

"Worse. Drunk Celeste is way more tolerable than crack Celeste."

She smirked.

"So, what else did Stevie say?"

"Oh god. This is all I'm going to hear about from now on, isn't it?"

"It's your fault… We should all do something again—the four of us. Troy is pretty cool."

"Yeah, I saw you guys bro-out all weekend. What's up with that?"

"I don't know… He's, like, a genuinely nice guy. He always tries to build someone up, make them shine."

"I know. It's weird, right? All I try to do is find weakness and then tear at it."

Alex laughed.

"You know, it's going to get harder with her before it gets easier." Celeste was earnest. "You think the press was bad last week? Wait until it really comes out…"

"What do you mean?"

"They'll be coming at you from every angle—friends, family, kids you went to high school with—they'll offer them money, anything to get them to spill some dirt for a story."

Alex sat quiet.

"You ever given a press conference? That's what it'll be like— you just got signed to Team Pearl. Dude, you're not ready for that —no one is. You should ask her for help—serious. She has a whole team for that, they can coach you."

"Coach me?"

"Not to be a dick, but usually the guys she dates are already celebrities—they have a lot of this shit worked out. You're not even going to be able to come to work—I'd seriously talk to Jim. He'll have to beef up security around here, maybe start letting you work remotely. He at least deserves a heads up because when this hits, shit's gonna go everywhere."

"Jesus…"

"I'm not trying to freak you out, but you need to know what's coming. The longer you can keep this on the DL, the better."

"I keep forgetting about all of that. Well, I didn't forget, but when it's just me and her—none of it seems to matter."

Celeste measured him, studying the intent within his words. "I just don't want to see you do something stupid. Walk away because the world blew up and you can't handle it."

Alex paused and then was deliberate. "We're so new… I know I like her, but we barely… It's too soon to be getting the world involved."

"I agree. You prudes haven't even made out yet." She prodded. "But just remember there's no one you can trust with this secret. The moment you tell anyone—you give Tommy shit and brag about New York pizza and private jets—the moment you fuck up and post a selfie with the edge of Stevie's pool in the background —it will explode."

"So, what am I supposed to do? I want to see her again, but how am I supposed to ask her on a date? There's no where we can go."

"Tell her that. Make sure she knows you want to see her. Stevie's a pro at this—she's been evading these assholes for years— she'll find a way to make it work. It's the minute you go rouge and do something you think is cute that will screw it all up."

"Good thing I don't do cute…"

"Just be smart. She likes you, Alex. Likes you like, woah."

Alex sipped from his iced tea and let her words rattle around in his brain. "So, I guess taking her to where the food trucks park is out."

"What, is that like the Alex Nopah starter pack? The go-to first date?"

"It's worked in the past."

"Oh, and to think I'm tied down with Troy… Hear ye, hear ye, all single women!"

"You like food trucks!"

"I do… Stevie probably would too. But, I doubt she's ever actually eaten from one… Just, I don't know—invite her on your stupid food truck date but then tell her there won't be any trucks. Or food. Or going out in public."

"Right. So just be like, *hey, are you free tomorrow—how about you and me stare at each other all night?*"

"Exactly. The point is you asked her out."

"That's pretty lame. I've got to do better than that."

"Don't. Get. Cute."

"A little cute."

"Maybe a little, but just let her know you want to see her again."

Stevie toiled within the basement of the estate. A sizable portion of her house had been converted into a world class recording studio. Adjacent from the gym, where she learned choreography and danced in front of mirrors, were several sound treated rooms. One was filled with recording equipment; a giant mixer, computer screens, impressive speakers, and a large picture window that overlooked the main recording area.

Doors branched from the centralized control room, tuned vocal and isolation booths surrounded the studio. The live room was the most spacious and served as the center of attention. Instruments were hung along the walls and a meticulous mix of engineered hardwood, diffusion, and absorption panels wrapped the room to manipulate the way sound waves were captured in her recordings. Tucked in a corner, Stevie sat alone at a piano. Her head was down and eyes closed as she continued to trigger a key, pressing a single note over and over again.

An arrangement ran within her mind and she whispered lyrics under her breath as she worked out cadence and time. A notepad covered with scribbles and crossed out words rested in her lap. The note from the piano resonated once more as she pressed the key.

In mid legato, Stevie arched her back and ran her fingers down the keys. The scale transformed into a melody, the melody into a movement. Her motion was effortless, finding each chord and note the same way she conjured words, a glance, or the syrupy timbre of her voice when lying next to Alex.

Though only a fraction of an idea, Stevie's performance would have captivated a stadium. A moment where everyone held their phones to the sky, casting a cool electric glow that could be seen from space. She imagined Alex standing off stage, an arm folded across his chest and the other hand limp, covering his mouth. Each night he would watch, studying, discovering something new about her and the way she conveyed her art. She would move him. He would swell with pride, electrified by thousands of voices aligning under a common song—their song.

Show after show, concert after concert, she would find him. She would lock onto his eyes in the sea of chaos and he would convey his heart with a subtle nod. His reassurance would cause a tremendous force to build within, every emotion she shared with Alex would leave her body at the crescendo—the slightest taste of her love being given to the world.

Stevie's mind was ejected from the fantasy. A vision so clear, catapulted by the grating sound of metal vibrating across wood. Irritated, she ended the concert mid stroke. She glared at her phone, at the audacity of someone calling during her performance. She looked down at the name on the screen and let out a huff. The phone continued to migrate toward the edge of the bench, levitating in frequency with each pulse of the ringer. She took a deep breath and answered.

"Shane."

"Stevie. Got a minute?"

"Umm, yeah… Just working on a new song."

"You're writing? That's what I like to hear!"

"I'm sure you do…"

"I won't keep you, but I just had lunch with Sylvia Preston. Executive and board member at Cosmo Global."

"Shane—I'm really not interested in talking with Cosmo ever again."

"She's not Cosmo Music Group—I'm talking top top brass. She sits on the board that oversees everything for the whole conglomerate; movies, video games, electronics, publishing, manufacturing, and yes—music."

"Okay?"

"I met her at a fundraiser a few years ago. One of those New York things. She gave me her card, but I don't think she remembered who I was. Her assistant really tried to brush me off —I think she was Googling me as we were on the phone." He chuckled. "Anyway, I finally got ahold of Sylvia and I basically begged for a meeting. Told her it was incredibly urgent. She was reluctant but agreed to a quick lunch."

"Why is salvaging anything with Cosmo so important to you?"

"Just listen. She wants to meet you. You've got to get back here, to New York."

"What? Why?"

"Stevie, what's more important than money? The one thing you don't have?"

A long pause filled the line, she wasn't about to humor him.

"Power. Real control. Creating your own destiny instead of serving someone else's."

"I thought we talked about this—I don't want to start our own thing. I don't care about running all of that."

"You won't. Everything stays the same except now you have rights. Major voting rights."

"What does that mean?"

"What if Sylvia gave you Kismet? Just handed over the record label—one hundred percent yours. Of course you'd still have to distribute with Cosmo, but you can do whatever you want with it —run it yourself, don't run it yourself—hire whoever you want, sign whoever you want, *fire whoever you want…*"

"I don't know… I don't have any interest in that."

"I know you don't. That's why we hire people who do. Keep it exactly how it is now—you're just an artist on the roster. The daily people you work with have been great—Mandy and Raj in marketing, all the guys over at the studio. The difference will be that you have the legal authority, ownership, to step in if you need to—no one can strong arm you."

"How is that different than just starting our own label? We can do all of that on our own without Cosmo."

"Well, that's not the best part." Shane was smug. "An equal share along with a full vote within Cosmo Music Group. She wants you to replace Ron Cohen on the board—Dallas Sachs' brother-in-law… She'll clean house, Stevie—she wants to open an ethical investigation, see who else was involved in *renegotiating* your contract."

Stevie rubbed her fingers along the bent spiral of the notepad, her eyes lost in the freshly written lyrics. "That's… unexpected."

"Don't you see? *This gives you freedom*. No more shitty deals with sponsors. No more threats, ridiculous code of conduct standards—no more slimy fuckin' executives exploiting, controlling how you live your life! You'll be changing the industry, Stevie!"

Stevie smiled at Shane's enthusiasm. "How did you...? Why is she doing this?"

"Well, it's not done, obviously. I just... I was just honest with her. You've made that company so much money. More importantly, you did it the right way. When I saw you with Alex the other night—I don't know, Stevie... you deserve this. Control of your future is so much more important than another big contract—that's what I fought for. The money will come eventually, I have no doubt that the backend of this deal will eclipse anything Apollo is offering. Ownership of Kismet, a share of CMG—are you kidding?! I don't know—I tried to find a way you could keep making music and have a life."

Stevie absorbed his words, nodding along to an empty room. "Wow... I just—"

"There's still a lot to figure out—I'll be buried in details—but Sylvia wants to talk to you. She won't move forward until you meet. It's important to her. Obviously, this is a massive move on her end, she'll have to present it and get the rest of Cosmo Global on board—but if this works out... what a bombshell for CMG. They fucked with the wrong girl!"

Stevie laughed. Right or wrong, she relished the thought of painting the ivory tower pink.

"Thank you, Shane. I'm not sure... I'm not sure if Cosmo could ever be an option again... but this is pretty big news."

"Get on the plane, sister! Get back here and we can start preparing!"

TACO TUESDAY
LIL JON

The phone rang as Alex rounded a corner in the Jeep. His eyes scanned beyond its windows, unfamiliar with the rundown street. Chain-link fences capped with razor wire ran alongside each side of the road while big tires slalomed potholes. He looked back down at the phone, the navigation screen that had been guiding him was interrupted with his mother's name splashed across the screen. He answered the call and her voice flooded the speakers.

"Alex?"

"Hey—sorry, I'm driving."

"Oh. Where are you going?"

"Good question…" Alex traced through the maze of back access roads of an industrial complex. "What's going on?"

"Nothing. Haven't heard from you in a while, thought I'd call."

"Yeah, it's been an odd few days…" Alex's tone was distant, his eyes shifting between the road and GPS on his phone. He was approaching the pin but couldn't fathom he was in the right location. "How's Tita?"

"Oh, I don't know… We just got back from the doctor. They're trying to get her medication dialed in but she never does what they say. Don't know if it's the medicine's fault or hers, but her numbers are all out of whack."

Alex acknowledged with a grunt; his mind focused on navigation. He had just passed the arrival marker on the phone and was now relying on directions Stevie had sent him in a text message. "What's she doing?"

"She refuses to take one of her pills—says it makes her stomach upset. But then she eats stuff she shouldn't, always has candy and sweets. It's probably my fault. I should just stop buying that stuff. None of us need it."

Alex made a left, the cracked pavement transforming into sloped concrete. "Eh—does it really matter? Let her have a fritter..."

The road narrowed and ran downhill, the Jeep descending along a single lane path toward a concrete cave. Weathered graffiti stained the walls. Broken glass glistened between plastic bottles and Alex nearly scraped the mirrors while avoiding an abandoned tire.

As he approached, the entrance of the cave revealed that it was nothing more than a long underpass of the sturdy bridge above. Thick retaining walls of concrete were built to withhold unimaginable weight. Engineered to spit in the face of San Andreas's Big One, thoughts of the Titanic sank within Alex's mind as he envisioned the bridge collapsing on top of him. Train cars twisted, metal snapped liked twigs, and the tracks for cargo trains that passed above pushed aside like a toddler moving on to its next game.

"I know..." The reception of the phone call fractured and crackled, Alex giving it some gas to reach the other side. "That's kind of...think too..her enjoy it. But the junk food is just going to make things worse. She struggles so much as it is."

Escaping before the call dropped, the single lane road spilled into a massive drainage system. As wide as the 405, the abandoned

L.A. River was a sea of concrete in every direction. Alex looked around with amazement, lifting his foot from the gas and allowing the Jeep to crawl down the cement bank. He glanced at Stevie's text message one more time to make sure he was in the right place. "What about Charlie? He get that axle fixed on the trailer?"

"No, not yet. He knows something's up—suddenly having money to fix things."

"He's known all along, Ma—he's not dumb. He confronted me at the gallery." Alex lurched as his tires reached the flat bottom of the river, pausing with the brake to look over his shoulder across the urban wasteland. Making a wide circle in the riverbed, Alex pointed the vehicle back toward the tunnel and then shifted into park.

"Jesus, Alex. Why didn't you say something?"

"What—you didn't think he'd figure it out? Tita suddenly getting a bump in Social Security?"

"I don't know—it was stupid. He's just so angry all the time. I didn't want to fight."

"Well... he knows." Alex's eyes continued to scan his surroundings. The sun was falling behind the high cement banks of the river. Any direct light that found its way through was casting long and distorted shadows. Everything about this place made him uneasy. "I'm going to come out this weekend. I'll talk to him."

The inflection within his mother's tone raised. "You're coming? Sunday?"

"Yeah." Alex reached his arm back into the footwell of the rear seat. He rummaged, finding the handle of a backpack and pulled it up from the floor, setting it on the center console.

"I'll make dinner. Any requests?"

It was hard to imagine the canal raging with water, but evidence swept up from recent rains was scattered across the dry riverbed. Trash, a large tattered patio umbrella, a few empty boxes, and a shopping cart littered his sightline. Alex unzipped the top of the bag and placed the backpack on the front seat next to him before looking at his watch. "You get chilies yet?"

"I did. A while ago. The freezer is full." Alex could sense that she was beaming.

"Nice. Let's do a batch of chili verde."

"Your favorite..."

"Need anything from The Big City? Tita still good?"

"Probably not, you know her..."

"Jesus." Alex shook his head. "How can she already be out?"

Kadence didn't offer a response.

"Okay. I'll stop by the dispensary before I head out. I gotta go, ma."

"Alright, I can tell you're busy. We'll see you Sunday."

"Yep—call if you need anything."

"Bye."

Alex cycled through his phone and pulled up his text messages. "*Yo—I'm here.*" He typed. "*Is Franklin going to kill me?*"

After a few seconds the dots began to pulse. Alex waited as Stevie crafted her response. "*Yay! 10 minutes. Oh, and I'd do it myself.*"

"*What is this place?*"

"*I told you, it's my special spot.*"

"*Special spot for drug deals...*"

"*Be there soon!*"

Alex put the phone in the cupholder and lowered the windows. He flicked the key back and killed the engine. A supreme quiet filled his ears, the bustle of the city vacant from the forgotten depths of the river. He adjusted his weight and leaned back, using the headrest as a pillow. Taking off his sunglasses, Alex rubbed his eyes long and deep. It had been an entire two days since he saw Stevie. They talked. Texted occasionally. But he hadn't seen her. This wasn't exactly the date that he imagined for her, but his heart began to beat like the climb of a rollercoaster. Each second another clack that built toward her arrival.

He looked at his watch again and then picked up his phone. He began scrolling through the apps, tapping on social media. He had learned to ignore the comments and direct messages, even going as far as to silence any notifications. His feed consisted of usual status updates from long lost acquaintances, photos of their lunch or kids that he could care less about.

He continued to scroll, seeing Troy's laughably introspective and artsy shot of the Bleecker Street Pizza sign. He gave the photo a like and began to comment. *Next time Joe's—I'll be the judge.* However, he hesitated before pushing send. He thought about his words, he thought about the consequences. As simple as the comment was, leaving it would place him at the pizza joint with Troy, and by extension associate him with Stevie. That was the kind of dumb mistake that Celeste had warned him of. He highlighted the text and then deleted the comment.

Alex continued to scroll, coming across a meme that his brother had been tagged in. The photo was of a barely clothed young African boy, shoeless and without a shirt or pants dancing in the street with his friends. The text read, "Alex Nopah Makin' It Rain". He looked at the name of the person who shared the post, it was one of his brother's friends from high school. They had played baseball together. He then tapped to read the comments; *Charlie Nopah: Homeboy left the rez long before he learn any rain dance.*

Alex clicked the button on the side of the phone and the screen went dark. His eyes adjusted to the falling sun and he scanned the concrete once more. The subtle sound of an engine echoed from the tunnel, tires kicking up loose gravel left behind from high waters pinged against the undercarriage. The front end of a silver Civic emerged and the car dropped down the embankment toward the bottom of the canal. Alex was cautious, its deep tinted windows making him apprehensive. He thought he recognized the vehicle from the night Stevie found him in the ally, but it just as easily could have been a street runner. The car slowed and pulled alongside him, lowering its driver's window.

"Dancin' Feet." Franklin nodded.

"It's Taco Tuesday!" Stevie shouted from the passenger seat, holding up a plastic bag filled with takeout.

Alex eased and greeted them with a smile.

"Pull down this way aways." Franklin angled his head and took his foot off the brake, the car rolling down the center of the river.

Alex turned the key and shifted into gear, swinging the Jeep around to follow. He tailed the Civic for a couple hundred yards until it neared a concrete wall. The car cut sharply and then braked, its reverse lights glowing as it backed toward the wall. Alex did the same and parked beside them.

Stevie was quick to pop her door and jump from the front seat. She was leaning in through Alex's driver's side window before he even had a chance to kill the engine.

"Wanna buy some drugs, man?" Her voice was raspy, trying to imitate every bad action movie she had seen.

Alex chuckled and shook his head. "Where the hell are we?!"

"What? You don't like it?"

"I give us 10 minutes before our first ass-raping…"

"Can't rape the willing!" Stevie backed away from the door, allowing him room to get out.

Franklin stepped from the car, the springs of the Civic rising as his weight hit his feet. He arched his back and looked around. "Think they took that dead body? I don't smell it no mo'…"

"He's teasing." Stevie reassured as Alex got out of the Jeep. She had him wrapped in her arms before the door could shut. "Missed you…" She whispered.

Alex squeezed tight and then rubbed her back. She let go and returned to the car, leaning in to gather an array of takeout. "Do you like Yuca's?" Her voice was muffled as she dug through the food.

Alex rounded the front of the Civic and greeted Franklin with a handshake.

"What up, Alex?"

"You guys come here often?"

"We like to get out from time to time. See a lil' bit of the city."

"Never seen this spot before..."

"Not many have. That's the point." Franklin leaned an ass cheek against the car, swinging his foot up onto the bumper.

Stevie began arranging food on the hood. She made a half dozen trips to the front seat, balancing styrofoam containers like a waitress and reading out their contents from the black magic marker written across lids.

"Whoa, whoa—what are you doin'?" Alex eyed her.

"What?" She juggled tiny salsa containers and a handful of napkins. "We're having a picnic."

"Not like this." Alex slowed with his hands. "Hang on a minute." He then went to the back of the Jeep and popped the lift gate. Tossing a few pieces of gear aside, he struggled to break free a set of camp chairs. Tugging at nylon sacks, he slid the chairs from their housing and then carried them back to the front of the car.

"For the big man." Alex handed Franklin a chair. "And the lady." He pushed the plastic feet into the cement and used his weight to spread its legs, opening the chair for Stevie.

"Look at you!" Stevie complimented.

"Hold on—we're not done yet." Alex went back to the rear of the Jeep. He wrestled like bull in a squeeze chute, the item he was after buried at the bottom of the cargo space with all of his expedition gear piled on top of it. After some maneuvering, a small folding table emerged. He returned to the front of the car, carrying it under his arm like a surfboard.

"What?!" Stevie laughed.

Lacking all sense of grace, Alex attempted to pop the table's legs in one fluid motion. Failing, and struggling more than he had intended, Alex eventually erected a makeshift dinner table in the middle of the concrete abyss.

"This is awesome!" Stevie flattered. "Well done!"

"Fuckin' prim and proper." Franklin chucked.

"Wait, wait, wait." Alex smiled and hid his pinched fingers behind his back. "There's more."

"Whatch yo' got over there—a clown car?" Franklin began to unfold his chair. "Dude's gonna be pullin' out a sink and fireplace next."

Alex returned to the rear of the Jeep once more. He unzipped a duffle bag and pulled out a battery powered lantern. He then stuffed an old blanket under his arm and fished into the side panel of the Jeep for a couple of glow sticks. He brought the items back to the group and began setting the table.

Stepping back, Alex whipped the worn blanket like a magician. With several snaps, a cloud of dust faded into the air and he then spread the blanket across the table. Playing up the five-star-service-experience, he coyly took extra care in arranging the brightly colored geometric fabric to match each corner. He then turned the lantern on low and placed it in the center of the table.

"Voila!" Alex grinned.

"I'm quite impressed. Easily the fanciest gutter dinner I've ever had!" Stevie gave him eyes. "You just carry all this stuff around?"

"Never know when you'll need it. Here." Alex tore the packaging of a glow stick. "Snap it and then shake it." He demonstrated and then handed the transparent plastic tube to Stevie. He tossed another to Franklin.

"Alex, this is incredible!" Stevie beamed.

"Ain't seen one of these in a while..." Franklin picked at the packaging.

Stevie cracked the capsule and then hopped in a circle to aide with the shaking. "Purple!"

Franklin laughed as he watched. "Imagine that. Stevie got her purple..." He then snapped his stick and gave it shake. "Orange? You kiddin' me?"

Alex snapped his within the package, keeping its color secret. He flaunted with each slow shake, building faux anticipation.

"What'd you get? What'd you get?" Stevie pranced.

Alex tore the corner of the package, using his hand as a shield. He then raised his eyebrows, teasing the big reveal.

"Green?" Franklin's tone dropped. His shoulders went limp like a toddler getting a smaller slice of cake. "Fuckin' orange... 'Ey yo, trade me. I need green."

Alex curled his brow. "What?"

"Here." Franklin pushed the orange glow stick toward him. "Gimme green—green like monay!"

Alex rolled his eyes and exchanged the glow stick.

"Fuck yeah!" Franklin wiggled the green glow stick in front of his eyes the same way kids in class turned pencils into rubber. "Got a green glow stick—gonna eat some tacos!" He slid the glowing rod behind his ear and then settled into the camp chair, its flimsy aluminum legs bowing under the weight.

"Taco Tuesday!" Stevie shouted, hooking her purple prize to the string of her hoodie. "You ever had Yuca's?" She asked Alex while tearing the lid off of a styrofoam container to create a makeshift plate.

Alex shook his head no.

"It's great." She prepared the food. "Maybe not in soggy to-go boxes, but it's my favorite... We got chicken, steak, carnitas—some chips and salsa. Franklin, two of each?"

"You know it."

Stevie pulled tacos from the various containers and arranged them in the lid. She added a couple cups of salsa and piled wedges of lime. "He likes lime." She noticed Alex staring at her.

"Oww oww!" Franklin got excited and scooted his chair closer to the table. "Taco Tuesday!"

Stevie giggled and hoisted the plate, gliding past the headlights to deliver the meal to Franklin. "Sit, Alex. Don't be shy."

He stepped back and looked over the impromptu feast, his attention shifting as he tried to read the graffiti behind the parked cars. Stevie fussed like a hostess on Thanksgiving, setting additional napkins in the center of the table and then going back to making plates. It was quite the contrast and it made him smile. "I got the chair for you. Get your tacos. Sit."

"Nope." She leaned over the hood, sprinkling cilantro like confetti. "I started you with one of each, but don't stop there." She admired her work. "I'm going to eat, like, four—maybe five." She then turned and handed him the styrofoam lid. "Sit. Enjoy."

Alex received the plate with both hands to keep the foam from flexing, but then hesitated.

"Get over 'ere." Franklin motioned. "She good."

The fading glimmers of twilight were being overwhelmed by the lantern glowing at the center of the table. The sun's absence allowed an evening chill but the air was calm. City lights reflected from a couple of lazy clouds, their warm incandescent glow out of reach from the low banks of the river. Alex took a seat across from Franklin, the man's sausage-like fingers covered in hot sauce from working the delicate creations like a surgeon.

"Good?" Alex cocked a brow.

"Ain't bad." Franklin sat back and licked his fingers. "'Ere, getch yo' a piece of lime." He offered by tilting his plate toward him.

Alex reached across and took a wedge, working a dribble across his tacos. Stevie joined them at the head of the table, using the hood of the car as her throne. She held the halved container close to her chin with one hand, twisted her head, and then used the other to guide the first bite past her lips.

"So good…" Her eyes were closed and she pointed her face toward the sky as she chewed.

Alex approached the pickup, looking for an angle. Folding the corners of the tortilla, he opened wide and brought the taco to his mouth. Before he could finish the bite, the bottom fell out and its innards slopped back onto the plate.

Stevie laughed, forcing breaths between swallows. She paused and then held a napkin in front of her mouth. "They're better there—at the shop."

Alex wrangled a plastic fork and reassembled what was left of the corn tortilla, taking solo bites of steak and peppers as he went. Silence fell over the trio as they enjoyed the night air and their tacos, each exchanging a knowing smile as they ate.

Franklin reached for a napkin and cleared his throat.

"'Ey, yo." He looked at Alex. "I 'preciate you bein' so cool meetin' us 'ere. This's my fault. This ain't typically how we run things… I got some problems back at the house." He leaned in on his forearms, jockeying for another grip on a taco. "Security ain't as tight as we'd like, too many eyes. Stevie got this big record deal goin' down—loose lips n' all that shit."

Alex slowed his chewing.

"She want to see you though—hangout. Ain't like I can drop you two off at the roller rink."

"Please don't think it's you." Stevie chimed in. "It's not that at all—I just need to keep a *very low profile* for the next few days."

"Is everything okay?"

"Yeah." She paused. "I'm working out a new record contract. In the past, any time I'm seen with a guy it creates this big fuss. We're just trying to avoid any distractions right now."

"There's pap camped out all around the house. Not sure if you've seen 'em, but they at yours too." Franklin nodded. "Ever since we gone to New York—they smell blood. Know somethin' up?"

"Shit. I didn't even notice this time."

"They bein' sneaky now. Hidin'. Lookin' for that shot… We can't trust the staff neither—we bring in a chef for you two, maybe someone workin' 'round the house sees you—they all good people but the price is too high. Someone'll talk."

"What do you mean?"

"Big money to whoever gets the story first. They pay the person who talks, or even better, gets a pic."

"I'm sorry about this, Alex. I really am." Stevie said.

Alex finished his taco and swallowed. "I'm not good at all this. I don't know what I'm doing."

The two remained silent, unsure how to reply.

"No one knows what the fuck's goin' on." Franklin muttered, casting an eye at Stevie.

She ignored his tone, picking at diced cabbage with her fingers. "Everything with my team is in flux right now." Stevie explained. "Normally we'd get together with my PR, they'd create a plan and be prepared for the increased attention—they'd do their best to manage it on our terms. We wouldn't do anything, we wouldn't be seen in a way we didn't feel good about… We try really hard—I try really hard—to protect the people I care about. But, I don't know if I'm able to do that… I can't trust them right now. They wouldn't have our best interest at heart—not until this deal is done."

"There's a lot mo' movin' parts than you think." Franklin's attention was latched back on his taco. "It ain't fair, neither. You guys just gettin' to know each other—can't even go get some ice cream. Do some normal shit. It's bad timin', Alex. A year ago we'd have this all smoothed over. You come over to the house wheneva yo' want, no problem. A couple months from now, no big deal. Right now though… right now, shit's gonna get crazy."

"I don't want crazy. I don't want to cause problems…" Alex met Stevie's eyes. "If—"

"No. Absolutely not." She leaned in. "You're not a problem—you're… The last week has been one of the best in a real long time. But I know how weird my life is. All this… I'm the problem."

Alex fiddled with the orange glow stick as he thought, twirling it between his fingers like a paintbrush.

"The week leading up to the galley was, well, miserable… I got hounded everywhere. People with cameras yelling at me from across the street, cellphones out when I tried to go shopping… Did you see any of the horrible, racist shit that was posted online? I was nothing but a joke to everyone… But you know the worst part? Underneath all that, I thought I blew it with you. That was the thing that stung the worst—and all the rest was just a reminder of that."

Franklin lowered his head and pushed half of a taco into his mouth. He tried to shrink in place and disappear from the conversation so the two could have a sincere moment.

Stevie's forehead ruffled and her eyes reflected the ocean. "You didn't blow it. I'm scared I'm blowing it."

Alex returned a reluctant smile.

"I'm not makin' it easy… I'll be gone the rest of the week. I have to go back to New York in the morning. Maybe you could call while I'm gone?"

"Each night—if you'll answer?"

"I'll answer."

Alex smiled and looked back down at his dinner. "These are pretty good. Chicken is the best."

"Told ya." Stevie's depth transformed into charm. "Have another." She passed the carton of tacos.

Franklin peered into the box. He then looked back and forth between the two, sensing his taco timing. "Any more carnitas? I just need one."

Stevie slid from the car and danced with the glow stick around her neck. *"It's Taco—Taco Tuesday."* She made up a song. *"Franklin wants carnitas, there's no, no more carnitas—because I ate 'em!"* She spun the purple stick like a propeller on the string, its blurred light creating their own private rave. "Just kidding!" She set the box down in front of him. "There's two left. I'm sure you can do it."

"Where's Gibby?" Alex asked.

"He stayed home." She sighed. "Someone had to stay behind and watch *Missing Thorns*. He promised he'd catch me up when I get home."

"Oh god, you watch that crap?"

"Crap?!"

"Here we go..." Franklin muttered, dressing the tacos with lime juice.

The two bickered about the show's writing and artistic principles while finishing their meal. Ironically, Alex knew quite a bit about the series for claiming never to have watched it. Franklin stood from the table and gathered empty plates, squishing the discarded takeout boxes back into the plastic bags they came from. He tied the top and tossed the trash into the backseat. Taking a step back, he observed Alex's Jeep. The chatter from Alex and Stevie played like a song in the background, a dolce duet occasionally pausing with the fermata of Stevie's giggle. He circled the vehicle, judging its lift and rugged mud tires. He then bent down and looked at the axles, using his glow stick as a flashlight. Returning to the front, he grabbed the bull bar and gave it a tug.

"Your Jeep's a tank." Franklin returned to the conversation.

"Thanks."

"You do it yourself?"

"Yeah. Most of it. It was something my grandfather and I worked on before, well, he passed."

"It's cool, man. Serious hardware under there."

"Alex is gonna take me for a ride in it someday. We'll see the stars." Stevie looked up; the sky was dark but the only lights above were from blinking planes in the distance.

Franklin gave a concerted stare, taking the two in while wiping the corners of his mouth. "'Ey, I gotta get some shit done but I ain't 'bout to leave you two down in this gutter... Let's wrap this shit up and get outta 'ere."

"What you gotta do, Franklin?" Stevie teased, knowing he was finding an excuse to give her some space.

"I got a life too... You two go do your thing—we meet up later when I'm done?"

"So, what? You just eat tacos and bail?" Alex snarked.

"Sounds like somethin' I'd do." He moved toward the vacant chair and began to collapse its legs. "Ain't too many places you can go though—the pap's gonna recognize that truck."

Stevie checked the time on her phone, contemplating places they could hide.

"I don't know how this works." Alex set the lantern on the hood of the Civic. "All the rules, places we can't go. I just wanna hangout. I mean—if you're still down?"

"Oh, I'm down." Stevie reassured. "Maybe we could drive somewhere?"

"Where you gonna go?" Franklin cocked his head. "Beach is out. It's still too early. Ain't no where off PCH you can go."

Alex folded the blanket. "What if we went the other way?" He suggested. "Mount Wilson. I ride my motorcycle up there all the time—fun road."

"Where's that?" Stevie asked.

"Nah." Franklin grunted. "Don't like it. Gettin' outta my bubble. Shit go down, no one gonna get there quick."

"Well, that's the point, right?" Alex said. "Topanga. Mulholland. Those roads are crawling with tourists seein' the skyline. The cameras are just waitin' for a drunk celeb to run one over. So, we go east. Avoid it all."

Stevie used her phone to look at the map. "It's an observatory?"

"Yeah, but we don't have to go in or anything. I just mean it's a good drive. Less people."

"It's only an hour away." Stevie rationalized with Franklin. "Even if we take our time, we'll be back by 11."

"Stevie..." Franklin pushed with his tone.

"I'm out of ideas." She was sharp. "We can't go home. You make sure everyone is out of the house—I'm sure most are gone by now —but lock it down. We stage vehicles and do drops, leave Alex's Jeep somewhere so we don't get tailed. I know they already went home, but get Knox and Mateo back—set them up as spotters by the tunnel. If we get the clear, *if*, we'll sneak Alex in. By that time, we hangout for 45 minutes before we have to sneak him back out, and then drive him back to the Jeep. *Fuck*." Stevie lost patience and looked around at the abandoned riverbed. "That's why we're here, Franklin. *Rats and smashed TV's weren't my first choice...* None of this is ideal. We're doing the best we can."

Franklin sighed and turned his back. He looked up, his eyes scanning for silhouettes against the crest of the riverbank on the horizon. "11 o'clock. He drop you back wit' me at our spot in Melrose."

Alex remained quiet, carrying the folding table back to his Jeep as the two negotiated. He pushed bags around and lifted the corner of a cargo carrier to slide the table in flat on the floor.

Stevie toed a few pebbles of pea gravel with her shoe. "I hate this, you know? It's not fair to you. It's definitely not fair for Alex."

Franklin faced her. "Ain't fair for you neither." He then walked to the rear of the Jeep, intentionally bumping Alex with his hip as he helped with the final push of the table. "Get outch ya phone."

Alex stepped back and pulled the phone from his pocket.

"'Ere. This my number. You call fo' any reason—k? Don't think twice."

Alex nodded.

"Not done. Just in case, here's another number. This emergencies. If I ain't answerin' for some reason an' bad shit happenin', you call this."

Alex saved the new contacts.

"Stevie—she good. She knows what to do… But when I ain't around, you gotta be smart. *Don't you ever be doin' shit that make her vulnerable.* People are weird, man… You gotta step up—always. 'K? Don't worry—whatever it takes—I getch you outta trouble later. You know what I'm sayin'?"

Alex met his eye. "I won't ever do anything to hurt her."

"I ain't worried 'bout you, man… You'll fuck 'er up in yo' own way. I'm talkin' 'bout you stoppin' shit. *Don't be 'fraid to regulate.*" Franklin's rock-hard fist prodded Alex's shoulder. "Never start shit. Always be finishin' it."

STOP!
AGAINST ME!

"I sent some flowers and left a voicemail." Stevie's mother pressed her lips together, staring at herself in a compact.

The SUV swayed while changing lanes, Mateo working the blinker and then glancing back at Stevie in the rear-view mirror. Her attention was lost out the window, allowing the sights of Queens to fade as the truck sped east along the 495. Franklin was riding shotgun, kicked back with his legs crossed. A dress shoe bouncing from his knee. The low drone of his voice harmonized with the road noise, his free hand directing a conversation on his cellphone like a conductor.

"I talked to her." Stevie replied. "It was hard. I didn't know what to say so I acted like everything was normal."

"What else can you say?" Kristen dabbed at eyeliner with her ring finger and then snapped the mirror closed. "Celeste must be so upset."

"She's not handling it well…"

"After this meeting, on your way home to L.A., why don't you stop into Austin? You haven't seen your father in weeks—we can all pay her a visit."

"Celeste is home this weekend. Janet's funny—I'm not sure she'd like that."

"You'll regret it if you don't. Especially if…" Kristen caught herself before she finished the thought. Her eyes became dovish and she reached for Stevie's hand. "I know there's nothing more I'd love than to spend some time with you girls."

Stevie looked over at her. "You're right." She sighed. "I'll make time… Thanks for coming today."

"Are you nervous?"

"Yes and no… I haven't felt this way in years—since the first tour. But there's also a big part of me that doesn't care. I'm so sick of these people and *the deals*."

"Be smart." Her mother cautioned. "Ultimately, you know we'll all be fine. You'll always make music… for as long as you want. You've earned that. But I don't think you're ready for the ride to be over—are you?"

"If it's living by their terms—I am. I'm not doing it anymore."

Kristen sunk into the seat, searching for words that would inspire.

"I don't want to get into it, Mom—but what they've done is unforgivable. I'm only doing this meeting out of respect for Shane."

Kristen bit the inside of her cheek as she thought. "Today is a fresh start. You're powerful now, Stevie. It's not like when you were a kid. You have something they want—make sure they give you what you want in return. Simple as that."

Stevie's gaze returned to the window. "I don't even know what that is anymore…"

The two sat quiet for a few moments. Kristen then broke the silence.

"You've proven your value and talent more than anyone they've ever worked with—now you must have their trust. You and Cosmo want the same things—commercially speaking—

you'd never do anything to sabotage that. But you also need a life. Freedom."

"Trust…" Stevie contemplated the word.

Kristen nodded, though she was blind to the depth within Stevie's tone. "Whatever you choose will be a leap of faith, there are no assurances or guarantees—you've seen enough broken contracts to know that they're meaningless if someone doesn't want to live up to them."

Stevie's eyes moved down to her freshly painted toes, her mind still hung up on the notion of trust.

How could I ever trust them after what they've done?

Her mind tallied the countless instances of exploitation. The one-sided deals, backroom negotiations, trying to sell her body through scandalous wardrobe when she was still a child—each of the memories piled effortlessly as she thought about her first record deal. The offenses only multiplied as her popularity grew, Kismet always at the center of her heartache. It was always a fight with them. The continual defense and protection of her image left behind a battlefield full of agents, choreographers, designers, promoters, and middle management. Now, all of it close to meaningless compared to the egregious threats by executives. What they had done to Alex. *Alex.*

Stevie's mind melted back to their moonlit drive. It had only been two days, but she missed him as if a war had torn them apart. His text messages read like love letters from back home, Stevie continuing to hold the front line until time and fate returned her to him.

She loved that he was still shy, such a contrast from the playboys ballsy enough to chase her from one side of the country to the other. Clearly, she adored him, and even told him as much, but she could sense the surge of energy he conjured when gaining the courage to hold her hand. They had just rounded a bend. Alex made sure the road was long and straight before daring to take a hand from the wheel. And then he wove his fingers between hers.

Stevie blushed, but she knew he didn't notice. The vehicle was dark and his eyes were pinned on the solid yellow line in front of them. He cleared his throat as if he were about to speak, but instead rubbed her thumbnail between his fingers. Stevie returned the affection, raising the back of his hand to her lips.

The two drove the Crest Highway, content with the hum of mud tires and a playlist shuffling low from Alex's phone. They shared quick glances, Stevie's heart skipping each time she met his eye. His preoccupation gave her a moment to study him. His movements were smooth, his left hand guiding the steering wheel rather than commanding it. His sense for the Jeep was outer-body, working the accelerator with each incline and only allowing the transmission to shift at its most easy moment. The way he worked the Jeep and held her hand was a microcosm, and an epiphany was settling deep in the pit of Stevie's stomach. Alex was considerate of the things he cared for, and it was clear that he was beginning to feel a great deal for her.

"Take the next pull off." She whispered. "We don't have to go any further."

Alex looked over at her from the corner of his eye. She smiled and gave his hand a squeeze. After a few more curves, Alex slowed the Jeep and pulled to the side of the road. The heavy suspension twisted through ruts, its big tires kicking up dust and gravel. Alex pointed the headlights out into the night sky, the world beyond the guardrail disappearing into an abyss. L.A. was in the distance, its skyline shimmering through the cool mountain air. Alex turned back the key, and silence washed over them.

Stevie's arm was limp across the center console, her palm raised with Alex's on top. She looked out over the dark canyon, then scanned the city once more before closing her eyes. She let out a long breath and faded into the seat. "I don't think I've ever felt this content…"

"You ready for bed? Want me to get you the blanket?"

Stevie smirked. Her eyes still closed and head propped up by the headrest. "I think you better stay right there."

Alex eased, unbuckling his seatbelt and settling into the cushion as well. "I feel pretty good too."

"I just wish it would all stop. Somehow capture this moment and live in it forever." Stevie twisted her body toward Alex, her eyes looking past golden hair that had fallen across her brow.

"I think I'd be okay with that."

"Just okay?"

Alex smiled and shook his head. "What am I going to do with you?" He studied the curve of her lips and single freckle on her cheek. "Can't even keep the hair out of your face." He brushed the blonde strands from her eyes, running his finger back along her ear.

Stevie reached with her cheek, pressing it against the palm of his hand. "Get over here." She whispered.

Alex leaned in, closing his eyes before his lips met her breath. He lingered, just for an instant, teasing with anticipation. Stevie trembled, pulling him closer until she had his lip between her teeth.

"That's why we're on our way to the Hamptons. That's why Shane insisted you meet with this woman. Are you even listening?" Kristen cocked her head.

"What?" Stevie woke from the memory. "Yeah, of course…"

"You've been distracted ever since I got here. What's going on?"

Franklin chuckled and twisted to get a view of the backseat. "She's in loooove—"

"Shut up!"

"Oh yeah—she gone." Franklin spoke directly to Kristen as if Stevie wasn't in the car with them. "She ain't told you yet? She all twitterpaded. Like high school all over again."

"What? Who?" Kristen questioned.

"Stop it!" Stevie huffed. "It's not like that!"

"See?" Franklin raised an eyebrow.

"I'm gonna kill you!" She halfheartedly punched the back of his seat.

"Who is it?" Kristen persisted.

"I'll let 'er tell ya." Franklin grinned.

"Ugh! I didn't want to say anything because there's nothing to say—I've been on lockdown dealing with this stupid contract ever since we met, so..."

"Who is it?!" Kristen lost patience.

"Alex. The guy I was dancing with at my party..."

Kristen's stare was blank until a slow smile crept from the corner of her mouth. "Yes. I remember him. He's quite handsome."

"Mom..."

"What? He's an attractive young man. You two have been spending time together?"

"A little. Not as much as I'd like."

"So, you like him?"

"Yeah..."

Silence fell upon the car. "Well, that's good. Right?" Stevie's mother eased.

Stevie shook her head. "This isn't happening right now. You're dead to me, Franklin."

The SUV gained access through the security gate and began the long drive toward the estate. A dense wooded thicket gave way to a manicured meadow. The lush grass ran for acres, edged in rings around sculpted trees. The truck passed stables with a barn suitable for a sultan before making its final approach to the beach house. The air became rich with salt and tall grasses plumed in the distance, golden strands waving in the onshore breeze.

Stevie's vehicle rounded the end of the driveway and parked at the entrance of the estate. Franklin stepped from the SUV, checking the surroundings as he buttoned his suit coat.

"Mr. Davis?" An attendant greeted Franklin. "It's a pleasure to have you, sir. Ms. Preston is ecstatic to be hosting Ms. Pearl. We've been beside ourselves waiting for your arrival."

"It's cool, man." Franklin nodded. "Whatch yo' name?"

"Me? Oh… My name is Royce."

"Like a Rolls?" Franklin chuckled.

Royce smirked. "Not quite, sir."

"Nice to meetch you." Franklin extended his hand. "Call me Franklin."

Royce met the greeting and was engulfed by a massive palm.

Franklin looked over his shoulder one more time and then nodded to Mateo who was still in the driver's seat. "We good here, Royce?"

"Certainly, Mr. Franklin. Ms. Preston has been notified of your arrival and is on her way to greet you. I'll happily show you and your friends into the home."

Franklin nodded once more and then popped the rear door to Stevie's seat. Royce was immediately met with bright blue eyes and captivating smile.

Stevie's grace poured from the backseat, the toe of her black heels making first contact with the pavers. She was dressed in a form-fitting sleeveless jumpsuit, black pants transforming into a black and gray checkered top, capped by a flowing silk tie that wrapped around her neck. Her hair was pulled back and hooped diamond earrings captured the sun. Mateo opened the door for Kristen on the other side.

"Hi there!" Stevie greeted.

"Ms.—Ms. Pearl." Royce stuttered. "We're so happy to have you!"

"Happy to be here. This place is beautiful."

"Welcome! Welcome. Ms. Preston is inside. Allow me to show you the way?"

Stevie nodded. She held a gray clutch in one hand and the other was slid into her pants pocket as they walked. Several stone steps climbed the estate's entrance, the group passing between massive white pillars that achieved their desired statement. Royce was quick to unlatch the front door and hold it open, Stevie grateful with a bow as she walked by. The group paused in the foyer, surrounded by impressive white woodwork and a ceiling that ran to the second level. Stevie knew wealth, and this home alone was worth at least half of all of hers.

With what seemed to be on cue, Sylvia rounded the corner and greeted her guests. Hugs all around, Mateo awkwardly obliging. Introductions were made and Sylvia lingered extra long while holding Kristen's hand. The woman was older than Kristen, probably in her mid-sixties but difficult to tell through all of the spa treatments. Her clothes were designer, light and flowing—the perfect complement to a summer beach home. The jewelry on her wrist chattered as she pointed out directions, promising to give them an entire tour of the grounds after lunch.

"You must be hungry." Sylvia insisted. "That drive from The City is horrendous. I told Shane that you are more than welcome to use the helicopter."

"Thank you." Stevie was gracious. "He did pass along the message, but I don't mind. Being captured in a vehicle is just about the only quality time I get with my mother these days."

Kristen blushed.

"I understand. That's important." Sylvia nodded. "Follow me. We'll dine on the back patio. The weather is absolutely beautiful."

Sylvia tweeted like a songbird as she led the group toward the rear of the home, commenting on various pieces of decor and art as they passed by. "My father won this at the Hampton Classic," she drew attention to the trophy, "always much more of an equestrian than I was."

The rear of the house opened to massive panes of glass that stood watch over the ocean, the patio doors held open allowing the fresh sea breeze to pass through. The sound of a waterfall trickling into an infinity pool snaked along the edge of the patio and large, blooming potted plants gave the illusion of a jungle.

"Over here." Sylvia led. An entire outdoor dining room had been assembled for her guests. "Please, take a seat." She gestured. "The menu's there for inspiration, but don't be afraid to create your own request. Timothy in the kitchen does a fantastic job. Royce, please let Samantha know that our guests have arrived. Have her bring a pitcher of iced tea and water, she can get the rest of the drinks when she arrives."

"Right away." Royce nodded and then vanished.

"You have such a beautiful home." Kristen complimented.

"Thank you—here, sit. Us girls on this end. You don't mind, do you, Franklin?"

"Not at all, ma'am. We appreciate you including us."

"Certainly. I'll have Stevie all to myself before the day is over, but I thought it was important that we all get to know one another. You've been her Head of Security for quite some time?"

"That's right. Almost a decade."

"You two must be quite close. I understand the relationship between a young woman and her bodyguard. Charles—Chuck as he insists—retired a few years back, but he was with me for nearly 40 years. Longer than any of my marriages, combined!" Sylvia cackled. "I still insist he be around at the holidays—I visit him quite regularly…"

Franklin pressed his lips. "That—that says a lot, ma'am. Him stickin' with you."

"He would have paid the ultimate price—thank God he was never called upon in such a way. Though I will admit, he did get me out of some precarious situations…" She smirked toward Stevie. "You and Mateo are always welcome here. Do you like island-inspired barbecue? Timothy makes some of the best. Everything that man does with a pineapple is spectacular."

"I know my way 'round some barbecue—I'll give it a shot."

"Franklin's a connoisseur." Stevie participated. "If you're not careful, he'll be back there showing Timothy a thing or two."

"Perfect!" Sylvia grinned. "He needs someone to keep him on his toes. Are you still in Austin, Kristen?"

"Yes—we are." Stevie's mother regathered herself into the conversation. "My husband and I, and Joey—Stevie's little brother. That's why I'm so captivated by this view—I miss it—not quite what I'm used to in Central Texas."

"It never gets old. Are you originally from Austin?"

"No. Ben and I moved there after college. He got a tech job right out of school and we relocated. I'm originally from New England, a little town in Massachusetts."

"Where's your accent?" Sylvia played.

"I was a speech therapist for many years with young children. Parents didn't want to hear their kids parhkin' the cah down by the gahden." She laughed. "Stevie still makes fun of me after a couple of beeah's."

"There it is." Sylvia smiled. "Fascinating occupation. That must have been rewarding?"

"Of course. Helping a child communicate—there's not many feelings like it."

"Where in Massachusetts? You must have made it over to the coast quite a bit growing up?"

"I lived on it. Plenty of summers out on Martha's Vineyard."

"Well, I'm sure Stevie could find you a nice little cottage—c'mon, Stevie. Buy your mother a beach house!"

"Then she'd never visit me."

"I made Ben promise we'd retire on the coast—wherever that might be. Though I'm not sure he'll ever retire…"

"You're so young—there's plenty of time. It's admirable you've both found careers you're so passionate about. Even after Stevie's incredible success."

"He's a nerd… but also a big reason why we're sitting here. He's a great father."

"Yes. You both must have done something right." Sylvia looked over at Stevie. "I'm envious. Not that any family is perfect, but yours does emit genuine resolve. If I were to do it over again, I'd settle for nothing less."

"Do, you have children?" Kristen toed.

"A son. However, he passed away from addiction. It was quite a while ago…"

"I'm sorry—I, I didn't know."

"No. No." Sylvia wagged her hand. "It's not your fault. It's mine… It's impossible not to blame yourself. Perhaps if I had chosen a better father—someone who inspired me to be a better mother—things would have worked out different. We were disgusting as young adults, both from money and privilege. Our parents basically arranged the union—another Manhattan power move by my father. It couldn't last, we despised each other. I withdrew into my work, and poor Marshall was left to find his way…" Sylvia locked eyes with Kristen. "It's the greatest regret of my life."

Kristen remained in shock, shaking her head with sympathy.

"We're getting to know each other today." Sylvia attempted to lighten her voice. "It's important you know who I am—and I'm not without flaws. Ah, Samantha." She greeted the young woman walking toward the table with her hands full. "Samantha, please meet our guests. This is the one and only, Stevie Pearl. This is her mother, Kristen, and these two gentlemen are Mateo and Franklin —her associates."

"It's such a pleasure to meet you, Ms. Pearl. Everyone else as well." Samantha met each of their eyes. "Ms. Preston has allowed me to gush for one minute." She held up a finger. "I just wanted to say that I'm your biggest fan! I have all your records and have been to your concert, like, four times. Okay—whew! Just had to get that out." She beamed.

Stevie laughed. "That's so sweet. Thank you. I'm flattered."

"Oh man!" Samantha cringed. "Okay—I can do this." She openly calmed herself, making light of her fandom.

Stevie blushed. "After lunch, why don't you come say hi? I'm sure Ms. Preston would allow us a few minutes?"

"That's very kind of you to offer—of course!" Sylvia nodded. "We've got all day."

"Oh my gosh—are you sure?!"

"I'd love to."

"Wow—okay—"

"Breathe, Samantha..." Sylvia said lightly.

"Yes, ma'am. Okay... okay. May I get anyone something else to drink? We have coffee, a full bar—smoothies, milkshakes—you name it."

"I'll, ah—I'll have a milkshake." Mateo pipped up. "Strawberry. What?" He glared at Franklin.

"Tea's fine." Franklin stared back at Mateo.

"A coffee sounds good. With cream, please." Kristen requested.

"I'm good with water. Thank you, Sam." Stevie winked.

Samantha blushed, mustering composure as she looked toward Sylvia.

"I'll have a coffee as well, the usual. Thank you, dear."

After lunch, Stevie made good on her word and spent a half hour chatting with Sam. A girl her own age was a pleasant distraction from the looming record deal. It gave her a moment to live vicariously through the stories of being young and single in the Hamptons. She wondered if she would have been a waitress, finding a summer job slinging slop to rich people in a beach town? It didn't matter, those thoughts were wasted energy at this point. Stevie finished by posing for a selfie—the two creating a mini montage before Stevie hugged her goodbye.

Sylvia took the group for a tour of the gardens and then called in a herd of golf carts for a ride around the stable. By late afternoon they were back at the estate, Sylvia inviting Stevie for a walk on the beach.

"You don't mind, do you? I imagine we'll get sandy."

"Not at all. I wasn't about to leave without touching the water."

"I've noticed you eyeing it. It's enchanting, isn't it? Come. We'll leave our shoes on the boardwalk."

Stevie undid the clasp of her heels and then rolled the bottom of her pant legs. Sylvia kicked her flats aside and she used Stevie for balance as the two descended the planks into the sand.

"It's warm." Stevie smiled.

"In July it'll give you blisters."

"I can't believe no one's out." Stevie looked up and down the beach, spray rolling in off in the distance.

"Yes. Pretty quiet around here now that school's started. I told you I'd get you alone."

The two took short steps down the bank toward the damp sand.

"Tide's out." Sylvia moved slow, her joints catching up with her age. "I want to apologize. That's mainly why I asked you here today. Shane filled me in on all your struggles with Kismet.

Regardless of what you decide, I'll be restructuring. I'm sorry for what they've put you through."

Stevie allowed the words to settle, relieved their conversation had finally turned to business. "Why didn't Shane join us today?"

"I asked him not to." Sylvia was blunt. "He's a good man—does right by you. You know, we met a while back when he was just getting started. Not really sure why I remembered him... A breath of fresh air, I suppose. When he called earlier this week about your deal, I was caught off guard. Quite brash. Was that his idea or yours?"

"His." Stevie was straight. "To be quite honest, it took convincing. I never wanted to speak to anyone at Cosmo again."

Sylvia smirked. "And yet here we are. Funny how things work out... It was fortunate that my lunch appointment had just been canceled. Timing is everything. He immediately rushed over the moment I hesitated—hesitation is a new quality I'm discovering about myself as I age. Perhaps it's consideration."

"For some reason this is important to him."

"It's not to you?"

"I'm... undecided."

"I see. Well, in that case, I think it's important that you and I come to an understanding—independent of Shane, the lawyers, and the rest of the executives."

Stevie tilted her head toward the old woman's direct tone. "We have a clear division of labor—it's not my place to be negotiating contracts. I pay Shane a great deal of money to handle these things for me."

"Shane may iron out the details, but as I see it, not much happens without your blessing. That's a good thing." Sylvia clasped her hands. "Are you even interested in a contract with Cosmo? The way it was explained to me, you're about to launch a publicity bomb aimed to sink the Music Group."

"Only out of retaliation. And they'd deserve every bit of it."

Sylvia shrugged her shoulders. "Probably so, but I don't see the good it would do anyone."

Stevie squinted through the sun. "It'd be good for the other women coming up behind me. So this stuff doesn't happen to them. It's good for the minorities that don't focus test well."

"A martyr. So, you're willing to be the sacrificial lamb?"

"I'm no lamb. And no longer working with Cosmo is not a sacrifice."

Sylvia grinned at the venom beneath Stevie's calm words. "Believe it or not, I'm on your side here."

Stevie's scoff was unconvinced. "You've been very kind to me today. Why? I know the numbers. The money I make for you is a drop in the bucket for Cosmo Global."

"Because you're important. What you represent is important."

Stevie's face was stone.

"There weren't many women in the game when I first went to work for Cosmo—at least none that had any power. My father was so angry… He was in real estate. Built this place back in the '50s after he made his fortune flipping buildings in The City. He eventually went on to bigger deals, skyscrapers and whatnot. He was so mad when I left him—*a woman will never be in charge of a multi-national*. He said. *You're wasting your talent—I didn't raise you to be some secretary*. I now own one of these estates on every continent—this, his, is the least impressive of them all. I keep it though, sentimental…

"As you said, Cosmo's a very large company. The Music Group is rather insignificant in our overall earnings. That's not to say what you do, and the impact you have, is insignificant. That's not the case at all. I'm just saying that the video game division alone brought in $45 billion dollars *more* than the Music Group did last year. We've also got motion pictures, publishing, and manufacturing—everything from engines, solar power, and the little nano chips needed for computers. The point is, name me one person in the video game industry or in manufacturing that's a household name? No one cares who they are as long as they keep pumping out the products—that's why you're so incredibly different. You have their attention. And, like in Samantha's case, their hearts."

"So, I'm another commodity? Like a microchip?"

"Of course you are, dear. You can't be upset with me for that. I didn't invent society. However, I believe you could be more than that. I believe your value exceeds the product you produce, and that has tremendous value for Cosmo."

"I don't understand."

"Mind if we sit? I'd like to enjoy this moment, rather than rush through it. All our walking today took it out of me... It's becoming painfully obvious, literally, that I'm no spring chicken."

Stevie looked around at the vacant beach. "Sure?"

"The sand—over there." Sylvia pointed as she moved up the bank. "When did I become such an old lady?" She chuckled to herself.

"You're doing fine." Stevie offered, moving slow along with her. However, the moment the compassionate words left her lips, they bit within her mind. Stevie knew that Sylvia was a wolf in sheep's clothing. The helpless old lady routine was a tactic. The shrewd businesswoman didn't amass an empire by being frail or out negotiated by her junior. Still, Stevie stood close, extending a hand and offering support as Sylvia plopped to the ground.

"Much better, thank you." Her breath was short. "Sometimes you have to sacrifice a nice pair of pants to make an old woman happy." She tugged at Stevie's pant leg. "Sit with me."

Stevie's gaze was reluctant, searching the sand with confusion. "Oh, what the hell..." She tossed her hands. In a single motion Stevie's legs contorted into pretzel and she sat cross-legged next to Sylvia, the sun brushing both of their backs as they looked out into the surf.

"I'm…" Sylvia hesitated, lost in the white caps. "Well, I'm not a good person." She frowned. "You start thinking about these things as you get older. 10 years ago I would have laughed Shane out of my office—if I even would have given him a meeting at all. Timing, as they say, is everything… I told you about the mistakes I made with my son. I've never been a champion for women—I never cared about any of that shit—I've always been about results—and ruthless in achieving them… Looking back, the majority of my failures and the things I'm least proud of have come directly from my lack of compassion. Not a tough formula to figure out, right?" She looked over at Stevie.

Stevie shrugged, unimpressed with the candor.

"*Great*, you're thinking. *Scrooge is having a change of heart.* I'm not that cliché, darling. I am who I am. But that's not to say you need to be like me to be successful. You're proof of that. It's not a zero-sum game."

"And what game are we playing?"

"Life, I suppose… God, I'm envious of you. So much still to come."

"Don't patronize…"

Sylvia nodded, realizing her conviction wasn't being well received.

"Your career, Stevie. The entire trajectory. You've been on my radar, at least in passing, for quite a while. To be honest, I don't listen to your music—I've heard it—but let's face it, I'm not your target audience. However, that's irrelevant. You've never allowed yourself to become something that you're not—a very difficult task in your industry. You've never sold yourself, you've never embarrassed yourself, you've never been caught up in some scandal or publicity stunt. *You've worked hard.* You've always made my label money and never once hesitated to put them through hell to defend and preserve your image. I admire that. I'm not saying mistakes haven't been made, but you've always made *right decisions*."

Stevie looked down at the sand between her toes. With the slightest bit of pressure she sent grains collapsing in on themselves. She observed the landslide that she instigated, lingering on how little effort it took.

"What is it that you want?" Sylvia finally got to the crux.

"What do you mean?"

"No life is perfect, even one as glamorous as yours. I've known nothing but wealth and power, yet that didn't help me achieve happiness or make the right decisions. If you could do anything, how would you improve it?"

"It's not so much about making it better—more comfortable..." Stevie hesitated. "It's about opportunity. Liberty."

"Explain."

"I want normal things, to go to normal places. I want to be able to walk into a restaurant and not have to run it by Shane, who then has to get approval from my lawyers that double-check to make sure there's not some non-compete clause with a sponsor, who then has to coordinate with my PR agent so they can prepare for an official public appearance... I've earned the chance to try new things; to expand and grow as a songwriter. I want those around me to have faith in what I'm doing—I want my own team to help me succeed instead of fighting me at every corner— squeezing me for every penny."

Sylvia was quiet. She turned and took a long breath. "I'm sure Shane has discussed my offer. Full ownership of Kismet, and a percentage along with full vote within the Music Group."

Stevie nodded.

"Stay with me, Stevie. I know you don't care about running a label, but I know of no other way that will help you get what you want. Signing with Apollo or someone else will only be more of the same—financial comfort without opportunity and liberty."

"Why?" Stevie shook her head. "Why would you help me? The deal you're offering is unheard of—especially the vote in the Music Group."

"If I help you, I believe you'll help me." Sylvia shrugged. "Simple as that. As I said, I'm looking well beyond your record sales. Cosmo Music Group needs major reconstruction. Music isn't dying, but the way we manage the industry is. There's no future for us without the proper leader. I need someone within its walls who knows what it takes to be a successful artist—who offers a vastly different perspective having been a young female artist. I need someone other musicians want to emulate and would be proud to be associated with, regardless of gender and genre. I'm not asking you to operate it, but I am asking for your powerful voice. I'm looking for an advocate to bring a bit of humanity back to the table... Knowing you, and with my support, you'll be able to whip that one vote into as many as you want."

Stevie maintained her stare straight ahead. Goosebumps from the breeze, or the offer, speckled her arms. She thought deeply and took a breath.

"I saw the report on Alex. I'm sorry, Stevie... Something like that would never happen under your watch."

She released the air from her lungs and then clenched her jaw. Just the mention of Alex's name from anyone at Cosmo made her spine stiffen.

"How could I ever trust you?" The reticle of Stevie's eye met Sylvia's, and she zeroed with indignant righteousness.

Sylvia looked away, methodically twisting the bracelets on her wrist. "You can't." The old woman's words were soft, unable to hold the glare. "That's why we're here. I'm trying to earn it. I'm trying to show you my flaws, share my aspirations for what I want the Music Group to become. You have no reason to believe me though."

"What do you get out of this?"

262 SEAN WILLIAM HAMMOND

"Besides atonement? Money, of course. I keep the biggest pop star on the planet. With your credibility as a prominent figure leading the Music Group, every decent artist will also want to sign with us.

"Regardless, I'm restructuring no matter what you choose. It's time. Like I said, I'm about results—and right now we're not achieving them if Stevie Pearl wants to burn us to the ground." She laughed. "Who knows, allowing you to topple the ivory tower with your own hands may be the incentive that separates us from the other offers—not out of revenge, but as you said, to really help the next generation coming up behind you. I know of no one more capable of enacting positive change—and this is how you change the industry, Stevie. Not be a product of it..."

Stevie closed her eyes.

"Oh," Sylvia nudged with her shoulder. "You have my word—there will be no backlash or fight from Cosmo if you decide to go elsewhere. I'll make sure of that. If we treated you better, well... if we had done a lot of things better, perhaps you wouldn't want to leave in the first place."

Stevie continued to push at the sand with her feet, the tumbling grains occupying the space her words were unable to fill.

Sylvia smiled and leaned back, propping herself up with an elbow in the sand. "Beautiful, isn't it? The constant motion is captivating. I'm sure there's a good metaphor—change, motion, renewal and the sort."

"I'm a bit more consumed by the irony..." Stevie maintained her fixation on the sand.

"There's also that." Sylvia laughed. "The great Greek tragedy... becoming the very thing you set off to destroy. That's how I know you'll do all the things I should have."

"What things?"

"A life beyond what's expected of you."

Stevie bit the inside of her cheek and avoided Sylvia's eyes, finally giving the woman the leverage she had been seeking.

"You'll consider consequences along with the bottom line. You'll find better ways to accomplish the same things we've always done. You will give opportunities to those who deserve them. You will love your husband, be loved in return, and you will nurture your children… You'll do all of this because that's who you are— you're not capable of being anything less."

Stevie shook her head. "How could I ever begin to forgive you?"

"By having real power. And then making better choices with it…"

I NEVER PICKED COTTON
JOHNNY CASH

Threading his bike through the yellow dotted lines, Alex took the same route home to Parker that he always took. The ride was long, but lacked its usual labor. This time the Mojave was more forgiving. He wore a leather jacket and praised the sun. His spirit reflected its brightness, his heart brimming with infatuation and thoughts wholly consumed by a gentle whisper and soft hands that pulled him close.

"Henry!" Alex pushed open the door to Woody's.

"Alex. You gonna give me that bike?"

"Sure—" He pretended to toss his keys.

The teenage clerk sprung at the empty air like a dog teased with a stick. "Not cool, bro."

"You're not cool, bro." Alex followed the worn path in the tile that led back to the cooler.

"Hey." Henry spoke louder so Alex could hear him. "Nice dance moves. You're like a nerdy white boy! You should take some lessons or somethin."

Alex cracked a bottle of water and took a swig.

"Shit—you're like one of those puppets from Sesame Street!" Henry cackled.

Alex smirked and took another gulp, walking toward the register.

"This is you!" Henry flailed like he was having a seizure, mimicking his arms being tied to marionette strings.

"You done?" Alex cocked an eyebrow. "See, when you do it, you just look foolish. Me—I only dance when I'm at a mansion. Next to a pool. Surrounded by supermodels. Oh, and with the hottest girl on the planet. You forget that part?"

Henry stopped his dancing and gave a blank stare.

"Yeah…" Alex set the bottle down. "You could be there with me, bro. You stop giving Mrs. Whatshername shit and pull your grades up?"

"Dude. How'd you even get into a party like that?"

Alex thought back to Celeste and the afternoon when she changed his life. Her coy way of gnawing on a sandwich while setting him up on a blind date. "They're… they're my friends."

Alex turned, stepping toward the shelves of candy for his brother's favorite chocolate bar. "Better get him two." Alex muttered under his breath, preparing himself for an uncomfortable conversation.

"Wait—so you actually know those people?" Henry was foaming with disbelief.

"Yeah. I work with Stevie's best friend. She's, like, really cool—my friend, too. Ask Charlie. He met her at the gallery." Alex placed the chocolate next to his water.

"No way. You're messin' with me?"

Alex shrugged.

"Have you hung out with her again—Stevie Pearl?"

"Do you hang out with your friends?"

Henry's mind exploded. "What?! This is crazy, bro! You just come in 'ere, tell me you're friends with, like, famous people and shit?!"

Alex couldn't help but grin.

"Fuck, man! That's so fuckin' cool! I'm comin' to L.A., bro! I'm comin' out there!"

"Dude—I told you. Get through this last year—get that scholarship—I'll set you up." Alex pealed a $100 bill from his wallet. "Go buy groceries—real food. No fast food bullshit. I'm counting on you to look after your mother and sister."

Henry looked down at the money, the amount was way more than the $20 Alex would usually leave him.

"You sure?"

"Hollywood." Alex put on his sunglasses. "You'll do the same someday." He slid the chocolate bars into his pocket and grabbed the bottle of water. "Be good, Henry." Alex walked toward the door.

"Hey, man—thanks..." Henry's voice faded as the door shut. Alex straddled the motorcycle and fired the bike with a flick of his thumb. The exhaust popped and crackled, Alex riding the shoulder of the washboard dirt roads to his childhood home.

Double checking that the gate was secure, Alex rode up the remaining length of driveway and parked under the tree. He lingered for a moment, fiddling with his saddlebags expecting Tita to greet him at the screen door. She didn't come calling for her medicine. He climbed the steps of the trailer and let himself in.

"'Eard ya comin'." Tita said from the couch, the TV flickering across the room. "Ankles are swollen as shit."

"You okay?"

"No. I'm fuckin' old."

"Let's hope that's all ya are..." Alex tossed a childproof bottle onto the coffee table.

"How's the ride?"

"It was good. Really good, actually."

"Finally got laid, huh?"

"Tita…"

"'Bout time. Now I can stop spreadin' them rumors you're gay."

"Who do you spread rumors to?"

"Anyone'll listen." She gave him a toothless smile. "Charlie's pissed. Have fun with that."

"He's always pissed."

Tita shrugged, accepting the statement as a common fact.

"Where's ma?"

"Around. Makin' your chili. She went out back a while ago to talk to Charlie."

"That bad, huh?"

"Let him win one. Your shadow's gettin' big."

"My shadow?" Alex ran his hand through his hair and then flopped into the worn recliner.

"Just sayin'."

"I'm not supposed to enjoy this? I'm not supposed to share it?"

Tita didn't offer a response, squinting through the skin tags on her eyelids as she watched TV.

"I'm not gonna feel bad for finally having a little bit of success. I've worked for years—"

Tita dismissed him with her hand and pointed at the show.

"Yep…" He muttered and stood up.

"He looked after you growin' up. Give him some credit for that."

Alex took a breath, thinking about all times his brother had pushed him to the ground. Yelled at him for chores. Left him behind when the older kids went swimming in the river. "He…" Alex bit his lip and then shook his head. "I'm not here to fight with him."

"Good."

Alex went through the kitchen, looking into the pot of stew and giving it a stir before heading out the backdoor. He trotted sideways down the steps and then kicked at rocks as he walked toward the barn.

"Alex!" His mother greeted, holding a flashlight for Charlie who was elbow deep in the front end of an old tractor.

"Fuck!" Charlie swore, his knuckles slamming into the engine block as he twisted the head off of a rusted bolt. "Fuckin' done now." He threw the ratchet to the ground and looked at his mangled skin. "Broke the goddamn bolt—no idea how we're gonna fix this piece of shit now."

Kadence turned off the light and took a step back, widening her eyes toward Alex with a warning that he had stepped in at the wrong moment.

"Whaddya think, Alex—we just go buy another one?"

"Hi, Charlie." Alex rolled his eyes and leaned against the horse trailer.

"How was the drive?" Kadence made light.

"Fine."

"Got your chili goin."

"I saw. It smells good."

Charlie paced as he wiped the blood from his fist with an old oily rag. "Can't get a torch in there to heat it up."

"Drill it out?" Alex suggested.

"Fuck that."

"Take a break, Charlie. It ain't goin' anywhere." Kadence offered.

Charlie shook his head. "Fine. If you don't care that we get the troughs moved—fuckin' herd watered. Maybe Alex can hookup with his motorcycle—drag 'em down to the south pasture?"

"Are you cranky? Do you need a candy?" Alex pulled the treat from his coat. "A Mr. Goodbar—your favorite!" He patronized.

Charlie continued to dab his fist.

Alex paraded the chocolate bar by dangling it from the corner of the wrapper.

"Well, fuck—you gonna toss it here or what?"

Alex smiled and threw the chocolate like a frisbee. Charlie caught it like a pancake and then used his teeth to tear into the wrapper.

"How's everything since the gallery? Have you started any of the commissions?" Kadence asked.

"Not really. Been pretty busy... Distracted."

"Those people are paying good money—you need to get them done."

"It's a process."

"Yes—don't rush the artist." Charlie chewed.

"See. He gets it."

"How's your friend—Celeste?"

"Not that good, actually. You know how she was super drunk at the gallery?"

His mother nodded.

"Well, she's been doing that a lot lately. Turns out her mom's got cancer. She went back to Austin this weekend to see her."

"That's—that's terrible..."

"Yeah. Doesn't sound good."

"That's the one who's friends with Stevie, right? Should get her to help."

"She is. Believe me. It's like her second mom. They're doing everything they can."

"What—no more, *how dare you speak her name in front of me?*" Charlie used the chocolate bar to point sarcastically as he talked. "You over all that finally?"

Alex ignored him. "I feel bad. I wish there was something I could do."

"That's how we lost dad..." Kadence vanished into thought, looking around at his old memories throughout the barn.

The boys stood quiet.

Kadence took an unsteady, quivering breath. "That's terrible, Alex. I'm sorry…" She hid her eyes. "Give her our best. I… I really need to check on the chili."

Kadence was quick to leave the barn.

"Good one, fucktard." Charlie studied the angles of the chocolate bar before biting off another square.

Alex crossed the dirt floor and flipped over an old five-gallon bucket, using it as a seat. "You could get the stick welder. Hold a nut to the end of that bolt. Should twist right out."

"I was thinkin' the same thing."

"Try not to ruin anything else while you're in there…"

"How'd you remember that trick?"

"I remember lots of things, Charlie. You seem to forget I was always a better mechanic than you."

"The fuck you are."

"Yeah, why'd grandpa always have me help with the truck? Sent you lookin' after the livestock."

"Because you have tiny, delicate hands. Good for small spaces."

"Uh huh…"

The two were quiet for a moment.

"This thing with Celeste really got me thinkin' 'bout him." Alex broke.

"Fuckin' sucks." Charlie crumpled the wrapper.

"I'm sorry, you know? I know you weren't ready for all of this."

Charlie didn't offer a word.

"He made me promise I'd finish school… But, I used that as an excuse. I know you needed me."

"He always did believe in you."

"He believed in you, too. That's why he left you this place."

"Didn't leave me much choice in the matter."

"He could have sold. The shit dragged on forever, he knew he wasn't gettin' any better. There'd been enough for Tita—maybe some to help mom out. But he knew you could handle it. Shit, as much as you bitch about it, this place is the only thing you've ever cared about."

"So I'm stuck takin' care of it?"

"Stuck? You're not, *stuck*." Alex talked with his hand. "You put that on yourself. What else were you gonna do? What dreams haven't you seen through because you've been workin' here? You'd just be somewhere else—workin' somewhere where no one cares about you."

"We all can't go off to Hollywood and be artists."

"Damn right. I'm lucky as shit—I know that. I also worked really hard. You suddenly have a talent for watercolor? You got this hidden Andy Fuckin' Warhol streak you've been keepin' from us? It wasn't like it was you or me—the family didn't give you the short straw."

"Fuck you."

"Yeah, fuck me..."

"Since you were little, you always got everything. Alex needs art supplies. Alex needs a new sketch book. They stopped at nothing to help you at what you were good at. I needed some new cleats—a fuckin' batter's glove—registration fees. Screw Charlie. He ain't goin' no where."

"Charlie, you spit in an ump's face! You got in a fist fight with the assistant coach. You were a great ball player, especially as a kid, but once it got time to get serious—you fucked off the entire way. The outside shot you had at a scholarship was lost when you started partying."

"Oh—I didn't sit in my fuckin' room all night—have no friends like you. I was such an awful teenager."

"I wanted out, Charlie. I saw what I had to do, and I worked really hard to make it happen. I sacrificed friends, girls—all the shit you were good at. No one in this town even knew I existed."

"That's because you didn't want to exist here."

"Fair. You did. You like it here. There's nothing wrong with that. Stop thinking there is and holding it against me for leaving."

"Pretty easy, wasn't it? Turning your back on everyone?"

"How did you ever come to that conclusion? I visit all the goddamn time—I come out and help you when I know you need it. Any extra money I have, I give to this family."

"So, you can just buy your place? Alex sends some cash—that makes up for it."

"*I'm not making up for anything.* I don't owe you shit, Charlie."

"We were gonna do this together, remember?"

"What? No. I really fuckin' don't. When did I ever say I was going to run this ranch with you?"

Charlie took a step back and bit his lip. "Well, why wouldn't you want to? Am I that fuckin' terrible?"

"Yes." Alex couldn't help but laugh. "You're absolutely fuckin' miserable—but that's not why. Me leavin' was never about you, Charlie."

"...I didn't give you much reason to stay."

Alex slowed his words and thought for a moment. "You think you pushed me away?"

"I did beat the piss out you regularly..."

"Yeah..." Alex nodded. "You did. But I idolized you. You're my big brother. All I ever wanted was to be cool enough to hang out with you."

"I know. And I never let you... Then one day you weren't here. And Grandpa wasn't here. And all my friends—well, most of them are in jail, but some went off to school. I got fuckin' left behind." Charlie turned his back. He began rummaging through tools on the workbench, using the meaningless movement as a distraction.

Alex couldn't help but smirk. "There's always mom and Tita..."

"Screw you..."

"Look, I get why you'd feel that way. But what else would you rather be doin'? Job out on the oil rig? That's the *best case*. I'd be workin' at Woody's my whole life if I didn't get out. You got this place—that means somethin'. Which one of your friends got anything close to a home? A place where they're needed. Somethin' that gives 'em a life?"

"I'm sick of barely existing. All this fuckin' work and I can't buy a goddamn wheel for the trailer. You talk about workin' hard —*I fuckin' work hard*. Don't mean you get rewarded for it. You come in, slip Mom some money—like I can't take care of it."

"She warned me." Alex shook his head. "Instead of accepting some good fortune in this family, you gotta sulk because it didn't come from you."

"Yeah—excuse me that I want my work to support the things I need."

"Grandpa worked his entire life—what you've done multiplied by another 40 years—this is all he got. You think you're better than him? Smarter than him? You deserve more than he got? It's a brutal fuckin' existence, Charlie. No one's ever meant to win out here, just get by."

"Yeah, well, I need a fuckin' win from time to time…"

Alex rubbed his head. "I want to help. We gotta figure out a way I can do that and you feel good about it."

"I don't *need* your help."

"Fine. But do you want it? Mom sure does—Tita seems to like it. Your pride gonna keep you from makin' this place a little better? Their lives a little easier? Jesus, Charlie—we solve a couple problems. Might give you a chance to go down to the bar and bring another one home."

"You gonna talk to me about women?"

"No. I'm not. Just want you happy. You deserve that. You're allowed to have a life too."

"I don't want a handout."

"How 'bout an investment? You figure out what you need, I figure out what I got—it ain't much—and you make it right when you load the trucks."

Charlie thought for a moment. "I dunno… That's better than you handing Mom a wad of cash."

"I'm always gonna hand Mom a wad of cash. But this way we do it right. No sneakin'. No lyin'. You can talk to me when you need some new parts for the tractor—maybe I can help, maybe I can't—but at least we'd be talkin' again."

Charlie stepped back, thinking about the proposition. "I ain't mad at you for bein' successful… I'm mad at me for not. I'm not sure I'd be a good investment."

"Jesus, Charlie… You've done the hard part. You've been keeping this place goin' since Grandpa died—what's that, a decade on your own? You've proven you ain't gonna take off, *like me*. You've earned it. You've made it work. You've earned all of us havin' faith in you."

Charlie looked past the tall barn doors and out into the corral. He nodded his head, preparing words. "This… this is somethin' I'll need to think about."

Alex rolled his eyes. "Well, okay then. Have your people call my people once you make up your mind. I'm gonna go eat chili."

Alex stood from the bucket. He circled the barn, taking in the worn hand tools. An old photograph was pinned above the workbench, his grandfather grinning with an arm around Charlie's shoulder. His brother was no older than 10, the same old tractor half out of frame in the background. Alex's heart sank.

He bit the inside of his cheek and walked toward the door. "You comin'?"

275 THE BALLAD OF STEVIE PEARL

Charlie walked down the driveway while Alex zipped his jacket. His brother undid the gate, waiting for Alex to catch up on the motorcycle. The exhaust snarled as Alex brought the bike upright. He coasted down the driveway, pinning the front tire an inch from his brother's boot. Charlie reached over and hit the kill switch with his fist, the quiet of the ranch recapturing the evening air.

"You done thinkin' yet?"

"Nope."

"Can I tell you somethin'?" Alex's eyes met Charlie through the clear glasses he rode with at night. "Don't... please don't say nothin' to ma or Tita—they can't keep her mouth shut down at the community center."

Charlie shrugged.

"Well, I'm sorta seein' Stevie Pearl."

Charlie's scoff turned into a muttering laugh. "Fuck off. That's who you were textin' with at the table?"

Alex nodded.

"This for real?"

"Think it is. That's why we've been so quiet about it."

"Sure she just ain't embarrassed of you?"

Alex didn't offer a reply.

"Jesus, Alex..."

"It's still new. But I think I really like her."

"What's there not to like?"

"I don't want to screw it up."

"Well, good luck with that."

"Charlie, I'm serious. I haven't been in a relationship since Emilia."

"I don't know, little brother..."

"You've always been better at this stuff than me."

Charlie wiped his lip. "Just... be her friend. Be the person she wants to talk to at the end of the day."

Alex looked down at the chrome speedometer.

"Don't pretend. Don't be somethin' ya ain't. You ain't gonna woo her with fancy dinners and jewelry—though that don't mean you don't try to make her feel special. Like she holds a meaningful spot in this world to you."

Alex nodded.

"Try this time, Alex. Don't be 'fraid of failin'."

DICE

FINLEY QUAYE & BETH ORTON

"You got to be absolutely fuckin' kidding me." Knox glared.

"I'm going as Deadpool." Mateo grinned.

"You gone covert before. Think of it as that." Franklin handed him what looked like the carcass of a sports team mascot.

"Yeah, in a fuckin' ghillie suit. Not some mutant rabbit."

"You're an abominable."

"Ahwhatable? Why does he get to be Deadpool?"

"Because that was the only costume that come in gorilla size. You think I like this tie dye unicorn shit I'm wearin'? Go put it on. We late."

"The face—it's disturbing." Knox held the giant head out in front of him. "There's Ironman, you know? He wears a mask."

"So do Hannibal Lecter—go get yo' ass ready."

Stevie paraded across the living room, twirling like a Disney character come to life. She wore a white skintight skirt with accents of fringe and fur that ran across her chest and thighs. A bushy white tail flowed from the small of her back and she wore faux fur boots that came just below the knee.

"Anyone seen my hands?" Her words were muffled. "Furry? With claws?" Her face was hidden behind a sexy fox mask that covered her entire head like a helmet.

"Who are you supposed to be?" Mateo stood like a gunfighter, holding the large utility belt that ran around his waist.

"I dunno. A snow fox?" The large animatronic eyes of Stevie's costume blinked, adding an eerie cartoon realism to the outfit.

Gibby sulked by her ankles, confused and upset by the large creatures that had invaded his home.

"What's wrong?" She bent down. "You don't like momma's costume?" The dog twisted his head at her voice, recognizing the sound but unable to associate it with the frosty blue eyes and large snout that stared back at him.

"Alex is already there." Stevie said to Franklin. "His panel is at 3."

"We got time. We good."

"I'd like to walk around a bit—check it out. I've never been to one of these things. These outfits were such a great idea—hiding in plain sight!"

"You ever been to a comic con before?" Mateo asked Franklin.

"Fuck no."

⚑

"Oh. My. God." Celeste drove her elbow into Alex's ribs. "That's them." She pointed.

"Ouch..." Alex glared and rubbed his side. "How do you know?"

"It's gotta be. The giant one's Knox—the tubby unicorn's Franklin. And look at fuckin' Deadpool skipping behind the sexy snow fox."

Alex laughed. "Oh, wow... He's really getting into character, isn't he?"

"This is amazing." Celeste pulled her phone from her pocket. "Proof of purchase."

Stevie recognized Alex in the sea of people and began to hop, her bushy tail following as she rushed up to his side. She pressed her furry face against his lips, popping her knee as the character kissed him.

"That's oddly arousing." Celeste greeted her friend with a hug. "You're fuckin' hot." She stroked the fur on her cheek like a dog.

"Thanks." Stevie giggled, twisting a hip. "It's no worse than what I wear on stage."

"Oh—my god." Celeste announced once more as the rest of the group approached.

"Put your phone away—no pics." Franklin held up a hoof.

"Don't worry—this is a fuckin' video." Celeste continued rolling. "Knox—I thought you were gonna dress up?"

"What's up, Celeste?" Mateo's tone was smooth and insinuating, Deadpool's lifeless white eyes staring into her. "See anything you like?"

"I do. Quite a bit, actually—in a train wreck sort of way."

"Where's Troy?" Stevie asked.

"Busy in the studio. Jimmy put him to work—I assume that's your doing?"

Stevie tilted her head and flipped her paws, acting unbeknownst to the answer. Her large programmable ears twisted automatically as if they had picked up a howl in the distance.

"Hold on, hold on—I'm not done." Celeste continued to circle the group like a cinematographer. "Franklin, you're majestic—trotting amongst the rainbows. Maybe point your horn a little toward the light…"

"That's quite the outfit." Alex eyed Stevie.

"What? You like this?"

He smirked. "I like you."

"Alright, alright—" Franklin lost patience through the horse mask. "What we doin' here? When's your thing?"

"The panel is in 45 minutes—I need to be there a little early. Our booth, which Celeste should actually be working, is over that way." Alex pointed. "We can hang out there, or walk around a bit?"

"Let's see your booth!" Stevie pranced with excitement, the white leather fringe of her mini skirt swaying like beads to a hippie's bedroom. "This is so much fun—I feel like a spy!"

"'Ey, 'ey." Franklin slowed. "We blow our cover, this'll get bad real quick. Keep your masks on—no accidents. That goes for you two." The unicorn eyed his crew. "The pap know who you are—if they see you here, they know Stevie here. Let's do this right."

The group hadn't taken more than a dozen steps before they were approached to pose for pictures, Stevie's arctic figure turning heads. Franklin stood like Eeyore while Knox was dumbfounded, people-watching a crowd that he never knew existed. Stevie enjoyed the thrill of no one knowing who she was. Her fluidity in front of a lens combined with her ease of posing with strangers normally would have been enough to captivate the shots. However, Mateo was the standout star. He reveled in the moment, fully embracing his character and putting on a wise-ass show for anyone willing to engage with him.

"This is a circus." Alex stood back and shook his head.

Celeste's eyes were wild as she looked on. "This is, by far, the best idea you've ever had. I'm so glad they let me come today."

"That's crazy Pam was cool with it."

"I know—*ambassadorship from the movie*? I came up with that bullshit on the spot. I asked. She said yes."

"Probably just wanted you out of the office…"

"Right? Look at fuckin' Deadpool…"

A group of guys hooted as they walked passed. "Hey-ay! Alex Nopah—*The Final Book* dude!"

Alex acknowledged with a nod and subtle fist pump.

"Why are all my friends famous?"

He shrugged.

"Jesus, Mateo's hilarious—look at him! This is what's been lacking in his life. Guaranteed, he starts going to all these shows now."

"There's an idea, match-maker. You should hook him up with a cosplay chick."

"That's actually brilliant." Celeste mentally ran through her contact list. "Totally balance him out. They'd make lil' Yoda babies."

"You can see Knox is so lost."

"Oh, he's freaked out right now—a deep fear in the Yeti's eyes..."

"He's, like, disappointed in America. You can see him looking around, questioning everything he fought for."

"They'll have to read him the Constitution on the way home, really hammer home that Second Amendment part."

"I bet if we found the right costume for him, you know? A character he really believed in."

"No." Celeste shook her head. "This is permanently traumatizing."

Stevie moonwalked over to Celeste, tugging on her jacket with a claw. "Where's your outfit?"

"Well, you see, I'm a *real* cosplayer. It takes time and effort—sewing—building the costume yourself. I didn't just go out and buy one this morning."

"I didn't buy this—I borrowed it from a music video shoot..."

Celeste rolled her eyes. "Much better."

"I didn't know you were coming or I would have got you one too."

"I'm good." She shook her head. "I'm a respectable adult who should be working. Speaking of which, let's mosey."

Stevie motioned to Franklin who was quick to follow, Knox right at his side. Mateo was left behind, still hamming it up for the cameras.

"I'm sweatin' my fuckin' balls off in this thing," Knox complained.

Franklin's horn jiggled from his head with each step. "I can't see out this goddamn mask."

"Alex Nopah?!" More people pointed while walking the other way. "Hey, man—can we get a pic?"

Alex's smile turned to a cringe, but he graciously accepted. He stood in the middle and wrapped his arms around the shoulders of both teenagers, all three grinning into the cell phone.

"Thanks, man—it's so cool to meet you. We love your work."

"Thanks." Alex bowed his head.

"Just hope they don't ruin the movie." The other friend teased.

"I resent that…" Celeste leaned in.

"Ignore her." Alex smiled. "Come to the panel—room 302. We'll be talking about it."

"We're on our way now—line's probably forever!"

"I'm sure you'll get in…"

"I don't know, man—rumor is they're going to announce the cast today."

"Want me to spoil it for you?" Celeste continued to angle.

"She's kidding." Alex forcefully shook his head at her. "It was cool to meet you guys. I'll be at our booth later if you want to come say hi."

"Right on, man—thanks again for the pic!"

Alex nodded and began moving forward.

Stevie squealed. "My boyfriend's a celebrity!" She snatched his hand through her paw as they walked, holding on to him tight.

"Psh, whatever…" He squeezed back, looking over at her black nose and whiskers.

"This is so cool, Alex."

Rays of sunlight pierced Stevie's white sheer curtains. A gentle breeze entered through the open balcony door, causing them to billow and release like Alex's breath. Birds chirped by the bushes, the flutter of their wings buzzing as they darted around plumes of flowers. Stevie found the rhythm of trickling water, matching notes in her mind to the automatic sprinklers that turned on each morning. She rolled over, tugging the silk sheets over her head.

She lay quiet, studying the knots of Alex's spine; she made constellations out of the freckles of his skin. She fought the temptation to touch him, to wake him. To press herself against his warmth and match her breathing with his. Her mind pirouetted to the night before, recapturing his command and her pleasure. She relented to desire. She stretched, then in a single motion wrapped him in both arms and pulled herself close.

Alex flinched and groaned, consciousness returning with the pleasantries of Stevie's touch. He settled deeper into the pillow, playfully biting her arm.

"Ou!" Stevie tossed.

"Sleepy time."

"Wakey time…"

The two lay still, conscious and sensitive to the pull tugging within their chest. Each had longed for this moment. To find that person who deserved their love, and in turn, allowed themselves to become vulnerable in accepting it.

Alex rolled to his back and Stevie's cheek settled into his chest.

"I can read your thoughts." She whispered.

"Oh yeah?"

"Uh huh."

Alex didn't bite.

"You're thinking about arctic foxes."

Alex chuckled. "'Fraid not. I'm pretty sure you liked that a lot more than me."

284 SEAN WILLIAM HAMMOND

"What do they call 'em? Furries?"

"You just like being invisible. It's crazy to think that you walking around in a life size fox suit gives you less attention than walking around normally."

"That is bizarre to think about... I did like that. People not knowing."

"I know."

Stevie pushed herself deeper into Alex, allowing her weight to settle on top of him. "I'm going to say something that isn't very romantic..."

Alex raised an eyebrow, squinting as his eyes were still adjusting to the light. "Sounds about right."

"Shut up!" She pierced her fingernails into his skin. "I just... I appreciate you. Like, fully."

Silence fell upon them. Before Alex could accept the compliment, Stevie continued.

"What is this, a couple of weeks? A few months? But I've never been more happy. That's because of you."

Alex pulled her close, leaning forward to kiss the back of her head. "I appreciate you too. I mean it."

"Are you happy?"

"Terrified."

"What? Why?"

"Terrified I'll lose you."

"Alex..."

"I am very happy... That's because of you."

"It's nice to have someone on my side. And be on someone's side." Stevie's simple reflection resonated.

"That it is. The world's hard enough. I don't want to remember what it was like when we weren't looking out for each other."

"It's awful. I remember..."

"Speaking of which…" Alex took a breath before he finished his thought. "I think we should go get tacos. Later today. Together. In public."

"Today's the day?"

"I'm ready if you are. You're certain everything is set with Sylvia?"

"It's been ready for weeks. I… I didn't want to pressure you."

"You sure Shane's got it all worked out? This isn't going to blow up on you?"

"I'll call him first, give him the heads up, but yeah—we are all set on that end. He's been biting his tongue, trying not to push me to make it happen. They're all ready."

"Good."

"Are you sure you're ready? This is going to be unlike anything you've ever known… It's going to get bad, Alex. People can be awful."

"We got each other's backs, right?"

"I've always got your back. I won't tolerate it any other way."

"It will be nice to stop lying to my mom—Tita."

"I know it's been unfair—I've been unfair."

"You haven't been unfair. This is a big fuckin' deal. I just wanted to make sure I could live up to it. I'm all-in, Stevie. I'm trusting you."

"I know you are." She turned and faced him. "I don't take it lightly. I love you, Alex."

"I love you. Let's tell the world."

BUSINESS EMINEM

Hello, I am Mario Cordova, and this is the Stevie Pearl Minute. Breaking news late this afternoon about beloved pop star, Stevie Pearl. Photos obtained exclusively by TMI *shows Pearl getting into a vehicle owned by Alex Nopah—the same footloose and not-so-fancy-free artist known from Pearl's infamous house party late last summer. Our cameras followed the couple where they drove to Malibu. Seen walking along Leo Carrillo State Beach with Pearl's internet celebrity dog, Gibby, the three enjoyed an afternoon in the sun and surf.*

While no comment has been given by Pearl or her staff, images suggest that she has become quite close with Nopah. Seen here holding hands, the glances they exchange are clearly reserved for only the most special. Is Alex Nopah America's sweetheart's newest heart throb? Tag TMI *and let us know what you think. For instant, breaking news about Stevie Pearl and a recap of all her past relationships, visit* TMI *online.*

"What did Shane say?" Alex held his phone, notifications pouring in like a typhoon.

"Hook, line, and sinker. Lisa and Kismet think I'm signing with Apollo. She actually sent the focus group testing to sponsors as she was yelling at Shane."

"Wow…" Alex shook his head.

"It's unbelievable. I mean—perfect—couldn't have worked any better—but I'm still in disbelief that they'd actually sink that low."

"This is insane, Stevie…"

"Told you—oh, wait—Shane's calling again. Hang on." Stevie marched to the patio, pacing as she coordinated with Shane.

"Welcome to the big time." Franklin popped the leg to the recliner and jabbed at buttons on the remote. He pulled up *Sports Center* and then sipped iced tea. "Better just turn that thing off." He nodded at Alex. "Ain't nothin' you need on there. You already talked to your momma, right?"

"Yeah." Alex tossed his phone onto the coffee table and took a seat on the couch. "I called her before we went to the beach. Wanted her to hear it from me first."

"Good man."

"I've played this moment out over and over…"

"Ain't nothin' what you thought?"

"Nope."

"Can't prepare for this type of shit. It ain't normal. Stevie's been swimmin' with the sharks since she was a kid. She'll take care of you."

"You think this is all a good idea? The sting?"

"Don't matter what I think… But, I'll tell you this, I can't wait 'till she take the stage next week. Those fucks finally gettin' some."

"You trust Sylvia?"

"Nope. She pragmatic though. This shit's comin' out one way or another, she might as well make Cosmo look like the hero. She went from federal investigations to social justice warrior. Plus, she get to keep Stevie Pearl—and Stevie always bring the money."

"Ha!" Stevie scoffed, stomping back into the room. "Apollo's restructuring the deal! Just knocked a third off of their offer! Clockwork. Wonder when one of these geniuses will realize, *wait*

—she didn't sign with Kismet, she didn't sign with Apollo, and she purposefully just blew up her career? Maybe there's something else going on..."

"Sponsors dropping yet?" Alex asked.

"They scramblin'. That'll be Monday or Tuesday." Franklin continued to channel surf. "Stevie'll get a call Monday morning—Kismet will be groveling for her to come back, all panicked 'n shit when they realize there's no deal with Apollo. They won't know what the fuck's happenin'."

"Shane said that Sylvia cleared her Thursday. That's our day. They're turning it into a big event. Keeping it quiet now, invites will go out on Tuesday. We'll fly out Wednesday night."

"A big event?"

"Typical corporate thing—like when a new phone or operating system is released. Big stage presentation—the whole company and media are invited—live streamed."

"You know what you're going to say? How could you even begin?"

"I have an idea..." Stevie's eyes narrowed. "A few more public appearances to stir the pot—but no talking to the press. Please, no one."

"Yeah." Alex shrugged. "I'm on lockdown with you. I talked to Jim this morning—he couldn't be happier for us. He's basically cut me loose anyway now that they've started production—just have to answer my phone, keep up on emails."

"Everybody on standby." Franklin nodded. "I've canceled all staff for the week—paid vacation—they like that. Mateo and Knox got their crews—you two don't do none of that public shit unless we there to regulate. Pap's going crazy, ain't gonna take nothin' for a mob."

Alex looked dumbfounded. He was dropped into the middle of a war room without the slightest bit of credibility or experience to justify his presence. "What... what now?" He asked.

"We wait." Stevie plopped down next to him. "There's nothing better than silence—let everyone run away with their imagination."

The auditorium's lights dimmed. The large, curved screen that wrapped the length of the stage began to flicker. Generic stock music pumped through the speakers.

"Welcome to Cosmopolitan." A movie trailer voice actor set the introduction. "Ingenuity, creativity, inclusivity, and environmental consciousness set the corner stones of our corporation. The world is, Cosmopolitan."

The crowd hushed, conversation fading to whispers as attention turned toward the stage. A brief video played recapturing Cosmo's important quarterly releases before Sylvia emerged into view. She walked slow. The hyped introduction fell short, leaving three quarters of her walk to the podium in silence. The crowd began to clap out of courtesy, but she instantly silenced them with her hand. She pulled up to the microphone, resting her forearms on the podium and stared into the crowd.

"I'm sure you're all wondering why you are here. There are no tech innovations to unveil—purchase orders from manufacturing plants in China haven't leaked any confidential information. The lineup of our fourth quarter releases for movies and video games are set in stone—there will be no surprises there. However, today will go down in history. Today will be remembered as one of the most forward-thinking events to happen in Cosmo's legacy. I wish I could tell you that I'm proud of it… I wish I could tell you that today is about celebration…

"The news our corporation is about to deliver is not mine to give. But make no mistake, the managing partners of Cosmopolitan Global fully support the new direction in which our Music Group is taking. Please allow me to introduce..." Stevie Pearl's latest single began blaring, the screen behind Sylvia flashing with images of overflowing stadiums with hundreds of thousands of people. "...our guest of honor, Ms. Stevie Pearl."

The crowd was paralyzed with shock and suspense, then erupted into chaotic noise. No one expected the pop star at an industry insider event. No one had heard from the pop star since glimpses were caught of her with her new boyfriend.

When the lights had returned to the stage, Stevie was standing at the center. She hid behind no platform, she stood behind no podium. Her hands were clasped, she waited for the audience to subside, and she began to speak.

"You are a disgrace." The massive woofers from the stage audio boomed. "Makes me sick—I'm so disgusted, I can't even look at her... Choke and die on Geronimo's cock. Fuck you, fuck you, fuck you... These are just a few of the things that have been said to me since last Saturday.

"I have been in a relationship with Alex Nopah since the end of summer. My record label, Kismet, along with my legal team at Hodges and Rhode, threatened to ruin my career if I dated him. Cosmo Music Group conducted focus group testing, they weighed their financial options against my personal life—against the man I love. They decided that Alex Nopah was not profitable—not someone who should be associated with my image—simply because he's Native American. Because his family isn't wealthy. They risked your retirement. They threatened to tank stocks—they threatened media and economic panic so ferocious that people would jump out of buildings because their livelihoods would be destroyed... They threatened to slut shame me—to make me so dirty, so undesirable that no record label would touch me.

"Perhaps they were right. When their report circulated about my involvement with Alex, Apollo Records—the largest competitor to Kismet and rival of Cosmo—retracted their original offer with me. They wanted to restructure. Just by seeing me with Alex, Apollo dropped their offer by 23 percent. Since Saturday, 6 of my sponsors, including the largest cosmetics manufacturer in the world, canceled their contracts. Many cited *market instability* as their reason, one was brave enough to cancel over code of conduct issues.

"These companies are saying that me playing in the sand with my dog and boyfriend devalued their product. I say, only if their customers are racist... Which they're not. This is collusion. This is price fixing. This is insider trading. All of these groups worked together to devalue me—in turn, devaluing you. Their threats at the negotiating table turned into vindictive action, and a federal offense—they sold off their stock high on Monday morning, and have hammered me in the media each day since. It's estimated that $2.8 billion dollars have vanished in three days, the ripples not yet known. I'll be happy to see each one of them in court.

"The last few months have shown me sides of our industry that I didn't know existed. I now realize I have been used in ways that I didn't even know I was being used. I was naive, and I am so ashamed that I was complicit in it. I know what these people have done to Alex, but I don't know what they've done to the rest of you. It's kept me up at night imagining it...

"As new majority owner of Kismet Records, the culture within our label is going to be much different. As owner, I set the priorities. We will once again focus on the music—not the slender image of teenage girls that we can exploit. Artists who sign with us will be treated with respect—our support staff will be compensated fairly. Most importantly, every executive complicit in the racist coup to coerce me into re-signing is terminated.

"Behind me, up on the screen, is a copy of their termination letter. And... with a wink and nod..." Stevie did her best *Bewitched* nose twitch impression, "the emails are sent. Thank you all for bearing witness to my first act as Owner, President, and CEO of

Kismet Records. If one of those little messages pops up in your inbox, *have your personal belongings removed by the end of the day.*"

The image of the termination letter transitioned to screenshots of emails, documents, and correspondences that served as evidence of her entire mistreatment.

"Moreover, Cosmopolitan Global has concluded its internal investigation, and due to its findings, they are restructuring the Board of Directors of the Music Group. The actions I described by Kismet were approved and coordinated by several prominent figures. These individuals are no longer welcome to represent the distribution corporation in any capacity. Their votes and seats have been revoked, effective immediately.

"Further, in light of recent events, with new seats becoming available, and with my ownership of Kismet Records—Cosmo Global has nominated me to take a position on the Board of Directors within the Music Group. I graciously accept. I vow to use my vote, and my voice, to foster positive change throughout the internal workings across all of our labels and brands. I will advocate for reformation to be implemented throughout the entire industry. I will not squander this unprecedented opportunity."

Stevie relaxed and began to walk the stage.

"I was scared, you guys. A few months back I was miserable. The biggest reason is because I had no hope. I saw no way for things to change. Even me, with all of my fortune and success, I was unable to control my own fate. There is no way that I can equate my struggles to yours. I won't begin to act like I know what it's like to be you—but we do share hope. Optimism. The notion that tomorrow will be better than today… I am still scared. After all I've seen, I'm skeptical. After all I've experienced—after the way Cosmo has treated the people I care about the most… I still decided to move forward with them. Sylvia and I have formed a friendship, and I trust her. She has given me the hope that I can do something about this mess—I have been empowered. With some hard work and careful consideration, I too can empower the next generation of musicians.

"I want to extend my cautious gratitude to Cosmopolitan Global. They recognized a severe problem internally and have gone to great lengths to correct it. This has been painful for everyone, but seeing their commitment has given me faith. I thank them for this opportunity and, in part, trusting me with the future of our dynasty. There's no questioning the artistry that has come from within these walls—I pledge to honor the musicians before us and continue to innovate without sacrificing and exploiting those most susceptible. I want to express my appreciation to Ms. Sylvia Preston—she made this possible—she is the leadership that Cosmo Global deserves. Shane—you did it.

"One final thing before I go, I want to recognize the millions who have supported me and Alex. You often get overlooked in the media, your goodness silenced by the negativity. You are the majority—you are the decent—and I hear you. I see you. I feel you. The numbers are in our favor, and it's your strength that has afforded me this opportunity. Keep doing the right thing, and I'll continue to try as well. It's literally as simple as that…

"Thank you to my forever family at Cosmopolitan and Kismet —there's a core group of you who have never left my side. I started with you, and I will end with you. I look forward to you stopping by my new office at the Kismet headquarters on Monday! I love you Mom and Dad—Joey. I love you, Alex." And Stevie waved goodbye as she exited the stage.

LOVER GIRL
RYAN BINGHAM

"Let's get out of this town. Drive out of the city, away from the crowds." Alex paced. "You and me, right now."

"You're serious?"

"Why not? The Jeep's parked out front. We'll sneak you out, bring Gibby."

"Where would we go?"

"I dunno… We've been talking about going for a ride forever, getting the tires dirty. Let's do it! We'll go east. I'll show you where I'm from."

Stevie bit her lip. "Franklin would kill me."

"He's been working as much as you have—I'm sure he's sick of us. Plus, it's Saturday, let him have a day off—he'll never even know we're gone."

"Just like that—we just leave?"

Alex shrugged. "Fuck these people. It's a beautiful day—the desert will be gorgeous this afternoon. No cameras, no mobs—just you and me and a dirt road."

"You're insane… I can't just…" Stevie caught herself.

"Can't just what?" Alex cocked an eye. "You crushed the evil empire, Stevie—you won. Enjoy it! That little smirk tells me you're down. Are you down?! Let's do this—celebrate!"

Stevie's smile morphed into a grin. "Okay, then." She nodded.

"Really?!"

"Why not? Well, maybe I should check with the boss first—oh wait! I am the boss!"

"Fuck yeah you are!"

"I don't need to get permission to go for a drive with my boyfriend." She justified aloud. "I don't need permission for anything." She said once more. "Yeah… Let's do it. Let's go!"

Alex moved quick before she could change her mind. He stumbled into his boots while throwing an arm through a pearl snap shirt. "Good shoes." He directed. "Hiking boots if you've got 'em."

Stevie fed off his energy and followed, rushing around the bedroom and pulling at anything she thought she might need for their adventure.

"Don't forget something warm—it gets cold fast."

"Will you grab Gibby's leash? Get his water bowl too. How long are we going to be gone—should we bring food?"

"I'll head downstairs and see what you've got—snacks are always good."

"Drinks. I've got a cooler somewhere."

"I'll figure it out. Hurry your ass up—let's go, let's go!"

"Hey now." Stevie twisted her head.

Alex was already out of the door. His heels skipped across the treads as he careened down the stairs. Gibby followed, darting with excitement while playfully nipping at his fingers. Alex rummaged through the kitchen cabinets, filling his arms with whatever looked good. He then leaned into the fridge and pulled out a couple cans of soda and water. "We've got stores…" He muttered, finding the task to be a waste of valuable time.

Alex pushed the button to the garage door and then began loading the Jeep. He moved junk that had cluttered the backseat and examined the footwell. He placed Gibby's items up front and then mentally ran through a checklist.

Stevie skipped across the driveway, a beach bag swaying from her hand with each step. "Ready yet?" She teased.

"Back there—whaddya think?" Alex pointed. "Lay down on the floor, I'll cover you with a blanket. Once no one's following us, you hop up front. They'll give up if they think it's just me— especially if I'm going east."

"Perfect. I've trained you well."

"*Human Trafficking: All You Need To Know* by Stevie Pearl."

"Don't forget my other classics—*Drunk In Fiji: A Memoir*, *How To Fire Your Agent*, and *Cold Case: Paparazzo*."

"Yeah, but I was kidding."

"Me too… maybe."

"What are we forgetting?"

"I think we'll be fine—you could restart civilization with this Jeep. We're only going to be gone for the afternoon, right?"

"Sure? Let's go then! Quit your bitchin' and crawl in there."

She slapped him in the chest with her bag and then jumped up into the Jeep. Stevie's body twisted and contorted as she wiggled down onto the floorboards. "This hump isn't very comfortable."

"Not what you said last night."

"Shut up…"

"Will a pillow help? A blanket on the bottom for padding?"

"No… Help Gibby up. I'll be fine."

"You sure? Now's the time."

Stevie shook her head.

Alex lifted the dog into the backseat. Gibby's wag swaying his entire body as he leaned down and licked Stevie's face.

"Ugh—stop it!" She squirmed to pushed him back, then sunk her nails into his fur to calm him.

"Awe… You're adorable." Alex jested.

Stevie looked up, squished into position. She began to laugh.

"Just keep the blanket on until we get through the security gate."

"Not my first rodeo."

Alex whipped the blanket out into the air, and then smothered her with it. He teased and tickled, Gibby barking as Stevie squealed. He finally released and then tussled the dog's neck, Gibby nosing him and panting from all of the excitement.

Alex hopped into the front seat and fired the Jeep. He reached back and placed his hand on Stevie's hip, giving a reassuring squeeze. He then shifted the vehicle into gear and they began rolling.

Stevie crunched on tortilla chips. She had a ball cap on backwards and wore a designer pair of aviators. Her tank top was speckled with crumbs and she grinned as she tried to annoy Alex with embarrassing questions.

"I'm just saying, 17 is a late bloomer."

"Not all of us were coked-out child stars!"

"I never did drugs. Even still, how was there not a game of Spin The Bottle that you could be a part of?"

"I thought you meant a *real kiss*—not some contrived teenage bullshit."

"Seven Minutes in Heaven? That shit was real. Celeste and I played all the time."

"You made out with Celeste in a closet?"

"No. I mean, like, all of our friends."

"Guess I didn't go to the cool parties."

"So, who was she? The *real* first kiss?"

"You're such a weirdo. Why would you want to know that?"

"You don't want to know mine?"

"Well, I guess there's a morbid part of me that's curious—and because I take an overall interest in you—but no, not really."

"Let me tell you anyway. It was a crisp autumn night, Halloween was just around the corner..."

"Fuck me."

Stevie cackled. "I think it's cute. Are you jealous?"

"Look—I know you're teasing, and I'm totally cool with it. We can talk about this stuff if you really want to... but I get insecure. I just... I don't compare to the other guys you've dated."

Stevie's face turned a bit more serious. "What do you mean? Which guys?"

"Well, all of your relationships are pretty public."

"You've been reading up? You get their side of the story but you don't want to hear mine?"

"That's not what I meant."

The Jeep hummed down the highway. The stereo came into focus as they both sat silent.

"I listened to a couple of chapters from that douche bag's book—the DJ." Alex admitted. "I saw it in the bookstore when we were in New York the first time, it just ate at me. From the moment I read the synopsis, I fuckin' hated him... Once I got into it, I knew it was wrong and I stopped listening."

Stevie sat quiet. "...Wish you'd just talk to me."

"I know... I stopped. I just... I get worried that I'm not doing this right. Being the guy who's supposed to be dating Stevie Pearl."

"None of those relationships worked, Alex. Don't be those guys. I never want to date those guys again."

Alex nodded. "I know. I'm sorry."

"There aren't books about your relationships..." She eased. "That's why I asked about your first kiss. I'm curious about you too—the girls you've liked… so maybe I could be more like them?"

Alex looked over and shook his head. "No. Don't be those girls —I like you just how you are."

"Understand now?" She grabbed his hand. "You're perfect."

Alex let the words settle. "Thank you."

"Pfft." Stevie sputtered. "I give you a, "you're perfect" and you give me "*thank you*"?" She teased.

Alex chuckled. "Should I have said, 'I know'?"

She grinned from the seat next to him. "Oh, your tender ego… such a house of cards."

"That shit's true, and I ask you kindly not to knock it over."

"Never."

"…I hate how those guys treated you, Stevie. God… it just… it wasn't right."

"No, it wasn't… but I'm glad they're assholes or I wouldn't be here with you."

"You keep sayin' nice things like that, I might start believing you."

"Your turn." She sat back in the seat. "I'm not fishing, I'm demanding—say something nice about me."

Alex laughed and shook his head. "You have no idea how every impulse inside of my body is screaming to be sarcastic right now —but I won't. That's old, shitty, The World Sucks Alex."

"The world doesn't suck anymore?"

"No it doesn't."

"Why's that?"

"I have a best friend, and I'm in love with her."

Stevie leaned across the center console and brushed her lips against his ear. "Well done." She whispered before biting his lobe.

"It's so beautiful…" Stevie huffed with a hand on her hip. She took a moment and sucked from a water bottle. "I've never seen an arch in real life. Just pictures."

"Never?" Alex contorted a shoulder and pulled off his backpack. "This one's kinda scraggly. There's way better ones."

"How'd you ever find it?"

"My grandpa started bringing me around here when I was a kid. These are called the Turtle Mountains."

Gibby pressed by Alex's legs, navigating the loose shale like a mountain goat. The dog was panting but a wild had returned to his eyes, his first true experience of fresh air and adventure.

Alex pulled a water dish from his pack and tossed it to Stevie.

"Thirsty?" She gained the dog's attention, pouring water into the bowl. "Drink?" Gibby swallowed the drool that had formed around his lips and began lapping from the bowl.

"It's like no one's been here in the history of the world. I've never been somewhere so remote."

"Lots of people have been here." Alex smiled. "We roamed this desert for thousands of years."

"I forget about that…"

"We all do. Half the rez has never even been out here."

Stevie stood quiet.

"It's okay. You can talk about it. Ask me questions."

"I don't know… I don't ever think about it, but then when I do, I feel ashamed for not thinking about it."

"You're not born knowing this stuff—it's not your heritage, why would you know?"

"I dunno… There's Google—I feel like I should have looked it up or something. Inform myself."

"You're not going to find much on there. A few archeologists or history professors that write a paper—that's not who we are… were."

"Where is it? The reservation?"

"That way." Alex pointed to the east. "Not far. The other side of the river."

"It's so quiet." Stevie looked around. "I've never heard anything like it."

"There's no way to describe it. You can hear a hawk flap its wings from a 1,000 yards away."

"It's… weird. Not scary, or eerie, but… unsettling. I've never experienced silence like it."

"Right?" Alex grinned. "I love it."

"Was it bad?" Stevie mustered. "White people? Settlers?"

"There it is." Alex chuckled. "It wasn't fuckin' good… We weren't a warrior people—not that cowboys and Indians shit you see on TV. We were peaceful. We rarely ever fought with other tribes—basically because it's a hard life out here. You're focused on survival. We were overpowered in an instant—all rounded up, put on reservations. That's when the bad shit really started to happen. Prisoners—our only crime was existing. We got fucked at every opportunity. Still are."

"I'm sorry." Stevie shook her head.

"Hey—it's not your fault. You've brought more awareness to my people in 5 days than we've had in 50 years."

"Chemehuevi."

"There you go! You got it now."

"I'd like to learn more…" Stevie's words were soft and shy. "If you ever want to teach me."

"There'll be plenty of time for that." Alex picked up his backpack. "Let's loop back. We'll be getting home late as it is."

Stevie took Alex's hand. He rooted himself into the dirt offering support as she hopped down from a rock. "Thank you, Mr. Nopah."

"Certainly, Ms. Pearl."

"Going down is going to be a lot easier."

"Careful. That's when you'll twist an ankle."

"I should come out here and climb mountains to get into tour shape—way better than the treadmill!"

"I'll bring you any time you want."

The two chatted the rest of the way back to the Jeep. Gibby wore himself out, chasing lizards and sniffing every rock along his path.

"Woah." Alex motioned, cutting his stride as they rounded the trailhead.

Stevie bumped into the back of him. He used his forearm to brace her. "What is it?"

"Shh." His eyes were trained on his Jeep. "There's another truck."

"So?"

Alex glared at her voice and then watched intently, looking for signs of life. He could hear chatter but couldn't make out the words. "Get Gibby on the leash." He directed.

Stevie unhooked the leash from Alex's backpack and called the dog softly. She clipped his collar and the dog shook his coat to straighten it, the ringing jingle of the metal contrasting against the barren landscape. The voices stopped and two men stepped into sight. Alex knew they were made and he began walking toward the vehicles.

The men were rough. One wore a green ball cap. He had a plaid sleeveless shirt with stained jeans and boots. The other wore a wife beater and gym shorts, he had white socks pulled to his knees and skate shoes. The taller of two, the one with the green hat, was leaned up against the tailgate of his truck. His arm was dangling into the bed. The other man had his hands behind his back. They maintained, allowing Alex and Stevie to get closer.

"Howdy." Alex offered.

"Well, hello there." The ball cap answered. "Lovely evenin' for a hike."

"Yes, it is." Alex slowed his steps. He noticed the rear passenger window of his Jeep had been smashed, glass sparkling across the sand.

"You two are quite aways from home."

The wife beater giggled at his partner's words, his teeth missing and rotten.

"Petey, get a load of that..." Ball cap whistled. "Fuckin' Sittin' Bull's got a nice piece of ass."

"Alex—your Jeep?" Stevie noticed the glass.

"Oh, that?" The man in the ball cap raised a shotgun from the back of the pickup truck. The wife beater flashed a handgun, pointing it sideways at Alex. "Yeah, looks like ya had little accident."

Alex pushed himself ahead of Stevie, using his body as a shield. The methhead cackled wildly.

"Ain't that cute?" The ball cap moved toward them with the shotgun planted in his shoulder.

Gibby began to growl, his hackles standing straight.

"Scalp 'em, Reggie!"

A blast shook the ether. The force of the buckshot yanked the leash out of Stevie's hand and the dog yelped, Gibby's body twisting to the dirt with a thud.

Alex charged, met with the stock across his face.

SAVE ME
THE LOVEMAKERS

Sound began to resonate. Frequencies formed shapes within Alex's mind. He swallowed hard, his consciousness returning to a throbbing skull. He reached to touch the pain but couldn't. He reset and tried once more. He felt his muscles straining, but his arms were stuck. They felt pinned behind his back.

Alex swallowed once more, allowing slits of light to enter his eyes. His left eye began to sting, flooded with a dark, syrupy fluid. He blinked several times, clearing the blood from his vision. Shapes morphed into objects, the moonlight casting shadows. It took him a moment, but he recognized that he was face to face with the wheel well of a pickup truck. The bed was rusted, beaten. Dents and dings running as far as he could see.

Alex rolled to his back, grimacing as his weight fell onto his wrists. He blinked several more times and took a breath. Stars, clear as signal fires, consumed the sky above him.

"Oh, shit!" He heard a voice. "Go getchya some sloppy seconds. I'm wore the fuck out."

Alex continued to listen. The sound of whimpering acting as smelling salt.

A jolt of energy surged through him. His eyes became wide and his mind crystal clear. He remembered chucks of flesh and fur flying through the air. He remembered a methhead pointing a gun a Stevie. He remembered a redneck slamming the butt of a shotgun into his face.

Alex leaned forward, poking his head above the side of the truck. He captured the image within his mind and quickly hid himself. His breath hastened and he closed his eyes, crystalizing what he had saw. There was an old tow behind camper trailer, dull lights glowing from the inside. Steps lead to a screen door, about two thirds of the way back. Crushed aluminum cans littered the gravel, their crinkled reflection acting as luminaries in the moonlight. He clenched his jaw and listened once more.

"What makes you think I want her now? After you and that fuckin' wagon burner?"

The screen door slammed. Alex heard the flick of a lighter, its striker grinding against the spindle several times before a long inhale.

"Reggie, I dunno man…"

"What the fuck, Pete?" The screen door slammed once more. Hollow footsteps stomped within the trailer. "I fucked her, now you fuck her! That way I know we in this together."

Alex began twisting his wrists, trying to wiggle free.

"Jesus—okay… okay. Put the gun down, man… Let me have another hit first."

"You fuckin' smoke more of that shit than you bake!"

"It's been a stressful day, Reggie! I wasn't plannin' on rapin' and killin' no one today."

"Boo-fuckin'-hoo. Goldie Locks fall in your lap and you ain't takin' a piece?"

Alex created some space, the duct tape stretching and loosening under his force.

"Just let me smoke. Get my head straight. She any good?"

"She real good."

Alex forced his hand free. He ripped the tape from his wrists and then stretched, trying to realign his joints. He took a couple of breaths, rubbing his hands while scanning the bed of the truck. The methheads had stolen all of the gear from his Jeep and piled it in the back with him. Alex clenched his eyes and said a prayer. He then reached for his backpack. Without making a sound, he unzipped the top pouch.

He slid his hand into the bag, his fingers greeted by kydex and a cold steel rail. He reached a little further, the polymer handgrip feeling like a handshake from God himself. He pulled the 9mm from the bag and press checked the gun. Good to go. He laid back, his hair matted with blood as he clutched the Sig close to his chest. He didn't breathe, listening intently to the men inside of the camper.

"That's enough!" He heard a growl. "We're already short this drop."

Alex clenched his jaw. In a single motion he moved to his feet and climbed over the side the truck. He used the tire as a step to soften his landing and then crouched, listening once more.

"This shit's... fuck—it's our best batch yet."

"Toss me 'nother beer."

Alex's steps were short and smooth, weaving past the cans and gliding over the gravel like a ghost. He pressed his back against the side of the trailer. His eyes were wide and focused, his ears tuned to the movement inside.

"None left—the rest's out in the cooler."

"You drank all the fuckin' beer?"

"There was two. I had one, you had one. There's another case in the truck. What? You wanna watch?"

Alex rose to his tip toes, angling to look through a window of the trailer. The skinny one in the wife beater stood from the table. He began rubbing his dick through his gym shorts. The large man in the green ball cap laughed, stroking the sawed-off barrel between his thumb and index finger.

"Won't be much to see. Your tiny little pecker'll pump three times, then splat."

"Shit..." The wife beater continued to prepare himself. "Get outta here, man—go get the beers." He shoved past the green ball cap, forcing himself forward through the camper.

"Get yo' ass in there." The man in the ball cap hooted as he kicked at him with his boot. He then turned and pushed himself through the screen door.

Alex immediately ripped the trigger, sending two rounds tearing in and out of the man's chest. His neck jolted and the hat fell from his head as he staggered and turned. The shotgun followed, kicking with a flare of powder that blew from the end. The man crumpled, falling down the steps and landing face down in the gravel. He tried to squirm and gasped for air. Alex put another round in the back of his head before rushing through the screen door.

The man in the wife beater scrambled, trapped in the small hallway. Stevie screamed in terror. Without hesitation, Alex lit him up. Round after round methodically pumped through flesh and bone, the green dot of the front sight fixed upon divine retribution.

Alex's ears rang as gun smoke swirled throughout the kitchen, a deafening silence once again consuming the desert. He trembled, pushing blood from his swollen eye. Staggering, he pressed his weight against a folding table, sending beakers and cook pots crashing to the floor. He then pushed himself forward, lunging over the man he had just killed and slipping in leaking blood as he struggled down the hall.

"Stevie?!" He shouted. "Stevie?"

Wailing poured from the bedroom.

"Stevie?" Alex forced the door open.

There she was, cowered in a ball in the corner. Beaten. Bloodied. Her clothes torn from her.

"Stevie!" Alex pushed once more and then slumped to the floor next to her. Her hands were shaking, her eyes hidden behind blonde hair. "Stevie." He held her. "It's okay. It's me. It's Alex."

She jerked away, fighting him as he repeated her name. She struggled to make sense of the face, the damage to his socket swollen and disfiguring. She found the shape of his jaw and a tone in his voice that felt familiar. Her arms slowed, her mind working to connect the pieces.

"It's okay—you're safe." He heaved. "I got 'em. It's all over. You're safe now."

Stevie's mind battled to focus, her comprehension glitching. She reached for his mangled brow, failing to find words. Her eyes then locked on to Alex's shirt. He was sopping wet. She saw that he struggled to breathe.

Alex continued to stare into her. His hands holding her tight. "You're okay now, Stevie."

"Alex…" She whispered.

"Yes—yes, it's me. You're okay." He nodded. "It's Alex. You're safe now."

"But—your chest?"

Alex looked down, finally understanding why it felt like the wind had been knocked out of him. He bit his lip and then shook his head. "Don't worry about that."

"Alex…" Stevie repeated his name, the habitual consonance solidifying his presence. "Alex, you need help." Her tone cleared.

"It's okay." He nodded. "You're okay now."

"No. I don't think so." She became frantic. "You need help— right now! Where's my phone?!" Stevie pushed herself to her feet, her bare toes smeared in his blood. She rushed out of the room, jumping over a riddled corpse that blocked the path of the hallway. She pushed bottles and cans on the counter, searching the camper for communication.

"Stevie—" Alex called.

"Hang on!"

"Come here—now!"

She hesitated, her eyes scanning each object around her. She could hear Alex cough.

"There's no cell service." Alex labored. "It doesn't matter..."

She ran back to him, crouching by his side. "We got to get you help."

"They got me too, huh?" He gave an uneasy smile. The gravity of his wound becoming more apparent by the second.

"You'll be okay—you'll be okay." Stevie trembled.

Alex shook his head. "Listen, okay? In the back of the truck. My backpack. There's a GPS with an SOS button. Go get the whole bag."

Stevie looked confused. Her entire being in distress.

"Back of the truck, Stevie." He grabbed her by the arm. "My backpack. Go."

She nodded.

She wasn't gone more than a minute, but minutes were more than Alex had. He understood that Stevie would soon be alone, lost somewhere in the desert and surrounded by the remains of unimaginable evil. Driving aimlessly in a beat-up old truck across dirt roads wasn't going to save him, and more importantly it wasn't going to save her. Without supplies—a clue of where she was or where to go—he knew buzzards would be the only thing to find her.

"Good. Sit with me." He directed.

"My god, Alex... come here." She propped his arm over her shoulder and held him up. His head bobbled and rested against her chest.

Alex fought for consciousness, rifling through his bag with one hand. His chest gurgled, his lung collapsing from the stray buckshot that sprayed wide and landed in the most unfortunate spot. He found the device and held it up.

"Knew I bought this thing for a reason." He made light while his bloody thumb held the power button.

"Let's drive—I'll take you back to town."

Alex shook his head. "No. Help's comin', Stevie. You wait right here with me. Promise? Promise you won't leave me." He activated the SOS function on the GPS, sending their coordinates to the nearest dispatch.

"How long?" Stevie pressed.

"Not long," Alex lied. "Help's comin' now. Don't you leave me until they get here."

"What can I do? I got to do something."

"Just wait with me... Just wait right here with me." He used his foot to kick at the little bedroom door until it closed, shielding her from the sight of the vacant stare of the toothless man that was missing the back of his head. He then looked up and clutched her hand.

Helpless tears dribbled down Stevie's cheeks. "Alex..." She squeezed back.

Hold Me (Alt. Version)
Zoli Band

The makeup around Celeste's eyes was smeared. Her breath sputtered as she held Stevie's hand.

The service for Alex was held in a tiny funeral home in Parker. Weeks had passed since the incident. The bruises on Stevie's face were concealed with toner, though the yellow discoloration that lashed her arms and shoulders were too much for the black dress to cover. She wore large black sunglasses to hide her eyes and a black hat that covered the patches where the hair had been ripped from her head. She sat motionless through the entire ceremony, except for squeezing Celeste's hand. She squeezed just as she had squeezed Alex's hand. The same way she held him as he took his last breath. The way she continued holding him through 'till dawn, when help finally arrived.

Later that day, in the hospital, Stevie was finally able to meet Alex's mother. His brother stood in the doorway, unable to hear about how much she loved him. How he had saved her life.

Today she sat in the pews next to them. Tita was there. Not a single joke fell from her lips. The old woman was broken with grief, crumbling when Charlie got up and spoke.

The room was filled with family and friends. People Alex knew from childhood, a few of his closest co-workers and friends he had made while creating art. Outside, lined up and down the street, the entire town was in attendance—the world for that matter. They carried signs, held candles, and placed flowers at the community center where his mother worked.

Troy stood in the back, his arm around Joey with Ben and Kristen at their side. They had only met Alex once. Stevie's Mom and Dad visited L.A. prior to the Cosmo announcement. Stevie ambushed Alex with their surprise arrival. She had already given Alex her heart, but she was looking for her father's approval. Alex handled it in stride. He met Benjamin with his eye and hand. He showed her father respect, and demonstrated an earnest effort in getting to know them both. Kristen gushed. She adored Alex without question. "Not what I imagined..." Her father finally said before they left. "You love him?" She nodded. "Good. Wouldn't be fair if you didn't—he's gonna marry you."

The service ended and people began moving around the room. Franklin stood close to Stevie, Celeste hanging on to his suit coat. Mateo and Knox worked the doors, their teams sprinkled around the exterior of the facility.

"Excuse me." A man approached. "Celeste?"

She looked up.

"I thought I recognized you. It's Sean. We met back at—"

"I know who you are..." Celeste extended her hand. "Fuckin' sucks, man."

Sean accepted and nodded.

"Stevie—this is Alex's only friend other than us..." She made the introduction. "He's the douchebag that wrote all that *Final Book* garbage. Him and Alex worked together forever."

Stevie leaned in for a brief hug. "I remember you... we've actually met before."

"Yes, we did." Sean smirked. "Hardly recognize you without your fox mask."

"You knew it was me?"

Sean nodded. "Alex and I talked a lot… I'm more of a Joe's Pizza guy. Bleecker Street is okay, but…"

"Fuck you." Celeste scowled. "The Nonna Maria is the best."

Stevie smiled. "That was a good night… I miss him, Sean."

"I do too… There's no words… You know, there's a scene that always tore Alex up—he hated drawing it for me. There's a dog in the book, Argo, and he gets put through some real soul-crushing shit. It's the only time Alex got truly philosophical—condemning me for even writing such heartache… putting something like that out into the world. Makes me think about Gibby—"

Stevie's nose twitched and her lip quivered.

"I'm sorry…" Sean stopped himself and rubbed the back of his head. "…I've got a ton of his work. Piles of the stuff. I was going to give it to Kadence, but I think you should look through it."

"Yeah?" Stevie mustered. "I'd like that."

"There's no rush. I'll keep it safe—whenever."

Stevie nodded.

Sean turned to step away but stopped himself. He looked back and met her eyes past his brow.

"Stevie—I have some other things you may like to have… want to keep? One day—even years from now—just let me know… It might give you a little idea where his head was at. How much you meant to him."

Stevie remained quiet. She shook her head. "…I…"

"He was never happier. *You*…" Sean cleared his throat and nodded, unable to finish his thought. He looked over toward Kadence and Tita. "I'm going to do all I can for his family—don't know what that means right now, but I'm in it for the long haul. He'd do the same for me…" He then brought his attention back toward her. "I'm sure we'll see each other again."

Stevie nodded. "I'm sure we will."

"Celeste—I'll see you at the premiere?"

"We'll save you a seat." Stevie answered before her friend could reply. "Thank you, Sean. It's going to take me a little while, but I will find you."

Sean nodded.

Stevie forced a smile and then broke away from the group. She moved across the room, scanning faces as she walked. A silhouette stood in the window that broke her stride. He was standing back to, looking out into the crowd who had gathered to offer their support. His hip cocked with the same cant, his hair curled in the same way. Stevie closed her eyes and let out a breath of air. She walked over and placed her hand on Charlie's shoulder.

"You look like him. Standing here."

"Always thought I was more handsome…"

"Impossible."

"That sure is a lot of people."

Stevie bit the inside of her cheek. "I can't do it. Not yet…"

Charlie put his arm around her.

"You takin' Tita home?" She looked up at him.

"Probably should. Mom's gonna stay—she's got more stuff to take care of. I keep tellin' her it don't matter—someone'll figure it out. She just has to keep busy."

"Mind if I come with you?"

"Back to the house?"

Stevie nodded.

"Uh? It's okay with me, but it's kinda wrecked…"

"I don't care." She plead. Her words were soft and hopeless. "I want to see his room."

Charlie looked down and nodded. "Okay… Let me take care of a few things, wrangle Tita. We'll get outta here."

"Thank you."

Stevie coordinated with Celeste and her family, she promised to meet them back in Havasu later that evening. Franklin sent his men ahead to patrol the property. He then took Knox and Mateo in the SUV and they followed behind the old Bronco, its windows still stained with crusted water spots. Tita rode up front, Stevie bouncing down the dirt road on the bench seat in the back. She lost herself in the distance, staring at the peaks of desert mountains.

A cloud of dust blew across the barn, the vehicles pulling next to the trailer. Stevie got out, studying the old ironwood where Alex parked his bike. She imagined him as a child, pushing Tonka trucks and skinning his knee on the gravel. Charlie getting mad at him for not doing chores.

"C'mon in." Charlie said, walking up the steps. "We've been spread a little thin…" He qualified. "Distracted."

Stevie waited for Tita. The old woman shuffled along, taking the steps one by one. "My husband built this place." She eyed Stevie, taking a break to rest. "Alex's grandfather put this thing together from nothin."

"He told me a few stories about him…" Stevie forced her words. "He showed me photos."

Tita licked her gums, studying Stevie long and deep. "He was a good man. Veteran. Hard worker… We'd get into it time to time, but we loved each other. He loved his daughter—always did right by the boys… But I don't miss him."

Stevie tilted her head.

"No sense in that. Selfish. He did what he's meant to do in this world—ain't fair for me to ask any more of him." Tita climbed the rest of the steps. "Missin' somebody only makes yourself feel better by feelin' worse. You comin'?" She held the door.

Stevie's legs trembled up the steps. She held onto the doorway while looking into the living room. The coffee table, the side stands, the back of the couch—every flat surface within the room was filled with cards, flowers, and baskets of well wishes.

Tita scuffed toward her chair. "Shut the door." She directed, using the armrest to ease herself down. "Goddamn feet." She kicked off her shoes. "Get in here. Now, that don't mean I forgot him. That don't mean I don't think 'bout him. But holdin' on to that feelin'—that he's missin' out—that you're missin' out. That'll tear you up, and tear you down… He don't want that for you." Tita reached for the television remote.

"Come on in." Charlie returned from the kitchen. "There ain't much room in here." He gestured at all of the well wishes. "You're just gonna have to move stuff. Everyone's been real nice. Got more goddamn apples than I know what to do with…"

"Feed 'em to the horses." Tita forced the power button, pushing it harder to make the TV turn on faster.

Stevie removed her sunglasses. The remnants of a black eye became more visible. "A lot of people care…" She continued to look around the room.

"It's crazy." Charlie shook his head. "We've been donating most of it. Don't know what else to do… C'mon. I'll give you the tour."

Stevie followed Charlie into the kitchen. More baskets and cards were piled on top of each other. The counter was filled with casserole dishes and Tupperware. Friends and neighbors providing meals.

"Well, this is it!" He laughed. "The tour's over. You probably saw the barn when we pulled up." Charlie pointed out the back window. "Down the hall is mom, Tita, and Alex—the bathroom." He began to walk. "I'll show ya."

Stevie followed.

Charlie turned left into the first bedroom. "Alex and I shared this room growin' up." He stood in the center, looking around. Stevie was unable to cross the threshold.

"I fixed up a spot and moved out to the barn when I started partyin'. Figured I'm out there all the time anyway... He basically lived in here. Drawin'." Charlie leaned down, fingering a pencil at the desk. "We kept it the same when he moved to the city. I mean, he was still out here all the time anyway. Helpin' me with the cattle and whatnot."

"May I?"

"Yeah—yes! Please."

Charlie watched as Stevie moved forward into the room, absorbing the posters on the wall. She studied the childhood trinkets and keepsakes that he was unable to part with. She then rounded the room, seeing ghosts of a young man growing up. Spending hours at his desk, mastering his voice and soul. Her eyes welled and she steadied herself at the edge of his bed.

Charlie sniffed at a runny nose and turned his back. He swallowed hard.

"Goddamn, Stevie..." He shook his head, unable to face her. He wiped his eyes with his sleeve. "Take all the time ya need." He walked quick, shutting the door behind him.

Stevie lowered herself. She sat hollow on the end of the bed, her eyes pinned on an old pair of boots. Her gaze shifted across the room once more, her longing and broken heart finding his pillow.

She reached for the corner and pulled it close, the faded fabric draped across her lap. She held the memory of his eyes looking up at her, the fearful smile as he used remaining life to clench her hand. She then wrapped the old matted pillow in her arms, buried her face and began to sob.

Stevie fell to her side. A shoe dropped from her foot as she curled into a ball, soaking her tears into Alex's childhood blanket.

WILDEST DREAMS (REPRISE)
TAYLOR SWIFT

The producer cut the feed. The crew stood paralyzed, onlooking with tissues in their hand. Stevie undid the mic pinned to her dress.

"May I?" Sarah stood, opening her arms.

Stevie obliged and gave her a hug.

"Okay people." The producer clapped. "Let's wrap this up. Don't want to wear out our welcome."

The bright lights for the cameras shut down. Cables began to coil.

Sarah stepped back, holding Stevie by the wrist with sympathy in her eyes. "I think you did well…"

"I've had some time to think about it." Stevie withdrew.

"Your recovery. I think it's going to be helpful for a lot of women."

"Every story's different." Stevie dismissed. "At least they know they're not alone."

"All the new treatment facilities… shelters. The awareness."

"It's just support—survival to get through the day. None of it will heal their heart."

Sarah nodded. "Well, if there's anything I can do…"

Stevie paused and thought for a moment. "Sure. Share other stories. If I weren't famous, no one would care. Just some Native American and a nameless victim. Statistics. That's wrong."

"You're right. Maybe we can start a series? We'll do the journalism and you can host."

Stevie scoffed and shook her head. "Thanks for the interview..." And began to walk.

Sarah frowned. "What? I didn't mean anything by it..."

Stevie turned and returned a glare fit for the gallows.

"I don't want to relive this over and over again each episode. *You didn't hear a single word I said tonight*. You nodded your head. You asked the right questions. You handed me a tissue when I needed it... I'm not okay, Sarah—*fuck you for asking me to do a show right now!*"

Sarah stood quiet.

"The whole point of doing this live was to get it over with. One and done. *I had to say something because of who I am*. I didn't *want* to say something."

"Okay." Franklin stepped in. "Interview over."

"God damnit!" Stevie clenched her fists. "I'm not the poster child for rape! Alex gets murdered and she's workin' me for deals to profit off it!"

"Let's go." Franklin guided. "Let 'em clean up. We take a walk on the beach."

Stevie snarled at Sarah as she picked up her phone from the end table. "I want Knox fuckin' *watchin' 'em*. Don't let these people out of your sight."

Stevie walked through the open doors, across the patio, and down the steps onto the beach. She tugged off her wooden heels and threw them to the ground. The sand was still warm under the surface, holding its heat from the long set sun. She closed her eyes and wiggled her toes, the sound of the surf impacting the shore like an 808.

Franklin caught up, slowing a few steps back.

Stevie sighed. "I overreacted."

"You acted just fine."

Stevie kicked the sand and flopped down. Franklin sat next to her.

"That interview was somethin' else..." He said.

"I'm still trembling." Stevie held out her hand.

"He'd have liked the part of you talkin' 'bout sneakin' up on him in the alley... at the gallery. I saw him square you up—that boy didn't back down."

Stevie smiled. She thought about the white string from her hoodie. The way she curled it around her finger as she made him apologize.

"I wish I never went that night..." A tear fell from her cheek. "At least he'd still be alive."

"This ain't your fault..." Franklin put his arm around her. "I told you he'd break your heart. Just didn't see it goin' this way..."

She leaned her head against his chest, wiping her cheek with the back of her hand. "What are we gonna do?"

"Keep on livin'.

A Word From The Author

No matter how many times I read this story, how many times I've gone back and made revisions—I'm always brought to tears. I can't even listen to the soundtrack without wiping my eyes. I love these characters. Truly. And I hate myself because somewhere I instantiated their trauma. In some many-worlds theory of the multiverse, Stevie and Alex are living out this story right now—and it's all my fault.

Inspiration is a fickle gift. To this point, I've never written a story for the sake of writing a story—rather, it's a compulsion. Stevie Pearl wedged herself into my marrow as I was careening down the canyon just south of St. George, UT. I was on I-15 headed toward Las Vegas and I saw the story from its ending. The final scene played so vividly in my mind, Alex waking up in the back of a pickup truck. His final moments with Stevie made it blurry to see, hard to keep the Jeep on the road. From then on, I was consumed. The entire book was constructed backward from that horrific moment. I spent the next several years discovering who these characters were, and I why I cared so much about them.

I hope a bit of them transcended through these words. I hope Stevie and Alex are now buried deep within you too.

ABOUT THE AUTHOR

SEAN WILLIAM HAMMOND spent his early career in the music industry as a marketing rep for Sony Music Entertainment and as a tour manager for Warped Tour. During this time, he compiled most of the tongue-in-cheek material for his first non-fiction coffee table book, *The Mixtape Manifesto: A Pop Culture Confessional*. These experiences were the synthesis of Stevie Pearl.

Hammond's first novel, *Gods*, was met with critical praise for being "a truly epic and skillfully written saga that will linger in the mind, memory, and imagination long after the book is finished." A controversial and blasphemous last chapter of humanity, Hammond reconstructs our creation stories while continuing to tug at our heart. Set in three periods–present day, the 1960s, and ancient Mesopotamia – this modern epic blends human history, ruthless mythology, science fiction, and the supernatural to tell a love story of the future.

Hammond runs an active website filled with easter eggs, photography from his journeys, and plenty of articles.

www.swhammond.com

www.ingramcontent.com/pod-product-compliance
Lightning Source LLC
Chambersburg PA
CBHW021536250626
47154CB00006BA/2140